CW01338560

e Cry
 the
vorm

Shi Naseer grew up in China unde
immigrating to Australia as a
earning a master's in mathemati
and a PhD in black-hole physic
currently divides her time bet
and lives with her husband a

The Cry of the Silkworm
Shi Naseer

atlantic·fiction

Published in hardback and trade paperback in Great Britain in 2024
by Atlantic Books, an imprint of Atlantic Books Ltd.

Copyright © Shi Naseer, 2024

The moral right of Shi Naseer to be identified as the author of this work has been asserted by her in accordance with the Copyright, Designs and Patents Act of 1988.

All rights reserved. No part of this publication may be reproduced, stored in a retrieval system, or transmitted in any form or by any means, electronic, mechanical, photocopying, recording, or otherwise, without the prior permission of both the copyright owner and the above publisher of this book.

No part of this book may be used in any manner in the learning, training or development of generative artificial intelligence technologies (including but not limited to machine learning models and large language models (LLMs)), whether by data scraping, data mining or use in any way to create or form a part of data sets or in any other way.

This novel is entirely a work of fiction. The names, characters and incidents portrayed in it are the work of the author's imagination. Any resemblance to actual persons, living or dead, events or localities, is entirely coincidental.

10 9 8 7 6 5 4 3 2 1

A CIP catalogue record for this book is available
from the British Library.

Hardback ISBN: 978 1 83895 966 1
Trade paperback ISBN: 978 1 83895 967 8
E-book ISBN: 978 1 83895 968 5

Printed in Great Britain by CPI Group (UK) Ltd, Croydon CR0 4YY

Atlantic Books
An imprint of Atlantic Books Ltd
Ormond House
26–27 Boswell Street
London
WC1N 3JZ

www.atlantic-books.co.uk

*For Niangniang, Gufu,
and all shidu parents*

China introduced a one-child policy in 1980 to curb population growth. Brutal enforcement methods, such as coerced abortion, resulted in countless tragedies. Across the nation, the victims' families sought revenge against family planning officials, some succeeding in murder.

Yuanfen

A predestined, fateful bond between individuals.

1
Shanghai
Winter 2002

Chen Di came to Shanghai to kill.

She hid behind a plane tree on the bustling pavement and fixed her gaze across the road on the sign: *Shanghai Family Planning Commission*.

She raised her arm to check and recheck her green watch and pulled up her green jacket's hood to hide her face. Any minute now, he could stride through the gate into the government building. It had ten storeys but was still more wide than tall, its glass walls allowing officials to see out but no one to see in. On a pole at the front fluttered a national flag as red as the jeep that had abducted Chen Di's beloved mother, her eight-month pregnant body folded away like a quilt. Hours later, they'd brought her back, limp, lifeless, her belly still bulging.

Motorcycles whizzed between honking cars. Plumes of exhaust permeated the grey city air at the start of another year. Nothing like Chen Di's village, nothing like the cotton field she'd left behind at age seventeen – three years ago today.

Dusty wind whipped her in the face as parents sped past on bicycles. On each of their back carriers sat a single, precious little one. Cared for. Doted on. Loved. Boy *or* girl. A sting inside her, she tore her eyes away from the passing children.

Mission first.

Chen Di gripped the handlebars of her tricycle. The attached cart was cluttered with DVDs that she couldn't care less about selling, each one in a plastic sleeve. All Hollywood, all bootlegs. She focused on the gate, the plane tree's leafless branches hovering over her, the north wind pricking her bones like wet needles. She rubbed her cold hands together and bent to rearrange the DVDs, assuring passers-by she was out hawking, and hawking only.

Across the road, the silver sliding gate opened just enough for one person to fit, or two if they were as petite as Chen Di. Officials arrived on foot and on bicycles, greeted by a guard. A bald man grinned as he sauntered inside, his mouth open like a puppet.

Which unlucky family would they destroy today?

Her muscles tensed. She had felt the small man approach from the right almost before she saw him. He wore a black overcoat and a knitted hat, and swung his briefcase like he had good news to report. His heart-shaped face was the one cemented in her mind, which had haunted her village like a malevolent spirit. The face of Mother's murderer.

Chen Di shuddered, a high-pitched chuckle echoing in her head, and she felt tears building. *Mother!* she almost cried like that morning in the village, alongside the bare field, slapping the window of the red jeep. They had both reached out to the glass, Mother's wrists tied, their fingertips matching before the vehicle had rumbled away.

Now Chen Di wiped her eyes fiercely as she registered the man's every movement, every swing of his arms and legs. After all this time in Shanghai, going up mountains of knives, down seas of fires, she had found him!

Finally, she was about to avenge Mother's death.

She stepped forward from the pavement to the road. A bicycle almost rolled over her foot and she dug her hand in her pocket, her fingers climbing around her Voyager flick-knife. Her only valuable. Made in America, its drop-point steel blade and fiberglass-reinforced nylon handle allowed for hand-to-hand combat and short-range throws. She felt the inscription on the handle, '98 *Lantern Fest*. The Lantern Festival of 1998.

The man passed through the gate.

He pulled off his hat, revealing a pair of square ears.

The wrong ears. It wasn't him.

A sudden emptiness settled inside her, her limbs stiffened. Slowly, Chen Di backed onto the pavement. Her fingers loosened around the Voyager and she pulled out her hand, her palm showing a pink line marked by the spine of the folded blade. She held the tricycle grip to steady herself, then punched the seat. She breathed. In. Out.

Every so often, she dreamed of being in Shanghai for something else, perhaps university. Once or twice, she'd even entertained the thought of getting a degree from America, as

Teacher Jia had. She still remembered his Statue of Liberty paperweight. But that would have to wait until her next lifetime. In this one, Mother had died.

'What are you daydreaming about, girl?' a shrill voice behind her said in Shanghainese, which Chen Di understood but couldn't yet speak well.

Chen Di spun around with the finesse of a martial artist. Before her stood a big-boned woman around forty. Putting on a smile, Chen Di replied in Mandarin, 'What would you like to buy?' To appear polite and friendly, she added to the stranger, 'Big sister.'

The woman stared at her, frowning. Everyone did. Chen Di raised her hand to hide the brown birthmark that covered a quarter of her face, from her forehead to her left cheek. Despite being female and twenty, thanks to the birthmark, she was rarely harassed. But she knew she wasn't ugly. Her large eyes held a rare shade of light brown, and her long brows complemented her jawline. Mother had told her once that her high forehead symbolised fortune.

'You wouldn't even know if your DVDs got stolen.' The woman's eyes flicked to a tall boy idling under another plane tree. He looked fifteen or sixteen, blatantly skipping school, a cigarette dangling from his lip. He puffed upward, trying to show off, but ended up coughing. His indigo blazer was the uniform of Wende Private Secondary School around the corner.

Little emperor.

'Whatever you want, I got it,' Chen Di said.

'I don't care for American films, hard to relate.' The woman clicked her tongue, scanning the cart, just as another woman came along, about Chen Di's age. The younger one grabbed five DVDs and didn't even bargain. 'You be careful now,' the older woman said. 'I'm telling you out of the goodness of my heart.'

'Thank you, big sister.' Chen Di put away her smile like a bank card after use.

Both women left, and Chen Di couldn't help but glance at that little emperor again. Even though his back was to her, something about him held her attention. Was it the way he angled his head? How he rubbed the left side of his chin?

He stopped at the eatery diagonally behind her, where a dozen out-of-towners sat at flimsy outdoor tables under the worn awning that read *Yuanfen Eatery*. The wall menu showed a popular saying on top: *yuanfen brings together those thousands of miles apart; without yuanfen we come face to face only to pass each other.* Chen Di laughed. As if a shabby eatery could set the stage for fateful encounters.

The boy raised his cigarette at the young waitress. 'I want a couple fried dough sticks.'

'Yes, brother.' The waitress's accent announced she was from Chen Di's home province, Sichuan, and she blushed, probably taken by the boy's good looks. Chen Di wanted to knock some sense into her. 'One yuan for two.'

'I said I *want* some, not to *buy* some.'

Two customers turned. One rose and tapped the boy's shoulder. 'Oi, young man.'

'Don't you touch me, xiangwuning!'

Disgust surged through Chen Di and she pushed her tricycle towards the eatery, her eyes fixed on the boy's back. Too many times she herself had been called a 'xiangwuning', a Shanghainese term reserved for the poorest out-of-towners: street sweepers, all kinds of labourers, those running cheap eateries, those eating at cheap eateries, hawkers on tricycles.

'Young brother, young brother.' The old owner rushed over, a towel around his neck, the mole above his lip symbolising ample food in life. He nodded at the boy. 'What's the problem? You tell me, and I'll do all I can to serve you.'

A motorcycle zipped into the nearby cycle lane. The boy brushed the dirt off his shoulder, dropped on a plastic stool, and crushed his cigarette on the table. 'As a Shanghainese, I'm giving you face by wanting your xiangwuning food. And you need me to pay?'

This was getting ridiculous. Spectators gathered, and Chen Di was so close to the boy she could touch his back. As if he could see behind him, he whipped his head around.

She flinched. His eyes, as black as burnt bark, were like her little brother's. And he looked at her the way her brother had, head tilted as if casting a judgement. These eyes knew her darkest secrets, secrets she'd buried deep and told no one, secrets that had forced her to leave Sichuan, brought her to Shanghai, and made her who she was today.

The world darkened as the boy rubbed his chin again with

the back of his fingers. She found it hard to breathe, the past rushing back, engulfing her. In her chest she felt a wet, chilly wind, like the howl of a female ghost.

Little Tiger...

Then her heart softened. It softened so much, so unexpectedly, that she bent down and reached out with an impulse to pull away the boy's hand as she had her brother's. All those years ago, Little Tiger had rubbed his chin because of a constant drool rash...

But this boy couldn't be her brother! He was far too old.

The boy didn't speak or move, just held her eyes. No, he was studying her face – her birthmark – though not in the way others did. As if in pain, he pressed a finger to his temple. She almost blurted, *Are you okay?* But he'd already crossed his arms and faced the eatery owner again. 'Would you ask your dad to pay to eat here?'

Who did he think he was? A big man at the next table asked his name.

'Family name Lin, given name Feng,' the boy said like in some martial arts series, before a fighting scene. '*Lin* written by doubling the character for *tree,* as in *forest. Feng* as in blowing *wind.* Forest wind, remember it well.'

The man pointed his chopsticks in the direction of Wende Private. 'Aren't you afraid, Lin Feng, that we go to your teachers?'

'Go to the police, for all I care.'

A bigger man strode over and raised a fist. 'I'll beat you up right here.'

The boy slammed a Swiss Army Knife on the table, and Chen Di could hardly control her urge to teach him a lesson. What was with these little emperors, acting like they owned the world, squandering life opportunities rural kids would die for? He turned his blade out at the owner. 'If you don't want your eatery gone—'

Chen Di snatched the knife out of his hand. It was a toy compared with her Voyager.

He sprang up but stared at her again before saying, 'Give it back.'

'You're better off without it.' She folded back the blade and held it away from him. She wished he weren't a head taller than she was. 'You don't use a knife to threaten good people.'

He tried to grab it. 'It's mine!'

'Is it?' She passed it to him. 'Then you must know how to hold it.'

The boy widened his eyes, surprised to see the knife back in his hand. He gripped it so tightly that his knuckles went white, probably thinking no one could pry open his hand without chopping off his fingers. Chen Di reached in fast, palm to his nose, while her other hand bent his wrist and squeezed his fist. His hand was unexpectedly cold. The knife fell only a few centimetres before she scooped it up.

'Once more?' Again she gave it back.

He smirked. 'Big sis, the look in your eyes, it's like you want to kill someone.'

Chen Di opened her mouth, cold sweat running down her back, and before she could dismiss it as a kid's silly guess, the boy turned out the blade and slashed it through the air, aiming at her arm. People cried out in terror, but she slipped behind him, jabbed her fingers under his chin, and caught his wrist from behind. She was sure he'd fall but he shifted his weight and steadied himself. Impressive. With some training, this boy might take her down.

The knife, though, had returned to her hand.

'You go, girl!' bystanders called out. 'You know martial arts?'

Alarmed, Chen Di scanned the crowd – two dozen people were cheering. A short man with chipped teeth panted as he told her that the same boy had vandalised his glassware shop last year. Of course. The kid was just out in the city trying to be tough, and it wasn't her job to help Yuanfen Eatery. She had only been watching this Xuhui District office of the Family Planning Commission for a day, she couldn't afford rash actions. Her Voyager and her training were not to be wasted on a little emperor and now she'd brought attention to herself.

'You deal with him.' Chen Di put the boy's knife in the eatery owner's hand. 'Don't let these brats do whatever.' She turned her tricycle around.

But the boy's dark eyes stayed with her. She shut her own eyes and raised both hands to clutch her head, a habit that helped her expel any unwanted thoughts.

Forget your brother. Mission first.

She walked off, one hand covering the DVDs with canvas. People shouted, but not at her. 'Oi!' they called. 'Wake up, kid!' Had the boy fainted? Chen Di forced herself to not look back, jumped on the tricycle, and pedalled off.

Tomorrow she'd come back.

Tomorrow she just might spot the monster. She just might spot Lü Yuandou.

2
Sichuan
Harvest 1990

'You,' Grandfather said. 'Get out.'

Chen Di's eyes snapped open. Against the moonlight, Grandfather towered over her small wooden bed and pointed straight at her. She shuddered, the way she did every time she saw that calloused finger. But he was only telling her to leave. It didn't look like he'd beat her. Rubbing her eyes, she quickly got out from under the quilt and hurried towards the door.

A moan made her turn back and she stumbled over a low stool. At the other end of the room, Mother, belly bulging, was twisted in bed like an injured animal.

Chen Di gasped. 'Grandfather, is Mother…'

'I told you to get out.'

'But is Mother about to—'

'Yaonü…' Mother said, exhaling heavily. *Darling daughter.* 'I'll be fine.'

'Get. Out.' Grandfather gritted his teeth like he wanted to yell, his unibrow knit in the middle, but kept his voice low and measured. Indeed, their wooden house had been quiet for months as Mother's belly swelled. 'No one needs to know about this,' Grandfather had said under his breath, 'in case it's a *girl*.' 'Girl' had sounded like a disease.

But those few months hadn't been bad. Neither Grandfather nor Father had hit Mother. Grandfather hadn't scowled much at anyone and kept a look of hope on his oblong face. Many times he'd even lowered himself to kitchen work, cooking congee topped with century eggs, gelatinous and nutritious, for Mother.

'What are you still standing there for, you little shit?'

'I-I'm sorry, Grandfather.' She threw on her coat and rushed out to the courtyard.

The double doors squeaked open before she could get out. She dodged Father as he stepped into the yard, wearing Grandfather's black polo shirt that made him look lankier than he already was. For a few seconds he held her gaze, and she his. She didn't like having his light-brown eyes, even though they were considered beautiful. Father glanced beyond her, at the house. If she hadn't been so short, she wouldn't have noticed the tremor in his left hand, the one missing a thumb.

Mother's moan came from indoors.

'Come in, come in,' Father said to someone behind him.

The midwife was a small old woman. She wore her hair in a low bun and shouldered a wooden box, lid open. The crooked pair of scissors reflected moonlight like her silver tooth. Her smile made Chen Di cringe.

'Can I help?' Chen Di asked Father.

'You're eight,' he said.

She stepped across the high threshold and outside, the doors shutting behind her.

Crickets chirped, louder than any other night. There wasn't even a wisp of cloud, only a full moon hanging above the vast hills of the village. It must've been past midnight. Chen Di stood on the stone steps before their shingled wooden house and listened to Mother's muffled cries. She clenched her fists, sweaty despite the wind. Only her feet were cool, her slippers too big. Her dull red cotton coat, with a patch at her elbow, was oversized too.

Across the arched stone bridge lay their soon-to-be-harvested cotton field, a field of dirty-looking white. The colour of death. Given the high humidity and the steep terrain that limited sun exposure, the crop was rare on the hills of central Sichuan. But ever since peasants, not the state, were allocated fields and had a say in what to grow, Grandfather stuck to it the way he stuck to everything.

Chen Di's arm tensed, her hand remembering the hard bolls that pricked her fingers every cotton harvest. It'd been an unusually sunny year, ideal for cotton. 'A good sign,' Grandfather had said, glancing at Mother's belly. 'We'll call him Little Tiger.'

Little Tiger. Would Chen Di finally get a brother?

Her eyes darted to a wall on the left of the field, the big writing on it bright red even in the dark. The words had been painted on the order of a man the adults called 'Lunatic Lü' more often than his official title, 'Chief Lü'. Even though

Chen Di didn't go to school, she could read it. Mother had taught her the simple characters: *one is good; a son or a daughter, equally good.*

An earthy smell wafted through the air. She paced down and up the three stone steps until Mother's scream sliced through the crickets' chirps. She held onto the door frame, either side of which had been pasted with red paper, showing a couplet: *prosperous family, prosperous people, prosperous business; booming fortune, booming wealth, booming luck.* Her legs trembled, her hands joined in prayer. *Let it be a boy, let it be a boy, let it be a boy.*

Then came the loud clank of an enamel mug hitting the floor, and Grandfather yelled, 'Useless woman – you shame my ancestors!' He lowered his voice. 'Now, can't you just—'

'I don't do anything that's going to bring bad karma,' the midwife said, followed by a shriek – a baby's cry, cut short.

Chen Di's heart jumped. Was that her baby brother, or…? A wave of fear washed over her almost before she knew why. Grandfather often banged mugs on the floor, but right now, it could mean only one thing: there was no Little Tiger.

'You then, Son,' Grandfather said.

Father mumbled something indistinct.

'What *but*? Only *one* more kid allowed, it's national policy. If we kept this one, you'd die sonless and I'd die grandsonless!'

Mother let out a wail, and Father mumbled some more.

'Shut up.' Grandfather restrained his voice but Chen Di could still hear his words. 'Who'd help us farm? Who'd carry our family name? And how would Xixi— How would your...' Chen Di had never heard his voice break before, but now, all she made out was him murmuring the saying, 'unable to shut her eyes in her death'. Unable to rest in peace. Then his voice grew steadier, harsher. 'Without a son, you can't hold your head high, can't even be buried in the ancestral grave. For your own good, do as I say.'

'Just be careful on the way,' the midwife added. 'It *is* illegal. You don't want to bump into Lunatic Lü.'

Before Chen Di could digest their words, Father exited, almost pushing her over. He walked fast, away from the house and towards the cotton field, faltering on the stone bridge, a white bag slung over his shoulder. No, the bag was really a holed shirt, corners tied together, gripped in his good right hand. Then it moved, the fabric stretched as if being pushed from the inside...by a little fist, or foot.

A chill passed through her.

The crickets hushed. The world stopped. Only Father slipped through the field like a nocturnal animal, hardly rustling the cotton plants.

'Father!' Chen Di charged across the stone bridge.

But he'd vanished, the crickets loud again. She stood in the white field, panting.

Where was Father taking her baby sister?

Chen Di staggered back and slumped on the stone steps, the moving shirt-bag etched on her mind. She was still trying to steady her breathing when the midwife came out, muttering about how delivering a girl meant half the pay for the same work. She cursed as she tripped over Chen Di, but Chen Di didn't move. She watched her hands on her knees, her small toes in her big slippers. Her finger traced the pattern formed by the dents on the steps, like scars.

Eventually, the day dawned. Orange, then blue. Her bottom hurting, Chen Di rose, pushed open the doors, and lifted each foot across the high threshold back into the courtyard. She entered the front room, hit by the sharp smell of hot-and-sour soup. A pot lay face down on the ground and liquid dripped from the wall portrait of Chairman Mao, as if the great leader was crying.

She bolted into the back room. Mother lay not in bed but on the concrete floor, her body at an unnatural angle, and she whimpered, foam by her mouth.

'Mother!'

'Yaonü... Just stay outside...'

Chen Di rushed over, but before she could reach Mother, her arm was yanked so hard she screamed. Grandfather shoved her to the floor. A part of her had seen this coming – Grandfather's rage was nothing new – but still she felt unprepared.

'You little shit,' he said, 'how dare you show your face in front of me!'

'Grandfather!' She fell to her knees and kowtowed to him. 'Forgive Mother, please.'

He pointed a coiled length of rope at Chen Di while scowling at Mother. 'We haven't served you for months for another one of *these*.' He raised the rope, the braiding coming loose at several places. 'Our Chen family will not end in your hands!'

Chen Di covered Mother's body with her own before the whips came down. Mother tried to push her away, but Chen Di didn't budge. The whips landed on her back, her bottom, her calves, her back again. Each whip a burn. She gripped Mother's hand and did not cry, determined to protect Mother the way Mother always protected her. Besides, though canes were more common than ropes, everyone got beaten. Children, of course, and grown-ups too. Like Mother, Chubby Aunty from Grandpa Li's paddy also got bruises often.

The door creaked.

Father came in, dishevelled, no longer carrying that shirt-bag. Half in shadow, he studied Chen Di and Mother on the floor, then nodded at Grandfather. 'It's done.'

'No Lunatic Lü?' Grandfather asked.

'No Lunatic Lü.'

More whips came down, giving Chen Di no time to think. She clenched her teeth until Mother pushed her away, the next whip hitting Mother's flabby belly.

'Please, Grandfather!' Chen Di begged.

He hunkered down and dropped the rope. 'I named you *Di – girl with younger brother* – to ask Heaven to give you a younger brother. Your existence is meaningless without a younger brother!' He pinched her cheek – her birthmark. 'What happened to Little Jade could've long happened to you.'

Chen Di shivered at the mention of the missing village girl.

'Do you know what *really* happened to her?' Grandfather said. 'She was a bad child during the day, so at night, the ghost woman slid out of the big pit and snatched her, right when Little Jade was squatting over the toilet. She didn't even get to finish her pee.'

This wasn't the first story Chen Di had heard about the ghost woman living in Daci Pit, the canyon beyond the jungle on the east, which her village – Daci Village – was named after. Goosebumps on her arms, she pictured the translucent ghost, how her long nails dug into the little girl she carried through air, how she stashed the girl at the bottom of the canyon and ate her for breakfast, lunch, and dinner.

Grandfather raised a foot but put it down without kicking Mother's pale face. 'I'll give you another chance, woman.' He stormed out. 'You want peace, give birth to Little Tiger!'

Slowly, Chen Di's hot back turned numb. The door creaked again and she looked up only to see Father come in. She hadn't even realised he'd left. His eyes met hers, and she'd never seen him look so sad.

She stumbled to her feet. 'Where did you take that shirt-bag?'

'I tucked in thirty yuan and waited for hours, Chen Di, hours at the bus stop until I saw a granny picking her up.'

Whenever Father said her full name, it sounded like passing secrets through a hole in a room divider. 'Your little sister will be taken care of.'

She felt she'd heard similar words before but wasn't sure. And she believed him, she wanted to. Some day, she just might reunite with her little sister.

Sunlight filtered in through a crack in the window shutter, along with the smell of hot-and-sour soup she'd noticed earlier, now turned bitter with the distinct odour of boiling Chinese medicine. Father helped Mother to bed.

'Did you soak the herbs first?' Mother asked.

'Once I got back,' Father said, a quaver in his quiet voice. He fetched a few clean cloths from a cabinet for Mother to tuck under herself, then sat beside her. 'It's on low heat now, it'll be ready soon. The huangqi and the danggui I got from Old Yang.'

'Old Yang from the county town? How expensive—'

'The important thing is you heal.'

Mother looked like she wanted to say more but only smiled at Father, who rose and turned to Chen Di, a stripe of sun painting his body.

'Here, this is for you.' In his palm was a metal hair clip, shaped like a leaf. 'I found it in a market in the county town...a while back.' It sounded as if he'd saved it for this exact occasion.

She waited before picking it up. The hair clip was green, sparkly in the sun, its jagged edge like a real leaf's. Before she realised it, Father had already clipped it into her hair. A wave of anger made her yank it off, pulling out a few hairs. 'I don't want it.'

'I'll dress your wounds.'

'I don't need you to.'

But he did.

That night, her back stinging, Chen Di lay on her side as Daci Pit sprang to mind again. She'd never visited the canyon before – all children were warned not to – but she'd heard people talking about the red cliffs, the snaking riverbed, the child-devouring ghost woman. Would the ghost come to get her the way she'd taken Little Jade?

The sound of a leaf whistle outside distracted her from her thoughts. She sat up and pulled open the window shutter a slit to see Father tucking a leaf between his lips, holding its two ends. His thumbless left hand quivered as the melody rose and fell, and, like magic, it soothed her. She lay back down and, like that, drifted into sleep.

In her dream, adult Chen Di stood at a huge intersection crowded with people and cars and tall buildings. She wore a ponytail and a green shirt dress and waved at a short-haired girl with large eyes, white teeth, and the brightest smile.

Her little sister. Alive and well.

3
Shanghai
Winter 2002

Chen Di stood before a glassy mall at Xu Junction. No fresh air, only exhaust. She fixed her ponytail and straightened her white shirt and red pencil skirt, her red tie looking awfully like the red scarves worn by the Young Pioneers at school. That Lin Feng boy at Yuanfen Eatery this morning would be too old to stay as a Young Pioneer, he was probably now a member of the Communist Youth League, except his bad behaviour could've got him expelled.

She clutched her head and shut her eyes. *Not your business.* But even as she went through Pizza & Apple Pie's automatic doors for her lunch shift, she wondered if the boy had recovered after fainting. How unusual it was for a well-fed little emperor to pass out on the street...

'Tilt your face, Young Chen,' Manager Chu said without mentioning her birthmark. He was a big man, hair parted in the middle. 'Show your good side, remember. Your good side.'

'Yes, Manager Chu.' She wished she could turn a deaf ear

to him, but she had to be patient about her life in Shanghai until she tracked down Lü Yuandou.

Chen Di served deep-pan pizzas, spongy crusts filled with prawns. A young mother with wavy hair complained the prawns were too small, and her son rolled a red double-decker toy bus all over the seats in the booth. After her break, more customers arrived for dinner. Day three of this year's Spring Festival had coincided with Valentine's Day, and the heart-shaped pizzas were still selling well. This evening, again, the better-off Shanghainese didn't disappoint, choosing hundred-yuan pizzas and pies over tangyuans, the rice-ball dessert which people traditionally ate on the Lantern Festival.

It'd been exactly four years since Mother's death and Chen Di couldn't wait to finish her shift. Tonight, she'd walk around to let the lanterns that filled the sky fuel her hatred.

The last table she served included a thin woman whose double-fold eyelids could only be the product of cosmetic surgery. 'My brother got his American green card!' the woman said to her friends. Chen Di wondered if it was easier for a Shanghainese to get an American green card or for an out-of-towner – a Sichuanese like her – to get a Shanghai household registration. The woman then lowered her voice as she brought up how white people mocked her brother's English.

Chen Di placed an apple pie on their table with a thud. How was it any different here? The locals had ridiculed her for blurting out Sichuanese. If Shanghainese helped you belong, good Mandarin showcased your education, then 'non-standard' Mandarin accents – or worse, Sichuanese – labelled you as a poor, uneducated xiangwuning.

After work, she put on her beloved green padded jacket. It was a gift from Teacher Jia. Even after all these years, thinking of his crinkling eyes and charmingly awkward smile sent heat through her body. But those emotions would have to wait until her next life. Right now the jacket was practical to her mission, that was all. Its hood helped her disguise herself and its old-fashioned round collar associated her with styleless out-of-towners, which was perfect. The less people noticed her, the better.

The malls on either side of the road were festooned with hundreds of round, red lanterns, all powered by bulbs instead of candles. She elbowed past the shoppers swarming the pavement and a little girl singing, 'London Bridge is falling down, falling down, falling down…' A white couple stopped before a young hawker, paying for a good-fortune knot at a ridiculous price. Above, clouds slipped past the full moon that accompanied every Lantern Festival. Most people missed their hometowns when they watched the moon, but Chen Di had no one left there to miss.

Once, the Lantern Festival had been a day of hope, where she and Teacher Jia and Mother had chatted away in a small school office, eating Mother's tangyuans. Then there was the 1998 Lantern Festival, when everything had changed.

She passed Saint Ignatius Cathedral and wove her way out of Xu Junction. Modern housing estates appeared, wrought-iron fences enclosing ten- to twenty-storey apartment buildings, nothing like where Chen Di lived. Precious only children strolled around with one parent on each side, pulling wheeled rabbit lanterns as if walking dogs.

Then she stiffened and stopped walking. Across the street, among all the families, a middle-aged man and a teenage boy sauntered down the pavement, their faces dimly lit by the street lights and the lanterns. The boy had narrow shoulders and wore square glasses, and his gait suggested a lack of sureness – so unlike that little emperor this morning, Lin Feng – but the man reminded Chen Di of Lü.

She stayed on her side of the street but resumed walking in the same direction as them. The man's brown quilted coat looked even more ancient than Chen Di's jacket, its half-standing collars hiding his chin, and his knitted hat covered his ears. This area wasn't far from that government building. It'd make sense for any officials there to live here, and if Lü really worked there…

But her whole village knew Lü Yuandou had no child!

The father bent his head to talk to the son, a humbleness in his posture, and Chen Di almost laughed at herself. Lü Yuandou, a humble father? No way. He had Lü's small frame and that was all. She must be tired, mistaking everyone in the world for that monster.

Except the man turned to her, perhaps having sensed her gaze. Chen Di snapped her head down and pulled up her hood, heart throbbing. She pretended to check her watch, even raising her other hand to cover her birthmark. But why did she need to hide if he wasn't Lü after all? Somehow, she couldn't look back up.

He *was* Lü's exact height and build…

It took a long while for her breathing to return to normal. The father-and-son pair disappeared around the corner, and she leaned on a fence and continued to watch the lanterns, each one a puddle of blood. Like the festival in 1998. She remembered Mother, Mother's lifeless body, on a makeshift bed, with make-up on. A sudden weakness in her knees almost made her fall, a dull blade twisting in her chest.

Now, hate! Hatred helps. All other emotions are useless.

Midnight, Chen Di entered her enclosed neighbourhood – her longtang – through an arched opening. It was a hundred-year-old compound of connected three-storey buildings – some of the lowest residential buildings in Shanghai. The inhabitants were mostly older-generation Shanghainese and out-of-towners trying to get by. They couldn't be more different from Chen Di's Pizza & Apple Pie customers.

She quickened her pace down the alley. Tomorrow morning she had aikido training and, of course, had to return to the government building.

She reached a solid iron door, opened the padlock, and unbolted the latch. A loud squeak. She tugged a string and the hanging bulb lit up her unpainted rental unit, converted from windowless storage. Her dumbbells lay under a small bamboo chair. An enamel chamber pot sat in one corner, a little coal stove at another. Few still used such stoves, but to

Chen Di, dragging hers outside whenever she cooked beat doing so in the gossip-filled communal kitchens.

Chen Di swung open the wooden door to her wardrobe, its surface covered with gouges from her knife-throwing practice, a large headshot of Lü Yuandou glued to its inside. Last year, seeing all the cybercafés springing up around Shanghai, she had paid a café owner to teach her to use computers and the internet. It hadn't helped her locate Lü, not exactly, but there he was, famous enough to be found online, having risen through the ranks.

In the photo, Lü Yuandou looked impeccable in his immaculate black suit, nothing like the quilted coat worn by that father on the street. He had neatly cropped hair, his small eyes smiling on his heart-shaped face. At first glance he looked almost kind. Too bad his notable ears – pointed, with unfittingly long lobes – were cut off at the edges of the printout.

Chen Di flicked open her Voyager, her fingers tracing the carving on the handle that marked not only Mother's death date but also the fifth and last time she'd confronted Lü in person, in Daci Village. *I'm so sorry, Yaonü,* Mother had said before being thrown into the jeep, her last words to Chen Di. Except Lü Yuandou was the one who should've been sorry.

She stabbed his forehead.

She retrieved her knife and banged shut the wardrobe. She was ready to face him for the sixth time, now in Shanghai.

But the shadow of that humble father flashed across her mind again. Why was she still thinking of that stranger?

Her wall displayed the largest map of Shanghai she'd been

able to find. Baoshan up north, Fengxian down south, Qingpu on the west, Pudong on the east. The map was mildewed, but the two dozen small red-marker circles – government buildings with offices of the Family Planning Commission – remained clear. All but four had been crossed out.

Chen Di had been spying on the offices for a year and a half, eliminating them one by one from outer districts to inner ones, spending weeks at each location to ensure she hadn't missed Lü because he was on a trip. Tomorrow, she'd return to the office she had started surveilling.

She pulled off her canvas shoes and lay on her small bed, satisfied. But as she drifted towards sleep, her ceiling morphed into a young face, with large and dark eyes, like two black holes. Lin Feng, again. She wondered if he was okay. Surely someone would have helped a collapsing child, even if he was a brat. Except she hadn't done so.

Chen Di remembered the way the boy had rubbed the left side of his chin, how he'd stared at her with his head tilted, like Little Tiger.

How she wished she could go back in time... To undo what she had done.

She flinched.

Yuanfen Eatery. It wasn't fate, karma, or coincidence, but yuanfen – a bond between two humans, a day-to-day concept in which she'd long since lost faith...

Well, there was no yuanfen between her and Lin Feng, who only *looked* like her brother. They'd never meet again.

Mission first.

4
Sichuan
Harvest 1991

At dawn, Chen Di trailed Mother out of the wooden house towards the cotton field. Mother's long plait swayed before her, and Chen Di's two short ones bounced on her small shoulders. She secured her fringe with her leaf-shaped hair clip. She didn't admit to anyone that she loved its sparkly green, that the gift Father had given to her last year had become her favourite.

They crossed the stone bridge and arrived at the field. Hardlock and boll rot made much of the cotton this year impossible to harvest. Grandfather had complained non-stop about the excessive rains during germination, lack of rains during flowering, and again excessive rains before harvest. But most of all, he hated the bollworms they'd tried and failed to kill.

'Use these.' Mother held out the pair of knitted gloves for picking cotton.

Chen Di didn't take them. Instead, she gazed at Mother, wishing she'd inherited more than just her high forehead, and reached towards her eye. 'Does it still hurt?' Last week, Mother had stolen money from behind the men's backs to buy the gloves for Chen Di, to protect her fingers from the pricks of the pointy bolls. But the theft had resulted in a bruise to Mother's left eye, first purple, now greenish. It stung Chen Di inside more than the plants ever could.

Mother caught her small hand and put on the gloves for her, then caressed her birthmark. 'With this bruise, we look more alike.' She made it sound as if Chen Di's birthmark was something cute that everyone wanted to have.

Chen Di smiled, determined not to let the gloves slow her down. Her short height meant she didn't need to bend, and she twisted out the cotton from a boll and put her little cloud into the sack hanging from her neck. 'I don't like them beating you.'

'Your father's hand is soft, he only pretends to hit me.'

'I don't think so. He's just skinny, but he tries whenever Grandfather tells him to.'

'A good son always obeys his father.'

'He's not even Grandfather's *real* son.'

'So he has to obey him even more.' Mother picked from many bolls before putting all the cotton in her sack in one go. She placed a hand on her belly. 'Anyhow, they'll stop soon.'

'You mean...'

'I'm expecting again.'

Chen Di said nothing, clutching a handful of cotton, her palm clammy.

'I have a feeling this time you'll get a little brother.'

'But what if it's another...' *Girl.* Her eyes darted to the wall on the left of the field. The enormous writing had been repainted twice over the year, but it showed the same bright-red words: *one is good; a son or a daughter, equally good.*

It simply wasn't true.

Mother reached towards another boll. 'It won't be.'

'But *what if?* Would Father again take her to the bus—'

'It won't be!' Still holding the cotton, Mother's hand trembled. 'It'll be Little Tiger. It will, I know it. I can't... afford to fail again.' She steadied her hand. 'Little Tiger will go to school and improve our lives.'

Chen Di imagined a little boy holding a pencil and a notebook, running to school, leaving her behind at the cotton field, and for the first time she envied someone who didn't even exist. 'Why can't *I* go to school?' she complained. Over the last couple of years, she'd sneaked to the village school a dozen times, but without Grandfather's consent, she'd been kept out. Last spring, the teacher – an old woman with a big nose – had smacked her head with the chalkboard eraser, sprinkling white dust in her hair, like lice. The pupils had burst out laughing.

Mother sighed. 'I'll keep teaching you.'

'But you don't know much yourself. You can't read the new couplet at Grandpa Sun's house.' Chen Di instantly regretted her words, seeing Mother biting her lip.

A screech cut through the dawn quiet. Chen Di and Mother exchanged a look and turned to the pair of loudspeakers mounted to a concrete pole across the field. Loudspeakers were all around the village but rarely sounded at this early hour. Generally they broadcast news and entertainment and announced weddings and funerals. The Party cadres even sang jingles to encourage patriotism. In the summer, a family was exposed over the loudspeakers for stealing their neighbours' bayberries, and a young man for not showing his father filial piety.

'Attention, villagers,' sounded a high-pitched man's voice, calm but chilling. Even children knew this was the tone Qing dynasty eunuchs used to announce the emperor's edicts. It was Chief Lü speaking. 'Family planning helps us cope with shortages of natural resources and consumer goods, it promotes our nation's economic growth. It is every citizen's duty to comply.' He chuckled. 'Now, shame on Li San and Wang Ting! Last night, the unruly couple disrupted family planning…'

All the adults talked about how the county had been divided into two eras, the one before Lü and the other after, especially in Daci Village. Before Lü, Daci cadres had 'enforced' the one-child policy by pocketing bribes and keeping one eye open and the other closed. But then Lü was posted from the provincial capital, Chengdu, down to the county to 'catch negative exemplar villages'. Technically he came with good news: the one-and-a-half-child policy applied to select rural areas, rendering a first daughter half a child, which meant if a couple's first baby was a girl, they could have another after a minimum of five years. But if their second was again a girl, then they'd have to settle with the two daughters.

People with one son wanted more to make sure they'd have at least one son who'd have a son, who'd also have a son. And the new policy infuriated all families with two daughters. If a boy meant prosperity, two girls meant twice the burden – twice the money spent on raising someone who'd eventually belong to another family.

Lü joined his subordinates frequently, on-site, to make sure the policy was enforced. He beat up anyone who tried to bribe him. He was a true believer.

Various rumours spread from village to village.

'Lunatic Lü's whole team broke in, kicked out the elders and the boy, and ripped down the roof. What could Red Flower do? She had to come back and get an abortion. They already have a son after all, can't try for another.'

'Six months! Lunatic Lü said try the needle. One shot, and it stopped kicking. The family cried their eyes out, Old Wu almost fainting on the spot, because guess what, it was a boy! Well, they'll have to live with their two girls.'

'When Lunatic Lü got there, they'd already buried the stillborn baby, but he didn't believe them – insisted they were playing the system and had taken the baby into hiding in order to have another. So they had to dig up the little corpse to prove it to him!'

Chen Di's heart pounded every time she heard such a rumour. They sounded as scary as the stories about Daci Pit's child-devouring ghost woman.

The loudspeakers stopped blaring, the cotton field was quiet again.

Chen Di had never seen Lü in person, but she knew the official thought pregnancy was a bad idea, like she did. Grandfather's rage after the birth of her baby sister was still fresh in her mind. It'd been a year, and no one, not even Mother, had talked about her. Except she knew Mother must've been praying, like she was, for the baby to grow up fine. Chen Di imagined the wrinkly face of the nice granny at the bus stop, who she hoped had taken the baby for her own family instead of giving her away.

Now, had Mother got pregnant again just to receive a few months of good treatment? This year, most of their beatings had been the fault of the bollworms. Generation after generation of the pests had eaten through the cotton bolls before they could ripen, and Grandfather's moods had never been worse.

'I wish there weren't so many bollworms,' Chen Di said. 'Then maybe they'd treat you okay, Mother, without you needing to get pregnant.'

Mother's hands stayed busy. 'There are good worms in the world too.'

'Worms are pests.'

'Not canbaobao.' *Silkworms,* or literally, *silkworm babies.* 'Silkworms spit out silk, and you can make clothes out of that silk.'

Chen Di considered it. 'So silkworms are like cotton plants?'

'You're quick, as always.' Mother described silkworms: black when little, then grey, white, and translucent before they spun cocoons. Chen Di pictured the caterpillars, not hairy, not greenish or pinkish like the bollworms. Babies. Babies who were loved.

The first rays of sunshine touched her face, the arc of the sun emerging from behind a hill that divided the dark field and the glowing sky. They both dropped the cotton into their sacks and looked to the east. The sun made its way up, lighting their world. Chen Di took in the earthy smell, feeling her lungs expand, contract, expand again. Her face warmed.

'Isn't it filled with life?' Mother's eyes were fixed on the sun.

The sunrise lifted them out of their sadness, and it belonged to the two of them alone. A rooster crowed. Chen Di wanted to talk to Mother more before others came. 'If silkworms are like cotton plants, then are there silkworm farms?'

The dry plants around them rustled. The cotton in Mother's hand almost flew away, but she promptly added it to her sack, which bulged like a pregnant belly. 'I grew up on one.'

'Really!' She only ever knew Mother wasn't from their village, and now it felt as if for years Mother had intentionally avoided talking about the silkworm farm. 'Do you miss it?'

Mother put her palm over Chen Di's eyes. Chen Di loved the touch, even though Mother's hand was coarse, bandages on half her fingers. 'Imagine flat bamboo baskets covered with mulberry leaves. Imagine the white and gold cocoons silkworms spin to trap themselves inside. Quite a scene.' She dropped her hand. 'But few silkworms get to become moths.'

'The rest?'

'Boiled alive inside their cocoons.'

Chen Di gasped.

Mother's gaze made her feel like a grown-up. 'After the boiling, silk threads are pulled from the cocoons. By then, the chrysalises would've long died.'

'But silkworms are good, you said!'

'They're good only for producing silk.'

'But don't they still deserve to live?'

'A silkworm has to make a hole in the cocoon – damaging the silk – to get out, so we kill the silkworm to save the silk.' Mother reached for a big boll and twisted out the cotton. 'Even if they do get out, silkworm moths can't fly anyway.'

5
Shanghai
Winter 2002

In the predawn darkness, Chen Di switched on her bedside lamp and flipped open a crumpled literary magazine to a story she'd read twenty times. It was about a smart and brave village girl from the 'Land of Abundance', Sichuan, who had a star-shaped birthmark beside her eye. The author used a pen name but every time Chen Di read it, she felt Teacher Jia talking to her. Again she lost herself in her memories and daydreams, picturing a reunion with him here in Shanghai. *I got a job offer at a publisher in Shanghai*, Teacher Jia had said.

She shut the magazine.

Aikido, then the government building.

She sprang up for her workout, wishing she could do so on the roof but confined to her unit instead, fearing other early risers might find her intense training suspicious. She started with easy stretches, then did squats and lunges, her movements precise. She pushed herself with long sessions of planks, sit-ups, and knuckle push-ups, and breathed through her dumbbell curls. Her muscles burnt and she touched her biceps, pleased with her body. She only wished her breasts would stop growing. She reached into her bra and squeezed them. Two inconveniences. Undesirable for fighting, for her mission.

To cool off, she walked through a few aikido wrist locks – critical to taking down Lü Yuandou. Her class was in an hour and she couldn't wait to throw and pin people.

Chen Di wolfed down a century egg. Most people couldn't stand the eggs' pungent taste on their own but then again, they hadn't been deprived of them in their childhoods. Holding her chamber pot, she exited into the alley and saw a mouse scurry past a door with a *Hygiene Model* sticker. She scrubbed clean her chamber pot at one of the public sinks located alongside the low-walled communal toilets, trying to ignore the sight of an old man peeing.

Half an hour later, she arrived at the Dragon Lustre area, at a six-storey building as grey as the sky. The front was a medicine shop, huge turtle shells fixed on the walls. She entered through a backdoor and pulled off her jacket, making sure her Voyager was hidden before hanging it up. She couldn't let it be seen again – she'd almost been banned from aikido. They weren't allowed to carry around weapons.

She appeared at the door to the dojo in a white uniform. A group of men and a few women, all around Chen Di's age, had already knelt on teal-green mats in a line. They faced their trainer, Master Mu, who had deep-set eyes and whose freshly shaven face made him look younger than his seventy years.

Chen Di took in the scene. Nothing had changed since that rainy day two-and-a-half years ago, when she had charged into this dojo, water dripping from her hair. She'd only had to try one aikido class to realise she'd found what she had been looking for.

Now she bowed and entered as usual, submitting herself to seiza – sitting on heels – and mokuso – meditation. For such pointless rituals, they might as well go to the nearby Dragon Lustre Temple. Master Mu then shared the quote of the day: *The way of a warrior is based on humanity, love, and sincerity; the heart of martial valour is true bravery, wisdom, love, and friendship.* His voice resonated like an old bell.

When real training finally began, no one in search of a partner looked in Chen Di's direction, apart from a baby-faced new girl, Shanghainese. She approached, dimples showing, before extending her arm. Chen Di gripped her wrist, not smiling. By trapping Chen Di's hand and bringing her own forearm over Chen Di's, the girl should be able to make her drop to her knees, but she couldn't.

'To start with,' Chen Di said, 'your stance is too narrow.'

'Really?' the girl said.

If only Chen Di had a female classmate who wasn't a joke. As to her male classmates, they'd initially treated her like any other girl but soon learned their lesson after being subjected to her wrist locks and witnessing her putting a run-over cat out of its misery with a neck twist. Behind her back, classmates now called her Mei Chaofeng – the female killer from *The Legend of the Condor Heroes* whose fingertips penetrated skulls.

'I'll take you down first so you see.' She gave her wrist to the dimpled girl.

The girl took it. Chen Di kept her motions slow and gentle until Lü Yuandou came to mind. She mentally replaced the girl's dimpled face with his heart-shaped one, her round ears with his pointed ones, long lobes hanging.

'Owww!' the girl shrieked, kneeling on the mat.

The dojo went silent. A guy pinned to the floor looked up, and students in the middle of throwing or being thrown stopped in funny positions.

'Oh no.' Chen Di let go, noticing the force in her grasp. 'I'm sorry.' But her hand stopped in mid-air before she could place it on the girl's shoulder. She shouldn't have apologised. She was training to kill, she needed to be able to hurt people.

Tears spilt from the girl's eyes.

'Young Chen.' Master Mu came to them. 'We are *training* here.'

She tried to look indifferent. 'I said I'm sorry.'

He directed her attention to the wall, to the photo of Morihei Ueshiba – a small man with long white beard and brows. 'The Great Teacher said: *to injure an opponent is to injure yourself.* Be mindful of others' well-being.'

But that wouldn't help any avenger. 'I got it.'

'You have not.' His eyes pierced her.

Master Mu asked the new girl to join another pair and

waved to Chen Di to follow him. Reluctantly she did, and they stopped by the wall rack of wooden swords.

'Please, Master Mu. Let me return to training.'

'An aikido practitioner *redirects* her opponent's force, you add too much of your own.'

Chen Di knew the basics. It was her choice to adjust things a little.

'Regardless,' he said, 'your grasp of the techniques is good.'

'I'm flattered.'

'What you need is a different kind of training.'

She felt her feet sink into the mat, impossible to escape under Master Mu's stern gaze. He'd said these words to her before, and she hadn't come for another one of his lectures.

'Fundamentally,' he said, 'what is aikido?'

'A martial art.'

'And what is a martial art good for, in this modern world we live in?'

She turned to the rack of swords – wooden swords – too blunt to really hurt people. Still, they were swords. 'I know what you're trying to say.'

'Martial arts are vehicles for the cultivation of life, not devices to take down people.'

But they are, if you're good.

Metres away, the three girls in class looked like they were doing a slow dance. Behind them, a stout teenager couldn't get into position to execute the move, and his thin partner wasn't helping. It crossed her mind the way that Lin Feng boy, though clearly untrained, had steadied himself in front of Yuanfen Eatery yesterday, despite Chen Di's intention to take him down. *He'd* make this class more interesting.

Then she shivered, her fingers remembering his cold hand.

'Young Chen, I'll be watching you.'

Chen Di snapped her head to Master Mu, relieved to be brought back to the present.

He asked her to join two crew-cut-sporting older guys, one of whom Chen Di had once overheard bitching about not wanting a girlfriend like her. As if she'd ever take an interest in him. She sighed. If only one-eyed Tang were still around. Tang was her favourite training partner who'd quit last year. Only his attacks were more brutal than hers, his one eye sharper than others' two. She could still picture his eyepatch sewn with a fake eye, complete with lashes.

The two guys' faces stiffened when they saw her approach. With Lü Yuandou in mind, she began throwing and pinning them.

After class, Chen Di pulled off her aikido uniform and threw on her Pizza & Apple Pie one, followed by her jacket, and walked with Master Mu towards his longtang. By the arched entrance, a bicycle repairman sat before an upside-down bicycle. Plucked chickens had been hung up to dry, attached to clothes hangers that dangled from overhead electricity cables.

Master Mu's videotape-VCD-DVD warehouse was the back of his home. Every morning, Chen Di loaded some bootlegs onto the tricycle locked outside. Street hawking was a perfect disguise for her to spy on the government buildings, and in exchange Master Mu let her come to aikido for free.

'The city inspectors are moving around,' he said.

'I won't get caught.' She reached for the bags of Hollywood DVDs she'd packed yesterday. 'Enjoy your visit to Dragon Lustre Temple.'

'Do you have five minutes?'

She checked her watch, the office was opening. 'Just five.'

Beyond a curtain, Chen Di smelled incense. A carved-root tea table centred Master Mu's living room, a bonsai on the windowsill. On the wall hung the ink painting of a woman in traditional dress, wide sleeves flying, though her layered short hair looked modern. Now deceased, she was Master Mu's Japanese wife he'd met during the years he had lived in Japan. If it wasn't for this painting, the room could've been part of a Buddhist temple.

A small photo was taped to a corner of the painting. Taken at Tiananmen Square, it showed a young man, hands on hips, and a young woman in a red sun hat, holding the man's arm. The couple smiled broadly against the giant red placard that read *Long live the People's Republic of China!* With darker skin and a narrow jawline that looked more Japanese than Chinese, the young man was Master Mu's son living in Beijing.

The least inspiring item was Master Mu's wooden wardrobe, similar to Chen Di's but without knife gouges. And she'd bet it didn't have Lü Yuandou's headshot glued inside either.

Chen Di sat down with her backpack strapped on her shoulders. Master Mu returned from behind the curtain and poured chrysanthemum tea for them. He took his seat across from her. 'You can stop selling the DVDs.'

She opened her mouth. 'Are you firing me?'

'Keep coming to my class, I won't charge you.'

'I would prefer not to owe you more than I already do.'

Master Mu sipped his tea, annoyingly calm. He tilted the cup slightly, put it down quietly. 'I wonder sometimes what you work so hard for.'

'To send money home.'

'You didn't even go home for the Spring Festival. Who in your family is still in your hometown?'

Chen Di stared into her cup, small flowers floating, cut hawthorns at the bottom. She didn't know the answer herself. Her spineless father, most likely. She could almost see him holding a leaf to his lips, playing the whistle, his nine fingers quivering.

This wasn't the first time Master Mu had asked such prying questions. She'd always felt he wanted to take on a guardian role for young out-of-towners like her. Perhaps he was compelled by his Buddhist beliefs or some martial arts philosophy, or maybe… She glanced at that small photo. Maybe he simply missed his son.

Not knowing what to say, she looked out the window. Two middle-aged women stood by the longtang's public taps and passionately corrected the way a young mother held her baby.

'Young Chen, exactly what are you in Shanghai for?'

'Money, as I said. Like all out-of-towners.'

'You're not at all like all out-of-towners.'

She looked at him. 'How so?'

'Your mannerisms, for one. Not many rural girls are as educated as you are.'

'I had a good teacher.' Chen Di clutched her jacket, the sudden heat in her chest like a boiling pot of hot-and-sour soup. Indeed, the only items she'd brought with her from Daci Village were this jacket and her education, one she wasn't supposed to have had. And the man who'd given her both might just be in this city right now, somewhere. 'I was lucky.'

'I'm sure it wasn't just luck.'

'Please, can we stop talking about me? We both know *you* are not selling bootlegs because you need the money.' Even longtang-living was his choice. He could opt for any elite housing estate, having built a successful business importing electronics from Japan.

'I'm sure you have your suspicions about me.'

Some of the DVDs were not only bootlegs but also banned in China. Master Mu had hinted that he wanted to share what he knew about the world with less well-off citizens. Which made sense. Back then, Teacher Jia had had a similar goal. 'I have,' she said.

'And I have, too, about you.'

Chen Di tensed. She picked up her cup, bothered by the aroma, but gulped the tea all the same. 'Mind sharing?' Master Mu might've felt *something* going on with her, but couldn't have known her mission. No one could.

'You're walking down a dangerous path.'

'I don't know what you're talking about.'

'Young Chen, you are not a hateful person at heart.'

How easy it was for Master Mu to talk about hate! What had he experienced in life anyhow – rich, powerful, pretending to live with out-of-towners? Outside the window, the middle-aged women and the young mother from earlier were gone. A fight broke out between two men, one cursing the other to 'die sonless and grandsonless'.

'Our five minutes are up.' She downed her tea. 'Enjoy Dragon Lustre Temple.'

But Master Mu picked up his cup again and glanced at her pocket. 'I forbid my students from carrying around weapons because it's a lesson in peace.'

She tensed again. She'd always felt he had a sixth sense. 'You can train with us on one condition,' he'd told her that first day at the dojo. 'My students do not carry around weapons.' Chen Di had clapped her pocket, wondering if he knew about her brand-new Voyager. And last year, he'd seen it fall out of her jacket.

She laughed at herself now. Today, at least, Master Mu had glanced at the wrong pocket. He knew nothing.

6
Sichuan
Winter 1991

Harvest ended amidst the smoke from crop stubble burning. Rumour went that the big-nosed old woman had retired from the village school, and an urban man had come to teach. Chen Di itched to head over there again. Chalk dust in hair was a small price to pay, and the new teacher might just let her watch from the window, for a day. The only hurdle was Grandfather's warning: 'Now is not the time to stir up trouble.' Even though Mother's belly still looked flat, Grandfather already forbade Mother from leaving the house. 'Don't let anyone see you.'

But despite the risk, one clear morning when Grandfather went to the county town for business, Chen Di sneaked out. *Just one visit. I won't stir up trouble.*

The mud paths to school were meandering and uphill, the terraced green fields contrasting with the red banners and red wall writing she passed on the way. A banner she could read, said, *Four to two to one will make China great.* The closer she got to the school, the more loudspeakers were mounted on high concrete poles. A pair screeched out an announcement right above her. 'Attention, villagers.' It was Lü's high voice again. 'You'll be granted a second birth permit only if your first child is a girl. *Girl.* And yet it looks like one abortion just isn't enough for you, Red Flower! We *will* find you. No birth without birth permit.'

Chen Di quickened her pace but couldn't forget the announcement. Mother had no birth permit. They could obtain one, having had only one registered female child, but Grandfather wanted to keep Mother's new pregnancy hidden in case it again turned out to be a girl.

Chen Di arrived at the school's one-storey building, calmed by the surrounding bamboo, which grew even taller than the pole holding the national flag. She tiptoed outside a classroom window. The large windows had no glass but were barred, and where she stood, one bar was missing. Inside, pupils sat on stools and chairs of unequal heights.

The new teacher was younger than she'd expected. He wore navy trousers like the villagers, but his checked shirt made everyone else's clothes look dull. His sleeves were rolled to his elbows, and he held a book in front of his face. The smallest pupils followed line by line as he recited a poem in not Sichuanese but Mandarin, his accent refreshing.

'É, é, é, qǔ xiàng xiàng tiān gē.'
Ganders, ganders, ganders, sing to the sky with necks curved.

Chen Di craned her neck and imagined his face. As if he heard her, he lowered the book and made eye contact with her. In his early twenties, the teacher had longer-than-usual hair, bushy brows, and light stubble. His high-bridged nose looked almost foreign.

'Girl with a sweet smile.' He approached the window.

Tentatively Chen Di asked, 'Me?' She hadn't been told to leave or called 'girl with a birthmark'. Only Mother had ever mentioned her smile.

'Why don't you come in?' He reached out his big hand – neither an accusing finger nor a palm ready to slap. An invitation. Chen Di had never before met a man who'd look at her like this. So far, when she thought of men, she thought of a bellowing voice, of beating, of the power to decide the fate of newborn babies. But this man before her... There was something unusual about his words, his gesture, his gaze. Something kind.

A rush of wind messed the teacher's hair. She gave him her hand, coarser than his, darker than his, with dirt in her nails. He laughed as he caught it, helping her onto the windowsill and inside. He let go, and she had an impulse to hold onto his hand again.

The classroom looked different from inside. Chen Di felt like she'd crept behind a waterfall to find treasure. Then she realised she might've misunderstood the teacher's gesture. 'I'm sorry, I should've come in through the door, teacher...'

'Teacher Jia. And the window's just fine, if you prefer.' He smiled, his eyes crinkling, his lips curling up with a trace of awkwardness that made him approachable.

'Half Face!' A freckled boy broke the momentary silence. 'You're here again.'

A familiar stone formed in Chen Di's chest. She raised her hand to cover her birthmark, knowing it was too late. But Teacher Jia spoke. 'Nobody. Nobody in my class shall call her that.' He looked back at her. 'Would you like to study with us?'

She nodded.

'Your name?'

'Chen Di.'

'You are staying, Chen Di.'

She loved the sound of her name in his Mandarin. She wanted to hear him say it again. She wanted to speak like him, to learn from him.

'Tomorrow I'll get your paperwork organised.'

'Oh... Tomorrow I can't come.'

'Why not?'

'I can come today only because my grandfather is away. He doesn't let me... He doesn't think I should study.' She glanced at the pupils. 'Please don't tell him.'

'And why,' Teacher Jia said, 'doesn't he think you should study?'

Chen Di scanned the pupils again, many more boys than girls. 'Well, boys get to study.'

'Boys get what girls get, there shouldn't be a difference.'

Why would he lie like this? 'Boys deserve so many things girls don't.'

'Like what?'

'They... They deserve to be born! Everyone wants sons.'

'*Everyone* isn't always right.'

She didn't understand. 'But they do want sons. Isn't that why if the family's first baby is a daughter, then they can have another? Like Chief Lü said on the loudspeakers—'

'The loudspeakers aren't always right either. I'll take care of it.'

Chen Di was helping Mother with sewing in the back room that evening when they heard a motorcycle, followed by determined knocks. 'Old Mr Chen!'

Her heart raced when she realised it was Teacher Jia's accented voice, a mix of emotions inside her she'd never experienced before. But would he really be able to persuade Grandfather? How scary it was to have hope. Chen Di glanced at Mother's not-yet-bulging belly, which, this time, might just bring a Little Tiger into the world. Or maybe not.

Mother removed Chen Di's hand from the handle of the sewing machine wheel. She glanced at the door. 'Go ahead.'

Chen Di slipped into the front room, not looking at Father or Grandfather's two mahjong friends, whom she called Grandpa Li and Grandpa Sun, cigarettes between their fingers. Grandpa Li was from a paddy, stout and hairy, nose and ear hair sprouting. Grandpa Sun was the opposite – bald and without even eyebrows – and lived at the neighbouring tobacco field. They sat at the square mahjong table, before scattered small green tiles.

Grandfather led Teacher Jia indoors. Teacher Jia pulled off his raincoat to reveal a checked sweater, and he gave Chen Di a nod that made winter feel like spring.

Father, Grandpa Li, and Grandpa Sun crushed their cigarettes and scooted to make room. In contrast, Teacher Jia's manners were so refined. He was like a big crane rising among the chickens of the village. But then he dropped on a stool and rested one ankle on the opposite knee, showing off the mud on his trousers and shoes. Not that elegant. Chen Di noticed the legs of his socks: one red, one blue. She almost laughed. Maybe Teacher Jia was more sloppy than refined after all, which made him even more approachable.

'Don't you know what to do?' Grandfather scowled at her.

'Yes.' Chen Di hurried out across the rainy yard to the ashy kitchen. She lit the carefully stacked firewood and boiled water while listening in on the conversation in the front room. The Kitchen God idol beamed at her promisingly.

'I've heard about you, Teacher Jia.' Grandfather spoke cautiously, as he did with new guests since the start of Mother's secret pregnancy. 'Are you from Guangdong Province?'

'Yes,' he said, 'the city of Shenzhen.'

'People get out of here and go to places like Shenzhen, you do the opposite. You give Daci Village too much face.'

'I'm here to learn as well.'

'What's there to learn here?' Grandpa Li laughed. 'Well, yuanfen brought you to us just as my grandson's turning five, it looks like he'll be taught by an urban man!'

Chen Di dropped pinches of tea leaves in five enamel mugs – for Grandfather, Father, Grandpa Li, Grandpa Sun, and Teacher Jia. When the kettle whistled, she poured the hot water into each mug, shut the lids, and set them in a tray. She hoped she was part of the yuanfen that connected Teacher Jia to the rest of them, that *she* would be taught by this urban man.

Back in the front room, she saw Father get up and ask Teacher Jia to take his stool instead at the mahjong table. Though she didn't quite believe it, he gave Teacher Jia an earnest nod as if saying, 'I'm leaving it to you.'

But even after Father left for the back room, Grandpa Li continued to blabber about his grandson, a grin stretched across his hairy face. Grandpa Sun, on the other hand, looked down, his bald head like a big brown egg. His son at the tobacco field had ended up with two daughters, named Tingting and Lanlan, which meant 'Grace' and 'Orchid'. Though they could also mean 'Stop' and 'Block'.

'Girls are good, less pressure!' Grandpa Li clapped Grandpa Sun's back as if to comfort him. He then looked at Chen Di sideways and said to Grandfather, 'You still have a chance, Old Chen. Zhang Si's medicine works, guaranteed boy.'

'Nonsense!' Grandfather stole a glimpse of Teacher Jia, then glanced at the back room, where Mother was. 'You want to get Zhang Si arrested? We don't mess with family planning here, it's national policy.'

'R-Right, I got carried away,' Grandpa Li said. 'We don't want Chief Lü to—'

'Shush!' Grandfather said. 'Family planning is good, the Party is infallible.'

The drizzle thickened, water pouring from the eaves, forming a curtain outside the door. While Grandpa Sun fiddled with a mahjong brick and kept his bald head down, Grandfather and Grandpa Li checked Teacher Jia's face. Sweat trickled from Grandfather's temple, and he picked his nose like a child, the way he did when he was nervous.

Teacher Jia put down his leg, leaving a patch of mud on the opposite knee. 'I'm not a Party member. I'm sympathetic to the villagers when it comes to family planning.'

'You're not with Chief Lü?' Grandfather's eyes drifted to the back room again.

'No, I'm not with Lü Yuandou.'

Grandfather pulled his finger out of his nose, his face loosening.

But Chen Di remained tense, the tray in her hands heavy. Exactly who was this Lü Yuandou, if he could scare even Grandfather? Despite all his high-pitched loudspeaker announcements, the family planning official remained as shadowy in her mind as Daci Pit's ghost woman – both with scary stories, neither she'd met in person.

Teacher Jia spoke. 'I came here today to discuss enrolling Chen Di at the school. She's already nine years old.'

All eyes fell on her. She rushed to set the mugs on the edges of the mahjong table and opened the lids one by one.

'Thank you,' Teacher Jia said, startling her. Had anyone thanked her, ever? A lid slipped from her hand and clattered on the floor. She bent to get it, but a slap on the back of her head made her kneel. She retreated to the side but looked up to see Teacher Jia gripping Grandfather's forearm. Suddenly the back of her head stopped hurting, her chest warm.

'No need to use hands,' Teacher Jia said.

Grandfather shook him off, while Grandpa Li waved his hairy arm. 'Her future mother-in-law is not going to be happy.'

Teacher Jia held out a palm. 'As I said, I'd like to discuss enrolling—'

'Teacher Jia, you're not from here.' Grandfather lit a cigarette. 'We have our traditions. Studying is for boys, girls will be married off! Uneducated women are virtuous women.'

'But times have changed.' Teacher Jia refused the cigarette passed to him.

'What change? We need helping hands here, especially during harvest.' Grandfather puffed towards the back room. He looked more and more relaxed, perhaps knowing now that Teacher Jia wouldn't report Mother's pregnancy even if he found out. 'She might even get busy all year round. Let's say she has a little brother to take care of...'

'Chen Di can bring him to school.'

'Whose side are you on, Teacher Jia? Didn't you say you were on ours?'

'It's not black and white.'

'Study, study, what study? This little shit is lucky to be alive. She hardly deserves to live.' Grandfather whipped around, his stool scraping the floor, and he pointed at Chen Di with his calloused finger. 'Aren't you grateful for your little life?'

'Yes,' she quickly said.

'Say it!'

'I am grateful for my little life.'

The room stilled. Teacher Jia pulled his ankle back on the opposite knee. He scratched the leg of the blue sock, then his head, his shaggy hair hiding his face.

Grandpa Sun looked up, edgy, showing his missing eyebrows. 'Old Chen,' he said, 'if we're not playing mahjong, then I-I-I'm leaving.' Maybe he wasn't just upset – he was hiding something, the way her family hid Mother's pregnancy. In fact, Grandfather, Grandpa Li, and Grandpa Sun exchanged glances as if they knew each other's secrets. It wasn't that easy to hide things in the village, after all, but there was a tacit understanding for villagers to safeguard each other in front of any common enemy.

'We *are* playing.' Grandfather tilted down his oblong face while his eyes looked up, his unibrow dipped in the middle like a wronged child. A child who only wanted to fill his belly after a harsh winter without food. 'Come, come, come, Teacher Jia! Give us face and join us for a game. What difference does one pupil make anyway?'

Teacher Jia looked up from his sock. 'What difference does one player make, anyway?'

'But it's a four-player game.'

'Yes, it is.' Teacher Jia rolled up his left sleeve, and his right. 'If I win, then tomorrow I'll see Chen Di at school. Is that okay with you, Old Mr Chen?'

'And if you lose?'

'Then I owe the winner a good carton of cigarettes.'

'Deal.' Grandfather laughed. 'When a word leaves your mouth—'

'Even four horses cannot bring it back.'

Chen Di stared at the back of Teacher Jia's checked sweater, her eyes tracing the pattern. He was fighting for her. For the first time, someone was. The mix of emotions inside became too much to bear and she wondered if she should kowtow before him to express her gratitude. But something told her Teacher Jia wouldn't want that.

She returned to the back room to see her parents sitting at the sewing machine, not sewing. Father stood and left again as if to avoid her, and she sat beside Mother, putting down the tray she'd forgotten she'd been clutching. Mother hugged her shoulders with one arm and caressed her own belly with the other hand. 'Yao'er,' she murmured. *Darling son.*

Chen Di had thought Mother was concerned about her chances of going to school, but of course her pregnancy occupied her mind. 'It'll be Little Tiger.' She tried to smile.

Mother smiled back. 'Yes, it will.'

The clatter of the mahjong tiles took away Chen Di's attention, followed by the sound of each tile hitting the table. She continued sewing with Mother, turning the machine's wheel. She could hear Grandfather shout 'chi' when completing a straight and 'peng' a set of three. She wanted to sneak a peek, but thought better of it.

The rain stopped, leaving a rhythmic dripping sound. And Chen Di jumped when at last she heard laughter and voices saying goodbye. Had Teacher Jia won or lost the game? The double doors creaked and she shot out straight to the courtyard, her big slippers landing in the murky puddles. Outside, Teacher Jia mounted his motorcycle.

She ran to him, panting. 'Teacher Jia!'

'It's all set, see you tomorrow.'

She almost cheered aloud but only gazed at him and nodded. 'Thank you for…coming all the way to our house.'

He gave his slightly awkward smile. 'You're worth it.'

'But I'm just a girl.'

'And a girl is worth it. You have worth, Chen Di, don't let anyone tell you otherwise.' Without getting off the motorcycle, he leaned down to her level. She felt his breathing by her ear, and it warmed her whole body. 'Next time your grandfather makes you bring him tea, spit in it.'

7
Shanghai
Winter 2002

Between her aikido class and her shift at Pizza & Apple Pie, Chen Di had only one hour to hawk bootlegs – to spy on the government building for Lü Yuandou.

She stood behind a plane tree further away from Yuanfen Eatery today, hoping the owner wouldn't recognise her. The steaming bowls of savoury soy milk made her mouth water. She would've bought one and added chilli bean paste if she hadn't got herself into a knife fight here yesterday. Her eyes cut to the sliding gate across the road, but she again glanced back at the worn awning that read *Yuanfen Eatery*.

Students flocked to Wende Private. One girl fixed the red scarf around her neck as she recited to her mother her speech on being 'a successor to the communist cause'. Shanghai couldn't be more different from Daci Village, but people here loved the Party all the same.

Just after nine, a boy ran towards her in track pants, his uniform blazer flapping. He extended an arm to hail a ride, but all passing taxis were full. Another pampered kid from

Wende Private, skipping school for Heaven knows what. His long legs darted, avoiding people, and leaped over a pile of foam boxes. Chen Di flinched as she caught sight of his face. Though he was at least twenty metres away, she recognised his eyes. Little Tiger's eyes.

It was none other than that little emperor yesterday, Lin Feng.

His school was around the corner, but she hadn't expected to spot him like this. And she caught herself sighing with relief. So he was okay after having fainted yesterday.

Lin Feng approached and she couldn't help but study all his features. He had a square face, his brows straight as if drawn by a calligraphy brush, his nose rounded at the end as if to secure everything in place. As he ran, his side-swooping fringe was swept back, exposing his forehead. His skin was so fair he could model for skin-whitening-cream companies – Chen Di had a bizarre feeling he'd become translucent one day, and vanish.

A tall woman in white called out and chased after him, holding her black satchel so it didn't swing. His teacher? Mother? Lin Feng almost ran past Chen Di when a sweaty guy zipped down the pavement on his bicycle, shouting at an old man in a beret walking a pug, 'Get out of the way!' Lin Feng stopped abruptly to scoop up the dog, barely dodging the bicycle as it whizzed by, one wheel rolling over his sneaker.

Ow. Chen Di felt her own toes ache.

'Child! Are you all right?' The old man took over the pug, horrified.

Lin Feng ignored the question.

The woman caught up to him. 'You!' She grabbed his ear, wrinkles deepening between her thin brows. Her old-fashioned bun had loosened, the jade hairpin about to fall out. Only a mother could look so desperate. 'You think running solves all your problems!' One hand still twisting his ear, she lifted her satchel and whacked him across his face.

Chen Di winced, feeling a surge of sympathy as the boy's cheek turned pink. Physical punishment was common, but out on the street? Didn't the mother care about losing face? Regardless of the kid's crime, he was her precious only child.

Passers-by stopped to gawk. The mother didn't care, her lower lip quivering. 'Run, run, run! Run to your death!' She massaged one temple as if she was getting a headache.

The boy yanked her hand off his ear. He glanced around, and his dark eyes stopped at Chen Di. She flinched again, the past she'd buried deep creeping in, unstoppable.

But this kid had nothing to do with her brother! Little Tiger was born in the year of the Monkey, he would have been only nine years old if he was still alive.

'You there, big sis!' Lin Feng waved a green note – fifty yuan. 'Give me a ride.' He limped closer and pressed both hands on her DVDs, his breath forming clouds in the cold.

Fifty yuan was almost a quarter of her rent. 'Excuse me?'

'Come on, big sis! Take me with you.'

She looked to his hands so she didn't have to look him in the eye, and she clutched her head, her nails hard on her skull. 'Cut it out.'

'Take me.'

'No.' She wasn't about to stray from her mission. She wouldn't forget her priority.

Behind him, the mother dropped down on an outdoor stool at Yuanfen Eatery, surrounded by others. When Chen Di looked back, Lin Feng was climbing onto the cart of her tricycle, one black sneaker already among the DVDs. She almost shouted at him to stop, but his mum cried out like a madwoman, 'Be grateful for your little life!'

Chen Di grimaced. She could almost hear her grandfather say these exact words to her. She jumped on the tricycle, the boy at the back, and sped into the cycle lane. Something thorny swirled inside her chest and she pumped the pedals hard.

After crossing an intersection, Lin Feng clapped her shoulder like an old friend. 'I saw you the day before yesterday too, on my way to school. You seem pretty awesome.'

'So you actually go to school.'

'How many DVDs do you manage to sell? It doesn't look like good business.'

'Don't you have better things to do than check me out?'

'Your birthmark...was hard to ignore.'

The following silence compelled Chen Di to look back over her shoulder. Lin Feng sat cross-legged among her bootleg DVDs, head down, rubbing his chin in that disturbingly familiar way. The pink on his cheek wasn't fading. Then he said, 'My sister has a birthmark on her face too, on her chin. She's about your age.'

'By *sister*, you mean *cousin*?'

'No, my real sister.'

Chen Di had thought family planning was a strict one-child policy in Shanghai. 'Look, Lin Feng, I'm not interested,' she said, as much to him as to herself. She was just getting an easy fifty yuan.

'You remember my name! What an honour.'

'When are you getting off?'

'We're really close, me and my sister. We did everything together until she went to Beijing for uni. She still calls me every day, though, every evening at eight.'

'And she'd be sad to find you in jail when she gets back.' Lucky girl, studying in Beijing, awaiting some high-paying job, supported by her forward-thinking urban parents who didn't necessarily prefer boys to girls. Rural girls would die for that kind of life.

'Anyway, big sis, are you—'

'Stop that.'

'Stop what, big sis?'

'It's Chen Di!' The way the kid called her 'big sis' got on her nerves, and it annoyed her how much she let it annoy her. 'I'm not your sister.'

A north wind tore through the leafless plane trees lining the road. She felt a hand gently placed on her back, then it vanished, and she looked over her shoulder again.

Lin Feng crossed his arms and smirked. 'I'll go with Boss Chen then.'

She laughed, flattered.

'Boss Chen, are you really just a hawker?'

'Precisely. I'm just a poor out-of-towner—'

'Who knows martial arts. What you did at Yuanfen Eatery yesterday was something. Are you in some kind of gang? Are you a professional?'

'Unfortunately not.'

'I'm not calling you Boss Chen for nothing. How about you take me as your apprentice?'

'What?'

'Teach me how you snatched my Swiss Army Knife.'

'No.'

'Come on, Boss Chen. I'll bow to you.'

'No is no.' Chen Di biked around a corner to avoid two men dressed in blue shirts and indigo suit jackets, national emblems on the sleeves. City inspectors. 'Don't mess with me, I'll bring you back to your mum.'

He huffed. 'I'm not afraid of that crazy woman.'

'It looked like you were.'

'I'm not. She hates me, that's all.'

'I haven't met a Shanghainese mum who doesn't love her child.'

Chen Di passed a news stand, a real estate agency, and a symmetrical European-style house. Deciding to stay close to the government building, she turned twice. Tall fences surrounded twelve-storey apartment buildings, the names of the housing estates engraved in red on large stones. Here last night, she'd taken a humble father to be Lü. She wondered if Lin Feng lived nearby, then felt him shifting behind her.

'Why were you running from your mum anyhow?' she asked.

'Because I have important business today! I have to see a bro down in Dragon Lustre. I don't have the time to deal with school.'

'You meant to say she caught you bunking off. No wonder.'

'No, my mum actually hates me. She hates me especially when I run and I just broke the one-hundred-metre school record, it set her off like crazy. My dad too, he also hates me, I haven't seen him in ages.' He cleared his throat. 'Only my sister likes me.'

Chen Di couldn't get involved. She shouldn't, mustn't, didn't care about his life. 'When are you getting off? I'm heading back.'

After a pause, he said, 'When do you want me to?'

She braked at a red light, a sharp screech.

'Fine.' The boy jumped off and signalled an aqua Dazhong taxi that was also stopped at the red light. 'I'll find out about you, Boss Chen.'

'What's there to find out about *me?*' Except she couldn't help but feel flattered again. It was as if he cared about her the way a real brother might…or maybe not. She hadn't treated Little Tiger all that well, even before the incident of the 1994 harvest.

She cringed, and clutched her head.

Lin Feng smirked again. 'You have a story, you're worthy of having an apprentice like me.' He then reached out and, with his fingertips, touched her birthmark. She should've slapped away his hand but only opened her mouth, her heart pounding. His fingers lingered on her cheek, the touch gentle but ever so cold, and for a second she glimpsed sadness in his dark eyes.

He retracted his hand and strode to the taxi, snapping his fingers at the driver like a gang leader.

'Pay up!' she said.

Without looking back, he tossed her a handful of coins.

'You said fifty!'

'Nope, I only waved it.' He climbed into the car and slammed the door.

Chen Di sat rooted to her tricycle and let an old man in rags pick up the coins with his frostbitten fingers. She should've taken the kid's money in advance. No, she should've kept watching the gate! But she only touched her own cheek. Her birthmark. She could still feel his cold fingers on her skin.

Bicycles swerved around her, ringing bells. She pushed her tricycle onto the pavement. That was when she saw the back of a small man, wearing a suit, holding a briefcase.

All her limbs stiffened. She felt as if she were falling.

He had pointed ears and long lobes that symbolised goodness. Lü.

8
Sichuan
Spring 1992

Despite Lü Yuandou's loudspeaker announcements, despite the fear of being found out, hope filled the house as Mother's belly swelled. No scowling. No yelling. No beating. If the mere prospect of a boy already brought so much joy, how good life would be if Chen Di actually had a little brother! They welcomed a small porcelain idol of the Bodhisattva of Compassion. She stood in white robes on a blooming lotus, a baby boy in her arms. Everyone in the family lit incense sticks and bowed before her daily, asking for a Little Tiger. Chen Di did so too, of course, willingly, wholeheartedly.

Moreover, though she still couldn't believe any teacher would suggest such a thing, Teacher Jia had been right: each time she spit in Grandfather's tea, home life *did* feel more manageable, school life even better.

Her notebook was always by her side now. She opened it by the enamel washbasin while washing clothes, kept it beside the stove while cooking, and left it in her lap while plaiting her hair. She held it in one hand while hanging laundry, in both hands while squatting over the toilet. Already she could read over a thousand characters, including many that Mother didn't know.

One afternoon in early spring, Teacher Jia caught up to her outside the school, saying she no longer needed to study with younger pupils but could join her ten-year-old peers. Chen Di held onto a bamboo stalk and gazed at him to make sure of his words. His hair was neater than usual, his head blocking the stars on the red national flag.

'Well done,' he said. 'You've learned so much so fast.'

All thanks to you. Her eyes became wet. Her life before Teacher Jia now felt like someone else's life – everything had changed. 'Teacher Jia, I've been meaning to ask you…'

'Ask away.'

'What if you lost that mahjong game last year?'

His lips curled up, his eyes crinkling. 'I would've given your grandfather a carton of cigarettes and tried again, I would've fought for you till the end. You are worth it.'

It was the same lie again, though it felt so good to hear it. 'Thank you…for saying that.'

'I'm not just saying it.'

'But I'm only a girl, I'm not worth it.'

'Not again, Chen Di.'

'But even *I* want a brother, I really do. Boys *are* worth more than girls.'

Teacher Jia watched her. 'Why?'

'Without a son, you can't hold your head high, can't even be buried in the ancestral grave.' She realised she was repeating Grandfather's words, and looked down, holding onto the bamboo stalk again. Well, it was a fact as true as the bamboo was green. 'Chief Lü was just repeating the rules on the loudspeakers that if a family—'

'That's enough.' Teacher Jia rolled his sleeves despite the cold, and he glanced around the schoolyard. There were no other adults nearby, only pupils. 'I'm going to tell you something now, and I need you to not repeat it to anyone because I think no one else will understand. But I believe *you* will, some day.'

She nodded. Teacher Jia was going to share a secret with her, and only her. It was as if he trusted her more than he did anyone else.

He leaned down and said into her ear, 'Lü Yuandou is a monster. Between our fellow countrymen's outdated mindset and the Party's authoritarian policies, he's found an opportunity to prey on people.'

Chen Di's heart thudded. She repeated the line in her head, unsure if she understood it, unable to picture how one might write some of the characters, but still she committed it to memory. A part of her wished Teacher Jia would've told her something personal, maybe about his family. She wondered what his parents were like, if he had brothers or sisters. Or he could've told her about his hometown, Shenzhen, surely an amazing city.

'So don't listen to the loudspeakers.' He held her eyes

so intently her face grew hot. 'And don't listen to your grandfather either. You have worth. Every child does.'

She wished he hadn't added the very last bit.

Chen Di headed home that afternoon, reviewing what Teacher Jia had taught in class, drawing out new characters in the air. Her finger dropped when she passed Grandpa Li's wooden house across the stream, decorated with strings of corn cobs. On one side stood Grandpa Li's daughter-in-law, Chubby Aunty, the bulging mole in her eyebrow visible even from a distance. She chatted with a short old woman while holding onto her fidgety son. At the front of the house, a tilted concrete pole held a pair of loudspeakers.

'Attention, villagers.' Lü Yuandou's high voice made both Chubby Aunty and Chen Di stop. Not listening to the loudspeakers was easier said than done. 'I call your attention to Du Daidi, carrying her third child, *third,* and nowhere to be found! Reporting permitless pregnancies is every citizen's duty – whoever helps her will be severely punished.' He paused. 'Now, Du Daidi, listen up! You can hide past the first day of the Spring Festival, not the fifteenth day. If you come forward for abortion, we'll make things easy. But if you do not cooperate, then don't blame me for what happens next!'

A bad feeling settled inside Chen Di. Du Daidi, whom Chen Di called Aunty Du, was Grandpa Sun's daughter-in-law from her own family's neighbouring tobacco field. Chen

Di had felt since Teacher Jia's home visit that Grandpa Sun, like her own grandfather, was hiding something. 'Du Daidi's going to Chengdu to give birth,' people had whispered. 'No birth permit?' 'Obviously not, it's her third!'

The loudspeakers continued to blare, reminding villagers about the Learn-from-Lei-Feng Day, urging them to follow the examples of Comrade Lei Feng, an eager-to-help model citizen. 'Today is the day to do good deeds!'

Chen Di hurried home.

From far away, she saw Grandpa Sun's house and field, lined with little tobacco sprouts. Was Aunty Du hiding inside? Nothing seemed unusual until Chen Di looked in the direction of her own house. They'd just sowed cotton seeds, the field quiet, but before the stone bridge was a black car almost the size of a tractor, four loudspeakers fastened on top. Two pointed to the front, two to the sides, and they were uniformly white, as if to announce death.

She wiped the sweat from her forehead. Before the double doors to the courtyard she stopped, hearing voices, and quietly pushed one open. It was Grandfather's voice and a familiar, high-pitched one. She'd heard it on the loudspeakers a hundred times.

Chen Di stumbled at the high threshold, but kept quiet. She tiptoed across the yard and poked her head into the front room. Grandfather was having tea with a small man whose back was to her, and who was flanked by two bigger men. The small man had short dark hair and wore a casual-looking dusty suit jacket. She couldn't stop staring at his ears: pointy on top, the lobes long. Only Buddhist idols had such blessedly long lobes, but their ears were never pointy.

'But they're your neighbours,' the small man said.

'I'm afraid we really do not know where Du Daidi is, Chief Lü.' Grandfather rarely spoke so politely. 'We will be sure to report to you if—'

'You're helping them by reporting them, you understand?'

'We do.'

'You don't.' Lü set down the enamel mug. 'It looks like Bald Old Sun has friends, good friends who are willing to be punished with his whole family.'

Chen Di shuddered and took a sidestep away only to knock a broom to the floor.

Lü Yuandou jerked his head around. His heart-shaped face looked almost kind at first, but then chilling. His ears were even weirder when viewed from the front. 'So this,' he said at an excruciatingly slow pace, 'is your granddaughter.'

Her hand shook as she tried to hide her birthmark, too late.

'She's, what, ten?' Lü said. 'Your daughter-in-law never had a second?'

'Never,' Grandfather said.

Lü chuckled, his eyes moving from Chen Di to Grandfather as if saying he knew exactly what had been happening. He checked his watch and looked outside before turning back. 'Let's forget Bald Old Sun and Du Daidi for a second. Where is *your* daughter-in-law?'

Chen Di's heart jumped, her hand still covering her

birthmark. Mother, with her growing belly, hadn't left the house for three months now.

'Where *is* your daughter-in-law?' Lü repeated.

Grandfather rose and headed to the back room. Within a minute, he returned, followed by Mother, head down, belly bulging. 'Chief Lü, my daughter-in-law is expecting, and we're just about to apply for a birth permit.'

'Really,' Lü said, his voice even higher. 'Congratulations.'

'But, Chief Lü, things happen. Miscarriages, stillbirths. We can only hope Heaven will protect this baby.'

'Regardless of its sex?' Lü glanced at their idol of the Bodhisattva of Compassion.

'Yes,' Grandfather said stiffly, a blatant lie. 'Regardless of its sex.'

Lü's small eyes were squinting. Chen Di first thought he was doubting Grandfather, then realised he was looking at Mother, something unseemly in his gaze. 'My mug is empty,' he said. Without thinking, Chen Di turned to head to the kitchen, but Lü stopped her. 'Would *you* make me another, Old Chen? That was an exceptionally good mug of tea.'

As soon as Grandfather went out, Lü rose and circled Mother and Chen Di, nodding. Chen Di trembled, taking hold of Mother's hand, only to feel that Mother too was shaking. She'd never imagined a time when she'd rather Grandfather were around. They backed towards the wall, with its new portrait of Chairman Mao. The great leader wore the same tunic suit as in the previous version, but in this he beamed more, his cheeks red.

'Your pretty face reminds me of a slutty fox spirit,' Lü Yuandou said to Mother, who kept her head down, her arm shielding Chen Di. He flicked the air before Mother's breasts, as if he was choosing a ripe watermelon. 'I'll be keeping an eye on you, big sister.'

It felt like forever before Grandfather came back with tea. Lü was still chuckling. 'All right, Old Chen.' He stood against the beaming Chairman Mao and raised his arms generously. 'Go and get papers signed and stamped. Bring your marriage certificate, household registration, resident ID, photos, and the first child's birth certificate. You'll need to fill an application form for another child.'

'Yes, Chief Lü,' Grandfather said to the table.

'*Make sure* you have a birth permit the next time I see you.'

'Yes, Chief Lü.'

Chen Di looked to Mother, who'd never appeared so small. Now that they were registering her pregnancy, they'd have to accept the outcome. Chen Di shivered and bent her arm to touch her back, feeling the scars from Grandfather's beating. *Let it be a boy this time, please!* She'd never wanted anything so badly, and Mother's clenched jaw showed she was begging for the same.

Lü quietly sipped from the new mug. 'Ahhh, good tea.'

A loud engine sounded from the distance.

'Chief Lü,' one of his men said.

'Time to go.' Lü stood and gave Mother another unseemly look before swaggering out with his men.

'Wait!' Grandfather chased after them. 'What are you doing to Old Sun?'

Chen Di went outside too. Lü got into his large car and it rumbled towards Grandpa Sun's house, leaving plumes of dust under the gathering dark clouds. Thunder roared overhead. His leaving should've made her feel relieved, but it did not. Before the tobacco field, the muddy path had been blocked by an enormous orange machine. An excavator.

Grandfather pressed a hand to his chest and staggered after Lü's car, his face reddening with worry. 'Old Sun shared bark and roots with me during the Great Famine...'

Chen Di followed Grandfather's unsteady steps across the cotton field and up the mud path. She'd never seen Grandfather like this before but knew the significance of the famine for him – memories of his rescue of an orphaned boy, Chen Di's father.

Lü's large car looked small beside the excavator. Chen Di and Grandfather joined the dozens of villagers standing around the house by the tobacco field, some angry, others curious. Four people knelt on the muddy ground in front of Lü: Grandpa Sun, Uncle Sun, and two girls in pigtails – Tingting and Lanlan – both younger than Chen Di.

'Old Sun,' Lü said calmly. 'Bring your daughter-in-law out if you don't want to end up houseless.'

'She is no longer here.' Grandpa Sun's bald head dropped to the ground. 'Forgive us, Chief Lü! I only have granddaughters...'

Tingting and Lanlan sobbed loudly, their small heads pressed down by Uncle Sun to beg for Lü's mercy. Lü raised a hand, signalling to the driver of the excavator. It rolled into the tobacco field, the engine louder than the onlookers' screams, crushing the tobacco sprouts, row by row, that lay in its path. It stopped at the side of the house and extended its arm.

'I'll count till three.' Lü looked almost bored. 'One.'

'Chief Lü, please!' Uncle Sun grovelled to touch his shoe, only to be kicked.

'Two.' The machine raised its excavator bucket above the house.

'Wait, Chief Lü!' Uncle Sun scrambled up, his eyes widening with horror. 'My mother is bed-bound. She's still in the house!'

'Three.'

The huge metal bucket pounded a hole through the shingled roof. Dust particles flew. Chen Di coughed, her eyes watering. Grandpa Sun and Uncle Sun rushed indoors as one side of the house collapsed. Lightning ripped the sky, followed by another crack of thunder, rain threatening to pour. The excavator raised its arm a second time.

'Stop!' villagers shouted. 'You're going to kill them!'

Tingting and Lanlan hugged each other, sobbing by Lü's feet. He glanced at them and chuckled. 'Your grandfather is so soft-hearted, isn't he? As much as he wanted to get around the policies, he didn't let the ghost woman take you girls.'

Chen Di felt goosebumps on her arms as she pictured the translucent ghost snatching the two girls, one in each of her bony hands, flying over the jungle, plunging down into Daci Pit, and devouring them in her bloody mouth.

Grandfather fell to his knees, surprising Chen Di. She'd never imagined he'd kneel for a friend's sake. 'I beg you, Chief Lü!' Grandfather kowtowed to the family planning official. 'Have mercy! They're good people.'

Lü ignored him.

'This is barbarous!' A middle-aged woman squeezed through, a jade pendant around her neck. She pointed at Lü. '*You* are barbarous! No wonder your wife left you, we've all heard.'

'How dare you?' Lü spat at her, losing his cool for the first time. 'Don't you dare mention that woman! You know nothing about that slut, that fox spirit!'

Before the excavator bucket could smash on the house again, Grandpa Sun and Uncle Sun appeared, carrying a wizened old woman outside. Grandpa Sun's head was bleeding.

The rain poured and Lü looked down as if annoyed his leather shoes had got dirty. But when Chen Di sneaked a peek at his face, his expression confused her. He wasn't looking at his shoes, only hanging his head, his eyes squeezed shut as if in pain. He rubbed his forehead.

'Consider yourselves lucky,' he announced, raising a hand to stop the excavator. His small eyes scanned the crowd. 'I'll be extra merciful today and give you a week to bring me the woman, before I tear down the rest of your house.'

He got back into his car and left with his men.

Grandfather bandaged Grandpa Sun's head, and for days, no one paid attention to a small scrape on his forearm. Only when he said his jaw was stiff and he couldn't swallow was he taken to the village health centre. By then, a week had passed.

Aunty Du never came back. Grandpa Sun never witnessed the rest of his house being torn down. And even after Grandpa Sun's funeral, the cotton field remained scarred to the point Chen Di felt sorry for Grandfather. But her sympathy lasted for only two months.

Then her brother – Little Tiger – was finally born.

9
Shanghai
Winter 2002

Shanghai had too little space, too many people, the roads wide but never wide enough. Cars and buses swerved and honked, motorcycles revved their engines, and bicycles raced on, everyone trying to squeeze everyone else out of the way so they could get ahead.

Chen Di walked her tricycle, which took up too much space on the pavement, and kept her distance from the man with the pointy-topped ears. When he went around a news stand, she glimpsed half of that heart-shaped face.

No mistaking it. It was Lü Yuandou.

Chen Di's whole body shook. She felt like a child rewatching a scary cartoon, the monster just as frightening, if not more, because she already knew what it could do. This wasn't like yesterday morning, when she'd spotted an official with Lü's face shape but the wrong ears. It wasn't like last night, when a humble father in an ancient quilted coat had somehow, ridiculously, reminded her of Lü.

This *was* Lü.

Her hands gripped the tricycle handlebars so tensely she felt she could break them off. She was only a few steps away from avenging Mother, avenging her whole village!

Chen Di felt tears building again and reminded herself this was not the time to be sentimental. What right did Lü have to remain alive when Mother had died? She'd hoped for an illness or traffic accident to claim his life, but she could, and would, kill him herself. After three years of hard work in this inhumane city, she'd toughened up even more than before. She could end his life on the spot! The simplest aikido wrist lock would force him to kneel. She could twist his arm behind his back and push her Voyager into his throat.

Only she had to be prudent. A passer-by might be more adept than she was and intervene. Ambulances, non-existent in Daci Village, were commonplace in Shanghai. And if she acted now, surrounded by people, she'd have little chance of getting away. She pictured a female prison packed with women who'd been physically abused and killed their husbands. What kind of life would that be? After the mission, she needed to live on, and live well.

Some day, she just might flee China.

So she couldn't rush it. She must complete her mission in stages, as planned, which included killing Lü Yuandou at his home and escaping without a trace.

Lü crossed the road. He *was* heading to the commission. He had to live nearby then, so close he didn't need a bicycle. Chen Di crossed the road too, her front wheel almost rolling onto a small boy's foot, and his mother cursed her. Just as she reached the opposite pavement, he turned. She ducked, pretending to check her DVDs, heart throbbing. She pulled up her hood before standing straight again and scratched her forehead to hide her birthmark.

Lü continued. She didn't know what had caught his eye, but he couldn't have recognised her. He wouldn't be expecting to bump into a Daci villager in Big Shanghai.

The government building appeared, the national flag flapping hard. But before reaching the sliding gate, Lü turned into an alleyway. She followed to see him walk through another gate, where he was greeted by a guard, before proceeding to a small side door of the same government building. Chen Di clenched her fists. She'd almost let Lü Yuandou slip away from under her nose! Thank Heaven, thank Earth today she had taken Lin Feng on her tricycle – she might never have known about the side gate otherwise.

The boy's smirk crossed her mind. She recalled the way he tossed her the coins but was unable to get mad. And she recalled his gentle but cold touch on her cheek, which she'd forgiven him for on the spot. He must've been thinking of his own sister who'd moved away.

Perhaps there was some yuanfen between them after all.

Chen Di served the wrong pizza twice during the same lunch shift. Step one was complete: she had found Lü Yuandou. After three years in Shanghai, eating bitterness, she had found him right here in Xuhui District! She laughed at herself now for having first surveilled the offices of the Family Planning Commission in outer districts.

For her afternoon break, she marched out the backdoor into the mall to get some time alone. To think. Crowds of shoppers sauntered past her as she mulled over her next steps.

Step two: follow him home.

Step three: execute him. She didn't allow herself to shudder.

Step four: escape.

In order to complete step two, Chen Di would need to quit Pizza & Apple Pie to free her evenings, and she'd have to carry out the rest of her mission before her savings ran out. Time to really focus. Except she saw a mother-and-son pair on the ascending escalator and thought of Lin Feng again, the way his mum had whacked him in public... How would he face her tonight? If she could get so physical with him on the street, what *wouldn't* she do at home?

Back at the restaurant, Manager Chu stood in his suit and fat red tie and wagged his finger. 'Your evening shift, you're three minutes late.' He moistened his lips and pointed to the right, his big silver watch reflecting light. 'You kept Mr, uh, you kept an important person – I-I-I mean, customer – waiting.' He blinked nervously.

She followed him towards a man in a beige sweater at a window booth, a grey wool overcoat folded beside him. Her jaw dropped.

'Master Mu?' She went to the table, where a pizza sat untouched before him.

'Sit.' He gestured, his deep voice at a different pitch from the surrounding chatter. She sat across from him and caught a whiff of incense, so out of place in Pizza & Apple Pie. 'Young Chen, you broke your promise to me.'

'What promise?'

'You're banned from the dojo.'

'What?'

'And you can stop your morning job, working for me.'

Now that she'd found Lü, she no longer had to pretend to be a hawker, but she needed aikido. 'Master Mu, I didn't get caught bootlegging. The city inspectors don't get up until the sun's burning their asses.' She shouldn't have said 'asses'. 'Please, don't ban me. I have more to learn.'

'Well said.' He slid aside the pizza and placed a pocket-sized book on the table. The white cover showed a large circle drawn by a calligraphy brush: *The Art of Peace* by Morihei Ueshiba. Chen Di had seen this book before, somewhere. 'You do lack training. Return after you have understood the Great Teacher's words.'

'At least tell me why, all of a sudden, you—'

'You still carry around that knife, the one carved with '98 Lantern Fest.'

So that was the promise she'd broken. How had he found out this time? 'But I don't carry it around anymore,' she said weakly. 'You can check my belongings.'

'I don't need to, because I have it.'

She almost stood. 'You stole my knife?'

Chen Di glanced at the locker room, then at Manager Chu, who was looking in their direction, blinking rapidly again. Had he let Master Mu enter the women's locker room, check her jacket pockets, and take her Voyager? This sounded absurd.

Shanghainese chatter filled the restaurant. A man insisted on using chopsticks for apple pie, mocked by his teenage son. A little girl rose to recite to her grandparents, 'May your fortune be as vast as the Eastern Sea, your life as long as that of the Southern Mountain!'

'It wasn't me who first took it,' Master Mu said.

'I'm sorry? Who took it then?'

'Lin Feng.'

Chen Di leaned back, her chest tightening at the mention of the boy's name. She felt as if Master Mu had found out a secret of hers. But how did he know Lin Feng? She thought back to this morning, before she'd spotted Lü Yuandou. Had Lin Feng pulled her Voyager out of her pocket while riding on the cart of her tricycle?

Master Mu spoke again. 'You don't need a knife like that for self-defence.'

'I cut vegetables with it!' She glanced around, regretting her loud voice. 'Instead of meddling in *my* life, why don't you head to Beijing and lecture your own son on a thing or two?' She'd meant it as a complaint, but the brief moment Master Mu averted his eyes made her feel as if she was the one prying. She quickly said, 'How did you know Lin Feng took my knife? Did you get it from him?'

Master Mu nodded. 'He was playing with it, and I recognised it right away.'

'Where?'

'Dragon Lustre.'

I have to go and see a bro down in Dragon Lustre, Lin Feng had said. Chen Di couldn't believe she'd let a kid snatch her Voyager, couldn't believe she'd been oblivious to its absence for hours. Spotting Lü should've made her more alert, not less!

Master Mu continued, 'I saw him on my way to Young Tang's recycling yard.'

'Tang-senpai?' The mention of Tang sent a thrill through Chen Di. She missed his merciless attacks, his comical eyepatch, and most important, talking to him about vengeance.

Master Mu furrowed his brow. 'I'm worried about Young Tang as I am about you.'

Chen Di said nothing. She admired Tang for more than his strength. Tang also had grudges in life, had people to track down, and only to him had she hinted at her desire for revenge. Master Mu slid *The Art of Peace* closer to her, and suddenly she remembered. Last year she'd seen this little white book at the dojo – beside Tang's spit.

That wintry morning, Tang had bounced in without bowing, just in time for real training. He looked over thirty with his bald head but was barely in his mid-twenties. Though average-sized and wearing the same white uniform as everyone else, he wore it in a crude style, the fabric wrinkled, the belt loose. It complemented his eyepatch.

'Yo, little sis!' He'd picked her out to greet.

'Tang-senpai.' She approached him with delight, having just been left alone as others had paired up. They glanced at Master Mu, who stood across the dojo instructing two students. 'It's good you came,' Chen Di said to Tang. 'Who'd take me down otherwise?'

'Then what are we waiting for?' His laugh was as rough as his techniques. He extended his arm, inviting her to grab it. The move Master Mu had demonstrated was incredibly basic. She seized Tang's wrist and he pulled her centre of gravity towards him, whispering, 'New development last night.'

She stopped. 'Is this about the family that took your eye—'

'And beat my uncle to death.' His other hand pushed her chin skywards. Still she saw his good eye narrow. 'And guess what, little sis, I nailed down the school the thug's son goes to.' Tang twisted her wrist and pushed down on her arm, forcing her to drop to her knees, painfully, impressively. He then rotated her elbow and straightened it and pinned her shoulder to the mat, followed by her entire body.

Chen Di panted. 'Con-Congratulations,' she said, despite being trapped in the uncomfortable position, her face against the mat. 'You'll have to teach the kid a lesson.'

'I'm not just going to *teach the kid a lesson*.'

His tone, filled with menace, gave Chen Di the creeps. Still pinned to the ground, she reminded herself Tang was a better version of her: stronger, crueller, shrewder, more experienced, and more resolute. He was the person closest to being her role model in Shanghai. And she was flattered he shared such information with her – she'd only talked in broad strokes about her own vengeance.

'You're right,' she said. 'An eye for an eye, a tooth for a tooth.'

'And a life for a life.' Tang's snigger worsened her physical discomfort. But it shouldn't have! Both his philosophy and his skill would serve her mission.

Finally he let go. But they rose only to come face to face with Master Mu. Unsure if he came to check on their training, Chen Di extended her arm to Tang this time. Except Master Mu caught Tang's wrist. 'Young Tang, you're often late recently. I need you to bow and step out, bow again before you step back in, go through mokuso—'

'Yeah, yeah, I've already done them at home.'

Master Mu didn't let go. He asked Chen Di to join another pair and led Tang to the front. She caught Master Mu saying words like 'complaint' and 'bruises'. In a corner of the dojo, two girls murmured to each other while pointing at Tang. How pathetic. Instead of improving their own skills, they must've reported him for hurting them during training.

'You old fart!' Tang's yell silenced the class.

Master Mu passed him a small book. 'If you still want to train with us, then read this.'

'Like hell I will! Tell you what, my recycling yard's a better training ground than this shit hole.' Tang spat on the mat and chucked the book, which landed with its white cover facing up. 'This time, old fart, it's a farewell.'

He walked out with a bounce, his agency leaving Chen Di in awe. She would never dare to talk or act like this in front of Master Mu.

'Little sis!' Tang looked back before reaching the end of the corridor. 'Come visit.'

She glanced at Master Mu and gave Tang a slight nod of her head.

That aikido class had ended up being Tang's last, and Chen Di had been meaning to visit his recycling yard. Now she stared at the book on the table before her, suddenly feeling honoured: Master Mu had asked Tang to read it too – she was being treated like her role model. It felt as if she was one step closer to becoming the person she admired.

'I appreciate your concern for us.' Chen Di avoided touching the book and held out her palm. 'Thank you for getting my knife back for me.'

'I'm keeping it in custody, for now.'

'Oh, please.'

Chen Di still remembered the dingy basement shop where she'd first flicked open the Voyager's blade, felt its cold steel. It had cost her four months' wages her first year in Shanghai, waitressing at a dark, damp eatery – hell compared with Pizza & Apple Pie – where an angry cook sprayed his sweat in Yangzhou fried rice.

'I'll give you a chance to have it back,' Master Mu said. 'But first, you are consumed by the desire for vengeance, that much I suspected the day we met.'

She swallowed. 'I don't know what you're talking about.'

'Anyone can tell you have few friends, few connections in the city. And based on the way you are at the dojo, anyone can conclude you are seeking revenge.'

'Only you can, Master Mu, and it's simply not true.'

He placed his hands on the table. 'My suspicion was long confirmed.'

'Because of my knife? That's hardly evidence.'

'Because of someone who knows you, though I promised to not reveal the identity.'

'*Reveal the identity?*' Master Mu wasn't the type to tell jokes, but this sounded like a line from some spy story. 'I don't know what grand secret you're guarding, but no one really knows me. You're right I don't have friends, and my family's mostly dead.'

'Are they?'

'Truth be told, only my father is alive, and he's in my godforsaken village doing Heaven knows what.'

'I'm sure your father cares about you. Deeply.'

She laughed. 'How would *you* know?' Father's leaf whistle sounded in her ears, like a calling from the afterworld. She clutched her head briefly and, remembering Master Mu was a father himself, added, 'I'm sure you care about your son, deeply, but you're mistaken if you assume all fathers are like you.'

Master Mu went silent, though his eyes remained probing. 'Young Chen, no good can come from vengeance.'

'There is no vengeance.'

'I don't want you to do this to yourself.'

'Do what to myself?'

He pushed *The Art of Peace* so close to her that she leaned back. 'Read it, and I'll consider giving your knife back to you. May the Great Teacher's words bring you some peace.'

Chen Di needed hatred before she could even begin to think about peace. She wished she could look daggers at Master Mu as Tang did with his one eye. She wished she could toss the book across Pizza & Apple Pie as Tang might. But she'd better keep quiet if she wanted her Voyager back.

10
Sichuan
Summer 1992

A weak ray of light came in through a crack in the window shutter. Chen Di lay still, tired because she'd gone to bed late last night – preparing for today's feast. A feast for Little Tiger. Her brother was now one month old – something to celebrate.

Her heart still drummed wildly whenever she thought about that life-changing instant. That night, she'd sat on the stone steps outside the wooden house, waiting in dread. Dread of another girl who'd be taken to the bus stop.

Then the midwife shrilled, 'It's a boy! It's a boy!'

'It's a boy!' Grandfather shouted after her, 'It's a boy, Xixi! Xixi!' And Chen Di wasn't sure if Xixi was supposed to be someone's name or just him laughing ecstatically.

Father called out too, the quiet person he was, 'It's a boy!'

Mother's voice quavered with delight. 'It's a boy!'

Before Chen Di knew it, she'd run inside and cried alongside everyone, 'It's a boy!'

Lying in bed now, she could still hear the firecrackers they'd set off that night, little explosions announcing to the world the birth of Little Tiger. The high spirits in the house these days made her feel light-headed, and she knew today would be even more exciting.

Across the room, Father and Grandfather slept soundly, but Mother and Little Tiger were gone. Chen Di sat up, alert, and pulled open the window shutter. In the middle of the field, Mother cradled Little Tiger, their silhouettes merging with the cotton flowers as she pointed out to her baby the dim glow in the sky before dawn.

Chen Di stiffened. A breeze brushed her face as a sense of betrayal cut through the joy she'd been feeling for a month. Sunrise belonged to her and Mother.

She got off the bed and marched out into the half-dark, the air unusually dry. She'd gone only a few steps before noticing the sky redden – the sun was about to rise. She ran into the field towards Mother, her uncombed hair flying.

'You're up!' Mother smiled. 'Come.'

'Mother!' Chen Di stopped before her and held onto the arm cradling Little Tiger. 'You should have woken me up. I want to watch the sunrise with you.'

'But you were so tired last night.'

'That's nothing. I'd rather—'

Her brother gurgled, taking away Mother's attention, and he drooled. Chen Di had never seen other one-month-olds do that. Mother wiped his drool, her lips curling up more. 'Of course you'll teethe early. You're our precious Little Tiger.'

Chen Di thought her brother was more like a monkey than a tiger, and this had little to do with him being born in the year of the Monkey. He was a small baby and his intense eyes stood out on his face. His irises were as black as his pupils, as if they could see her darkest secrets.

Little Tiger looked from Mother to Chen Di, his head tilted, his dark eyes like a warning. She felt forced to let go of Mother's arm. 'Mother, can I ask you something?'

'Of course.' Mother's eyes lingered on Little Tiger.

'Do you love me or my brother more?'

'Oh, Yaonü...' Mother reached out her spare hand and smoothed Chen Di's hair, combing it with her fingers. 'I love you both.'

'But if Little Tiger and I both fall into water, who would you save?'

'Well, you can swim.'

So she'd save Little Tiger. For the first time Chen Di wondered why she'd felt so happy the last month. A boy's birth was supposed to be a good thing, but what did it mean to her? In fact, why *was* it a good thing? She could almost hear Teacher Jia ask that. Grandfather had talked about getting buried in the ancestral grave, for example, but who'd set the rule that you couldn't be buried there if you had no sons?

'You and your brother are both my precious children,' Mother added.

A gust of wind whooshed past them, briefly flattening the cotton plants. Mother tightened her hold on Little Tiger. Chen

Di gazed into Mother's eyes, her dark-brown irises more like Little Tiger's than Chen Di's lighter ones. 'And my little sister? Is she your precious child too?'

Mother's lips parted. She turned away and her gaze fixed on a whole area of wilted cotton flowers. 'You don't have any sisters.'

'But I have one!' she said, too loud.

Mother turned back, a faraway look in her eyes.

Chen Di continued, 'Isn't she just...growing up somewhere else?' With a nice granny who lived in a huge house, lots of children jumping around her, broadening the smile on her wrinkly face. *I tucked in thirty yuan and waited for hours, Chen Di, hours at the bus stop until I saw a granny picking her up. Your little sister will be taken care of.*

'Oh.' Mother's eyes softened. 'Right, all I mean is that your sister isn't with us anymore, but I'm sure she's living a good life somewhere, in a rich family in the city, hopefully, that treats girls well. Here though, I have two children, and I care about both of you.'

Chen Di nodded, and accepted Mother's answer.

They held each other's gaze until Little Tiger squirmed. The arc of the sun appeared above a hill, casting rays of gold over the field, over all three of them. In the quiet, Chen Di again felt a moment of tenderness, a 'now' worth living. Nothing had changed. It was still the same sunrise – *filled with life,* as Mother had said.

Chen Di inhaled. Exhaled.

At least I'm alive.

Some time later, they all went back inside. The sun wasn't yet high, the feast not until hours later, but Father and Grandfather were already setting up round tables in the courtyard and outside the house. A few village women came to help Mother cook – they'd be wok-frying dishes of chicken, duck, fish, and pork, reddened with chilli bean paste.

'Stay out of the way,' Mother said to Chen Di. 'And mind your brother.'

In the front room, Chen Di held Little Tiger in a red swaddle, his head in the crook of her arm. She stopped before the Bodhisattva of Compassion and watched the way the bodhisattva cradled the baby boy until she recognised an uncanny similarity between the idol and herself. Compelled to change position, she lifted up her brother and rested his head over her shoulder.

Grandfather came in, his steps light. One hand holding her brother, Chen Di arranged three incense sticks in the burner and bowed. Grandfather's silence meant his approval. Over the last month, like a miracle, he'd approved of everything she'd done.

But suddenly Little Tiger squealed like an animal on fire. Startled, she lowered him from her shoulder. He tried to roll and his hand wiggled out of the swaddle, the strength in his small body catching her off guard. His pudgy arm swept through the air and slapped the Bodhisattva of Compassion to the ground, smashing the idol into pieces. A bad sign.

Grandfather scowled, his unibrow knit in the middle as he stormed over. Until this moment Chen Di hadn't felt protective of her brother, but she really didn't want to see such a little baby punished. She hugged him close.

'What use are you if you can't even hold a baby?' Grandfather raised a hand as if to slap her, but it stopped in mid-air, instead pointing a calloused finger at Chen Di's nose.

Of course, Grandfather blamed *her*. He didn't smack her only because he didn't want to risk hurting precious Little Tiger, who was still in her arms.

Mother rushed in. 'Yao'er!' she cried. She didn't even look at Chen Di but took over the swaddle and examined crying Little Tiger frantically, left and right. 'Is he all right?'

'He is, don't worry,' Grandfather said, a slight touch of respect in his voice. Mother's position had risen in the family.

'But what happened to him?' Mother wouldn't stop asking. 'Did he injure himself?'

While Grandfather reassured Mother, Chen Di felt numb. Mother had always protected her, but now it felt as if she took Grandfather's side and was protecting Little Tiger *from* her. While Mother cradled Little Tiger to the back room to breastfeed him, Chen Di swept away the broken porcelain, feeling Grandfather's gaze burning into her skin.

'Be careful now.' Mother returned and kissed Little Tiger before reluctantly passing him back to Chen Di. 'Go sit at a table outside, and hold him tight.'

As the summer sun rose higher, warming the air, Chen Di's heart grew colder.

The first guests arrived at the outdoor tables. They waved palm-leaf fans and snacked on cream-flavoured watermelon seeds, sunflower seeds, pumpkin seeds. Everyone came to Chen Di to pinch Little Tiger's cheeks as if he were a jade sculpture that brought good luck to those who touched it. It made him drool more and caused a rash to appear on his chin.

'Chen *Di!* Chen *Di!*' A stout man raised a finger. 'Heaven did give you a younger brother!'

Villagers laughed, patting her head as if saying, 'Good job!'

Father and Grandfather set off firecrackers. Red debris covered the uneven ground, a sea of blood, matching everything from the baskets of boiled eggs to the characters for *Fortune* stuck on the walls. Chen Di ignored them all, focusing instead on the notebook she kept on the table. She not only reviewed the characters she'd learned last week but also previewed new ones she'd be learning in the coming week, which she had copied from Teacher Jia's textbook.

A sudden hush fell over the space. She looked up to find the guests staring in the same direction. But all she could see was the familiar field of cotton flowers. It wasn't until she rose, Little Tiger in her arms, that she made out something unusual. A person. A small man. He swaggered through the cotton field and crossed the stone bridge towards them.

Lü Yuandou.

'Congratulations,' he said calmly. Chen Di did all she could to stand strong as he stopped before them. 'Lucky family, a girl *and* a boy.'

Mother appeared from behind her and took Little Tiger from Chen Di's arms.

'Hello there, big sister,' Lü said. 'Don't go so fast.'

Mother froze, her arms tight around Little Tiger. Lü pinched his cheek like everyone had, and for a second Chen Di wanted Lü to take her brother away from Mother.

Grandfather came forward. 'How may we help you, Chief Lü?'

'Old Chen, Old Chen, aren't you blessed by Heaven?' He glanced at Little Tiger. 'With all these little *boys* born around the village, the ghost woman's been rather hungry.'

'You're welcome to stay for the feast,' Grandfather said stiffly.

'I won't spoil your fun.' But Lü took the seat beside Chen Di, poured himself a cup of baijiu, and downed it in one go. 'Ahhh.' He quietly set down the cup, the lack of sound sending a chill through her. 'Good liquor.'

He poured two more cups and eyed Grandfather. 'Join me?'

'No, no, Chief Lü, I still have to—'

'Join me.'

Grandfather did, and picked his nose in his nervousness.

'To Old Chen and his grandson.' Lü reached out to clink Grandfather's cup. 'I really wanted you to have another grand*daughter*,' he said in a whisper, and yet Chen Di was sure all guests heard it. 'You'd applied for a birth permit, even the Party was expecting the baby, so how would you get around things? Fake a stillbirth?' He chuckled. 'I can hardly keep up with all you villagers' smart ways to defy the system.'

Grandfather remained silent.

'All right, off I go.' Lü Yuandou stood and swaggered away as quickly as he'd arrived. In no time he crossed the bridge and vanished beyond the cotton flowers. It was as if he'd come to bid them farewell. They had only done what was allowed, after all, having had one daughter followed by one son. Their trouble was over.

A few guests reassured Grandfather. 'You'll never see Lunatic Lü again.'

But Mother was still clutching Little Tiger.

And somehow, Chen Di couldn't sigh with relief either.

More guests arrived, and the fearful atmosphere grew lively again. Chen Di fixed her plaits, her notebook now in her lap, and waited for the one person she most wanted to see. She knew Teacher Jia felt boys and girls were equal but today almost wished things were different – that he valued Little Tiger's birth like Grandfather did – just so he'd come. She hadn't realised how much she wanted to see Teacher Jia today. Every day.

The tables were filling up with food: cold plates and hot dishes and bowls of steaming rice. Like a wedding. Cups clinked, chopsticks clacked, and words of congratulations flew through the air. Grandpa Li's family sat at the same table as Chen Di and her parents, his grandson crawling underneath it.

'Let me predict,' Grandpa Li said to Grandfather, waving his hairy arms. 'Your Little Tiger will go to *university*.'

'By the time he does, your Little Dragon would've graduated!'

The two old men drank cup after cup of baijiu. It was as if they'd both forgotten Grandpa Sun's recent death. Grandpa Li cut his chopsticks into the fish belly for a large bite. 'Life is so good now. Thinking back to the Great Famine—'

'Let's not talk about the famine today,' Grandfather said.

Chen Di scanned the other tables, some quieter than others. Without exception, families with daughters sat together and chatted about mundane matters. Those with sons also sat together, but they flattered each other, expressing goals and dreams for the future. City life. University. Lots of money. Chen Di couldn't chopstick even a bite of rice.

A loving voice sounded beside her. She almost said, *Yes, Mother*, when she realised Mother wasn't talking to her. 'Yao'er, Yao'er, Yao'er, Yao'er,' Mother sang to the baby in her arm, rolling her tongue, her voice oversweet. Chen Di's heart tightened. She wanted Mother to let go of Little Tiger. Drop him. Now! As if Heaven heard her, while Chubby Aunty waved Mother to lean over to her, Little Tiger struggled out of his swaddle and fell face-first onto the muddy ground. His shriek made everyone turn.

Chen Di rose, washed over by a sense of guilt, even though she didn't believe her wish had caused this. A swarm of adults came to help Little Tiger, checking for injury. None, thankfully. Grandfather banged his cup of baijiu on the table. 'You!' He pointed at Chen Di as if it really had been her fault instead of Mother's. 'Go! Wash him up.'

'Y-Yes, Grandfather.'

Holding Little Tiger, she hurried inside only to crash into Father. A blue booklet fell from his hand and Chen Di stepped on it before steadying herself. She moved her foot. The booklet had stitched binding and read, *Diamond Sutra*.

Father bent to pick it up and brushed the dust off its cover, then studied her and her brother. He didn't ask about Little Tiger's muddy face. With a tremor in his hand, he removed her leaf hair clip, smoothed her hair, and clipped it back. The gesture felt almost comforting, contrasting with everything else that'd happened – happened to her – today.

But then he went out to join those at the tables too. Chen Di held her brother in one arm and found herself pulling off the hair clip and re-clipping her hair. She wasn't sure if she did it to remember Father's gesture or to remove any trace of his touch. Last night it'd been the sound of his leaf whistle again that had taken her into dreams.

Finally, she carried a bucket from the kitchen to the back of the house and poured the water into an enamel washbasin. Little Tiger's pudgy arms and legs poked out from the red fabric covering his body, tied around his neck and waist. Mother had embroidered it with a plump boy riding a qilin, a dragon-like beast of legend with the body shape of a deer. And it was Grandfather who had dressed him this morning, making knots with womanly patience.

Chen Di untied the piece. If only she could switch places with her brother...

Flies buzzed and incessant laughter came from the front of the house. She sat on a low stool and placed Little Tiger in the washbasin, water brimming over the sides. Supporting his head, she washed him with a red-and-white-striped towel, rubbing him harder than needed.

He smiled. She winced.

Beside them lay a large pile of poplar branches, a few tied together in a bunch. They were put around the cotton field to attract bollworms, to be killed. In front of them, nails poked out of the house's back wall, some hung with the tools that they used to butcher chickens. Chen Di's eyes lingered on a dangling pair of scissors. The handles were rusty, but the blades reflected sunlight. She gazed down at the little thing between her brother's legs, the thing that somehow meant he was better than her.

Her heart pounded.

Chen Di let go of the towel. She continued to support his head but leaned forward and reached for the scissors. She unhooked them, put her fingers through the handles, and opened them. Her eyes returned to the one difference between her and her brother.

Scissors in hand, she sat straight again. Little Tiger's head wiggled in her other hand. He stopped suddenly and watched her with his dark eyes, almost no white showing, his small head tilted, as if reading her thoughts. Except Chen Di had none. She couldn't think. She felt herself dropping into a trance, her limbs not in her control. Her hand shook, her thumb and index fingers opened wide, blades pointing.

Little Tiger reached up.

She pulled back so fast she tossed the scissors into the tall grasses behind them.

Her right hand was still trembling. She raised it and clutched her head, hard, unable to believe she was capable of such an idea, the most horrible one she'd come up with in the ten years of her life. Her nails digging into her skull, she shut her eyes and tried to think of something else. Teacher Jia. His refreshing Mandarin, his awkward smile, his red sock and blue sock. In a recent dream with a mishmash of colours and ideas, he'd taken her to Shenzhen to see her little sister, who'd shocked them with her incredibly long arms and legs.

Finally, Chen Di let go of her own head, and her hand dropped to her lap. *You have worth*. She savoured Teacher Jia's words despite doubting them. She couldn't wait to go to school tomorrow, to learn from him, to impress him.

She dressed her brother and brought him back to the feast.

11
Shanghai
Winter 2002

Chen Di picked up the small tube beside her pillow and unscrewed the lid. She'd been sleeping with her eyes open since the age of twelve. Even doctors in Shanghai couldn't diagnose it, having only prescribed tubes of ointment. She pulled down her left lower eyelid and squeezed some ointment into her dry eye, then repeated the steps with her right eye. She shut both for thirty seconds – during which she made up her mind to give her three-week notice at Pizza & Apple Pie. Then she could really put one hundred percent into steps two, three, and four.

With her savings and her last pay, she'd have enough money for one month of rent and food, plus a train ticket to head south to Shenzhen. Teacher Jia's hometown, supposedly.

How he'd fooled her back then.

Chen Di pulled over a literary magazine, whose earlier issues she'd first seen on Teacher Jia's desk in Daci Village. That was how the magazines had caught her eye at a newsstand in Shanghai. And soon she'd noticed a regular writer: Four Three.

The majority of Chinese writers used pen names instead of real names, but *four* was *si,* and the character for *three* rotated by ninety degrees was *river, chuan.* Sichuan. She left the magazine beside her pillow and again thought of Four Three's only piece of fiction, whose protagonist had Chen Di's exact background and personality and looks. There was even a teacher character, a man from Shenzhen.

Chen Di's heart dissolved as she speculated about who Four Three might really be, a powerful sensation rising in her heart. Again she daydreamed of reuniting with Teacher Jia in Shanghai. What would he think of her now? She didn't expect him to approve of her mission, not fully, but would he be proud of her otherwise, as an adult, as a woman?

She felt like a schoolgirl again. She buried her face in the pillow and murmured, 'Teacher Jia... Teacher Jia...' She imagined him holding her with his big, smooth hands, loving her with his whole body. She allowed herself five minutes before the fantasy swallowed her.

Afterwards, she warned herself that fantasy was fantasy. The yuanfen between them had long ended, or rather, it'd been nothing special to start with.

Chen Di proceeded to do her workout, focusing on the dumbbell curls. It was Tang who'd taught her the routine two years ago at his recycling yard down in Dragon Lustre. Master Mu put no emphasis on strength training, and Chen Di and Tang agreed his approach was nonsense. It'd been a few months since Tang's breakthrough with his own revenge, having found his target family's whereabouts. She would've expected her role model to be done by now, except Master Mu's words at Pizza & Apple Pie hadn't suggested that.

She'd better get on with her own. Chen Di crossed her arms as her eyes fell on her map of Shanghai and stopped at one small red circle: Lü's workplace. She no longer needed this map. She detached it from the wall and folded it up, then took it outside with the rubbish.

Waste sorting was a recent measure, and her longtang was one of the first in the city to carry it out. She put out her empty bottles of chilli bean paste for recycling but tossed the map as food waste. May Lü rot with it.

'Young Chen, that's not food waste.' Grandma Chu strutted over in her bob wig and black flats, as proper as what society expected of women in their sixties. She was a neighbourhood committee member and Manager Chu's aunt. It was really thanks to her that Chen Di had got her job at Pizza & Apple Pie two years ago.

'Sorry,' Chen Di said. 'I was distracted.'

Grandma Chu's rimless bifocals made her both serious and exaggeratedly friendly. 'Here.' She reached inside the bin with her disproportionately long arm.

'I'll do it,' Chen Di quickly said. 'Don't dirty your hand.'

Grandma Chu let her take over. 'Ayo! Is this a map? It looks big.'

'Y-Yes but it's mildewed.' Chen Di quickly chucked it for recycling. She should've burnt it. This map linked her with

Lü Yuandou – it could come back to bite her. She sneaked a glance at Grandma Chu as a bad feeling rose inside. With too much spare time in hand, Grandma Chu patrolled the longtang, looking for faults, reporting people, adding cooking oil and vinegar to spice up any gossip. But Chen Di would look suspicious if she now pulled the map back out of the recycle bin, and it'd only make Grandma Chu want to take a better look at it.

'What a waste. Chairman Mao's clothes had patches, he never left a grain of rice in his bowl.' Grandma Chu clicked her tongue. 'Why did you need such a big map anyway?'

'To…learn about Big Shanghai.'

'It reminds me of some crime series, a big map on a big wall at the police station. Or maybe at the criminal's home, some serial killer—'

'By the way, I must pay rent.'

'No rush at all.' Grandma Chu's dentures showed, and she waved off the idea. 'Are you living comfortably? Is my nephew treating you well at Pizza & Apple Pie?' She asked the same two questions every time just to make sure Chen Di felt indebted.

'All is well, thank you.' She'd better first speak to Manager Chu about quitting. 'I'll bring the rent tonight.'

The dentures vanished. 'I'm busy tonight. February's short, tomorrow's March.'

'I'll bring it right away.' Chen Di should've known by 'No rush at all', Grandma Chu had meant 'I'm waiting'. Shanghainese never said what they meant.

Chen Di visited the bank and bought a used men's bicycle, too big for her but the cheapest item in the shop, to replace Master Mu's tricycle she could no longer use now that he'd fired her. Her feet could barely reach the ground, but she didn't mind. She was flying.

At the neighbourhood committee office, she stopped to pay her March rent. Grandma Chu was on the phone, gushing about a young couple stealing electricity. 'We need to respect out-of-towners,' she said. 'Who else is going to serve us Shanghainese?' On her desk, a stand displayed two miniature national flags. On the wall behind Grandma Chu's chair hung a yellow-rimmed red pennant: *Serve the People*. Finally, Grandma Chu hung up.

Chen Di handed over the cash. 'Please count it.'

'No need, no need,' Grandma Chu said, counting.

March meant spring, and the weeks passed fast. On her last day at Pizza & Apple Pie, Chen Di awoke in the morning to smell the night rain. Tomorrow would be her big day for step two: following Lü home. To make that easier, today she'd try to figure out his typical workday routine by catching him on his way out of the government building.

Only her weapon was gone. She punched her bed, wanting to find Lin Feng at Wende Private and twist his ear the way his mum had, but that wouldn't solve her problem. Master Mu was keeping her Voyager in custody. She glanced at *The Art of Peace*, its dusty white cover, the large calligraphic circle. Even if she read it, would Master Mu really give back her knife or first test her on the book? Besides, replacing dojo training with a book was about as useful as praying to the Buddha for your room to be cleaned.

But this little book *could* help her, today.

During her afternoon break, Chen Di biked to Lü's workplace again. The air was still, the budding plane trees looking like bad sculptures, the national flag flapping feebly like a dying man's hand. She stopped at a corner of the building so she could see both the main gate and the side one, and flipped open *The Art of Peace*, holding it in front of her face as she pretended to read. It hid her birthmark while allowing a wide field of vision.

She couldn't help catching a line or two. *A good stance and posture reflect a proper state of mind.* Chen Di had already adjusted how she held herself, straightening her spine. This wasn't so bad. She turned to another page. *An attack is proof that one is out of control.* Vexed, she flipped away, but she stopped again only to read, *The essence of the Art of Peace is to cleanse yourself of maliciousness.* She almost shut the book in annoyance, when she remembered it was her disguise.

Officials exited from both gates. Having spent years watching people *entering* gates, she felt she now lived life backwards. The difference between everyone's morning and afternoon looks struck her. The smiles they put on before work were fake – just a show to keep up appearances. Now, they revealed their real smiles that reached their eyes.

Students dispersed from Wende Private, two passing boys tittering about a video of topless Japanese girls at a pool. Spontaneously Chen Di looked down the road, and she recognised him from his back.

Lin Feng.

Warmth surged through her, not how one should feel about a knife thief. Lin Feng stood at the corner in a singlet and track pants, a school bag on one shoulder. The feeling inside Chen Di grew stronger, swirling around her body. It was as if she missed him. Her muscles moved before her mind could catch up, and she pushed her bicycle over.

Half a dozen boys surrounded him, and two long-haired girls waved at him and giggled as they passed. Chen Di cut through the students, but behind his back, she paused. What did she want from him now? He no longer had her knife.

Before she was ready, he whipped around.

She spoke first. 'Do you know how high the sky is, how thick the earth is? Stealing from me?' She didn't sound as mad as she wanted to be.

He tilted his head. 'Who are you?'

She opened her mouth.

Lin Feng looked to his left and right. 'Do you guys know who she is?'

'Are you kidding me?' She hated how she sounded like she was begging.

A plump boy put a potato crisp in his mouth. 'I'm sure I would've remembered such an ugly birthmark.'

'It's cute enough.' Lin Feng's eyes fixated on Chen Di, and she didn't know what to make of his words. Only one thing was for sure: if she'd had even one per cent doubt that she'd had the wrong person, she didn't any more.

'Come on Feng Bro,' the plump boy said. 'You don't have to tease her this much.'

'I said, it's cute.' His serious tone made everyone stop.

'Well, you also said,' Chen Di continued, 'that you wanted to be my apprentice and that I looked like your sister.'

'His sister?' A thin boy laughed as if he'd just heard the funniest joke. 'When have you ever got yourself a sister, Feng Bro?'

A third boy stepped up. 'Your apprentice has no sister.'

Chen Di felt her lips part. Lin Feng had no sister? And why would he pretend to not know her? It hurt more than she'd like to admit, and she suddenly wished he'd touch her birthmark again, no matter how cold his hand was. Did he really find it cute? Exactly what was with this kid?

Thinking back, demanding free food and threatening Yuanfen Eatery was outrageous even for a brat, and he didn't have to expose himself by wearing his uniform or announcing his name. It was as if he stirred up trouble in order to get caught, as if fighting another teenager just wouldn't have done the trick.

She watched as he strode away, clapping two boys' backs, saying, 'Nope, no one's going to be home tonight.'

Chen Di imagined some elite housing estate where he lived, his apartment fancy but empty. She clutched her head and shut her eyes, trying to think straight. She headed towards the government building only to look back. Lin Feng, too, was glancing back at her. Suddenly he looked like someone else, not the leader of his school gang but a disturbed kid, something wistful in his dark eyes. He rubbed the left side of his chin and they both turned away again.

Back at the gate, Chen Di leaned her bicycle on a plane tree and flipped open *The Art of Peace*, reminding herself that her mission came first.

Just as she worried if Lü might've left, she saw him emerge from the main gate. Shivers ran through her, his high-pitched chuckle ringing in her head. She breathed in, and out, and gazed at him. He walked off in the direction he'd come from the other morning, and she checked her watch, proud to be ready for step two, tomorrow. But she was already pushing her bicycle after him, intrigued by a stain on the back of his grey suit jacket. Mud? No, more like soy sauce. It felt out of place, a flaw too human for someone like Lü.

Only when he stopped at a red light did Chen Di realise she'd come too close, and as he turned to cross the road, she stiffened more. The expression on his face was similar to that of everyone else leaving the site: his eyes smiling like he couldn't wait to see someone.

It was as if Lü Yuandou had a loving family waiting.

12
Sichuan
Harvest 1993

At school, Chen Di sat at the back with one-year-old Little Tiger. She was allowed to continue her schooling as long as she also took care of her brother: rocking him to sleep, feeding, changing, and bathing him. The cotton harvest had ended, a good yield this year. Everyone said Little Tiger had brought the sunshine, and it made Grandfather laugh like a child. It was only today, after the crop stubble had been burnt, that the darkest clouds gathered.

In the afternoon, the rain flooded the school grounds, making the surrounding bamboo look as if it was growing out of water. But Teacher Jia's presence kept Chen Di's day bright. He waved goodbye to every leaving pupil and stopped her inside the door. 'Will you two be okay?'

Chen Di's one hand held Little Tiger's, her other gripping an unopened umbrella. She wanted to look at her teacher like before but only dared to steal a glance, her whole body blushing. She couldn't pinpoint when things had changed, but his smile struck her now as beautiful. Every day, she pictured his face in her mind after school, his voice echoing in her head. Every night, she went to bed savouring his words of praise about her good answers, brooding on those she'd tripped up on. He appeared in her dreams, good ones, bad ones, ones that woke her in the middle of the night and made her flush.

Chen Di moved closer to him, half a step, her body tugged by a sensation her mind couldn't catch up on. 'Yes, we have a big umbrella.' She wanted to add something intelligent, to talk to him more, but she glanced up only to look down again.

'What is it?'

She summoned her courage. 'What's the climate like in Shenzhen?'

'Oh.' Teacher Jia's frozen expression made her wonder if she'd asked something she shouldn't have. He turned to say goodbye to three other pupils and stared out into the rain. 'You remember the city I'm from.'

Of course she did. Only he looked as if he wished she'd forgotten it.

'Well,' he said, 'all those places down south are warmer than here and even more humid.' He used his teaching voice, almost detached. Then he opened their umbrella for them. 'This *is* big.'

'Yes, and we'll be okay.'

His eyes crinkled. 'I know you're capable.'

'It's all... It's all thanks to you, Teacher Jia.' *You changed me*, she wanted to add. *You made my life worth living.* But Little Tiger's cry broke the moment.

Enormous raindrops drummed the world. Chen Di tied her brother to her back and headed home, balancing an umbrella between her head and shoulder. She couldn't help but wonder if Teacher Jia disliked Shenzhen. Was that why he'd come here?

Walking turned into wading. Muddy water soaked her feet, her ankles, and at one stage her shins. Well, as long as her brother stayed dry.

Before Grandpa Li's house, the stream rushed, and the loudspeakers blasted again with Lü Yuandou's high voice, promoting the financial benefits for families to have only one child. It should have become background noise by now, but an image would always come to mind, of a small man with pointy ears and long lobes flicking the air in front of Mother's breast.

Then Chen Di felt something on her ankle. She glanced down and yelped, seeing her bloody feet. Half a dozen leeches were clinging to her ankles. She shuddered, wiped her face, and re-clipped her hair. She tied Little Tiger tighter to her back and broke into a sprint, terraced fields blurring past. She took a break and ran again, all the way to the cotton field. She panted as she held onto the wall that read *One is good; a son or a daughter, equally good.*

The rain stopped just as she stepped into the wooden house, and her brother wasn't even that wet. She felt proud as she entered the front room and let him down.

Mother, Father, and Grandfather were all there, and their faces changed.

Chen Di thought they were worried about the leeches still on her feet, the blood only partly washed away. 'It's nothing—'

'What did you do?' Grandfather scowled, while Mother rushed over to pick up Little Tiger. Chen Di realised only then her brother's cheek was scratched – perhaps by some low twigs, somehow. Worse than the scratches was a red wound on the left side of his chin. He'd been rubbing his drool rash non-stop. Little Tiger tilted his head, his dark eyes judging her, seeing through her.

She lowered her head. 'I'm sor—'

A slap made her dizzy, and she almost fell. Grandfather's finger shook, more calloused than she remembered. 'One more scratch on him, and I'll put ten on you!'

She nodded before Teacher Jia's face came to mind. *You have worth.* She felt a sudden desire to overwrite Grandfather's words with Teacher Jia's.

'You're your brother's cow, his horse!' Grandfather said. 'Understand?'

Chen Di nodded again, forcing his voice to enter her head from one ear and exit from the other, leaving no impact in between. And it worked like magic.

'Say it! Say that your whole life you're—'

'My whole life I'm my brother's cow, his horse,' she said, trying not to believe it.

Mother sat with Little Tiger in her lap and asked Father to bring some antiseptic. 'Yao'er,' she murmured. 'Yao'er.'

Chen Di's heart tightened, and she had the urge to slap Little Tiger the way Grandfather had her.

She slipped back out into the courtyard, slid against the wall to the wet ground, and rolled up her trousers. Seven slimy leeches gripped her legs, their mucus making her retch. She gripped one on her ankle but its sucker remained tight on her skin. She dug her nails into its body and yanked it out, blood streaming down her foot.

'This is not how you do it.' Mother appeared and squatted before her.

Chen Di looked at her. *You care?*

But of course Mother did. She fetched salt and sprinkled some on each of the leeches. Their suckers loosened, and they fell away. 'Maybe...' Mother didn't look up. 'Maybe you don't have to go to school these days, the weather's so bad.'

'Because of all the leeches?' Chen Di said hopefully.

'Because of what happened to your brother too. And don't let him rub that rash on his chin again, it's your responsibility.'

Her heart grew cold.

Chen Di went to school again the next day anyway. And she was glad she did since Teacher Jia announced that if it poured again, he'd give rides to pupils living in certain areas.

With Little Tiger strapped to her chest, she sat behind Teacher Jia on his motorcycle that afternoon, marvelling in the fresh air and rain that had so daunted her yesterday. She gripped his waist as they zipped through water, feeling as if a small furry animal zoomed around her body. She wished she lived several villages away. She stared at his beautifully shaggy hair, wet from the rain, annoyed that her brother was sandwiched between them.

The next day, though, Chen Di spiked a fever and couldn't go to school. It wasn't yet evening, but she'd slept in the back room for hours, woken only by the big group of mahjong players, men and women, who'd set up a few tables of the game in the front room.

'Chief Lü *is* making our lives better here,' said a scratchy man's voice. 'Fewer babies means fewer mouths to feed—'

'Which means more food, more money,' said a woman.

'Right!' Grandpa Li said, clapping the mahjong table. Thinking of his hairy face and arms sickened Chen Di more than she already was. 'We get richer, the whole of China gets richer. Family planning makes us *rich*.'

'But Lunatic Lü is a baby killer!' a different woman shouted, then lowered her voice. 'I hear he's sterile. I bet he doesn't want us to have kids because he can't have one himself.'

'It's more than that,' said an old, measured voice. 'Lü Yuandou called his own wife – ex-wife – a fox spirit, sleeping with everyone, making him lose face, and his whole family mocked him. I say he simply has no love in life, only his work gives him meaning.'

Grandfather spoke. 'The shot hits the bird that pokes its head out. To save ourselves from trouble, let's keep our heads down.'

Murmurs of agreement were followed by the clatter of mahjong tiles.

Chen Di opened her eyes. *Lü Yuandou is a monster. Between our fellow countrymen's outdated mindset and the Party's authoritarian policies, he's found an opportunity to prey on people.* No one else seemed to describe the official the way Teacher Jia had.

'You're awake.' Mother appeared.

'Not everyone thinks Chief Lü is bad anymore?' Chen Di said, her body still aching.

'Oh, Yaonü, that's adults' business. We have you, we have your brother – family planning policies have nothing to do with us anymore.' Mother perched on her bed. 'I just hope your brother will grow up safe and sound.'

'I'll keep him safe and sound.'

Mother smiled. 'Are you cold?'

As if on cue, the window shutter flew open, making Chen Di shiver. Mother hurried to a cabinet and fished out an old cloth. She reached up to stuff it around the window frame and shut it tight. Across the room, Little Tiger drooled as he napped, his hands resting on the sides of his head as if he were surrendering. Mother didn't even look at him.

'I'm warm.' Chen Di gripped Mother's hand. 'Being sick isn't so bad.'

'Don't be silly.'

'I just wish I didn't have to miss Teacher Jia's classes.'

Mother studied her own hands, which grew more wrinkled after every cotton harvest. 'You only missed a day. You already know so much more than I did when I was eleven.'

Which wasn't much, Chen Di almost said.

Then came the sound of a motorcycle, approaching, stopping. Her heart raced. The towel slid from her forehead and she pushed herself up only to fall back down. She wished she didn't have to look so weak, her hair wasn't so messy. And before she was ready, she heard Teacher Jia refusing Grandfather's invitation to mahjong. Then he appeared at the door to the back room, in his checked sweater.

'Teacher…Jia…' Chen Di's heartbeat wouldn't slow. Her fever felt like nothing compared with how she was burning up right now.

He smiled at her and gave Mother a polite nod. 'Big sister.'

The greeting vexed Chen Di. If Mother were Teacher Jia's older sister, then Chen Di would be his niece, meaning a generation below. He wasn't old enough to be her father. It'd never bothered her before the way people addressed everyone like relatives.

Mother went to bring tea while Teacher Jia sat on a stool and rested one ankle on top of the opposite knee. Chen Di noticed his red sock and blue sock again, the red one with white stripes, in fact, and the blue one filled with little stars. She'd come to love his sloppiness.

'Chen Di.' He leaned closer, his lips curling up with a trace of awkwardness again. For an instant she thought he'd plant a kiss on her cheek, but he only tapped her shoulder. 'I brought you notes from today's classes.' He clicked open his briefcase and pulled out a few sheets of paper, the top one with English words. The school had never offered English classes before Teacher Jia's arrival. 'I'll leave soon so you can rest.'

'Don't,' she blurted. 'Wh-What did you teach us in English?'

'We studied the verbs *to like* and *to love*.' He explained the words, and her attention shifted to his high-bridged nose. 'Can you put either of them in a sentence?'

'I love Beijing Tiananmen,' she said.

'You are quick, as always.' Mother had praised her in the same way, but it sounded different coming from Teacher Jia. She rubbed her hot cheeks, hoping her face looked normal.

Mother returned with an enamel mug of tea for him, then went to sit beside napping Little Tiger. But she continued to watch them with concentration. Chen Di wished she'd leave. Mother had never studied English before, so it made no sense for her to listen in anyway.

An example on the sheet of paper read *I love the house but I don't like this room*.

'Can you make a sentence in that structure?' Teacher Jia asked.

'I love China but I don't like Chairman M—' Chen Di clapped her mouth. 'No, no, of course I love Chairman Mao, I wasn't thinking. Loving China *means* loving Chairman Mao, loving China *means* loving the Party.'

'According to the loudspeakers?'

'Everyone knows.'

Teacher Jia scratched the leg of his blue sock. 'Grammatically, it does make sense to say, *I love China but I don't like the Party*.'

That evening, Chen Di closed her eyes only to feel Teacher Jia's presence. She thought about his beautiful smile, his gentle tap on her shoulder, as well as what she'd learned. She should've given the example: *I like my teacher*. The thought made her burn even though her fever was receding. Her mind drifted to the way Mother had listened in. She'd seemed both eager and hesitant, like a starving man presented with a bowl of poisonous rice.

The door creaked. She opened her eyes a slit to see her parents enter. Mother put down Little Tiger, who climbed up the bed and tried to hide himself in a quilt. Father pushed aside his blue booklets of sutras on the bed and sat alongside Mother.

'You used to sneak to school too, didn't you?' he whispered to her. 'But when the Cultural Revolution started, that was that.'

Chen Di stiffened. It'd never occurred to her that Mother had wanted to study too. And in recent years, as Chen Di learned more and more, a part of her had started to look down on Mother's illiteracy... A wave of guilt coursed through her.

'But things are better for girls now, thanks to the Party,' Mother whispered back. 'And thanks to you. What a great idea you had that time, asking Teacher Jia to bet our daughter's schooling on a game of mahjong. Nothing else would've worked on her grandfather.'

Chen Di felt her fists clench. She recalled Teacher Jia's first home visit, where Father had given his seat to him and nodded as if saying 'I'm leaving it to you.' She hadn't quite believed it then. And to think that mahjong game had been Father's idea…

Across the room, Father gripped Mother's hand and… What?

Were they kissing?

Chen Di hadn't known her body to be capable of such stiffness. Her parents had never shown each other affection before – no parents kissed in front of their kids, ever. It was as if Mother and Father really, truly loved each other.

What else didn't she know about her family?

Just then, Grandfather walked in with loud footsteps, cutting off her thoughts. She squeezed her eyes shut, ready to be bellowed at for getting sick, failing to take care of her brother. She heard him make Little Tiger shriek with laughter, and when the steps stopped before her bed, her heart jumped. But a calloused hand only touched her forehead, and her quilt was pulled up so it covered her shoulders, keeping her warm.

Tears leaked from her eyes. She felt as if she'd been given a taste of what it was like to be her brother. If it was all because of her fever, she'd rather stay sick forever.

That night, Chen Di dreamed again of Daci Pit's ghost woman sliding through her, her body translucent, her hands bony, her mouth bloody. Yet when she awoke she felt no goosebumps on her arms. She no longer believed in any child-devouring ghosts. It was as if she'd finally grown out of it. Then she realised it was already morning, and she'd recovered from the fever.

In the ashy kitchen, the Kitchen God idol beamed as usual, lips red. Little Tiger's breakfast had been prepared: congee topped with a century egg, a sprawling pattern of pine branches on its black surface. Chen Di reached for the bowl, planning to wipe the wet worktop, only to have her hand slapped.

'Not. Yours.' Grandfather eyed a pot of plain white congee and slammed down a jar of blood-red chilli bean paste as if that was all she deserved.

This wasn't new, but she thought of him fixing her quilt last night and sensed an unfamiliar cruelty inside herself, the urge to smash her brother's bowl. *I'll keep him safe and sound,* she'd promised Mother. But did she really want to? Did she even care?

13
Shanghai
Spring 2002

On March 21, Chen Di woke with a jerk. She was free from all other duties. She'd journeyed two thousand kilometres and waited for three years. Now she had one good spring month to end it once and for all. This afternoon she would follow Lü home.

She squeezed ointment into her dry eyes and completed her workout with diligence. Except her body ached for aikido. She stood, one foot forward, and imagined an opponent grabbing her wrist. But imagining was simply not enough, and she grew angry. She needed to calm down.

The Art of Peace sat on her chest of drawers. A boring book might just do the trick, and reading it *was* a prerequisite for Master Mu to give back her Voyager, after all. Her mind drifted to its thief, Lin Feng, who pretended to not know her... Chen Di clutched her head, eyes shut, then grabbed the book.

To practise properly the Art of Peace, you must:
Calm the spirit and return to the source.

Cleanse the body and spirit by removing all malice, selfishness, and desire.

Be ever-grateful for the gifts received from the universe, your family, Mother Nature, and your fellow human beings.

She read the page twice, lying on her bed, and felt calmer. Page by page, Chen Di continued reading without analysing, and soon she reached the end. She doubted anything had gone into her head, but at least she'd read it now. There was enough time today before Lü finished work. She could pay Master Mu a visit and see if he'd actually give back her knife.

Wolfing down a century egg, she threw on a jade-green cardigan, jumped on her bicycle, and sped out towards Dragon Lustre.

In no time she arrived, the same bicycle repairman sitting at the longtang's entrance as she'd seen the last time she was there.

'Look who's here!' Tang emerged pushing a bicycle, his biker jacket unzipped, his eyepatch charming Chen Di as always.

'Tang-senpai!' she said, delighted.

'Yo, little sis.'

'It's been a while, I've been meaning to visit you.'

'But you haven't yet.'

She joined her hands. 'Sorry!' She lowered her voice. 'Any news since your breakthrough?'

He sniggered. 'Let's talk somewhere else, little sis.'

'Good idea.' She glanced into the longtang. 'Did Master Mu tell you to visit?'

'To warn me I'm "walking down a dangerous path".' Tang laughed, while Chen Di remembered Master Mu saying the same line to her. 'Man, I'm sick of the old fart's lectures.'

'Trust me, I know.'

'And you, little sis? Why are you here?'

'Oh. I just passed by.' Chen Di felt embarrassed. She didn't want Tang to know that she'd let Master Mu take her knife.

'Want to grab breakfast?' they said simultaneously.

The north wind was gone, the day almost balmy. Tang walked with a bounce even as he pushed his bicycle, and Chen Di followed him, heading further and further away from their master. Tang broke off a plane twig that had just begun budding.

Dragon Lustre Temple's pagoda came into view. A guide held up a megaphone with his twig-like arm, surrounded by tourists with Beijing accents rolling their tongues. Behind them, distinctive flying eaves topped five giant connected red gates. The guide said Dragon Lustre Temple was the oldest temple in Shanghai. 'It's *such* a peaceful place!' he announced, and revealed that Japanese soldiers had used it as a base during their invasion of China, sitting around Buddhist statues while devising battle plans.

Tang laughed. 'The old fart's favourite spot in town.'

Chen Di could almost see Master Mu in his grey wool coat, entering through the open red gate, holding a large bunch of incense sticks. She didn't feel comfortable making fun of his

Buddhist beliefs. Not that she feared divine retribution.

The guide held up the megaphone again at the fenced cemetery next door to the temple: Dragon Lustre Martyrs Cemetery. His thin arm indicated its name, calligraphed in gold at the gigantic stone entrance. 'Comrade Xiaoping named the cemetery!' Oohs and aahs came from the tourists raising cameras. 'It's *such* a peaceful place!' the guide announced again, and added that before the founding of the People's Republic of China, the Nationalists had executed the Communists there.

Tang led Chen Di past retailers, an internet café, and a fancy restaurant whose flying eaves imitated the temple's. At a roadside eatery, he paid for her bowl of savoury soy milk.

'I hear you don't train with them anymore.' He took a bite of his glutinous rice cake before sitting down at an outdoor table.

She sat across from him. 'Master Mu kicked me out.'

'The old fart's going to go out of business if he keeps kicking out his best students.'

Chen Di added a spoonful of chilli bean paste to her savoury soy milk. The waiter looked at her strangely. She didn't care, glad Tang thought she was one of the best.

'But guess what,' Tang said, 'it's good you got kicked out.'

'Sorry?'

'You're better than that class of weaklings. Besides, the less you have to do with the old fart, the better. Today he takes your knife, tomorrow—'

'You know he took my knife?'

Tang finished his rice cake and belched. 'I saw it on his windowsill, by the bonsai.'

'I...see.' Chen Di looked down, her cheeks hot, and swirled the soy milk with the ceramic spoon. The cut dough stick, seaweed, and pickled mustard stems bobbed up and down. 'Next time I see him, I'll get it back.'

'You're still going to see him?' Tang's laugh embarrassed her even more. 'Chances are, he won't give it back *and* might just find out another thing or two about you. You know he's onto us, don't you? He knows what we're up to.'

She gripped her spoon. She'd only ever told Tang she had 'a problem' with someone that she had to resolve. She'd never revealed her mission to Master Mu or anyone else, not even in broad strokes. 'Only vaguely though. Right?'

'He knows the exact family I have a problem with. Does that count as vague?'

She stared at him. 'You can't be serious.'

'You're sure he doesn't know about *your* plan more than you let on? I'll let you judge for yourself if you want more to do with the old fart.'

Chen Di didn't need a Made in America knife exactly to kill Lü – her Voyager had turned into a symbol over time, and really, any blade would do. 'You're right, Tang-senpai.' She lifted the bowl and poured some hot soy milk into her mouth. Delicious. 'I was about to quit the class anyhow, I'm leaving Shanghai soon.'

'Should I say congrats? You're about to finish what you came for?'

'Don't congratulate me just yet,' she said. 'Now, what did you end up doing to the son of that thug?'

Tang slowly peeled his tea egg. 'I didn't move a finger.'

'I never knew you to be so nice.'

He savoured the egg, making noises with his tongue and lips. 'You'd think I'd at least gouge out one of his eyes, wouldn't you? Given his fucking daddy's taken mine.'

She forced a laugh despite the chill passing through her.

'Sometimes, little sis, words kill better.' He sniggered. 'All I did was tell the kid a story and send him a couple text messages.'

'What story?' She let go of her spoon. 'What messages?'

'Long story, another time.' Tang slurped his hot milk. 'Don't you worry. I'll make sure my eyeball and my uncle rest in peace, only I won't get my hands dirty.'

His menacing tone gave her the creeps. But then she clapped the table, feeling that her own mission had been validated. 'Well then.' She poured the rest of the soy milk into her mouth, the bowl as clean as if it'd been washed. 'I just want to let you know you're pretty much the only one I admire in this hellish city.'

'Honoured,' Tang said. 'If you need me, you know where my recycling yard is.'

She gave a cold smile. 'I may need your advice, and I miss training with you.'

'Be my guest.'

As they stood, he extended his hand and she took it. The second their hands connected, his grip tightened – he was testing the strength in her grasp. She controlled her breathing, resisting the clutch that might have shattered someone else's bones. Each second felt longer than the last, her arm burning. Suddenly Tang's index finger lifted.

'Ow!' Chen Di failed to retain her grasp as his fingertip tickled her palm.

'Tactics, little sis. Tactics.'

She panted. Her hand had turned pink. 'I'll remember—'

'Like her.' He pointed across the street. A one-armed female beggar sat in a tattered coat, and an old couple bent to give her coins.

Chen Di looked back at Tang, confused.

'She hid an arm in that coat. Like that old beggar at the metro station, faking blindness with a cheap pair of sunglasses. It's all about tactics.'

'I'll remember it, Tang-senpai.'

'I'm not your senpai anymore, call me Tang Bro.'

'Good luck, Tang Bro.'

'And to you, little sis.'

In four hours Chen Di would follow Lü home. She bought tofu and dragged her coal stove out to the alley, lit some newspaper, set the beehive coal – a twenty-two-holed briquette – and flapped the palm-leaf fan. Unlike in her village days, she could now afford the minced meat that went with mapo tofu. And, of course, she added extra chilli bean paste.

After her late lunch and a good nap, Chen Di stepped out to find heavy clouds, so she packed a single-use raincoat along with her kitchen knife and *The Art of Peace*.

She was ready.

She rode towards Lü's workplace again. Her bicycle felt lighter, and she couldn't help but think it was because she'd spent her morning with the right person, a fellow margin-walker more competent than she. A true role model. Chen Di zipped past the plane trees, their bark like cancerous skin, their yellowish buds looking like they were already dying. She held the bicycle grip single-handed and, like Tang had done earlier, snapped off a new twig.

At the corner of the government building, she leaned her bicycle on a plane tree and started rereading the little book she'd already read in full.

Ten minutes. Twenty. Half an hour. Students dashed out of Wende Private, some picked up by eager parents. Again she spotted the man with a heart-shaped face like Lü's, but with round ears. Lü Yuandou, however, did not appear. Had he gone home early? Had he been delayed? Two children bumped her bicycle as they ran past, and it fell. Chen Di picked it up again, but the chain had dropped. And before she could fix it, she saw him.

Not Lü Yuandou, but Lin Feng.

Lin Feng stood tall in his uniform blazer, his school bag on one shoulder. Chen Di stepped back, feeling as if she'd been stabbed. When he'd denied knowing her, she'd given up on any yuanfen they might've had. But now, his reappearance shook her with ten times the strength, like a breeze that had calmed only to return as a typhoon, engulfing her. Entwined with her past. She looked back at her book, warning herself.

'Boss Chen,' he said, 'I came to see you.'

She wanted to keep her eyes in her book but couldn't. 'I thought you didn't know me.'

'You're my secret. How can I reveal it to others so easily?'

Again, she didn't know what to make of his words. A part of her felt relieved. Glad, even. It was as if she meant more to him than his school friends did.

'Boss Chen, I met the boss of your gang.'

'I don't have time for this nonsense.'

'Come on, it's not like I'm going to report you or anything.' Lin Feng rubbed his chin again. 'I think you're awesome.'

'Thanks for the compliment. You can go now.'

'So you've forgiven me for taking your knife.'

'I have not.'

'But your boss gave it back to you, no?'

Chen Di said nothing, realising that by 'boss of your gang', Lin Feng referred to Master Mu. She raised the book before her eyes. 'I said you can go now.'

'You quit Pizza & Apple Pie.'

Lightning flashed overhead, partly blocked by the plane leaves, and it took seconds before thunder swept over them. She shut the book with both hands. 'How do you know I worked there?'

'I said I'd find out about you.'

'Don't you play games with me.'

'Okay, okay. When you biked me that morning, I saw your Pizza & Apple Pie uniform under your jacket. There's only one Pizza & Apple Pie nearby, in Xu Junction, and when I went there today, they said you'd quit for good. It doesn't take Sherlock Holmes to figure that out.'

Chen Di eyed him, flattered he'd gone to the trouble to find out about her. It was as if he truly cared, like any kid might care about their cool big sister. Suddenly she wished she really were his sister.

'You know, Boss Chen, I used to go to that Pizza & Apple Pie with my sister.'

'Is your sister your secret too?'

'You could say that.'

'What's the point of hiding your sister from your friends?'

Lin Feng crossed his arms. 'Kids at school, they don't really know me.'

'And you suppose I do just because I also have a birthmark?'

That seemed to stop him. He looked into the distance, and she couldn't tell if he was thinking of something serious or nothing at all. Then he smirked. 'You might not know much about me yet, but I do know a lot about you.'

'Like how I worked at Pizza & Apple Pie.'

Lin Feng tilted his head, and pointed at the sliding gate. 'And the fact that you're here for that official. The one with those funny ears. Called Lü.'

14
Sichuan
Harvest 1994

Every harvest, Chen Di tried to like her brother. If it wasn't for him – her responsibility to take care of him – she'd have to pause her schooling and pick cotton instead. If it wasn't for him, Grandfather would've been in a worse mood all year round. If it wasn't for him, their cotton field wouldn't have had the fortune of another year of sunshine. She doubted the last claim but knew better than to argue. Secretly she'd been praying for heavy rain if it meant she could ride Teacher Jia's motorcycle, an excuse to hold onto his waist. Even with a small person dividing them, touching Teacher Jia thrilled her more than anything else.

On one afternoon of the 1994 harvest, the sky was empty but the strong wind forecast a change in the weather, and they headed home from school. Two-year-old Little Tiger could now walk half their journey, though he spoke little and drooled excessively while his peers no longer did. No matter how Chen Di scolded him, pulling his hand away, he continued to rub the rash on his chin. And for any of his wounds or infections, she was smacked.

Little Tiger pulled at her trousers when they were across the stream from Grandpa Li's house. The house now had redbrick walls and was hung with strings of corn cobs as well as chillies. Only the concrete pole at the front was still tilted, holding the same pair of loudspeakers.

Chen Di knelt on the cobblestones behind some reeds to change her brother's nappy. Rubbish poked out here and there, flies swarming. She tried not to look at the little thing between his legs. While most toddlers simply wore open-crotch pants, Grandfather had put on a childish smile and cut up an old bedsheet to create reusable, multi-layered nappies for Little Tiger. The same leathery hands he used to thrash her.

Chen Di scrubbed the dirty nappy in the stream, the water unexpectedly cold. Mother's 'Yao'er, Yao'er' thrummed at the back of her mind like a distant air-raid siren.

But screaming brought her back to reality. 'Let go of me!'

Across the stream, several people materialised before Grandpa Li's house, including none other than Lü Yuandou. Chen Di's heart jumped. She hadn't seen the official since she was ten, two years ago, but his heart-shaped face hadn't changed one bit, the ears as weird as always.

Then there was Chubby Aunty with the same big mole in her eyebrow – plus a bulging belly. Chen Di couldn't believe it. Chubby Aunty was pregnant again? They already had a son, so there was no way they'd get a birth permit. Grandpa

Li, while playing mahjong with Grandfather, had announced recently that his son and daughter-in-law were about to move to the county town for his son's work. Now Chen Di knew that Grandpa Li had only set up a lie to explain his daughter-in-law going into hiding to give birth.

Only before Chubby Aunty could leave, they were already caught.

Chen Di knelt rooted on the cobblestones, knees hurting. Chubby Aunty escaped a man's grip and bolted into the house on her short legs, and Lü followed. One man and one woman waited by a black jeep, partly covered by the reeds, but the four white loudspeakers on top of the vehicle were fully visible.

The last time Chen Di had seen this car, she hadn't yet known it was called a jeep. She thought back to the afternoon Lü Yuandou had torn down Grandpa Sun's house…

More screams.

'You're causing your whole family to lose face,' Lü said from inside the house, his high voice louder than the stream, making Chen Di tremble.

'It'll be over in no time, child.' Grandpa Li had never sounded so timid.

'No!' Chubby Aunty said. 'You can't do this to me!'

'Sure I can,' Lü said. 'I haven't even filled my quota—'

'Lunatic Lü! You won't die a good death!'

'How dare you, woman? Criticising me is criticising the Party. The Party does everything for the sake of your own future, can't you tell?'

Two men and two women hauled Chubby Aunty out of the house, one person grabbing each of her limbs. Chen Di shuddered. She'd seen villagers transport pigs this way for slaughter. Chubby Aunty kicked around, forcing them to let go, and she fell to the ground and rolled towards the stream, her face muddy, as if she'd rather drown than be taken by Lü.

But she was yanked up again. A man dragged her by her hair, and a woman slapped her so hard a bloody tooth fell out of her mouth.

They carried on.

Chen Di's fingers dug between the cobblestones where she was still kneeling, barely holding herself up. She felt she was witnessing the continuation of what had happened at Grandpa Sun's house two years ago.

But no, this was just another case. One of many.

Grandpa Li and most of the family came back out too, some sobbing, others with a resigned look, an old woman crumpling to the ground. Lü gave orders behind his team, expression unchanged. By the time they shoved Chubby Aunty into the jeep, she was almost naked, her white belly exposed like a piece of evidence.

Still kneeling, still shuddering, Chen Di wrapped her arms around her own body, wanting to hide. But Little Tiger let out a short cry of complaint.

Lü noticed them, his small eyes catching hers. 'Girl with a birthmark.'

Her body tensed.

'I remember you,' he said.

She was afraid to look at him, but terrified to turn and expose her back to him. But then she remembered a fleeting pain she'd seen on Lü's face when he'd torn down Grandpa Sun's house. Maybe, just maybe, he could be reasonable.

Chubby Aunty screamed from inside the jeep.

'What are you doing to Chubby Aunty?' Chen Di said, surprised by her own courage. She clenched her teeth and fists, and rose.

Lü stepped closer. She almost thought he'd wade across the stream, but he only raised his arms generously. 'So, how many of your sisters got chucked into the big pit?' His gaze moved between her and her brother. 'At least three, yes?'

Chen Di stood still, unable to wrap her head around his words. Her *three* little sisters? And Daci Pit, the canyon beyond the jungle on the east that all children were warned not to set foot near? Her heart throbbed almost before she knew why.

Her sisters had been 'chucked into the big pit'?

'You're wrong!' she said. *I tucked in thirty yuan and waited for hours, Chen Di, hours at the bus stop until I saw a granny picking her up. Your little sister will be taken care of.* She'd held onto Father's words, word for word, year after year. She'd dreamed of reuniting with her sister, in a big city, surrounded by tall buildings.

'Am I?' Lü turned to the family. 'Old Li, your grandson wasn't your first grandchild, was he? Did you take the first to the big pit? Or did your son?'

Chen Di shivered. Lü Yuandou might've been wrong about a lot of things, his words untrustworthy, but everyone in Grandpa Li's family looked like they knew what he was talking about. All these years, had she simply been holding onto what she wanted to believe in? She hadn't seen that granny at the bus stop, hadn't heard any gossip about her. And she *had* felt like she'd heard Father's words more than once...and still felt that way.

Lü chuckled. 'Realising something?'

Her teeth chattered despite her tight jaw.

'Well, girl, the ghost woman spits out bones.'

Chen Di felt she was about to puke. But her village was named after Daci Pit, *da* being the character for *big* and *ci* the one for *benevolence,* so the canyon couldn't have been such a bad place... Or could it? She'd never seen Daci Pit with her own eyes, but now villagers' descriptions came to mind. The red cliffs, the snaking riverbed, and the child-devouring ghost woman whom she no longer believed in.

Then it clicked. The ghost woman *was* Daci Pit.

She knew that every rumour, every story, every myth came about for a reason. Villagers must have created the ghost woman to explain the fate of missing little girls.

Chen Di could barely breathe. She imagined Father standing on a precipice, a shirt-bag in his good hand. Gripping the bag, he swung it forward, backward, forward again, like a child playing with a sack of rubbish. When he got bored, he let go.

Father had let her baby sister – no, sisters – go.

'You should thank Heaven you're alive, girl. You're not your brother.' Lü pulled open a door to the jeep and stepped in. 'Give your mother my regards.'

The door slammed, and the jeep thundered away.

Beyond the half-open window shutters of a neighbouring house, eavesdropping heads moved, and downstream, people chattered. Villagers were as nosy as always. Many had been watching the commotion, except unlike before, they hadn't stood up to Lü Yuandou. Some no longer opposed him, while others simply wanted to protect themselves.

Chen Di slumped on the grass, Chubby Aunty's screams and Lü's high voice echoing in her head. And she remembered one moonlit night, the way a white shirt-bag moved, pushed from the inside by a little fist, or foot.

The night of her sister's birth. And death.

Her body now reduced to bones at the bottom of the canyon.

Chen Di wiped the sweat on her forehead, messing her hair, and she yanked off her leaf hair clip and clipped it back. She rose and gave her brother her hand, and they walked away, under red banners, past red wall writing. *Fire safety is everyone's responsibility! Long live the Communist Party! Reward for families with one child or two daughters!* Little Tiger rubbed his rash. He tilted his head and stared at her with his dark eyes as if he could see through it all.

You should thank Heaven you're alive, girl. You're not your brother.

Brother. It was always about her brother, while her sisters had been thrown into Daci Pit before they could live. Was there nothing she could ever do about all this?

A will, the inkling of an idea, emerged from somewhere deep inside her, a place in her mind, her soul, that she never knew about. It boiled, it brimmed, it burst. Very quickly, it grew in detail and strength. Of its own, it became a conviction.

I shall live, and live well.

She would never be dragged around like Chubby Aunty. She would never live like Mother. *You have worth*, Teacher Jia had said. Yes, she would do better, much better, than thanking Heaven that she was alive. Her murdered sisters, her worshipped brother – the unfairness ought to be corrected, the broken world ought to be fixed.

Chen Di was not a silkworm.

She refused to be boiled alive inside a cocoon.

A rusty taste settled in her mouth, like blood. She dropped into a trance, her legs moving of their own accord. The mud paths had never felt so long and she felt she wasn't going forward, that the world was retreating from her. Dark clouds scuttled across the sky as if competing in some kind of perpetual race, the afternoon dreary, shadowy, inauspicious. A storm was coming. A wet, chilly wind whipped her face. Her blood froze.

Chen Di was no longer herself. She was overtaken by a force so violent, so primitive, it felt unhuman.

A female ghost howled in her ears.

And when she arrived home, she was alone.

15
Shanghai
Spring 2002

Chen Di hadn't been aware of the rain until water entered her parted lips. She was found out. Lin Feng knew she had Lü Yuandou in her sights. Lightning brightened the sky above the plane trees, and rainwater dripped from Lin Feng's fringe. A true killer would grab his jaws, force open his mouth, and cut off his tongue so he couldn't tell anyone about what she was up to.

People scurried, dull umbrellas crowding the pavement, raincoats shielding the bikers. The rain poured on them but she didn't move. Neither did he.

'You're shivering,' Lin Feng said.

'I'm not,' Chen Di said.

'Are you cold?'

Only Mother had cared enough to ask whether she was cold.

'So, Boss Chen, I found out your secret. Now you'll have to take me as your apprentice.' He extended his hand.

She had the urge to grip it. Even now, much of that afternoon of the 1994 harvest remained blank in her mind like a new notebook, without even lines or grids. But one thing was for sure: if only she'd kept holding that small hand, then she'd be living a different life right now, with not only Little Tiger but also Mother by her side.

She flinched, judged by the eyes before her.

Chen Di didn't shake Lin Feng's hand but wiped the rain from her face and looked down, murky water pooling in a crack. How strange it was that she wanted to hold the hand of someone whose tongue she should be cutting off.

'You better go home,' she heard herself say. 'Your parents would be upset seeing you like this.' But she couldn't let him go! Exactly how much did he know about her mission? And how on earth had he learned Lü Yuandou's name?

'They wouldn't,' he said, calm.

'Excuse me?'

'My parents wouldn't be upset. I don't need to go home.'

He didn't have those indulgent Shanghainese parents Chen Di had originally imagined. She'd known that for a while now, but still she grimaced. Water seeped into her canvas shoe, and she noticed only then his black sneakers were not only dirty, the supposedly white swooshes brown, but also worn, the uppers thinned, one sole starting to come off.

A desire to protect him overwhelmed her, then forced her to take a huge step back. The kid had the pocket money to get himself new shoes! She shouldn't invest emotions into his family situation, she couldn't afford to get involved. She had questions for him about her mission, and her mission only.

'Why don't we talk at your den?' he said, as if reading her mind.

She glanced at the rain-washed sliding gate and the government building beyond. Her unit did seem the safest place for such a conversation. *Tactics, little sis,* Tang had said. *Tactics.* Indeed, she should keep her role model in mind as she proceeded to the later steps of her mission.

And it'd help no one if Lin Feng caught a cold. Chen Di pulled from her drenched backpack the single-use raincoat, shook it open, and put it over him, the hood protecting his face. He watched her, her birthmark, but didn't reach out to touch it. Was he thinking of his sister again?

'Where are your parents?' she asked.

He gazed at her a moment longer, then smirked. 'Work.'

'What time do they get home?'

'Eight for Mum. Dad hasn't come home in ages.'

Again Chen Di thought of his mum whacking him on the street – this street. She couldn't help but ask, 'What does your mum do?'

'She writes short stories but hasn't published in forever.' He huffed and crossed his arms. 'Her novel's hopeless, it's never going to work out.'

Chen Di had pictured writers to be more restrained kind of people. 'And your dad?'

'More a businessman than a scientist.'

'You're awfully frank answering strangers' questions.'

'You're not a stranger.'

His dark eyes forced her to look away again. 'Come—'

She cleared her throat. 'Come with me then.' And she almost took it back, no longer trusting herself she could handle this kid, emotionally. But she had to.

Lin Feng was already squatting by her bicycle, examining the fallen chain. He pulled down the derailleur, wrapped the chain back in position, stood, and lifted the rear wheel off the ground. When he reached for the pedal, Chen Di grabbed it first. For an instant their hands overlapped. His skin was smooth but still so cold.

She spun the wheel. 'Can you stop rubbing your chin?'

He dropped his hand, embarrassed, as if having just realised what he was doing. A patch of black from the bicycle chain remained on his chin.

'Hop on.' She held the handlebars and eyed the back carrier.

'I'll bike you this time,' Lin Feng said, taking the handgrips from her, and jumping on the bicycle. It fit him much better than her. Chen Di kept her guard and sat on the back carrier side-saddle, legs pressed together. He raised the back of the transparent raincoat to pull it over her head, shielding her too. She felt no warmth from his body.

'Straight ahead,' she said from inside the raincoat. She held onto his waist, shocked that his body felt like a hollow shell, as if his fancy uniform had nothing inside.

Her arms trembled.

The rain thinned. At her longtang's arched entrance, Chen Di got off, and Lin Feng pushed the bicycle into the alley. The compound of low-rise buildings must've been nothing like where he lived. He looked up at the maze-like overhead cables and glanced around at the ads stamped over the walls. *ID Arrangement, Teacher Kang Tutoring, Cure to Sexually Transmitted Diseases*. One was stamped over a plate that read *Advertising Forbidden*.

She took over the bicycle. 'Yes, people live here. People who weren't born as lucky as you to have a private bathroom, a private kitchen.'

'It's awesome,' he said.

'You don't have to—'

'No, seriously. My mum looks miserable cooking in our *private kitchen*.'

Chen Di hadn't expected such a response. At her iron door, she opened the padlock and unbolted the latch. She pushed in the bicycle, leaned it on the wall where her map of Shanghai used to be, and tugged the string to turn on the hanging bulb.

'Wicked.' Lin Feng stepped in fast and shut the door behind him. 'It reminds me of cargo containers where drug-dealing or kidnapping happened.'

She laughed. 'You'll know to be careful then.'

He pulled off the raincoat and glanced around before spotting a nail on the wall from which to hang it. He put down his backpack and studied the knife gouges on her wardrobe, then her chamber pot, then her coal stove.

'It's a stove, young master.'

'Is this your gang's base?' He made a silly face, sticking out his tongue.

Chen Di couldn't help but laugh again. She went to fetch two green-and-white-striped towels hanging from a rope across the wall, used one to dry her hair, and passed the other to him. But Lin Feng stood still. He must've grown up not touching anything out-of-towners used, and suddenly she felt relieved. But then he took the towel and wiped his face with it.

She turned away to yank off her wet cardigan and T-shirt, and put on a green cable-knit sweater over her bra top before turning back around.

Lin Feng was blushing. 'The scars on your back look like tree roots.'

She rarely thought about Grandfather's beating anymore.

'What happened, Boss Chen?'

She hadn't brought him here to talk about this. 'I don't have tea, not even hot water.' She sat on the bed, crossed her legs, and pointed him to her small bamboo chair. 'About my interest in that man, does anyone else know?'

'You have good back muscles,' he said, and flushed.

'Thanks for the compliment. Now answer me.'

'I ditched my friends yesterday and turned back and saw you follow him, that's all.' He sat on the chair obediently, and his tone shifted. 'I'm good at observing people.' He sounded as if he was doing a job interview.

'But what made you think I followed him? Was I too close? Was it the way I walked?'

'Your knife. And how you glared at him.'

Had she really *glared* at Lü? She nodded, making a mental note to be doubly careful in the future. 'And how did you know his name?'

'His colleague called out to him after you left.'

Really? Somehow, this little piece of information made everything feel more real.

'About your knife, Boss Chen, sorry but you first took mine at Yuanfen Eatery. And that day, I only went to Dragon Lustre to see a bro, I didn't expect to bump into—'

'Enough of my knife.'

'But that old guy, he's the boss of your gang, no?'

'Enough of him as well.'

'What's so special about the 1998 Lantern Festival?'

Chen Di had carved Mother's death date on her Voyager's handle to help her focus on the mission, but she shouldn't have needed the reminder.

'And Boss Chen, who exactly is that man?'

'Feel free to think of him as "the boss of our gang", I don't care.'

'I'm talking about Lü.'

The air in the room thickened. Chen Di uncrossed her legs, clapped her knees, and leaned forward. 'He's no one to me, and no one to you.'

'Actually, he's my distant neighbour.'

'That's an oxymoron.'

'He lives in Phoenix Sea Court, building 1, unit 406.'

She sat up, heart pounding. So Lin Feng had completed step two for her, saving her the trouble of finding out where

Lü lived herself. *Good job,* she almost said, but only made a mental note of the address and made sure she didn't look too pleased. She'd passed Phoenix Sea Court before, a short walk from both that government building and Xu Junction. One final month of luxury for Lü Yuandou to enjoy. 'I know where he lives,' she lied. 'The question is, how do you?'

'I live in Dragon Lake Court. They're in the same area, a couple of streets apart. All the housing estates there are built by the same developer. And yep, I trailed him.'

'Did you, now?'

'Yep. I'm good at stalking people, and don't worry, I was very discreet.'

'You're good at poking your nose into others' business.'

Lin Feng looked as if he'd been praised, which almost made her laugh again. He seemed to want to say something but held back.

'What?' she said.

He smirked. 'Are you going to kill him?'

Chen Di lunged before she could think. She pulled his wrist and, applying pressure, forced him to stagger in circles until he fell face down to the floor. She jammed her foot under his shoulder and pinned her knee on his bent arm.

'You can choose to live or die, Lin Feng.'

He barely looked up, his cheek shoved into the cold concrete, the glow from her hanging light bulb reflected in his dark eyes. She didn't loosen her grip.

'I said you can choose to live or die. If you choose to live—'

'I never deserved to live,' he choked out.

One second. Two. Three. Four. Chen Di's hold loosened. Lin Feng flipped around and faced her, and inhaled, exhaled. They stared at each other, her body hovering over his. The sadness in his eyes hit her like a slap.

Then, a knock on the iron door, eerily soft.

16
Sichuan
Harvest 1994

Hours after she'd arrived home, alone, Chen Di found herself trudging through a dark, wet jungle, among other villagers. One of her eyes was swollen shut from Grandfather's slaps, and she had only a vague awareness she needed to find Little Tiger, that she'd failed, horribly, to fulfil her responsibility.

Then she saw him: Lü Yuandou.

In the light cast by the group's torches, his ears looked even pointier, the lobes even longer.

'Chief Lü,' Grandfather said, 'are you here to help us with the search?'

A high voice. 'Nice show you're putting on, Old Chen.'

'My son is missing!' Mother wailed.

'People come up with all kinds of stories to get around family planning,' Lü said. 'Old Chen, you're smarter than Old Li, you know better than to directly go for a permitless pregnancy. I must say, I'm impressed by the trouble you're willing to go through to get yourself another grandson.'

Mother didn't seem to understand, but a few others looked like they did.

'This is no joke.' Grandfather's fists shook.

'You really think you can fool me,' Lü said.

Grandfather threw down the torch and panted, pressing a hand to his chest.

Lü chuckled. 'Take care of your old bones, I say, and your old brain. Change your old ideas.' Then, in a condescending tone adults might use when talking to children, he added, 'Nice seeing you again so soon.' Singular *you*.

He had to be talking to Chen Di.

Suddenly she felt she was trapped in a thousand-year-old cave, the air stuffy, the earth soggy, malevolent spirits drifting about. The cave rumbled. Rocks fell. She backed up a step only to tread on Father's foot.

He looked at her. 'You saw Chief Lü recently?'

She didn't nod or shake her head, a numbness buzzing inside.

Lü Yuandou disappeared into the dense vegetation. Some villagers abandoned the search, too, following after him, but others remained, keen to help, and they split into a few groups, Father going off on his own.

'Is this just a show you're putting on?' asked two of Grandfather's mahjong friends.

'Please.' He clawed their arms. 'Believe us.'

Lü Yuandou's take on the matter explained the village cadres' inaction – not even a loudspeaker announcement. They all believed the family had taken Little Tiger out of the village and into hiding so they could claim his death and go ahead to try for another son despite the one-and-a-half-child policy. It wasn't a new idea. And Chen Di's earlier words had only made things worse: 'When I opened my eyes, he was gone.'

She'd been saying this ever since she'd got back to the cotton field. Everyone had been outside then, finishing up the day's work as dark clouds rolled in. Father, standing closest to her, dropped his sack of cotton and rushed off with a few other workers to search nearby areas. Grandfather scrunched up his unibrow and looked like he couldn't breathe, then he stormed over and smacked her hard, left cheek, right cheek, his face scarlet with rage. Mother's eyes widened in horror before she chased after Father.

Soon, the thunderstorm started, and her family headed for the village committee office, where the cadres were based, to report the incident.

'When I...' Chen Di stood swaying. 'When I opened my eyes, he was gone.'

The two cadres, a man and a woman, exchanged a suspicious look. The woman with white teeth asked, 'Why did you shut your eyes? Were you asleep?'

'I...don't know. When I opened my eyes, he was just gone.'

'Magic, wasn't it?' The cadre sat back in her cane chair as thunder roared outside. 'Now why don't you give us the location of the magic show?'

Chen Di said nothing.

'Where did you lose your brother?'

She didn't know. It was all blank.

'I'm telling you to speak, girl!'

'When I opened my eyes, he was just...somehow...gone.'

The male cadre laughed, his mouth opened sideways, showing his yellow teeth. Chen Di had seen him with Lü at Chubby Aunty's capture – the last event she remembered with clarity. 'Why are we wasting time on this?' He gave the female cadre a look and turned to Grandfather. 'Old Chen, Old Chen, Old Chen, what do I say? We know you and Old Li, what you folks want. One grandson just isn't enough. You're too greedy. Now asking your twelve-year-old granddaughter to lie for you? She's not too bright. Come up with something better.'

Grandfather pinned Chen Di to the wall. In the struggle, she pulled off the red pennant that commended the village as a fine collective.

The cadres had shoved them out.

The search continued through the night, torches beaming, dirt and sweat clinging to everyone's clothes. Before dawn, the groups met up, none having been successful. They'd looked almost everywhere: the fields, the jungles, even three neighbouring villages. Last year, a small boy visiting relatives from the county town had fallen into a well and drowned, so they'd made sure to inspect every well. And nothing. Might Little Tiger have fallen into… They didn't want to think the unthinkable: Daci Pit.

When they emerged from the jungle on the east and arrived at the canyon rim, Father was already there. He leaned on a crooked pine tree, the only tree in the bushy area. Near the precipice, the earth was bare and scattered with gravel. A few men squinted across the chasm at the opposite cliffs: dark red under the predawn sky, menacing. A large black bird flapped its wings and swooped down, letting out a piercing call that echoed between the cliffs. The riverbed wasn't visible unless you moved to the edge of the clifftop and craned your neck. A young man did and slipped on the loose gravel, barely saving himself.

Years ago, four curious villagers had climbed down into the canyon from a spot further out of the village, where the rock face was less steep. They'd never returned, rumoured to have turned into evil spirits.

Everyone sat around the low bushes and shared water and cigarettes. Grandfather's eyes were as red as Mother's. 'I'm sorry, Xixi,' he mumbled incomprehensibly. A thin man flopped down, exhausted. A stout man took a long drag on his cigarette. 'Kidnapped,' he said, his sweaty round face turning left and right. 'That's the best-case scenario.'

Chen Di sat hugging her knees, trying to breathe, still feeling stuck inside.

'You.' Grandfather's calloused finger. 'Go down, find your brother.'

The first sun rays on her face felt like slaps. 'Sorry?'

'I said go down. It's your job to stick to your brother! Have you forgotten your whole life's purpose – that you're his cow, his horse? Now go down.'

'To wh-where, Grandfather?'

'Go down into the canyon! Which part of my sentence don't you understand?'

She choked down her sobs.

'Nobody can climb down there,' Mother said. 'And she's just a girl.'

Grandfather pushed himself up on his knee to rise, and he grabbed Chen Di's plait and yanked her up too. 'I'll throw you down there, you, you…' He seized her other plait and dragged her from the bushes towards the precipice.

Two more metres, she'd be gone.

Chen Di shut the one eye she could still use. This was it then. She felt sorry for leaving Mother behind, so sorry. Then a new wave of sadness drowned her. She would never see Teacher Jia again, the only kind man in her life. No, it wasn't just his kindness. It was the fire in her chest, warm, slightly painful, whenever he was around. She wanted to hold his big, smooth hand again, to feel it against her skin. And in that moment, Chen Di realised this must be what people meant when they whispered about romantic love.

She was in love.

'Teacher Jia,' she murmured, 'what should I do?'

How could she give up! She grabbed the bottom of Grandfather's black shirt, tearing it, as she struggled to get out of his grasp.

Mother hurried over and knelt, clasping Grandfather's leg. 'I've lost enough children!'

Others also came to calm Grandfather. He continued to

hiss at Chen Di as he tried to shake Mother off, but Mother didn't let go and she looked to Father, who was now sitting under that tree, half in shadow. Chen Di remembered the night Father had gripped Mother's hand and kissed her. Well, if he cared, now was the time to act. Yet he seemed absorbed in himself, staring at his thumbless left hand.

At last, Grandfather let go of her plaits. With hair blown around her face, she fumbled to hide behind Mother, but inside she was resolute. She would live on, and live well.

She heard a laugh, first quiet, then loud, hysterical.

It was coming from her.

Apart from Father, everyone stared at her.

'W-We'll come again.' A short man from a neighbouring village broke the silence. People dispersed, leaving Chen Di with Mother, Father, and, of course, Grandfather.

Grandfather gave her parents a glance each. 'We go home and sleep too.'

Just as Mother took Chen Di's hand, he whipped around, pointing at Chen Di's nose. 'I did not say *you*. You murderer! You killed my Little Tiger!'

Chen Di flinched.

'No she didn't!' Mother wept. 'She only...lost him.'

'Is there any difference?' Grandfather yelled. 'There *are* no kidnappers here to "save" him. He's two! So small, so helpless... All the jungles, the canyon...' Tears streamed down his agonised face. 'Losing him *is* killing him!'

Chen Di flinched again. The fact washed over her like a bucket of freezing water, cutting through her numbness.

Grandfather's finger shook. 'Your brother doesn't come home, *you* don't come home.'

Without even looking at her, Father left with Grandfather, his ripped sleeve swaying like a dog's tail. Mother sat under the crooked pine tree, Chen Di's head on her thigh. She wiped the dirt off Chen Di's face, careful to avoid her swelling eye, and told her to sleep.

Chen Di fell asleep, eyes wide open.

17
Shanghai
Spring 2002

'Stand up,' Chen Di said to Lin Feng at the sound of urgent knocking on the door from the outside. 'Don't speak unless I tell you to.' Tang would've added 'or I'll kill you' but she couldn't. *I never deserved to live.* The words echoed in her mind, swirled in her chest. She couldn't imagine what would've made a little emperor say such a thing, except Lin Feng wasn't exactly a little emperor, was he?

Once he'd scrambled to his feet, Chen Di opened the door. 'Grandma Chu.'

'Young Chen.' The dentures smiled. 'I need to talk to you.'

'Yes, what is it?' Chen Di stood blocking the doorway as usual – she never let anyone in. Except... She glanced back at Lin Feng, who *was* in.

'Ayo?' Grandma Chu adjusted her bifocals. 'Who is this?'

'My nephew.'

Chen Di gave Lin Feng a nod, and he said, 'Hello, grandma.'

'What a lovely boy. See that milky white skin, he looks like a Shanghainese child.' She spoke to Chen Di but was looking

Lin Feng up and down, patting his arm. She'd probably pat his head if he weren't so tall. 'I never knew you had a nephew here.'

'He's my second nephew, more precisely.'

Grandma Chu's eyes stopped on his uniform blazer. 'Ayo! You go to Wende Private?'

'Yes,' Chen Di said loudly to get her attention. 'My cousin earned big.'

'What business?'

'Tea exports. So you want to talk to me?'

'Right, come with me for a moment.' The old woman again smiled at Lin Feng, leaning in as if she was about to put a sweet in his mouth. She backed off reluctantly.

'Stay put,' Chen Di whispered to him. 'If you touch anything—' Again she left the sentence hanging.

In the alley, some residents were out now the rain had stopped, and an old man sat fanning his coal stove, the smoke making Grandma Chu cough. Chen Di followed her bobbed head, which nodded to everyone the way a benevolent Party leader might a dung worker.

'You should interact with people,' Grandma Chu said to Chen Di as they ascended the steps to her unit. 'Here in the longtang, we're a big family.'

Chen Di mumbled her agreement noncommittally.

Upstairs, one door led to Grandma Chu's unit and another to a so-called communal kitchen, which was often locked, only Grandma Chu having a key. She opened the barred iron gate to her unit, then a wooden door, and they both changed into slippers.

The living room looked more like a modern apartment than a longtang unit. The TV showed Shanghai opera. The hardwood floor was newly waxed, slippery. A display cabinet showcased a Qing dynasty tea set painted with blue lotus flowers. During the Cultural Revolution, Grandma Chu must have defied orders and stashed it away rather than destroyed it.

On the far wall, among yellow-rimmed red pennants that commended the longtang as a fine collective, were a dozen photos taken during community events. Old residents played Chinese chess on the roof, men practised tai chi while women did Mulan boxing, and everyone ate together at round tables, under celebratory red banners. Chen Di wasn't in any of them – she'd never joined any events in this longtang or her previous one.

'Sit, sit, sit!' Grandma Chu said.

Chen Di sat on a couch draped with a red throw, and Grandma Chu went to bring tea.

'Please don't go to any trouble,' Chen Di said, and meant it. Except she knew she'd only said the words expected of any guests even if they desperately wanted tea.

Minutes later, Grandma Chu returned with steaming oolong tea as well as chocolates and mandarins and sunflower seeds. Eating too much would be a mistake. She'd heard enough gossip about guests 'not behaving'.

'You quit Pizza & Apple Pie.' Grandma Chu sat down beside her, not muting the TV.

So Manager Chu had told her. 'I was going to tell you when I paid my rent.'

'That's what I mean by saying you should interact with people. If we know better what's going on in your life, then we can help you better. If I have to hear from my nephew—'

'I'm going back to Sichuan to get married.'

'Plenty of rich men in Big Shanghai.'

'It was so decided. I'm moving out by April thirtieth.'

Grandma Chu glanced at the floor sideways, then looked at Chen Di as if she'd stolen something. 'Come for a second.'

She stood and signalled Chen Di to follow. Through the windows, Chen Di noticed a flimsy extension of the balcony. Grandma Chu was building a new room even though she lived alone, widowed for years. There were talks about the longtang getting demolished, and every owner would be compensated with an apartment whose size matched that of their current unit. An extra room meant a bigger apartment.

Chen Di followed her into a side room that smelled of leather, and her jaw dropped. Her old map of Shanghai was spread out on the desk. The small red-marker circles were obvious even before the light flickered to life.

'I wanted a map,' Grandma Chu said. 'This is perfect, but what are the circles for?'

She couldn't give a rash answer. She really should've burnt it! How un-Shanghainese of the old woman, to keep something an out-of-towner had thrown away! The Party had really driven frugality into some people.

'Why are some crossed out?' Grandma Chu asked. 'I told you it reminded me of what detectives use on crime shows. Now with all the circles, it's like a serial killer eliminating—'

Chen Di forced a laugh. 'Sorry but I don't have time for this, I need to take my nephew home.' She spun around and cut through the living room to get to the door.

'Wait. This isn't the only reason I asked you to come.'

She looked back, one foot in her shoe.

'Young Chen, I know you have some powerful people behind you, but you see—'

'Who's behind *me?*'

'Nothing, nothing.'

'I'm on my own here.'

'I know, I know.' Grandma Chu waved it away, then bared her dentures. 'You're moving out at the end of April, so I need your March rent within forty-eight hours.'

'Excuse me?'

'And I need your April rent by the end of March, not the end of April.'

But Chen Di always paid rent before the start of each month. 'Of course I'll pay for April by the end of March, but I already paid for March back in February.'

'Don't joke now, that was your February rent.'

Shanghai opera blared out from the TV, unintelligible. 'I'll bring the receipt.' Chen Di put on the other shoe. The old fox had some nerve, messing with her.

'If you can't pay on time, I'll have to give your unit to someone who can.'

Chen Di stood perfectly still. Seriously?

'I have people lined up,' Grandma Chu said. 'A young couple from Zhejiang who're willing to pay more than you.' She gave two sideways glances, left and right, and her eyes flicked back to Chen Di. 'You know, I'm quite free this Sunday. I think I'll check out those circled places on your map.'

'You can't be serious.'

'But I am. I'll be touring around.'

Chen Di stared at her. Was Grandma Chu, like Lin Feng, like Master Mu, also onto her? She couldn't dismiss this as an empty threat. Everyone knew Grandma Chu had a passion for patrolling and gossiping, she might just figure out that all the circles corresponded to government buildings. She shuddered at the possible turn of events – after Lü's death, this map could be incriminating.

She'd have to get it back.

The old fox was real trouble. Chen Di rushed down the stairs, along the wet alley, and back to her unit. She pulled open her iron door and was taken aback: Lin Feng was gone. Had she allowed someone who knew her mission to escape? She didn't yet know what to make of it when she moved around her bed and found him lying on the ground, facing away. 'Is my furniture that intolerable you have to lie on the floor?'

No response. She crouched down and tapped his face, noticing a pink mark under his chin. Lin Feng didn't move. She checked for his breathing. Normal. He'd lost consciousness. Master Mu had taught them the basics of first aid. She unbuttoned Lin Feng's blazer, pulled over her small bamboo chair, and raised his legs onto it. That empty shell, again.

He had fainted at Yuanfen Eatery as well. Was it low blood pressure? Low blood sugar? Drugs? She fetched Lin Feng's school bag and unzipped it to check for medicine. There wasn't even one book or notebook. Some student. She pulled out a single sheet of paper covered with ugly pencil writing, like chicken footprints.

> *I am ashamed of my behaviour. After the Yuanfen Eatery incident, I thought about a lot of things and reflected on a lot of things and realised my mistake. I accept criticism. My teachers have such great expectations for me to become a builder of our socialist motherland, but I failed them, failed the collective of my class. As a member of the Communist Youth League*

An incomplete self-criticism. So someone had reported him after all.

A red pack of fancy Chunghwa cigarettes lay at the bottom of the bag, and a white pharmacy box contained two blister packs of tablets. Chen Di read the label – the medicine treated 'all types of depression', 'obsessive-compulsive disorder', 'panic disorder with or without agoraphobia', and 'social anxiety disorder', among other things.

Before she could absorb the situation, she heard something beep. She pulled out a sleek phone from Lin Feng's pocket and flipped it open to find a new message.

> Fengfeng, in the fridge there's tomato and egg stir-fry, braised pork belly, and snow peas. We have a lot of work today, I won't be back until nine. Mum

Chen Di again pictured the tall woman holding up a black satchel. Lin Feng's mum would've looked elegant if it wasn't for her ugly expression, the wrinkles between her brows.

The phone beeped again.

> It'll be more like ten. Tomorrow I'll call a maid aunty over. Be good. Mum

Honestly, what an exception among all the Shanghainese mothers who treated their children as pearls in their palms. Chen Di studied Lin Feng's face again, his skin smooth and fair, and cold. She squatted and tapped his arm. Still no reaction. She reread the mother's words and accidentally opened an older message.

> If life is too hard, you can always find a way out, little bro.

The phone felt heavy in her hand, she couldn't make sense of the message. And when she checked the sender's name, she tensed and clutched her sweater. She opened a few even older messages, all from the same sender.

Tang Bro.

Just checking in. Thinking about your poor sister?

Good, little bro. Very good. No point now brooding over how she felt back then, day-to-day, living her painful life.

Don't feel guilty about your existence.

Lin Feng made a sound and stirred, and Chen Di almost dropped the phone. She flipped it shut and shoved it back into his pocket. 'You're awake? Your mum messaged saying she wouldn't be back until ten.'

He opened his eyes and massaged his temple. 'Are you okay?'

'*You* are asking *me* that?' Then she softened her voice. 'Do you faint often?'

'Sometimes.' He stared at her ceiling.

Chen Di's heartbeat was still fast. 'Tang' was a common family name, but... *All I did was tell the kid a story and send him a couple text messages.* Then suddenly everything became clear: the other day, Master Mu had already told her that it was on his way to Tang's recycling yard that he'd taken her knife from Lin Feng.

'Lin Feng,' she said unsteadily, 'the morning you took my knife, you said you went to Dragon Lustre to meet a bro.'

'I thought you didn't want to talk about your knife anymore.'

'The bro you met up with – who was he?'

'An awesome dude.' Lin Feng tried to sit up but couldn't. 'He's good at fighting, has a team of musclemen as his minions, and has a badass eyepatch.'

18
Shanghai
Spring 2002

'Are you okay?' Lin Feng asked again from the floor. Chen Di clutched her head with one hand and shut her eyes, trying to get her thoughts in order. Tang's grudge against Lin Feng's family had nothing to do with her. She was in Shanghai for Lü, and Lü only! She had to stay focused: deal with Grandma Chu and move onto the execution.

Mission first!

She went around her bed and pulled out a cardboard box from underneath. She wasn't used to having another person in her room, but the silence between her and Lin Feng felt companionable, calming. She picked out her stack of rental receipts, each of which was stamped and stated her address, Grandma Chu's name, and the amount paid. But they showed only one date: the date of payment. Nowhere did it say which month the rent was for. She looked into every envelope. No rental contract.

Chen Di punched her bed. She'd always considered herself one of the most capable out-of-towners in the city, but she wasn't. She didn't have two months of rent. Now she had no evidence she was being charged extra, and if the old fox banged on her door daily and bitched about her owing rent, she'd be in serious trouble. No, that was the best-case scenario. Grandma Chu had threatened to give her unit to a young couple from Zhejiang.

Chen Di had thought she had over a month to kill Lü. Now she had ten days.

More urgent still was her map. She doubted Grandma Chu would willingly give it back, and asking for it would only arouse her suspicions further. What could she do before the old fox went on her 'tour' this Sunday?

Something inside her clicked. She looked at Lin Feng, lying on the floor across from her bed. Grandma Chu had patted his arm with so much affection, her old eyes lingering on him as if he were the grandson she never had. Chen Di could make use of this.

She poured Lin Feng a mug of water from her Thermos, and went to his side. With his help, she could do something subtler than outright robbing the map or tearing it into pieces in front of Grandma Chu.

Lin Feng pushed himself to a sitting position and accepted the mug, wrapping his hands around it as if no one had ever shown him such kindness. For a second Chen Di forgot her plans, again hit by the urge to protect him, and as he gazed at her birthmark, she felt a sudden relief. Though his sister had moved to Beijing, it sounded like they had a real bond. She hoped the girl would take on their parents' role to make sure her brother didn't end up on the wrong path.

She couldn't believe she was thinking like Master Mu.

'So, Boss Chen, can you take me into your gang?'

She tried not to laugh. 'I'll think about it.' Except Tang's messages jumped to mind. She stared at his pale face and shivered, doing her best to resist an even stronger urge to protect him. 'Tell me, what makes you faint?'

'Low blood pressure due to anxiety.'

'What might've brought that on today?'

'This.' Lin Feng pulled out something from under her bed – one of her old literary magazines, flipped open to a short story. 'Here, my mum wrote this.' He passed it over to her and pointed at the author's pen name: Dried Bamboo Shoot. 'It's lame, I know.'

'Good for her.' To be published in the same magazine Four Three was published in. Memories of Teacher Jia rushed back, sending heat through her body.

'No, read it, Boss Chen.'

Replaced

Fireflies circle the resting place of my birth parents. I come here every Qingming, always in the evenings, the air wet and alive. I kneel before the graves, my foster parents behind my shoulders. They help me brush away the leaves and wipe the headstones. They kneel beside me, their palms joined like mine, their foreheads pressed to the mossy ground, like mine.

I never say my prayers aloud, not when I was nine, and not now, six years later. Only the fireflies know my mind, their feeble blinking a chorus of life's impermanence.

And permanent irreplaceability.

I clap one to death. I look to the human beings on my left and right. 'Father,' I call the man. 'Mother,' I call the woman.

'Tomorrow let's go to the animal market,' he says, cheerily.

'Your favourite animal market,' she says, more cheerily.

As if they could replace my real parents...

Chen Di finished reading fast. *Replaced* was about a daughter's inability to love her foster parents, who never managed to replace her dead birth parents in her heart.

'Good story,' she said.

Lin Feng was silent, though his face said he needed to talk.

She poured him another mug of water. 'Was this a real story?'

'No, but I've been to that animal market. The pagoda the characters see poking above the vendors' sheds is Dragon Lustre Temple's pagoda. I just remembered it all.'

'You *just* remembered it?'

'That's probably why I fainted.' He looked down. 'That time I sat on my dad's shoulders. He was fit, even handsome, I don't know how he turned into an obsessive cookie eater. And my mum was smiling and didn't wear a single hairpin. Her hair fell to her waist.'

Chen Di couldn't reconcile a smiling, long-haired mum with the madwoman whacking him on the street. 'And then?'

'And my dad was smoothing my mum's hair, which was crazy. They *never* touch each other.' Lin Feng gulped the water and stared at her. 'My sister was there too. She took my hand – her hand was so soft and warm, I can still…feel it.' His shoulders shook. 'And she put a stack of mulberry leaves in my palm.'

'For silkworms?' Chen Di said, hit by nostalgia. 'You kept silkworms?'

'As pets. I've kept them for as long as I can remember, every single spring. I have some at home right now.'

She didn't expect him to run a silkworm farm. Keeping silkworms as pets was probably a popular pastime in Shanghai. At least he seemed serious about the hobby. But how could such a harmless memory have caused enough anxiety for him to pass out?

Chen Di recalled his antidepressants.

Lin Feng finished another mug of water and said, more to himself, 'It was as if there used to be love in my family.'

'Lin Feng,' she said, 'maybe your dad and mum no longer love each other, maybe they're too busy to show you much care, but at least your family's well-off. And you still have your sister, who you said calls you every day.'

'But she left me.'

'To study in Beijing!'

He didn't look up. 'She's at Beida, you know? She's super smart and hard-working. She's studying literature, not that she's inspired by Mum. She takes it apart instead of putting it together. She's going to do a master's, a PhD, and—'

'And I'd gladly switch places with her!' Chen Di said, only her mind zoomed to Tang's messages again. *Thinking about your poor sister? No point now brooding over how she felt back then, day-to-day, living her painful life.* But Lin Feng's sister couldn't have been 'poor', her life 'painful'. Chen Di pictured a city girl of her age, wearing a fine dress, cradling a stack of books. 'You should be happy for your sister. If it makes you feel any better, all my siblings died. *Died.*'

'What?' He reached out. 'We're so similar.'

'We're *not*. Our circumstances can't even be compared, young master.'

'But out of your siblings, was there a little brother?'

Chen Di froze.

'There was, wasn't there? How did your brother die?'

She hated the direction of their conversation. 'He was... just lost.' *By me.* Even now, all she remembered from that afternoon was opening her eyes at some point, dazed, to find herself alone. She couldn't even recall when she'd shut her eyes or how she'd got home.

'Have you tried to find him?'

'He's been dead for years, in all likelihood.' As Chen Di said it, tears built all of a sudden, catching her off guard. *He's two! So small, so helpless... All the jungles, the canyon... Losing him is killing him!* She chewed on her lip, her chest tight. She needed to change the topic but could only stare down at her feet.

'But you never know, Boss Chen. Maybe a rich family found your brother.'

'That's too good to be true.'

'Well, he could've been kidnapped then sold to a rich family. Many parents want to have kids but can't. He might be across the country now, or even living overseas.'

Her family *had* wondered about this scenario, an extremely unlikely one.

'How old is your brother if he's alive?' Lin Feng asked. 'My age?'

'Nine.' Her voice cracked as she pictured a younger version of Lin Feng grinning at her. But she shouldn't, she should stop answering.

'I hear a lot of foreigners adopt Chinese kids.'

'Enough.' There was no point fooling herself. She hadn't lost her brother in the bustling streets of modern Shanghai but in Daci Village, and back in 1994. She knew the most probable scenario by far: Little Tiger was dead.

'But do you want to see your brother again? Do you dream about—'

'Enough!' Chen Di kept her voice hard, not meeting his eyes. 'I get you like talking about your smart sister, but I do not like talking about my brother. You're the one who fainted out of the blue. I'm helping *you* here.'

'But are you okay?' he asked for the third time.

'Of course.'

'Are you crying?'

Chen Di stiffened. 'Of course not.' She breathed and turned to him. 'Listen, Lin Feng, that Grandma Chu likes you an awful lot. I need you to come back the day after tomorrow, Saturday, at four-thirty. I have a task for you at her place.'

'A task?'

'A shady task involving a map. Are you brave enough?'

'Are you taking me into your gang?'

'I work alone.'

He smirked. 'So you aren't running an errand for your boss – you're the mastermind! Like one of those martial heroes, no? Here in Shanghai to hunt down an evil official like Guo Jing did Duan Tiande in *The Legend of the Condor Heroes*.'

Chen Di laughed. 'Whatever you say.'

'Then an assassin's apprentice I shall be.'

Lin Feng left after eight, and Chen Di lay on her bed. Now that she had Lü's exact address, ten days *would* be enough to kill him. Tomorrow she'd check out Phoenix Sea Court and on Saturday, Lin Feng would help her remedy the map situation at Grandma Chu's, which she could call step two-point-five. She'd leave no loose ends before moving onto steps three and four. Apprentice or not, Lin Feng was useful.

Chen Di watched her ceiling, the light bulb dangling to one side, her bedside lamp casting a shadow on the other. The air felt chilly now that she was alone again.

She couldn't help contemplating those messages. *If life is too hard, you can always find a way out* sounded like a call to suicide. *Don't feel guilty about your existence* sounded like *You should feel guilty about your existence*. Exactly what was Tang's plan?

She noticed a crumpled sheet of paper on the floor that must've fallen from Lin Feng's bag, and headed over. She expected to see that note of self-criticism but smoothed it open to find an award. Lin Feng had come first in his school's 100-metre dash, 12.74 seconds. 'Good job,' she said to her empty room, feeling like a proud big sister.

Then his mum's words came to mind. *Run, run, run! Run to your death!*

Chen Di spread her literary magazines on her bed and flipped each one open to the table of contents. Her fingertip moved down the authors' names and stopped not at *Four Three* but at *Dried Bamboo Shoot*.

She perched on the bed and read another story by Lin Feng's mum, one she vaguely remembered reading last year. The narrative was refreshing, the main character not a person but a plain white mug. The mug broke, prompting the husband and wife to visit every shop in town to find a replacement. They found one but were afraid to use it.

The new mug reminded them of the broken one.

19
Sichuan
Winter 1995

Alone, Chen Di stood on a precipice, eyes forced open. She looked up at the dark, tumbling clouds, pierced by lightning, and looked down at the threadlike riverbed. Her legs were paralysed, her feet glued to the loose gravel. At any moment she could slip down the red cliff, and she half-expected herself to, almost wanted to. Yet she didn't. Gusts of wet, chilly wind whipped across her face, howled in her ears.

'Nooooo!' she screamed.

Chen Di woke with a jolt from her afternoon nap, panting. It had been yet another nightmare. She wiped her forehead and found herself on the small bed in the school office – her home since Little Tiger's disappearance.

Your brother doesn't come home, you don't come home.

Four months had passed since the 1994 harvest, since Little Tiger's incident, and it felt like a different era. No one had noted Chen Di's exact birthday, but she was born just in time to make it to the year of the Rooster, so she must've turned thirteen, and she'd had her first period. She tried to tell herself her brother's birth had presented her with a new life, and his absence now with yet another. For four months she'd been living at school. For four months she'd been having the same nightmare, night and day. For four months she'd been sleeping with her eyes open.

She reached for the mug on the desk but accidentally knocked down Teacher Jia's paperweight. It was a little statue of a woman in greenish robes, wearing a crown and holding an ice cream. Chen Di stood it back up, then dipped her fingertips into the mug of water to wet her dry eyes. It didn't help. She rubbed them only to make them itchy. She sat up and tied a high ponytail, a radical hairstyle in the village. She didn't know how she'd lost her leaf hair clip, but she no longer needed it, her hair secured by an elastic band.

Her mind lingered on the nightmare.

She ran out of the office.

Lü Yuandou's banners and wall writing had taken over the landscape, glowing red under the late afternoon sun. Chen Di wasn't sure if their number had doubled over the years or if she simply could read them all now. Some that had confused her no longer did: *Coils are to be fitted. Procedures are to be done.* At that, she sighed with relief because Mother, like all village women who'd had two children, was no longer physically able to have babies.

Once Chen Di returned, she pulled out from under the bed a feather duster, a few cleaning cloths, a broom, and a mop. She fetched a large bucket of water and brought them all to the classroom, which she cleaned with the diligence she put into her studies.

After Little Tiger's disappearance and Grandfather forbidding her from coming home, Teacher Jia had proposed an arrangement to the school: for Chen Di to clean the grounds in exchange for lodging and a small allowance to buy cooking ingredients. If she was frugal, she could even save up a little for stationery and other essentials.

After completing her cleaning job, she sat back on her small bed and leaned on the newspaper-pasted wall. Teacher Jia visited his hometown, Shenzhen in the Guangdong Province, twice a year, always for a very long time. In the stuffed desk drawer, she'd found pieces of lined paper covered in his handwriting – sentences, paragraphs, whole articles – largely incomprehensible. Then there were magazines with serious-looking covers and few pictures, with articles filling every page, Teacher Jia's notes in the margins.

She smoothed the bedsheet. The bed frame was made of poplar wood, its shape distorted. Teacher Jia had put it there for her – he must've slept on this bed before. The thought sent electricity through her, a new sensation rising between her legs.

The door squeaked, and she sat up in a fluster.

'Hi,' Teacher Jia said. Chen Di wasn't sure if her face had already been burning or if it was the *hi*. She'd yet to hear him say *hi* to anyone else, he was usually more formal. He put down two clear plastic bags, the red lanterns inside still in their collapsed form. 'Would you help me put these up?'

Younger pupils had clamoured for lanterns this morning. 'The kids would be thrilled.'

She loved that he called them 'kids' in front of her. It meant he didn't consider her in the same way.

They went out to the front of the school, Chen Di holding the bags of lanterns, Teacher Jia carrying a bamboo ladder, his sleeves rolled. He set the ladder against one side of the building, and she expanded one of the lanterns, touching its silky surface.

'Is this real silk?' she asked.

'It is,' he said.

She held the lantern, remembering the silkworm farm in Mother's childhood. Many silkworms must've been killed to make this lantern...

Chen Di opened the rest of the lanterns and Teacher Jia lodged candles inside. He then climbed the ladder, hooked them under the eaves, and lit the candles. From below she noticed his odd-coloured socks.

'Now we can welcome the pupils this evening too,' he said.

Teacher Jia ran an evening class for older pupils who didn't attend the secondary school located in the county town. Chen Di, in her sixth and final year of primary school, already attended their sessions. The Spring Festival had just ended and today was the Lantern Festival – most pupils had said yesterday they wouldn't be able to come to class. She wished no one would. Then she'd have Teacher Jia all to herself.

He climbed down and checked the silver pocket watch he'd brought back from his recent holiday. He shielded it whenever opening it, as if his time was not to be shared, and he smiled in a new way. His eyes crinkled, his lips curling up, but it didn't look awkward. He was happy, truly happy. Something about the smile made Chen Di feel threatened.

'Where did you get the watch?' she asked.

He snapped shut the case and dropped it into his pocket, though she glimpsed a picture inside, with something red and blue that reminded her of his socks. 'It's from Hong Kong.'

'Is Hong Kong close to Shenzhen?'

He gave a surprised nod as if he'd expected her to have forgotten the city he was from. Not again. She'd mentioned his hometown multiple times, but he'd never said much about it.

She seized the opportunity and kept talking. 'Do you miss home?'

'I only just visited.'

'Does Shenzhen change a lot every time you visit? How did you feel, going back there this time? And how do you feel, coming back here?'

'It was good to go back. It's good to be back here too, of course.'

'You don't talk about yourself.'

He scratched his head, making his hair messy. 'Well, after university I wanted to see the real China.'

'And how is it?'

'We're heading towards a free flow of money and goods, but as for the sharing of ideas – well, what do you think?'

She pondered it. 'Maybe not as much. I think I'm starting to understand. I really liked it when you asked us to rewrite articles from different perspectives.'

'I'm glad.' He rolled his sleeves even higher.

'I want to hear more about you, not China.'

'Well, I wanted to work in rural China for a couple of years, so I ended up here.'

'You've been here for three years.'

'You're keeping track.'

Chen Di smiled. When they talked like this, one on one, she felt they were friends. The light grew dim. She remembered him calling her 'girl with a sweet smile' on her first day at school, and now she wanted her smile to shine for him the way the sun had. She wanted to do so much for him, and it wasn't just to show her gratefulness. Every passing day, his face occupied more of her thoughts.

'I felt the duty to stay,' Teacher Jia said. 'That's what I tell people. But in truth, I'm also afraid to face the bigger world and be changed by it.'

'You can get scared too?'

'I can. I do.'

Chen Di's heart squeezed. She was sure she understood him, and she wanted to hold his hand, to close the gap between them. 'Stay here, Teacher Jia. I'll protect you the way you protected me. And don't worry, you won't change, you are already perfect.'

'I'm not.' He looked up above the bamboo and into the orange sky. 'I'm still young.'

She laughed. 'Of course you are.'

'I'm not complimenting myself. As a teacher, I know all too well that I myself have yet to know better. I can't help but think I've yet to learn the full Chinese story.'

'You are being modest.'

The glow from the lanterns lit his face. 'I'm not.' Then he turned back as if having suddenly realised what he'd been telling her. 'I've talked too much, you must be bored. Why don't you go back in and—'

'I'm not bored.'

But he said no more. A gust of wind rustled the bamboo, then everything returned to quiet. The area darkened, the bamboo merging into one silhouette. The school building alone remained bright, lit by the lanterns.

A figure appeared. Chen Di was disappointed until she realised it was Mother, carrying two plastic bags that took a bowl shape. Mother hadn't been able to visit her on the first day of the Spring Festival, but she had on the second and the sixth.

'Mother, you came!' Chen Di saw no bruises on her face, but when she touched Mother's shoulder, it jerked.

Then Mother looked up. 'Silk lanterns!'

'Happy Lantern Festival,' they all said, like an afterthought.

In the office, they turned on the wall bulb and set down Mother's two large bowls of tangyuans – one filled with pork, the other sweet sesame – originally intended for the evening pupils on this festival. They moved the furniture so Mother and Chen Di sat on the bed on one side of the desk, across from Teacher Jia. Mother scooped the rice balls, round and sticky, still a little warm, into three small bowls. Chen Di would've gobbled had Teacher Jia not been there.

'Teacher Jia.' Mother put down her spoon. 'Yuanfen brought you to our village...'

And to my life, Chen Di couldn't help but think. She pictured the yuanfen between Teacher Jia and her as two braided red strings, and the idea made her blush.

Mother continued, 'We're all very thankful to you for teaching here. Little Leaf's mother said they invited you to dinner. Why did you decline?'

'I didn't want to impose,' he said to his bowl.

Chen Di wondered if he had better things to do, thinking of his writing in the desk drawer. When her bowl was empty, he rose to scoop more food for her. Her heart raced faster and faster as she watched his big hands, his jawline. She leaned closer with an impulse to touch his light stubble, she could barely control herself.

'You're my guest,' Mother said. 'Let me do it, Teacher Jia.'

'Big sister, this is school. You're my guest.'

'You're both my guests,' Chen Di said. 'I sleep here!' She looked from Teacher Jia to Mother. 'You're my family, my real family.'

Mother's hand trembled. She accidentally knocked her spoon off the desk.

Teacher Jia gazed at Chen Di with a tender expression. 'You've been through a lot.'

'But right now, I'm happy.'

Her eyes welled, and she started sobbing. She'd never cried like this before. She'd never felt safe enough. She wanted to keep Mother by her side, and she wanted to embrace Teacher Jia, feel all of him, give him her all.

She *was* happy. Even if, tonight, she still had to see the same nightmare.

Even if she still had to sleep with eyes open.

The electricity was cut before Teacher Jia could move the desk and chair back in place. Mother collected the bowls and waved Chen Di to follow her outside. The evening was tranquil, the weather still too cold for the insects. They looked up at the full moon.

'The Lantern Festival was my childhood favourite,' Mother said. 'On our silkworm farm, the mulberry trees always budded on the Lantern Festival.'

'Really?'

'Yes, it was like magic.'

Chen Di realised it was her favourite too, taking place at the opposite end of the year from the cotton harvests she had never enjoyed. Careful not to touch Mother's bruised shoulder, she moved forward to hug her, despite the fact that it wasn't the norm for people to hug each other, not even mothers and daughters. Then they gripped each other's hands.

Everything was fine, or as fine as it could get.

'Where *is* that silkworm farm?' Chen Di asked. 'Can we visit some day?'

'It was burned down,' Mother said without a pause, and Chen Di almost gasped. 'The whole farm, all the mulberry trees. People hated it for how well it was doing. My parents were just workers but lost their livelihood too.'

'What did you do then?'

Mother smiled. 'I came here. I wasn't much older than you now.'

'So your parents...'

'My parents gave me to your grandfather as his future daughter-in-law.'

Chen Di opened her mouth in shock. So Mother had been doing chores for Grandfather ever since her teens, before marrying Father. She scrutinised Mother's smile now and detected something dark underneath. 'Is there something else?'

'Not...really,' Mother said, seeming to change her mind. 'Just take care of yourself.'

'There *is* something, isn't there?'

'Well, after Little Ti...' Her voice quavered, her eyes watering.

'I'm alive, Mother! Isn't that enough?'

'I-It is, but you—' Tears poured down her cheeks, her unspoken words clear to Chen Di: Mother blamed her for losing her brother. As Mother raised her hand to console her, Chen Di cringed, reminded of Grandfather's calloused finger. *Losing him is killing him!*

Mother shook her head. 'After your brother's birth, they did a procedure.'

'I know.' Chen Di's voice was rigid. 'You can't have babies anymore.'

'But your grandfather has been—'

'I don't want to hear about Grandfather!' Words gushed out of her, unstoppable.

'Oh, Yaonü, your grandfather is a kinder man than he appears.'

Chen Di must've misheard her. 'Sorry?'

Mother's eyes were serious. 'If he hadn't taken your father in during the Great Famine, your father – not just his thumb – would've been eaten by the dogs.'

Father's four-fingered left hand flashed across Chen Di's mind. She couldn't imagine anyone giving up a son today. Father's being adopted might've been a reason for his mindless filial piety, but it was not an excuse! And Mother had no reason to defend Grandfather.

'Yaonü, you owe him too.'

'I do *not* owe him.' What had got into Mother? How could she forgive Grandfather for his actions? Had the loss of Little Tiger, somehow, changed her thinking?

The bamboo rustled, the air even colder. Mother turned to the night sky. 'Some villagers gave up their baby girls even before the one-child policy came along.'

Had they? For how long had Daci Pit been haunted?

Mother turned back. 'The policies made the situation worse, but—'

'Why are you telling me these things?'

'I'm trying to explain why you owe your grandfather.

Unlike many others, he was kind enough to let us keep our first child: you.'

Chen Di froze. She felt as if the sky was crashing down on her, pinning her to the ground. *She hardly deserves to live,* Grandfather had said about her many times. But if villagers had always got rid of their baby girls, even in the old days, then he'd merely stated a fact. She inhaled, and exhaled, and even breathing felt strange. If she really was supposed to be grateful to Grandfather, then she no longer understood the world she lived in.

'You were…going to tell me something else,' Chen Di managed to say.

Mother held her eyes. 'Your grandfather is asking for a grandson again.'

Chen Di's knees wobbled and she stepped back, almost tripping over a thick fallen branch. She hadn't thought Mother's words could disturb her any further. Lü Yuandou still believed Little Tiger had been hidden away in safety. They'd never be granted another birth permit, and Mother knew as well as she did what that meant.

'But you're right,' Mother said gently, perhaps seeing her face. 'Your father and I aren't able to have more children, so there's nothing to worry about.'

Mother's smile was anything but reassuring.

20
Shanghai
Spring 2002

Chen Di squeezed the ointment into her dry eyes as she recalled the famous military general Zhang Fei, who, impatient to avenge his sworn brother's death, gave two subordinates three days to prepare white flags and white armours or they'd be beheaded. Knowing it was impossible, the two men decided to assassinate their commander instead. At night, they arrived at his tent with daggers, but the commander lay with his eyes vigilantly open. His snores, however, gave him away: Zhang Fei always slept with eyes open. The subordinates stabbed him to death.

Chen Di didn't want to think a similar fate awaited her.

She sprang up and bent over to stretch her hamstrings, knees straight, forehead touching her shins. She *would* pay Tang a visit to find out his plans for Lin Feng's family. It served her no good to keep wondering, she might as well get to the bottom of it, today, before she put Grandma Chu off her trail tomorrow, with Lin Feng's help.

She lost balance during a lunge, shocking herself.

And she'd run out of century eggs.

Chen Di zipped out on her bicycle, wind ruffling her hair. She bought a flatbread and held it in one hand, taking bites while steering. At Dragon Lustre, she passed the aikido dojo, the medicine shop at the front not yet open. She also passed the cemetery's stone entrance and the temple's pagoda and red gates, but she avoided Master Mu's longtang.

She caught a whiff of urine as she biked into an alley, the character for *Demolition* painted in big white circles all over the walls on either side. It'd been a lively longtang the last time she'd come to find Tang. She noticed clothes hanging outside a second-floor window, even though half the building had been torn down. Poor family, forced to move.

Then came the crisp sound of tools hitting concrete, and she saw a figure – the back of Master Mu's overcoat. She swerved into a smaller alley and hid herself, stiffly holding her bicycle. Tang had warned her that the less she had to do with Master Mu, the better. Still, she hadn't expected herself to be so afraid she had to hide. Was it her guilty conscience? He still owed her the Voyager.

Chen Di peeked to find he was already on his way out. She kept her back glued to the wall, and when he passed, she glimpsed his furrowed brows and stern eyes.

She continued to Tang's recycling yard – a cemented area piled with bricks and steel rods. She let her bicycle fall on a pile of three-holed bricks. Beyond, the one-storey shed looked like its upper levels had been knocked off by a typhoon. Two brawny young men sauntered over, their thin coats and trousers mismatched. From behind a heap of unsorted steel came another, whose buzz cut and large nose she vaguely remembered.

'Little Sis Chen.' He approached. 'Long time no see.'

Chen Di had forgotten Big Nose's name. 'Hello, big brother. Where is Tang Bro?'

'Yo, little sis.' Tang emerged from the door frame of that shed in his biker jacket and eyepatch, walking with a bounce. 'You came fast.'

She almost asked about Master Mu but decided against it, knowing he wanted Tang to stop 'walking down a dangerous path'. 'I came to hear that story you told the kid.'

Tang looked at her with narrowed eyes, then led her into the shed, whose interior looked much more presentable than its exterior. They took their seats on opposite sides of a frosted glass desk, Tang on a rocking chair and Chen Di on a swivel one. A desktop computer sat by the window. On the wall hung a calendar embossed with the character for *Fortune*, written upside-down to signify its arrival.

'So keen you are,' he said, 'about that story.'

Big Nose brought a clay teapot and opened the lid for them before walking out. It was Dragon Well tea, the steam carrying a refreshing aroma. Tang poured for them both.

Chen Di took a sip. 'There is someone I want to... eliminate.'

Tang rocked back, looking unsurprised, even though she'd never said anything quite as direct. 'Here in Shanghai?'

'Here in Shanghai.' Chen Di would rather bring up her

mission and pretend she needed his help than reveal she knew Lin Feng. She put down her small cup, and it hit her that Lin Feng might've hidden her from his friends because he felt the same way about her. Warmth rose in her chest. What they shared was almost sacred, like a family secret – one between two siblings, bound by blood – that others wouldn't understand.

'And?' Tang's harsh voice brought her back.

'Right.' Just what was she thinking? She'd brought up her mission because she and Tang were in the same boat when it came to vengeance. 'I thought you could teach me a thing or two. I can't imagine how you get your job done without getting your hands dirty.'

Tang didn't touch his tea. He pulled out a pack of cheap Hongmei cigarettes and lit one. 'What I told the kid was just a real-life story.'

'*Your* real-life story?'

'And it's nothing special.' But he sniggered as if he had something special to share.

'Do me the honour, please, Tang Bro.'

'That I will, little sis, because I like you. You remind me of my younger self.'

'I'm honoured you think that.'

Wind sent a plastic bag flying outside. Tang kept the cigarette between his index and middle fingers and gazed out at one of his men digging into a chunk of concrete for rebar. 'I was thirteen when me and my uncle came to Shanghai.'

'I remember.' Chen Di sipped the tea.

'Most of the time people sold the cans and bottles to us, but in one housing estate, we'd often get them for free. You know those old enterprise-supplied housing schemes.' Right. *Buying* apartments was a recent phenomenon. Before, you were *supplied* with one through your workplace. Tang took a drag and flicked the ashes. 'No residents dirtied their eyes by looking at me. They walked with their chins up, and I wasn't a tall kid even though I'm a Northeasterner.' He laughed. 'I didn't hate them, not at all. I wanted to become one of them.'

Chen Di downed her tea and poured herself another cup. Like how the Shanghainese at Pizza & Apple Pie talked about emigrating to places like Australia and Canada, too many out-of-towners dreamed of becoming Shanghainese.

'And I people-watched.' Tang rocked his chair. 'Family planning is no joke in Shanghai – one child and that's all you get. On sunny days, Daddy and Mummy held a parasol over the little one. On rainy days, they lifted the little one across dirty puddles.'

'Little emperors.'

'That they were. But one family stood out – they had two kids! The son was little, about five, the daughter older but somewhat younger than me at the time.'

Lin Feng's family? Chen Di picked up her cup but didn't bring it to her lips. 'Is that the family that made you lose your eye and caused your uncle's death?'

'Correct.' Tang pointed the cigarette at her. 'But let's not get ahead of ourselves. Little sis, how do you think they got around family planning policies?'

'They're not ethnic minorities...'

'Not at all.'

'Well, they must've paid an exorbitant fine.' Even in Daci Village, a few extraordinarily sneaky mothers *had* managed to give birth in hiding. Lü couldn't 'force an abortion' on a living newborn after all, so he would fine the family the equivalent of their years of earnings. It was a nightmare, but at least the baby got to live.

'Not that easy,' Tang said. 'Otherwise all rich Shanghainese would be having babies after babies.'

'True...'

'Having a second child here means the parents lose their jobs and homes and faces.' He puffed, giving her time to think. 'I concluded the kids weren't actually siblings – the girl's parents must've left her with relatives. First, she was so thin it was like they didn't care to feed her. Second, many times the parents strolled around with only the boy.'

'You mean, they were not the girl's parents?'

'Only the boy's, that's what I thought.' Tang dropped the cigarette butt and crushed it with his shoe. 'One day in late spring, me and my uncle saw that girl with a different woman, wealthy-looking, plump in her polka-dot dress. I thought that must be her real mum. When the woman chucked a Coke can into the trimmed bushes, of course I ran for it. I picked it out and shook out the remaining drips. But who would've thought? Two drips splashed on her sleeve.'

'Oh no.'

'"Little xiangwuning bastard!" She slapped me like a mad bull and shoved me into the bushes. "I just got this from The Pacific!" she screeched to announce to the street she could afford stuff from that mall. Something thorny cut my arm, not a big wound, but deep. I was bleeding. My uncle hurried over with a cloth and tried to wipe the woman's sleeve, saying sorry over and over. "Get your xiangwuning hands off me!" she hissed and strutted away. Behind her, the girl turned back to look at us. Something in that look made me hate her mum less. "Why did you apologise?" I asked my uncle, but he only pressed his cloth on my arm to stop the bleeding. I hated, hated, hated my uncle then.' Tang's voice broke. He pulled out the pack of cigarettes and lit another. 'My uncle crouched low to get by, unlike me. I wanted to be Shanghainese.'

Chen Di swivelled on the chair, admiring how Tang cracked his way into Shanghai society. He now spoke Shanghainese more fluently than some Shanghainese kids forced to speak Mandarin at school.

'Then, guess what, the girl came back.' His hand flipped around, the cigarette now between his thumb and index finger, as if holding a fragile petal. 'She came up to us and sat down on the same filthy pavement *everyone* used. I tried to act normal and told her we'd already apologised to her mum. "She's my aunty," she said. Then she reached out to me and put a little plaster on my cut.' A dreamy look appeared on Tang's face. 'And I noticed a birthmark on her chin.'

'A birthmark?' So he *was* talking about Lin Feng's sister, the lucky girl now studying in Beijing. But was Lin Feng her brother or not?

'My uncle called her a reincarnated Bodhisattva of Compassion.' Tang returned the cigarette to between his index and middle fingers. 'That night I kept thinking about the girl. Had her parents died? I had no answer.'

Neither did Chen Di. She poured herself yet another cup of tea.

'Before that incident, my uncle had to drag me up every morning. After, I couldn't wait to get my ass back to the housing estate, just to see her again. I'd go to the boy's building, even knowing the girl only lived there sometimes, and look from one window to the next, and some aunties would always tell me to piss off. When summer came, I finally saw them again, and I was so happy I blocked the pavement. The daddy shooed me aside, but the girl flashed me a smile and pointed at her arm, like she was checking if my wound had healed. I gave her a thumbs up. Suddenly nothing else mattered.' Tang stared at his cigarette. 'I saw her three more times that summer. Every time, we smiled at each other. I'd never felt so hopeful.'

Hope rose inside Chen Di too. She sat forward and wrapped her hands around her cup, almost forgetting why she'd come. 'And then?'

'Then she disappeared. The wind was so crazy that autumn it was as if it'd blown her away. I crushed the cans so diligently it confused my uncle. I was just staying busy, you know, hoping tomorrow I might see her again.'

'Did you?'

'One day in the winter, when I was working at the opposite end of the housing estate, she showed up. She wore a white coat and one of those furry hats that are so popular up north, and guess what, she brought me a whole bag of cans for recycling. Sprite, Coke, Fanta. I was so excited to finally see her again. She told me she did live there, with her parents and little brother – so she really did belong to that family.'

'Wait. So the girl and the boy had the same parents after all?'

'Correct. They *were* siblings. So I asked, "How come you get to have a little brother?"'

That would have been Chen Di's question too. A gust of wind swept through the shed, rustling the wall calendar. She looked from that *Fortune* back to Tang as everything returned to stillness. Tang kept his head down, smoke rising from the cigarette between his fingers. His tea had gone cold. 'She told me it was because she was no good, because she was going to die soon. She asked if I'd go to her funeral.'

'What?' Chen Di blurted, too loud.

'I just stood there. I didn't know what to say. I grabbed her bag of cans and took off.' Tang dropped his carefully held cigarette, the ring of red slowly fading. 'The next day I saw her again. She told me about her family, and I told her about mine, my dead parents and my…my uncle. She was fascinated by how things worked up north, the kang bed-stove we slept on and ate on. Then I asked about her illness. She said it was her heart, she was born defective, and even in Shanghai the one-child policy has exceptions.'

'Which means…' Chen Di's voice shook.

'Which means her parents were allowed to have another child.' He didn't light a new cigarette, though his thumb and index finger stopped in mid-air, his face dreamy again. 'Then it snowed. I didn't know snow was supposed to be rare in Shanghai. She cheered and tried to catch the flakes, and I watched her pale hands and remembered her putting a plaster on my arm. "How come you're so different from other Shanghainese?" I asked. "Because I'm dying," she said. "Dying lets me see things others don't." A decade in Shanghai, that was the only day I cried. When she said she had to go, I just knew I'd never see her again.'

'But you did!' Chen Di said, surprised by her own urgent voice. Lin Feng's sister must've been cured long ago and had lived in Shanghai until she'd left for university in Beijing.

'No, she died.'

Chen Di couldn't move, sitting rigidly on the swivel chair.

'She died on the first day of the 1992 Spring Festival. It was the morning before I lost my eye, before my uncle…was beaten.' Tang's good eye narrowed. 'And, little sis, it was at this point I revealed to the kid I was talking about his own family.'

Chen Di felt she was hearing Tang through water. 'I don't get it.'

'This is the story I told the kid, remember?'

'But didn't he know it had to do with his family?'

'Not at all. He'd forgotten his sister until I enlightened him.'

'You mean, the sister died, and the brother forgot about her?' Chen Di let go of the cup, relieved – this couldn't be about Lin Feng, whose sister studied at the famous Beida. But a voice inside told her it was. His friends thought he'd never had a sister, while Chen Di thought his sister lived in Beijing. Neither was the truth.

'That's the gist of it. But the kid's remembering now, bit by bit.'

Chen Di recalled Lin Feng's fainting episode at her place, how he'd woken, telling her about visiting an animal market with his family, which he'd 'just remembered'.

'Except,' Tang continued, 'he doesn't like what he remembered, not one bit, especially not the fact that his sister died.' Tang pushed aside his untouched cup of tea and sniggered. 'The kid just needs a little push, and I'll get what I want.'

'Which is?'

'I told you I'd make sure the family went down so my eyeball and my uncle could rest in peace.' He rocked his chair, back and forth. 'The master plan, little sis, involves exploiting people's guilt. How I get my job done without getting my hands dirty? By guilting a kid who's already depressed – and, should I say, suicidal. After all, his sister's defect gave him the right to be born. He never deserved to live.'

21
Shanghai
Spring 2002

Chen Di refused Tang's invitation to spar and walked her bicycle back towards Xu Junction. Plane branches shook in the wind like the arms of an inept conductor. Gravity seemed to have doubled its strength, her legs heavy as if dragging two bags of rice. Tang couldn't have made it all up, however unlikely it sounded for a can-collector boy to connect with a Shanghainese girl.

She stopped at a roadside eatery for Yangzhou fried rice and chicken-and-duck-blood soup, unsure if Tang had answered or raised more questions. Even if Lin Feng had lost his sister in his early childhood, their parents would've talked about her. Surely he couldn't have blocked out the truth for so long? It made little sense that he was only now, thanks to Tang's 'enlightening', starting to recall his sister.

Chen Di raised the bowl to gulp the soup. She finished the rice without having even asked for chilli bean paste. And she continued on her way, passing more plane trees and a red-shingled European-style house. One thing was for sure: Tang wanted to harm Lin Feng. Or rather, his master plan involved Lin Feng harming himself.

If life is too hard, you can always find a way out, little bro.
Just checking in. Thinking about your poor sister?

Good, little bro. Very good. No point now brooding over how she felt back then, day-to-day, living her painful life.

Don't feel guilty about your existence.

Chen Di walked against the wind, listening to the traffic noises, breathing in the exhaust. A plane twig almost poked into her eye and she blocked it, remembering the way Tang had broken it off. Lin Feng had said he didn't deserve to live, unbelievably, but now she understood: he felt guilty about his sister.

The sound of a gunshot stopped her. Chen Di found herself behind the wrought-iron fences surrounding Wende Private Secondary School, brought here by her subconscious. She leaned her bicycle on the fence and looked inside.

Between two yulan magnolias – Shanghai's city flower – she saw a crimson running track, a class above other schools' cinder tracks. Beyond were multi-storey school buildings hung with banners urging students to study. A pole stood on one end of the sports field, the national flag flying high. On the far side, eight students were running, watched by a dozen others and a teacher. The gunshot had just been a starter pistol.

On the sixth lane was none other than Lin Feng. Staying low, legs extending, he sprinted ahead in a singlet and track pants and his old black sneakers.

THE CRY OF THE SILKWORM

'Go, Feng Bro!' a few boys shouted behind the runners.

'Lin Feng, you're the best!' shrieked a girl flipping on the nearby parallel bars.

He *was* the fastest. Chen Di made sure she wouldn't be noticed behind the trees and the fence, and observed him. The one-and-a-half-child policy applied to select rural areas. In this day and age, to a kid in Shanghai, having a sibling was only a concept, an outlandish one. Lin Feng wouldn't have been born if it wasn't for his sister's misfortune, and he thought he didn't deserve to live... His sister did.

Only one child per family did.

And what had his sister felt back then? Chen Di scanned all the kids, running with all their might. None of Lin Feng's sister's friends would've had siblings. She must've felt weird among all the only children, constantly reminded of her defect, her illness, her looming death, which had made her parents have a second child.

She'd been replaced.

Chen Di gripped the fence, leaning so close she smelled paint. Lin Feng's mum had written about replacement parents, about a replacement mug... The stories must've been her emotional outlet, her way to cope with her reality.

The runners passed Chen Di's end of the track, but Lin Feng's feet slowed as he took his time, looking down at something in his path. When he accelerated again, it was too late. Three others had passed him, and it was only a 400-metre dash. Boys and girls surrounded him nonetheless, and he threw a kick at the boy who'd come first and pointed a finger gun to his nose.

The bell rang. It was probably the end of their lunchtime break, but Lin Feng waved away those who asked him to come along and downed two bottles of water. Alone, he headed back along the sixth lane to the spot where he'd slowed. He crouched and picked up something and walked in Chen Di's direction.

She ducked, only to realise he hadn't spotted her. He squatted under one of the yulan magnolias before putting down the item – a dead sparrow – and digging at the soil with his hands. So he'd slowed down seeing a dead sparrow on the track. Chen Di was reminded of Teacher Jia talking about the time Mao had ordered all sparrows in the country to be killed.

Lin Feng laid the sparrow in the hole and covered it with soil, piling it into a small mound. Then he looked around and flattened the soil so the area seemed untouched.

He turned to leave.

'Lin Feng,' Chen Di called before she could stop herself.

He saw her, his eyes alert. Then he cut between the yulan magnolias and strode over. 'Boss Chen, you honour me with your gracious presence. Here to talk business?'

'No, I mean, yes. But don't you have a class?'

He huffed. 'Just Ideology and Politics.'

The only class Chen Di would rather all kids skipped, no doubt filled with the Party's indoctrinations. 'Well, I came to remind you of your task tomorrow.'

'The one involving a map? Come on, I'm not going to forget it.'

'Also...' She looked down, not knowing how to bring up his sister, and ended up studying his battered black sneakers. The left sole was really coming off from the front. 'Why don't you get yourself new running shoes?'

'My feet stopped growing.'

'That doesn't mean you wear the same pair forever.'

He kicked at the soil. 'I don't know, these're like a part of my body now.'

'But you run so much.'

'Exactly! I feel like as long as I wear these, I'll always be able to run. Fast.'

Chen Di caught herself smiling. 'Sorry that I made fun of you when you mentioned your sister. I'd love to hear more about her, even now.'

Lin Feng stopped, then reached across the fence and felt her forehead. 'Do you have a fever?' he asked, deadpan, then laughed.

'No!' She slapped away his hand before realising his touch wasn't as cold as before. Well, he'd been running. 'I'm actually curious. I've never met anyone else who also had a birthmark on her face.'

'Really?'

'Really.'

He turned around, crossed his arms, and leaned on the inside of the fence. 'I'm going to visit her pretty soon.'

'In Beijing?'

'Yep, it'd be cool to have her show me around the Great Wall.'

Chen Di bit her lip. This time, she didn't fight the urge of wanting to protect him. 'Why don't you tell me about you and your sister's past?'

'Our past?'

'What did you guys do together when she was still...' *Alive?* '...in Shanghai?' Chen Di glanced at the spot on the soil. 'Did you take care of animals together?'

Still leaning on the fence with his back to Chen Di, Lin Feng tucked his muddy hands in his pockets and looked up at the grey sky. 'We had lots of pets. I can't believe that for years...I didn't remember that.'

As Tang had said. 'But you remember now?'

'There were silkworms, as I told you. Also, like, heating a cardboard box to keep chicks through winters, making a plywood birdhouse to hatch parakeets, separating adult guppies from newborns to prevent filial cannibalism. She taught me all that.'

Chen Di nodded.

'The first time we took care of animals together...' Lin Feng continued without her asking. 'The first time *I remember*, I was only maybe four. But the way that market vendor smothered the pigeon to death stayed with me, how it flapped and twitched.'

The aspiring-gangster kid sounded like someone else as he spoke, his tone gentle but eager. Chen Di thought of a pressure cooker finally being allowed to vent.

'It was a cold afternoon,' he said. 'Mum bought a pigeon to cook, and I just sobbed and sobbed until my sister pulled me to her room and showed me a cardboard box under her bed. Inside, a lamp was shining on two small white eggs on a pink towel. She told me we could incubate the eggs and I could be her little apprentice. The box felt like a wonderland to me then, like the Flowers and Fruit Mountain in *Journey to the West*. The lamp was the sun, the towel was a floor of peaches, and the eggs were magical stones that gave birth.'

It surprised Chen Di that he used words like 'wonderland' and 'magical', as if he'd forgotten to feel embarrassed. Lin Feng continued talking, unaware he was rubbing his chin with his muddy fingers. He told her how he'd crawled into his sister's bed that night, knowing there was a pair of lives in the box underneath, and how he'd reached over to trace his sister's birthmark – shaped like a pigeon egg. For days, they had watched the lamp warm their wonderland.

The temperature rose. Sparrows chattered. Though Lin Feng kept his back to Chen Di as he spoke, his feelings were clear from his tone.

He really loved his sister.

'Did the eggs hatch?' Chen Di loosened her grip on the fence.

Lin Feng turned back to her and grinned in a new way, white teeth showing, his lips – and eyes – softening. A happy child. The grin was so natural she could almost imagine she lived a normal life and was just hanging out with someone she cared about.

For a long while they stood in the warm afternoon, facing each other.

A muddy patch showed under his chin. 'What's this habit of yours anyhow?' She raised her own fingers to rub her chin.

'Nothing.' He flushed. 'Just a habit.'

'Strange habit.'

'Stop teasing me, Boss Chen.'

She laughed and looked to the sky. 'I hope you'll get to go to Beijing soon.'

Chen Di headed home that day thinking about Tang's story, about the memory Lin Feng had divulged. For the first day in years, killing Lü Yuandou hadn't crossed her mind.

22
Sichuan
Harvest 1997

Wooden and mud-brick houses transformed into burnt-brick ones. Dirt roads became concrete ones, and mud paths paved ones. Mountains opened, three-wheeled trucks coming and going. Increasingly, cotton became a crop of the Xinjiang Uyghur Autonomous Region up north, and Chen Di's family were the only cotton farmers left in Daci Village. Production and transportation costs soared, but Grandfather wouldn't hear any suggestions.

Villagers proposed digging a tunnel to better connect the village to the outside as many left to work in the provincial capital, Chengdu, and many more left the province altogether for cities like Shenzhen, Guangzhou, Shanghai, and Beijing.

And Chen Di turned fifteen. A young woman.

This afternoon she sat on a sturdy new chair in the school office, marking second-year homework – a task she proudly helped Teacher Jia with besides her assigned work of cleaning the grounds. She didn't put down her red pen when the loudspeakers sounded in the distance, announcing a funeral.

She couldn't remember the last time she'd heard public shaming of villagers disrupting family planning. Rather, various families were praised for obeying the policy, their business and children's academic achievements showcased. Banners were removed, wall writing no longer repainted – people obeyed them without being reminded.

Talks of an orphanage in the county town replaced stories of Daci Pit's ghost woman, and rumours about Lü Yuandou carried a new, positive air.

'They should kowtow to Chief Lü with gratitude for not breaking their legs.'

'I'm not sorry Red Flower bled to death! She asked for it, breaking the rules again and again, making our whole collective lose face. Chief Lü only did what he had to.'

'Chief Lü's ways aren't all that humane, but he has his reasons.'

Recently, a quack in the county town was condemned for taking bribes to 'remove permanent coils' and 'reverse procedures'. Chen Di remembered Grandpa Li telling Grandfather years ago about someone's medicine that 'guaranteed boy'. Unlike before, such gossip was no longer for sharing information on various quacks' services. Instead, people applauded Lü Yuandou's 'speedy arrest' of such uncooperative citizens.

Villagers reported each other.

'Are they all brainwashed?' Chen Di had asked Teacher Jia this morning, receiving a stack of to-be-marked homework, thinking he'd agree, or better, she'd said the exact words he would've said. But he'd only touched his chin, clean-shaven today, and studied her as if she were some sort of specimen. A gust of wind had made him unroll his sleeves.

Now Chen Di put down her red pen and looked up from a pupil's terrible handwriting, recalling Teacher Jia's serious expression earlier. What had he been thinking? She remembered once, a few years ago, he'd told her he had yet to learn the full Chinese story.

The door squeaked.

'Hi.' Teacher Jia came in, his shaggy hair hiding his face.

'Hi,' Chen Di said before noticing a tinge of sadness in his eyes. She rose, wondering what had happened, how she could ask.

Then she jumped, seeing someone else enter: Father, hair grey, face sallow. He stopped beside Teacher Jia, and the way the two men stood side by side in this office jarred her so much she almost fell back into the chair. Father looked directly at her, and she realised all over again how much her eyes resembled his. The light-brown irises, the single-fold eyelids. People with single-fold eyelids generally had small eyes, but not the two of them.

'Chen Di,' he said, urgent yet distant. She hadn't heard his voice in so long it felt unreal.

Father, she mouthed, more like a question.

'I've missed you, Chen Di.'

He'd missed her? He had to be putting on a show in front of Teacher Jia. With what agenda? But as her gaze moved between the two men, it struck her that in all these years,

Father and Teacher Jia could've spoken at times, behind her back.

'Chen Di.' Teacher Jia took a step towards her.

'Yes, Teacher Jia?'

'Your grandfather is calling you home.'

Her heart jumped. She didn't care what Grandfather wanted, but it stung her hearing these words from Teacher Jia. Did he want her to move away from the school? She glanced at Father again, who stood behind pathetically. It had to be Father's idea. 'I'm not surprised,' she said carefully, facing Teacher Jia. 'It's harvest time.'

But Father stepped up too. 'Would you come back and live with us again?' His voice was unusually eager, no tremor in his hands.

'No.' She turned to him. 'I would not.'

'Your grandfather—'

'Grandfather, what?' *He sent his pawn to deliver a message.* Chen Di had learned to be assertive over the years, but she glimpsed Teacher Jia and, to save Father's face, refrained from saying it aloud. 'I don't plan to obey more orders from my abuser.' Except she stiffened as soon as her words left her mouth. *He was kind enough to let us keep our first child: you.*

'Chen Di,' Father said, 'for all that you did…'

She flinched and for a while didn't even know where to place her hands. She held onto the chair back.

'We don't blame you anymore,' he said. 'Come home.'

'I am not going back to my— to Grandfather.'

Outside the window, the sun dipped behind the bamboo.

Father shifted his body, the dwindling daylight reflecting in the eyes she'd inherited, and she saw the same sorrow she'd known since childhood. 'I still have hope for this family.'

She said nothing.

'If you come back, I will make sure this time—'

'I will not come back.'

'But—'

'And you do not miss me, Father. You miss my help.'

'It's up to you, Chen Di.' Teacher Jia's voice cut through, and her limbs loosened. He wasn't here to help Father with his agenda but to protect her from being pushed into doing what she didn't want to do.

'It is.' She nodded. 'And I'm used to living at school.' *Used to being around you, Teacher Jia. Even if no one in the world wants me, as long as I have you...*

Father looked around the office, and she felt as if he was slipping behind her room divider to see her naked. The walls were no longer pasted with newspapers but painted, decorated with a red, upside-down character for *Fortune*. Her single bed hadn't changed, a quilt folded at one end. The desk was the same old one too, except Teacher Jia had removed his paperweight at some point, the one she now knew was a model of America's Statue of Liberty.

Father's gaze stopped at the homework she'd been grading, and she caught a glimpse of pride on his face. Before she could deny it to herself, she remembered he'd been the one asking Teacher Jia to bet her schooling on a game of mahjong with Grandfather.

Father left without another word, hanging his head.

Chen Di let go of the chair back. Even if she needed time to process Father's reappearance in her life, the balance of the world seemed to have been restored. But her heartbeat slowed for only a few seconds. She became more aware than ever of the space shared between Teacher Jia and her, the two of them alone.

'Thank you.' She smiled at him.

He smiled back in the same awkward way she loved, then held out a puffy bundle. 'This is for you, Chen Di.'

'For me?' She received it with both hands and unfolded it to discover a padded jacket. Round collar, deep pockets, a zip to replace old-fashioned buttons, plus a hood. No jackets she'd seen had hoods attached. Besides, it was in the colour of pines, her favourite.

'I didn't have many choices,' he said.

'I love it.' The thoughtfulness of the gesture warmed Chen Di even before she put on the jacket. It was a little large, which was perfect since she was still growing. This way she could wear it always.

'Do you want to take a walk?'

She said yes, more dread than anticipation inside her. It had to do with Grandfather wanting her back. Teacher Jia had never asked her to go for a walk before, and she sensed that after this walk, things wouldn't be the same again.

Chen Di fixed her ponytail and kept the jacket on as they went out, the ground partly lit by the last few sun rays peeking through the bamboo. The sky was clear, its emptiness daunting. Teacher Jia chose a hardly visible trail and trod alongside high grasses, and she followed. She watched the wrinkle on his checked sweater, appearing, disappearing.

'Chen Di.'

Her heart tightened. She wasn't sure if it was just the serious way he'd said her name.

'You're already fifteen,' he said. 'Have you thought about getting out of here?'

'Some day,' she said. So this wasn't about Father's visit.

They came out of the high grasses to find a wider path, able to walk side by side now, ripe fields beside them. Paddy, corn, rapeseed, all in shades of gold. His arm brushed against hers at times, and each touch lit a small fire inside her.

Teacher Jia seemed to want to say more but looked ahead. Would he tell her a way to get out? Would university be an option for her? The sky dimmed. Chen Di listened to the loose rocks clatter under their feet, the dry leaves breaking into pieces. She stopped walking, shivers running down her spine. Teacher Jia stopped too and looked back.

'You're leaving,' she said.

His silence was enough of an answer. The surroundings chilled. She stepped forward and grabbed his wrist, wanting so badly to hold onto it, but she let go, knowing the inappropriateness. Her arm trembled. A stone formed in her chest and expanded, heavy. So he *had* teamed up with Father and did want her to move away from school – for a reason much worse than Grandfather wanting her back.

Teacher Jia didn't continue walking until she did. Five minutes. Ten. Chen Di cried soundlessly. She didn't want him to see but noticed him noticing. She'd believed in their yuanfen. How could it end like this?

They forged ahead, downhill.

'So you're going back to Shenzhen.' She did all she could to keep her voice even.

'I'm not, and I owe you some truth.' He scratched his head. 'Before the British handed over Hong Kong several months ago, my parents had feared Chinese policies might affect them negatively, so they'd moved, to Canada.'

'You mean…'

'I'm from Hong Kong.'

Suddenly everything made sense, all the times he'd avoided talking about Shenzhen… 'But why did you have to lie?' And what had his parents feared, even if they were from Hong Kong? The handover of the special administrative region from Britain back to China had been repeated on the loudspeakers. It was something worth celebrating. Clearly, every Hongkonger had longed for 'Motherland's embrace'.

'I just didn't want to complicate things. I first thought some Mainlanders would think of us Hongkongers as capitalists who sided with Britain, but it turns out everyone here treats Hongkongers as fellow Chinese comrades.'

'Because you are. So you're going back to Hong Kong?'

'No, I got a job offer at a publisher in Shanghai. Teaching here – meeting you – has been rewarding, but with this new job I can really make something of myself.' He looked in the direction they'd come from. 'Also, my wife is back in Shanghai now, so things lined up.'

For a long second Chen Di was puzzled, as if he'd been speaking a foreign tongue. Then her heart stopped. The stone in her chest vanished, replaced by a black hole.

'You never mentioned your wife,' she said, brusque.

'She's Shanghainese. We met during our bachelor's in Boston.'

'*Boston...*' He had studied overseas?

'Yes, it's an American city. After graduation, I wanted to help rural China, while my wife – fiancé at the time – wanted to study more in America. So we only spent summers and winters together. My six years here, she earned her PhD. But she is back now and we're going to settle, in Shanghai.'

The summary felt like too much detail. *But I love you!* a voice inside Chen Di exploded, but she only stood there, motionless. The evening wind blew through her, reeking of burning crop stubble even though it was still early in the season.

Teacher Jia pulled out his pocket watch the careful way he did.

'Show me that,' she said.

He passed it to her, though the chain was still attached to his button. She flipped open the metal cover to see a young woman in a huge red-and-blue striped headband, white little stars filling the blue. Chen Di opened her mouth. She looked down, but Teacher Jia's trousers and shoes covered the entirety of his socks. Her eyes returned to the photo. The young woman had large, confident eyes, her face without blemish. Full of light. No matter how sweet Chen Di's smile was, she could never beat this person.

'Do you love her?' she asked.

'I do,' Teacher Jia said.

'How much? How much do you love her? How much?'

He looked unsure of her intention. 'I wouldn't be me without her.'

And I wouldn't be me without you, Teacher Jia!

'Are you…okay?' he asked, when she didn't respond. 'I'm so sorry to leave like this, but I hope you can keep learning. Maybe some day you will see an opportunity to get out of this village and further your edu—' He sighed. 'I know it's easier said than done. How I wish you were born in a good family in the city… You are the best student I've had.'

She was his best student. Nothing more.

On their way back, Chen Di was surprised to find herself not crying. She observed him and caught herself doing so. Teacher Jia walked ahead, passing the golden fields that looked grey in the dusk, his posture upright, his gait faster. The rising moon lit the side of his face she couldn't see, and not once did he look back towards her.

If only she had evidence he'd been taunting her, seducing her. But she knew it wasn't true. The kindness he'd shown her, he would've shown it to any pupils in her circumstances. She hadn't been the only one he'd invited into the classroom, she hadn't been the only one riding his motorcycle on rainy days, and she hadn't been the only one attending his evening class. Chen Di closed her eyes and saw two braided red strings untangle as they burnt into ashes.

It made her hate him – him and his beautiful wife – hate herself, hate the village, the entire world. How silly she'd been! She wanted to shred the stupid jacket, the way his words had shredded her heart. With every step, a piece of her fell to the cold ground.

Back in the school office, Teacher Jia said she could have all his books and asked her to keep reading with older pupils. Chen Di nodded, and nodded, and nodded. They did not sit.

'Moving is probably good for my personal development.' He picked up his briefcase and scrutinised the ceiling. 'I tell you guys nothing is black and white, but have I myself really…' He seemed to be debating something with himself, some big idea she couldn't care less about, not right now. 'I've been questioning a few things, like how so many of us Hongkongers wrote off our ancestral ways and adopted those of our British colonisers. Is it really right to judge the Party with Western values?'

Chen Di stopped listening.

'Kiss me,' she said, cutting him off.

A look of alarm appeared on his face. He turned to the wall – that *Fortune* glued on it – and back at her. He blushed until an understanding came to his eyes, then they grew sorry.

'I said kiss me.' She didn't want his pity.

He leaned down and, gently, kissed her cheek. Her birthmark.

'Goodbye, Chen Di.'

23
Shanghai
Spring 2002

'Nooooo!' Chen Di woke and found herself screaming in her small unit in the longtang.

The red cliffs, the threadlike riverbed, her expecting to slip on the gravel but not moving, the wind whipping her face like a ghost's slaps, howling in her ears like a ghost's cries. It was the same nightmare she'd been having since the 1994 harvest. But this time, it had included a rustle in the bushes, someone approaching from behind.

'So you came to kill me?' he'd said in his high voice, calm but chilling.

In the dream, Chen Di had pinned down Lü Yuandou only to hear him chuckle. She'd yelled at him, 'What's so funny?' without getting an answer.

What's so funny? What's so funny?

Her own voice echoed in her head and she tugged her bedsheet, her body as tight as her mind. Hands unsteady, Chen Di picked up her tube of ointment and unscrewed the lid. She pulled down her left eyelid and squeezed, too much.

She wiped it only to squeeze too much again into her right eye. Though the dream had recurred for years, she'd remained the only person in the dreary landscape. But now... What did it mean, for Lü to be there too?

A dim line of light appeared under her door, and a draught made her shiver. She clutched her head to forget the nightmare and jumped up for her workout. She doubled her number of push-ups and sit-ups and added thirty seconds to each plank, her heart rate high, her muscles burning. Sweat dripped from her nose.

Yesterday she'd visited Tang's recycling yard and Lin Feng's school. How *could* she? What had she been working for all this time, eating bitterness in Shanghai? Not to protect Lin Feng, but to kill Lü Yuandou! If Tang were in her shoes, he would've long freed himself from any unnecessary emotions. He would've been done by now, would've fled Shanghai.

Chen Di had one week left before losing her unit.

She'd put away her jacket from Teacher Jia, but today was cold again. It vexed her she had to pull it back out. She threw it on and zipped out on her bicycle.

After hours of queuing at the bank, she withdrew all her savings. Then she stopped at a stationery shop to buy another of the red markers she'd used to draw and cross out circles on that map. With Lin Feng's help this evening at Grandma Chu's, step two-point-five would be easy. And tomorrow she'd head to Phoenix Sea Court even if the sky collapsed.

Chen Di returned to her longtang. While opening her padlock, she heard two women whisper around the corner.

'Poor old thing,' one of them said. 'When will she ever get to see her two grandsons?'

'Only her nephew remembers she's alive,' said the other. 'If only her two daughters bothered to visit her, then she wouldn't have the time to go around digging out problems.'

'And she wouldn't behave like such a petty—'

'Quiet! Speak of Cao Cao.'

Chen Di heard someone's flats slapping against the ground. She quickly pushed in her bicycle and shut her door, realising only then the women had been talking about Grandma Chu. She'd thought Grandma Chu had no grandchildren.

Lin Feng would come soon. She lay on her bed, opened one of her magazines and reread a non-fiction piece by Four Three. That his articles weren't censored made her even sadder than if they were: the Party knew most Chinese readers wouldn't pick up on the sarcasm and would take at face value his words with sentences like, *It's the man who's gone insane, not the society in which he lives.*

Sharp knocks on her iron door. As she got up and moved over in quick steps, delight rose inside. She needed Lin Feng to deal with the old fox, but a part of her simply wanted to see him for the sake of seeing him. He had become…like a real brother to her.

Lin Feng appeared in a grey quarter-zip sweater, a backpack on his shoulder. He looked even taller. 'Boss Chen!' he said as if bumping into an old friend.

She laughed. 'Hi.' She led him in, a gust of wind swinging her bulb.

He put down his backpack. 'Let's talk business.'

'Right...' It jarred her that she had to orient herself as if she were the guest.

'What map do we have to deal with?'

She perched on the bed, shut the magazine she'd been reading, and signalled him to sit. 'Bed or chair, or your favourite floor.'

Lin Feng sat on the bed too, moved a bit closer to her, then a bit further, which made her laugh again. She poured him a mug of water, hot water today, and held it out. But his eyes fixated on her magazine. She wondered if he was thinking of his mum's writing when he said, 'So you like Four Three?'

'How...' It felt as if Lin Feng had walked in while she touched herself.

'You dog-eared all his writing.'

Of course. 'I do like Four Three, he's brilliant.' Perhaps she'd always wanted to say these words aloud. Memories of Teacher Jia flooded over her again. Her mind, her body. *I got a job offer at a publisher in Shanghai.*

'You're smiling,' Lin Feng said, his voice so earnest it was out of character.

Chen Di felt exposed again. 'Excuse me?'

'I'm saying you look happy, which isn't how you usually look.'

'I'm not *happy*.'

He glanced at the magazine again, which forced her to push it away. He looked back at her. 'Do you know Four Three, like, in real life?'

Was Four Three Teacher Jia? She didn't know the answer herself.

Lin Feng continued, 'My mum works with him.'

'What?'

'My mum writes with him, that's what she says.'

Chen Di's heart raced, the sensation in her chest familiar from years ago. She pictured Lin Feng's mum not holding up her satchel but sitting with Teacher Jia, writing.

Suddenly she was afraid to find out about Four Three, terrified her dreamscape would shatter. Perhaps Four Three was just some man, or woman, whose writing she enjoyed.

But that short story's protagonist came to mind again: the smart and brave Sichuanese village girl with a star-shaped birthmark on her face, abandoned by her family, living at school. The only part different from Chen Di's life was that jarring ending: the girl grew up, got out of her village, and realised everything her teacher had taught her was wrong.

'You're still smiling,' Lin Feng said.

'I'm not.' Enough. She hadn't asked him to come and talk about Four Three. She hadn't journeyed to Shanghai to find Teacher Jia and resume a romance that never was.

'Anyhow,' she said, 'here's our task.'

Down the longtang, up two sets of outdoor stairs, Chen Di reached through the barred iron gate to knock on Grandma Chu's door. Beside her, Lin Feng smirked at the door the way a cigar-smoking gangster would at a frightened family.

'Who?' Grandma Chu's voice sounded from inside.

'Me, Chen Di.'

The door opened to show Grandma Chu's hard face. But then her eyes fell on Lin Feng and her lips curled up in such an unguarded way Chen Di wondered if this was how she'd smile at her own grandsons.

'Ayo,' the old woman said to him, 'you're here.'

'Hello, grandma,' he said. 'My parents are busy, so I'm here with my aunty again.'

Chen Di smiled inside at Lin Feng calling her aunty, while Grandma Chu glanced at her sideways as if to tell her she wasn't good enough to be the beautiful boy's aunt.

'What's your name?' Grandma Chu asked Lin Feng.

'You can call me Fengfeng.'

'Come in, Fengfeng. Sit, sit, sit!'

Lin Feng changed into slippers and placed his black sneakers neatly on a shoe rack, prompting a sudden wave of uneasiness in Chen Di. *As long as I wear these, I'll always be able to run,* he'd told her. It was as if by taking them off, he wouldn't be running again.

But just what was she thinking?

Grandma Chu nodded approvingly at Lin Feng and turned to mute Shanghai opera. She never did when Chen Di came alone. A good sign.

Chen Di sat on the couch. 'I'm not here to argue about rent.'

'Since there's nothing to argue.' Grandma Chu looked to Lin Feng. 'Have you eaten?'

He sat beside Chen Di. 'No, grandma.'

'Perfect. Let me feed you.'

'But we came after your dinner precisely because we didn't want to impose.'

'What a well-mannered boy you are. Go sit over there.' She pointed at the rectangular dining table before the balcony. 'The more you refuse, the more I want to feed you.' She let out a string of laughter and headed out of the unit, to the communal kitchen next door.

Chen Di exchanged a nod with Lin Feng. He followed Grandma Chu out while she went straight to the side room, marker in hand. Threads of moonlight filled the room, the leather smell strong even though nothing seemed made of leather. And there it was, the map. She'd expected Grandma Chu to have tucked it into a drawer at least, but it was neatly folded on the old wooden desk, beside a brown handbag. The old fox *was* ready to go on that 'tour' tomorrow.

She opened the map while listening to the talking outside. Lin Feng must've left both the unit door and the communal kitchen door open. Smart move to help her keep track. She heard bowls being put down on the worktop, Lin Feng asking, 'What is this?'

'Bullfrog legs,' Grandma Chu said.

'You must be an amazing cook.' Flattery always worked.

Another string of laughter. 'It's just a common dish. Don't you people from Sichuan prefer spicy food? Your aunty puts chilli bean paste in everything.'

'I prefer Shanghainese food,' Lin Feng said promptly. 'The

sweeter the dishes, the better. Shanghai is the best, it's the Pearl of the Orient! I even learned Shanghainese.'

'Ayo, say something.'

He switched from Mandarin to Shanghainese, in praise of Grandma Chu's cooking.

'You sound Shanghainese, Fengfeng!'

Chen Di was worried they'd be found out, but Grandma Chu continued, overjoyed, 'You could be a real Shanghainese, unlike your aunty.'

'Unlike my aunty?'

Grandma Chu clicked her tongue. 'Don't tell her, but my nephew and I helped your aunty more than she herself could imagine.'

Chen Di resisted the impulse to trash the old fox's room. Map spread out on the desk, she pulled off the marker's lid, having decided to add just enough circles so no one could figure out a pattern. She'd focus on outer districts like Songjiang, Qingpu, and Jiading. It'd take a while for Grandma Chu to get there. As to central districts like Huangpu, Jing'an, and Xuhui, she'd add only two or three at the most touristy spots.

Grandma Chu was laughing again. 'You'd better eat and get strong.'

Lin Feng mumbled something.

'What is it?'

'I usually have food very hot, but it's okay, let's bring the dishes over.'

'We can't do that! We'll heat it up to as hot as you like.'

Chen Di heard Lin Feng's footsteps – he must've walked

out as if he meant what he'd said. What a good actor. She continued to add circles and cross them out.

'Stop right there, Fengfeng!' Grandma Chu said, as expected.

The microwave door opened and closed, and just as it dinged, Chen Di drew the last circle she thought necessary. But she was about to fold up the map when she noticed the new circles took on a darker shade of red compared with the old ones. The microwave dinged again. She needed to trace over all the old circles with her new pen.

'I'll bring the dishes over,' Grandma Chu said.

'Let me bring the first two,' Lin Feng said.

The new and old markers had the same thickness, she couldn't rush the tracing. She tried her best to steady her hand and heard Lin Feng return and set the dishes on the dining table. When he barged into the room, she still had a dozen old circles to trace over.

'Quick, Boss Chen,' he whispered loudly.

'Why are you here?' She didn't look up. 'Stop Grandma Chu!'

'She's coming in ten—'

'Where did you two go?' Grandma Chu's voice sounded in the living room.

Chen Di snapped her head up to see Lin Feng picking up a penholder. He drew out a retractable knife and slashed it against the back of his hand. Ow. Blood oozed. He dashed to the living room. 'Grandma, I cut my hand! My aunty's looking for bandages.'

Chen Di continued with her task.

'This is bad!' Grandma Chu shrieked. 'So much blood!'

Last two. Last one. Done! Chen Di folded up the map, following the previous folds. She placed it back beside the handbag one second before Grandma Chu flicked on the lights. 'How do you expect to find bandages in the dark?'

'True,' Chen Di said as calmly as possible. 'Where do you keep them?'

They returned to the living room, the table heaving with bullfrog legs, tomato and egg, pea greens with shiitake, eels, rice, plus a medical box. Chen Di found a cotton pad and pressed it to the back of Lin Feng's hand, an ache inside her chest. She'd rather she herself had got cut and almost regretted asking him to do this for her.

Grandma Chu clamped her lips together as if she'd eaten something rotten. Steam from the microwaved dishes clouded her bifocals, but still Chen Di noticed tears in the old woman's eyes. It was as if her own grandsons had got hurt. And to think she had two ungrateful daughters who never let her meet their boys...

Chen Di reminded herself the old fox was her enemy.

'Come.' She grabbed Lin Feng's wrist and pulled him out of the room, leaving Grandma Chu behind. She rinsed his wound at the tap in the communal kitchen. 'Have you had a tetanus shot?'

'Yep, I'm all good.'

'You're not *all good*. Is it hurting a lot?'

He was silent, and Chen Di swallowed the urge to blame him for his reckless act. She rolled up his sleeve to avoid wetting it and saw a bruise on his forearm, blue with purple blotches. From his mum? School fights? Or...had he done it to himself?

'It's nothing,' he said, 'compared with the scars on your back.'

Suddenly she wanted to cry.

The kitchen was quiet apart from a dripping sound. Chen Di applied ointment to his wound, more carefully than when she dealt with her dry eyes, and wrapped gauze around his hand. She was reminded of what Tang had said about Lin Feng's sister bandaging his arm.

Chen Di finished dressing his wound but didn't let go of his hand. She felt he didn't want her to either. 'We have to go back,' she said.

'Right,' he said, rubbing his chin again with his spare hand.

Neither of them moved. Then she did.

'Eat now, Fengfeng,' Grandma Chu said when they returned. 'Young Chen, I assume you didn't come just to get Fengfeng's hand cut.'

'I came to pay this month's rent.' Chen Di chopsticked a bullfrog leg. 'And of course, I'll pay for the next month within a week, before this month ends. Thank you for always letting me stay before paying, how very kind of you.'

The evening sky was cloudless, the air refreshing. Chen Di and Lin Feng walked side by side down the stairs, up the alley. She found herself staring at his bandaged hand, then saw him grinning at the ground. She should be happy too – she could now safely carry out the rest of her mission. But she wasn't all that happy. She couldn't recall when anyone else had hurt themselves for her sake. Who would do that for another, anyhow? A lover, a parent, a child, or perhaps a sister or brother.

Back in her unit, Lin Feng raised his left hand, the one without the bandage, palm facing her. Their high-five turned into a left-handed handshake. His hand was warmer again.

'Give me another task,' he said. 'The shadier, the better.'

She looked at him, wanting to laugh and cry at the same time. She forced the words: 'You fainted the other evening and I helped you, and you have now returned the favour. We owe each other nothing.' But she glanced at his bandage again.

'It's not about owing.' Lin Feng unzipped his backpack, ripped out half a sheet of grid paper, and scribbled a number. 'I'll work for you.'

'Who do you think you are?'

'Your apprentice. I'm good at it, you can't fire me.'

She laughed despite herself and hated how it scared her she might never see him again. 'You've left your number,' she said weakly.

'Give me yours,' he said.

'I don't have a phone.' She hardened her heart. 'Go now. Don't you have other things to do?'

He pressed his back into the wall. 'My sister's calling me at eight.'

A lump rose in Chen Di's throat. For how long did he plan to continue the lie? She tried not to sigh but did. 'Is there nothing else you need to do? Homework?'

'Well, I need to get a bunch of mulberry leaves.'

'For your silkworms?'

'They just moulted, they're running out of food soon.'

'I know where to find the trees, I can bring you the leaves.' A place that gathered all trees in Shanghai was Dragon Lustre Martyrs Cemetery. Then she breathed and made sure she understood that her returning the favour was only secondary to her mission: Lin Feng lived in Dragon Lake Court and she had to look into the nearby Phoenix Sea Court anyway.

'You'll bring me mulberry leaves? Really?'

'If tomorrow morning isn't too late.'

Lin Feng took a huge step closer as if he'd shake her hand again. 'Tomorrow morning is perfect! Can you come at nine? I mean, eight-thirty if you can stay for a bit. Actually, between eight-thirty and eight-forty-five would be perfect.'

'Do you have something going on?'

'No, no, no, I don't go to Sunday cram schools.'

'You sound like you know the exact time for your leaves to run out.'

Lin Feng opened and closed his mouth, obviously hiding something. No matter, it wasn't her business what he did on Sundays. He swung his backpack on one shoulder and turned around before saying, 'Yep, I kind of do.'

'That's too late for me. See me downstairs at seven-thirty.'

And by nine, Chen Di would be an expert in the layout of Lü's housing estate.

24
Sichuan
Harvest 1997

Crops ripened. Leaves fell. It'd been one week since Teacher Jia had left, and it'd felt like the longest week in the fifteen years of her life. A proverb said, *Once a teacher, father for life*. But it wasn't just about that, about gratitude. She didn't even like her own father. Besides, proverbs were dog farts. *Uneducated women are virtuous women. The rod produces a filial child. Of the three unfilial acts, the worst is not having an heir.* Teacher Jia had called them gibberish. And every time she thought of his words, of him, she felt a stabbing pain.

She didn't help the new teacher – a young woman with thick glasses – mark homework but did continue to clean the school, to live at the school office. Tonight, she reached under the desk and flipped open Teacher Jia's wooden box of books. But seeing its contents stung like soap in her eyes. She remembered the day he'd pulled her into the classroom through the window, the smooth touch of his big hand. The same hand had held these books – touching them was like touching him, but he was gone. For ever.

She flopped on the bed, imagining the door swinging open, him stepping in and pulling her into his arms, pressing his lips to hers, telling her he was leaving his wife. In the middle of the night, she slammed the book box shut and punched it, over and over, her fists pink.

Why hadn't Mother come to comfort her?

Chen Di put on her old cotton coat, too small, with shallow pockets and no hood, its red faded to pink. She buttoned it wrong and re-buttoned it and shot out of the school office. She hadn't thought she'd walk those meandering paths to the cotton field again, but she did in moonlight, downhill.

After three whole years, she was going for a visit.

By the time she arrived, her trousers muddy, she'd calmed. The sea of cotton looked grey in the twilight. She stood in the partly harvested field, as still as a scarecrow. The bollworms had been bad this year, excessive rains having led to hardlock and boll rot. She spotted a well-cracked boll and twisted out the cotton. Funny how some skills stuck with you for life.

Ahead, shingles scattered on one side of the wooden house, and a corner looked like it'd collapse. So it had deteriorated while most village houses had been upgraded. It was as if her family alone had been left behind by time. Chen Di recalled her younger self and Mother in white hats, carrying large sacks. Then she thought of her leaf hair clip, a gift from Father. She still didn't know how she'd lost it.

'Chen Di.' Father materialised metres away, a number of cotton pickers far behind him. She hadn't noticed him rustle through the cotton. Well, his recent visit at the school office being an exception, Father had never made much sound in her life besides playing the leaf whistle.

'Father,' she heard herself say. *It's weird to see you again so soon.*

Almost simultaneously they both turned to the east. The sun emerged from behind the hill, bathing the cotton field in dawn light. A moment of tenderness, a 'now' worth living. Neither of them spoke as the world glowed, gold.

Chen Di inhaled. Exhaled.

At least I'm alive.

A rooster crowed. She took a sudden step backwards, irritated that she'd shared this sunrise with Father. She felt she betrayed Mother by doing so. Sunrises were their special time together.

'The sunrise is filled with life, isn't it?' Father said without looking at her.

Chen Di hadn't misheard him. For an instant it felt as if Mother was there, talking through Father's mouth, or perhaps they'd been Father's words all along. She stared at his profile, his light-brown eyes tinged with sorrow.

'Where is Mother?' she said.

His eyes were still fixated on the sun. He then turned, a tremor in his hands. 'How have you been, Chen Di?' he said, as if he hadn't seen her in years. Or perhaps he was concerned about her, knowing Teacher Jia had left.

'Great.' She didn't need his worry.

'Good, good. We're also doing all right—'

'I'm asking where Mother is.'

'She's inside. Have you decided to live at home again?'

'No.' Chen Di marched towards the house, ignoring Father's 'Wait!'

The 'no' sounded more resolute than she felt. In truth, she'd been considering coming back to live with Mother, now that her alternative had become painful. But a part of her resisted it. The meaning of 'home' had changed – the school office was her home – and every time she washed herself, touching the scars on her back, fear crept over her.

Across the stone bridge, the stone steps before the house were still there. The pattern formed by the dents had deepened, like an ugly map, and the double doors had blackened, one of them splintered. Rain had made the pasted couplet unreadable, but on each door, a new character for *Fortune* was stuck upside-down.

She knocked.

'Who?' Grandfather's voice.

Chen Di pulled the doors open. The threshold was lower than she remembered. She stepped into the courtyard, hung with laundry, piled with a heap of cement. Then her eyes met his. Grandfather was half-visible by the kitchen door, his head poking out, and he held a large red Thermos. A strange sight.

'Grandfather.' She gave half a nod.

He didn't put down the Thermos, his unibrow knit with suspicion.

'May I see Mother?'

He pointed, and that calloused finger sickened her. But as he angled his head, dim light reflected a cloudiness in his eyes that made him look old, truly old, almost forgivable.

In the front room, a *Fortune* was pasted right side up on the wall, as if to cancel those on the double doors outside. There were no idols. Three lit incense sticks stood in a burner before a brand-new portrait of Mao, a ring of light around his head. It was glossier than the old portraits, resilient to weather extremes.

On an edge of the mahjong table lay sheets of paper, and Chen Di recognised Father's handwriting. It read *Heart Sutra* on top. As much as she liked reading, she couldn't take passages and passages of lines like *Form is emptiness; emptiness is form.*

In the back room, Mother lay in bed. She'd always been an early riser. Was she sick? Chen Di leaped to her bed. But up close Mother looked well, her cheeks rosy, her hair thick. Neither her face nor her exposed arm showed any bruises.

Mother's eyes opened. 'Yaonü!'

'Good morning, Mother.'

'Why are you here?' She sat up but stayed in the quilt.

'You look great,' Chen Di couldn't help saying. Then she checked for Grandfather and perched on the bed. 'It's just… You know Teacher Jia left, don't you?'

'Oh, I know how much he's helped you.'

Chen Di had an impulse to confess her feelings for him and the whole story of his wife, but she only leaned closer to Mother. Mother moved away.

'More bruises?'

'I'm fine,' Mother said. 'Just take care of yourself.' She smiled gently. 'You had feelings for Teacher Jia, didn't you? You always turned red around him.'

Chen Di's cheeks burnt. 'I-I liked him as a teacher.' She thought she'd kept her feelings well hidden, but being found out by Mother didn't feel so bad.

'Some day, you'll meet someone special.'

'Mother…' Chen Di gazed at her, more thankful than embarrassed. At least she still had Mother, who understood her, who was on her side. She reached towards Mother, but Mother moved away again. 'What's wrong, Mother?'

Mother held onto the quilt and glanced around at the beds, the stools, and the sewing machine which now had a foot pedal, as if searching for something. No, she was just anxious to change the topic.

Grandfather entered, an enamel bowl in hand. He set it on the stool beside the bed, placed a pair of chopsticks across the bowl, and walked out with childishly light steps. The congee was topped with a century egg, and Chen Di's mouth watered.

Then she froze.

Steam from the congee vanished into the air. She rose, shaking, awareness coming over like droplets of water. Father in the field. Grandfather in the kitchen. Mother sleeping late. The century egg. In fact, there had been clues even before. Grandfather had wanted her back because he needed help during harvest, but that wasn't all. He had forbidden Chen Di from coming home only because she'd lost her brother, except

Little Tiger was just one son. The prospect of a replacement had halved her crime.

'This isn't... This isn't what I think it is, right?'

Mother only looked at her. 'Yaonü...'

'Right, Mother? Right?' Chen Di clasped her arm and shook it.

Mother's expression gave the confirmation she didn't want. Chen Di slowly let go and straightened her stiff back and walked backwards, one step, and another.

'Don't go yet.' Mother pushed on the bed to rise. The quilt fell to the floor, exposing her slightly bulging belly. Four months? 'Don't go...'

'They still think Little Tiger is alive!' Chen Di's scratchy voice didn't sound like hers. 'They won't give you a birth permit, and to give birth without a permit is to put one foot in the grave. You know that, Mother. You know, I know, everyone knows!'

'We'll...keep it hidden. I'll fake illness, or leave—'

'Can you? Even pregnant couples running around the whole country are getting caught and forced to abort. Things have changed, Mother, people report each other. Haven't you heard? When you do, you get rewarded and praised on the loudspeakers.'

'But if we manage, then once the baby is born, they can't "force an abortion" anymore. Whatever the fine—'

'But you said you could no longer have babies!' Chen Di was panting now. Villagers had talked about quacks who 'removed permanent coils' and 'reversed procedures'.

Was it actually possible? 'What have you done to yourself, Mother?'

Mother said nothing.

'What has Grandfather done?'

Mother said nothing.

'What has Father done?'

Mother said nothing.

Chen Di looked away from Mother's belly, from Mother, and slowly, step by step, backed out of the room, across the yard, over the not-so-high threshold, through the double doors, and away from the cotton field. The lie on that wall was long gone, but she saw it in her mind again. *One is good; a son or a daughter, equally good.*

She forged uphill, her breathing ragged, and cut through a funeral procession. A rooster was tied to the coffin. An old man played suona, the music loud enough to burst her eardrums. The more she tried to avoid them, the more people she bumped into. They held up a white flag, carried white flowers, and wore white garb with white head cloths draping to their shins.

She clutched her head, and ran.

25
Shanghai
Spring 2002

Chen Di skipped her workout and sped out. Today she'd bring Lin Feng some mulberry leaves and investigate Phoenix Sea Court.

Along the streets, plane branches twisted and forked, the leaves growing thick and maple-like, nursed by the sun and the rain. Several yulan magnolias stood majestically in front of Saint Ignatius Cathedral. Mulberry trees lacked their sturdiness and elegance, but they were needed too – for the silkworms.

She braked at an intersection. The sun, veiled by smog, had risen between two tall buildings. Chen Di had never before seen such a low sunrise in Shanghai. She fixed her eyes on it, reminiscing watching the sunrise with Mother from the cotton field, until her mind zoomed to the only time she'd done it with Father.

Irritated, she biked on.

Beyond Dragon Lustre Martyrs Cemetery's walls, she saw trees, trees, and trees. An oasis in the middle of Big Shanghai.

She walked about. The nation's struggles were depicted by gigantic stone sculptures, an eternal flame, and a memorial pyramid. A wide stone structure showed Chairman Jiang's words calligraphed in gold: *heart and blood dedicated to the people.* A wave of loneliness washed over Chen Di as she watched a kindly-looking old woman touching the stone, explaining each word to her excited granddaughter. Chen Di didn't belong, left out of the patriotism that united everyone else, in cities, in villages. But was it patriotism or just love for the Party? To what extent could you truly separate the two, in this nation?

On the eastern side, she stopped at a pair of solid wooden gates three times her height, locked with a chain. The gates probably opened into Dragon Lustre Temple, which was why they were locked. The temple asked for a ticket while the cemetery didn't.

She almost walked away when she felt something under her foot: two wet twigs laden with...mulberry leaves? She removed her foot and crouched. They really were the leaves Mother had described and drawn for her, leaves common all over Sichuan, apparently, even though she'd never spotted any in Daci Village. Around her were only trimmed bushes, so the twig must've come from behind the gates – the temple.

Chen Di picked them up. Lin Feng kept silkworms as pets, so he probably had no more than a few dozen. These leaves would be enough. Then it occurred to her that he could simply buy mulberry leaves from an animal market. She'd been the one to suggest picking from the trees and bringing him the leaves, but still… The kid had an agenda.

She headed back to the entrance, plucking the leaves from the twigs and putting them in her pocket. She held up a small leaf, green and sparkly, its edge jagged.

How had she lost that hair clip?

Chen Di didn't have to pass Lü's housing estate to get to Lin Feng's, but she did, taking a detour. Across the street from Phoenix Sea Court, she got off her bicycle and pushed it slowly. Inside the three-metre-tall fences were twelve-storey apartment buildings and an impressive amount of planned greenery. The characters *Phoenix Sea Court* were engraved in red on a large stone.

Above a set of marble stairs, between pillars, the entrance to building 1 – Lü's building – boasted the air of an art gallery. A thin out-of-towner laboured up the stairs to deliver a twenty-litre water bottle. She looked up to the fourth floor, wondering which windows belonged to unit 406. Lü Yuandou could be having tea in his apartment right now.

She was so close. So close.

The fence on the far side was shared with another housing estate, with older, shorter buildings. The security would be laxer there. Chen Di turned at the end of the street and continued walking her bicycle. *I'm Chen Xiaoli from the Family Planning Commission, here to see Chief Lü for an urgent matter.* That should work, or, if she could climb over the fence, sneak into the building from the back, and knock on Lü's door directly, it'd be even better.

She was still planning when she saw the sign to Dragon Lake Court, so she followed it and turned again.

'Boss Chen!' Lin Feng met her downstairs as agreed.

'Hi,' she said. 'How's your hand?'

'All good.' He raised it to show her. He'd taken off the bandage, and the cut was recovering.

'Stop acting so recklessly in the future.'

Lin Feng stuck out his tongue, then grinned in that childlike way again, making her heart soften. She leaned her bicycle on a pole and caught herself wondering if her brother would have grinned in the same way.

She clutched her head and shut her eyes, then looked back. 'Here.' She picked up Lin Feng's uninjured hand and put the stack of mulberry leaves in his palm.

'Excellent.' He looked up from the leaves. 'Where did you find these?'

'Dragon Lustre Martyrs Cemetery.' His grin lingered in her mind. 'I didn't see the mulberry trees, only found twigs on the east side, by a pair of locked gates.'

Lin Feng nodded slowly as if to make a mental note of it, then pointed behind him. 'Come see my silkworms.'

Chen Di knew she'd already got more involved in his life than she should have, but one glance at Dragon Lake Court told her it bore an uncanny resemblance to Phoenix Sea Court. They were like sister housing estates – studying one would tell her about the other.

'Who should I be to you?' she asked Lin Feng. 'What are you going to tell your mum?' Speaking of which, what had his mum said about his bandaged hand?

'She didn't come home.'

Chen Di grimaced. 'Let's go then.'

'I'll say you're my teacher when Mum— when the guards ask.'

Her old seaweed-green sweater and jeans didn't look very professional. A maid might make more sense, but for an employer's child to escort a servant? She let down her ponytail and parted her shoulder-length hair off-centre, hoping to appear a couple of years older. Indeed, this was a good practice session for her big day of step three.

'Chinese teacher,' she said. 'I can't do maths.'

They crossed the street, and Chen Di locked her bicycle at a pole. Up the marble stairs, the foyer looked like a hotel reception, the chandelier bright, the artificial fragrance profuse. Two guards wore light-blue shirts and indigo trousers and looked more relaxed than the guards at the government buildings. They carried no guns, only batons. The older guard sat back behind the counter, his scalp glistening under the chandelier. The younger one stood up, his cheeks full of pimples. Tang would've deemed them clowns.

'I'm back, uncles.' Lin Feng slammed his forearm on the counter.

The young guard threw a questioning look at Chen Di.

'This is Teacher Chen,' Lin Feng said.

'Working hard, Teacher Chen.' The guard scanned her head to toe. 'It's Sunday.'

'It's my duty,' she said.

Lin Feng met the young guard's eyes and leaned closer as if to remind him who paid his bills. The guard swallowed, then invited them to go through the glass doors.

Beyond, Lin Feng pushed the button for the lift. A nearby stairwell led up and down. Assuming Phoenix Sea Court was the same, the basement would be a good escape route.

They stepped into the lift, and Lin Feng hit the lucky number 8. An upward acceleration, a rebellion against gravity. The doors opened, revealing a marble-floored hallway with a double-glazed window, a door to the stairwell, and three doors to the apartments. Before one door lay a doormat that read *Welcome* in English, and before another sat three pairs of shoes. Lin Feng pulled out a key to open a solid, white, metal door.

They both changed into slippers as they entered the living room, Chen Di glancing at his battered black sneakers again. A wall clock ticked loudly. The curtains were shut but the hardwood floor remained glossy. There was an eight-seat round mahogany table, chairs with carved backs, a leather corner sofa, a glass tea table, and a wide-screen TV with tower speakers. Furnished to impress. She saw no family photos, and the place smelled sterile.

Though Chen Di had never set foot in such a nice apartment before, she felt no jealousy.

Somehow she didn't think Lü Yuandou's apartment would look like this. In fact, she couldn't picture Lü's living space at all.

'The silkworms are in a tin on my dressing table.' Lin Feng pointed at the door to a bedroom, then went into the kitchen, which had a double-door fridge and a water dispenser. 'I'll clean the leaves in case of pesticide.'

'Not likely,' she said.

'Still.'

How careful he was.

Instead of checking out the silkworms, Chen Di considered how Tang might proceed and snooped around. A living room, three bedrooms, two bathrooms, two balconies, a kitchen, even a laundry room and a study. The only familiar bit was the upside-down character for *Fortune* on the doors. Then she noticed an ugly knife gouge on the mahogany dining table, deeper and wider than those on her wooden wardrobe. She felt it with her fingertips as she imagined Lin Feng swinging down a cleaver.

Lü Yuandou wouldn't need such a big apartment...unless he had a family. The idea had crossed her mind before but now jarred her again. A monster like Lü would never be loved, be a part of a family. If he were, it only meant others in his family, too, were monsters. Whoever supported someone as evil as Lü deserved to die just as much.

It wouldn't change Chen Di's plan.

The study had simple furniture that didn't fit, white like a funeral. The single bed was unmade, the desk unkempt, the wall calendar outdated. Chen Di stopped before the computer and clicked the mouse. The machine rumbled to display a document.

difference between short stories and novels. A novel demands character arcs; it is not about a character's one emotional state. You are a skilled short story writer, Author Peng, but the characters in your novel need to grow. They are *stuck*.

Stuck. Author Peng had to be Dried Bamboo Shoot – Lin Feng's mother – who just might know Teacher Jia.

Chen Di went out of the study and was startled by a quiet tapping sound. In the bathroom, she squatted to find a plastic container under the sink. Two turtles with brown shells crawled, necks extending, heads nodding, beady eyes blinking.

'They just woke from hibernation,' Lin Feng said.

She rose in a hurry and felt like a burglar. 'R-Right.'

'They're Chinese pond turtles, females. The big one's Comrade Xiaoping, the small one's Little Comrade.'

'That's blasphemous.' Chen Di laughed.

Lin Feng fetched a bowl of tomato and egg stir-fry, sat on the edge of the bathtub, and dropped a spoonful of the food into the container. 'They prefer raw meat but also eat this.'

The turtles devoured it, Comrade Xiaoping accidentally biting Little Comrade's foot. The tomato suddenly looked like blood, the container red like a mini-Tiananmen Square. Lin Feng dropped another few spoonfuls, and the turtle heads collided as they prodded at the food. Comrade Xiaoping won every collision. Sometimes she looked like a kind teacher, nudging Little Comrade to eat, while other times she looked like a battle tank ready to roll.

'Quite a few housing estates in this area look just like this one,' Lin Feng said. 'Some Tiger Court, Lion Court, and of course, Phoenix Sea Court.'

Chen Di stepped back. 'What do you mean?'

'You can look around, it's okay.'

She wanted to snap at him but found herself rather pleased, impressed he could read her thoughts. Not a bad apprentice. Now that she had a grip on his housing estate's layout, the buildings' structures, the apartments' feel, she felt more confident about Lü's. She could move onto the execution tomorrow. *No, tonight,* Tang's harsh voice said in her head.

Yes, tonight.

'I did want to show you my silkworms though,' Lin Feng said.

Chen Di headed into his bedroom, which was bigger than her whole unit. There was a large bed with a mahogany frame, mahogany bedside tables, and a mahogany dressing table. A digital clock quietly sneaked away time. She'd expected a Game Boy, Jay Chou's CDs, or the Harry Potter books kids at Pizza & Apple Pie talked about. But on the bedside table was only a blister pack of tablets – his antidepressants.

She noticed a fishbowl on the dressing table. Five tropical fish had round, colourful tails. One was triangular, striped like a white tiger.

'Guppies and angelfish.' Lin Feng scattered food pellets. A guppy caught a pellet only to have it sucked out of her mouth by the angelfish. He pointed to a river shrimp at the bottom, with a nice pair of pincers. 'My mum bought live shrimps to cook, and I saved one. I wish I could've saved them all. Isn't it unfair they're born to be eaten?'

'But you changed this guy's fate,' she said.

'I did.' He grinned again.

Chen Di snapped her head away. She should get going – she was liking the kid more and more. He was not her real brother and she had her mission to carry out! 'Hurry up and show me your silkworms.'

'There.' He pointed at a mooncake tin across the dressing table.

Lin Feng had already put in the mulberry leaves. The silkworms looked just like the bollworms except they were grey and didn't have hair. One made a hole in a leaf as it nibbled, eight pairs of legs moving softly, its body expanding, contracting. What Chen Di had thought was the caterpillar's mouth was really its entire head, a head capsule. This was the first time she saw silkworms with her own eyes, yet she felt she'd always known them.

'Only four?' She lifted the leaves. 'Did some die last night?'

'No, only four hatched to start with. I saved about a hundred eggs last year, I don't know what happened…' Lin Feng pressed his hands on the dressing table. 'But they grow fast, and they're less vulnerable now.'

'They are most vulnerable as chrysalises.' *Boiled alive inside their cocoons.*

He nodded. 'My mum made them once.'

'Sorry?'

'Crunchy silkworms. Chrysalises cooked with green onion and chilli oil.'

A delicacy, of course. After the silk threads had been drawn from the cocoons, the chrysalises boiled to death, all that was left was for them to be eaten.

'Don't worry,' he said. 'Nothing will happen to these.'

But even if these silkworms got out of their cocoons, they could only turn into flightless moths. She felt a surge of sympathy for them and admiration for the bollworms. At least bollworms put up a fight for the chance to fly.

Lin Feng was watching her.

'What?' she said, again wishing he wasn't so tall.

'Have you kept silkworms too?'

My mother, Chen Di almost said. She took in the fresh smell of the mulberry leaves and listened to the silkworms' faint nibbling.

'It's just you're smiling again,' he said, 'like when we talked about Four Three.'

'I'm not smiling.'

'You look good by the way, with your hair down.'

This kid – he liked her too much. Chen Di spun around, but Lin Feng took her wrist. Outside of Master Mu's dojo, no one had grabbed her wrist before, and escaping a grip was her forte. But she didn't try. 'What do you want?'

'Take me with you,' he said.

She cringed.

'I'll learn to cook on your coal-ball stove. My parents don't give a damn about me, the only one who cared—'

'Was your sister?'

He flushed, as if suddenly aware of what he'd said. The air in the room was still. The silkworms continued their breakfast in the mooncake tin, one making a new hole in a mulberry leaf, another enlarging a hole, and the other two tracing the jagged edges of the same leaf.

'Lin Feng, I'm not your sister.'

'I know,' he said.

His small voice hurt her in a way she couldn't explain. *Though I'm not your sister,* she wanted to add, *I wish I were.* But she only said, 'I'm sorry.'

'Nope, you're right. How can I ask for anything if I don't even deserve to live?'

That line again. Chen Di had the urge to tell him otherwise, that the world was broken, not he. But Lin Feng spoke again. 'Can I tell you another memory?'

'One with your sister?'

He nodded at the silkworms. 'I remembered it only last night.'

26
Sichuan
Winter 1998

The 1998 Lantern Festival arrived – four months since she had learned of Mother's pregnancy. Chen Di, now sixteen, woke before dawn in the school office, her eyes dry. She gazed out at the bamboo that rustled in the wind, in darkness. She, Teacher Jia, and Mother had spent the last three Lantern Festivals together, eating Mother's tangyuans. This was the time of year when mulberry trees budded. This was the time of year when she usually felt hope.

Not this year.

She trembled, picturing Mother's big belly, knowing the danger for her if she were found out by Lü Yuandou. Might Mother have left the village? Dozens of pregnant women without birth permits had tried to run away from Daci Village to give birth elsewhere, mostly resulting in capture. And Mother, who never went anywhere, would only arouse suspicion if she did. But even if she managed to hide her pregnancy until labour, would any midwives still dare to help with a permitless birth? Things had changed.

Why had Mother agreed to have another child anyhow? *I'm alive, Mother. Isn't that enough?* Chen Di had asked her. *It is,* Mother had said. Lied.

And how that hurt.

At least Chen Di still had Teacher Jia's books. Light filtered in, and she lay in bed and flipped the pages of the classic, *Dream of the Red Chamber*. She was sickened by the family hierarchy and the over-sentimental heroine's tantrums, her calling an old peasant woman a 'female locust'. She shut her tired eyes. How such a heroine captured the hearts of Chinese men *and* women was beyond her. She knew she didn't belong to Daci Village and now felt she didn't even belong to China, which she wasn't sad about – or so she told herself.

Her stomach rumbled, and though it was still morning, she headed to the school kitchen to make mapo tofu. She couldn't afford the minced meat that went with it but had bought pickled mustard stems. And by now she was so used to the taste of chilli bean paste she could hardly eat anything without adding extra. Still, the food tasted bland.

'Teacher Jia,' she murmured, 'what should I do?'

A clamour outside made her jump.

'Chen Di!' a girl called, one of Teacher Jia's former evening class students.

'Cleaner girl?' said a guy's voice she didn't recognise.

Yet another voice said, 'Come out! Your family is in trouble.'

She dropped her chopsticks and one rolled away. She bolted out to find a sunny day and half a dozen young people. 'What happened?'

The evening class girl leisurely braided her hair. 'Go and see for yourself.'

'We'll go with you.' A short guy rubbed his nose as if waiting for a show to start.

Panicked, Chen Di ran in the direction of the cotton field. Red-lantern-decorated houses blurred past, as well as bamboo scaffolding, a bulldozer moving earth, and a billboard reading, *Daci Village 1996–2000 Rural Development Work Plans*. Her steps slowed a little. Five men were building a pumping station, and a group of children shrieked in laughter, rolling an old tyre. The happy scene made her wonder if people at the school were playing a joke on her. It'd happened before, and she'd never got along with any of them.

But Mother's swollen belly came to mind again.

Chen Di jerked to a stop by the stream, across from Grandpa Li's house, now a two-storey brick building. Strings of corn cobs and chillies hung at the front, just like on that fateful day in the 1994 harvest. She recalled Lü Yuandou's jeep, his team of men and women, Chubby Aunty's screams, her being carried like a pig – hair in a mess, clothes torn, belly exposed – and forced into the vehicle. She shivered. In her mind, the mole in Chubby Aunty's eyebrow vanished, her face morphing into Mother's.

The stream rushed as if it were summer, not winter. The concrete pole was no longer tilted, now attached with a new pair of loudspeakers. Suddenly it blared with children singing 'On the Golden Mountain of Beijing'.

The doors flew open. Out came Chubby Aunty, her short legs moving fast as she sang alongside the loudspeakers: '...*Chairman Mao is the golden sun... How warm, how kind...We walk on a happy socialist boulevard!*' Her son followed her out. His county-town-school uniform included the Young Pioneers' red scarf. They both carried happy red lanterns. So they'd come out only to put up lanterns!

Chen Di might've been the target of some prank after all.

Well, she did want to see Mother, who must've been forced by Grandfather and Father – Mother wasn't the one who wanted another child. And today *was* their favourite festival.

She trod through the foothills, and a new motorcycle whizzed by, painted on its sides with rooster blood, which supposedly guaranteed a safe trip. She decided to talk normally with Father and Grandfather and to smile at Mother.

Far ahead, their field appeared under the late-morning sun, bare. Except a bright-red jeep was parked before the stone bridge, four white loudspeakers fastened on top, two pointing to the front, two to the sides. Beyond, villagers chattered.

Chen Di's whole body tensed. She ran to the jeep, stunned by just how clean the red vehicle was. She pushed through the crowd and hurried across the bridge to the house. A row of red lanterns decorated the front as if they were there to welcome her. The air was still, but as if on cue, one lantern dropped to the ground.

From inside came a high voice.

'Check the outhouse,' Lü Yuandou was saying, followed by other voices. One was none other than that of Uncle Li –

Grandpa Li's son, Chubby Aunty's husband – who generally stayed in the county town. Villagers had reported Mother's permitless pregnancy.

Chen Di shuddered, her palms clammy.

'There you are.' Lü's calm voice mixed with Mother's cry. 'Maggots under, spiders above. How impressive you hid by a toilet for that long.'

Chen Di couldn't breathe. Lü appeared at the double doors and swaggered out. Behind him, two men and two women hauled Mother outside. Villagers surrounded them, something unkind in their eyes. Mother's hair was everywhere as she tried to break free.

'Mother!' Chen Di shouted, but her shaky voice was drowned out by the villagers' clamour.

Mother didn't notice her. Neither did Lü.

'I promised to keep an eye on you.' Lü turned to Mother and raised a finger to make the point, and chuckled. 'You haven't aged a day, still looking like a fox spirit.'

Mother struggled to no avail. 'Heaven will punish you!'

'I work for the Party, I enforce justice *on behalf of Heaven*. Can't you tell the whole county's got richer? Thanks to what?'

'To Chief Lü!' two villagers sang. They'd once helped look for Little Tiger.

'No, to the Party. Family planning is national policy.'

'Yes!' Uncle Li gestured with his arms, as hairy as Grandpa Li's. 'The Party is right: better one son living well than a few starving together. I'll send my only child to university!'

'Not just sons.' An old woman hobbled over with the help of a cane. 'To be frank, Chief Lü, I resented you, my whole family did, I've always wanted a grand*son*. But then we accepted our fate and put all our money into the girls. And who would've thought my big granddaughter was such leadership material! Now she's settled in Chengdu and managing a team in *exports*.'

A few others cheered, men and women. 'Yes! Life *is* better.'

Chen Di wanted to cry. Years earlier, when Lü had torn down Grandpa Sun's house, villagers had taken the family's side, pleading for mercy. Later, when Lü had abducted Chubby Aunty, villagers had watched from far away, sparing themselves. Now, villagers accused her family and took Lü Yuandou's side.

What had happened to Daci, her village of big benevolence?

Then she recoiled, almost tripping over the fallen lantern. Could she really ascribe it all to brainwashing? Teacher Jia had taught her that absolutely nothing in the world was black and white, but she felt she was losing her ability to reason.

I'll send my only child to university.

We accepted our fate and put all our money into the girls.

Life is better.

Lü asked everyone to calm down. His team lifted Mother horizontally, her eight-month belly to the sky, and continued on to the stone bridge with her suspended between them. Grandfather staggered after, pressing a hand to his chest, his eyes cloudy. 'Please, Chief Lü!'

'Mother!' Chen Di squeezed through the team carrying Mother. 'Mother!'

Mother turned, her face sweat- and tear-soaked, and finally she saw Chen Di. 'Yaonü!' She struggled to reach out, but her wrists were tied together, as were her ankles. Chen Di extended her hand to Mother's shoulder before Lü pushed her away. She fell on the bridge.

'Yaonü!' Mother twisted, in vain.

Chen Di sat still on the ground, forgetting how to cry.

'I'm so sorry,' Mother said. The team muscled their way towards the red jeep. Mother turned her head but could no longer see Chen Di. 'I'm so sorry, Yaonü,' she said again before being thrown into the vehicle.

Chen Di felt each slam of the doors inside her chest. Teeth chattering, she staggered up and lurched across the bridge towards the jeep, but Lü blocked her.

'Girl with a birthmark.' He clicked his tongue. 'I thought I warned you.'

'Don't take Mother! Please.'

'Slap her,' he said to a stout female subordinate. The woman raised her thick hand and smacked Chen Di so hard she tasted blood.

She steadied herself and looked Lü in the eye. 'Don't take Mother!'

'Haven't I told you? You should thank Heaven—'

'It's kicking!' Mother wailed from the jeep. 'It's kicking right now! Please...'

Lü stood still as if remembering something, then returned to the vehicle. Chen Di followed, pushing through the villagers, to find Father already in a front seat, hands joined, thumb touching his nose, mumbling. Lü's team also allowed Grandfather to go with them.

Chen Di slapped the windows desperately, but it was Lü's face she saw. She almost backed off, yet his expression confused her. It reminded her of the fleeting pain she'd seen on his face when he'd torn down Grandpa Sun's house, an expression she'd almost forgotten. Lü rubbed his forehead now, eyes shut, and when they opened, they were vacant.

She gave the glass another clap. 'Mother!'

Finally, Mother's face came into view from the back, and they both reached towards the window, all four hands, Mother's wrists still tied. Their fingertips met, and Chen Di felt a sudden emptiness inside her.

The vehicle rumbled away.

A plume of dust blurred her world.

When Chen Di came to her senses, she was running, not after the red jeep but towards the jungle on the west – a shortcut. She knew the village health centre, she must go to Mother. She followed a path, then a trail through the jungle, through the tangled vegetation. She puffed and panted, forgetting the pain on her cheek. The branches and thorns cut her all over. Patches of sunlight appeared and disappeared.

A thick vine before her feet, her heart in mid-air, she tripped over.

27
Shanghai
Spring 2002

They watched the silkworms as Lin Feng talked, rubbing his chin again as he thought back to his childhood.

He remembered his horror after crushing a silkworm underfoot, its flat body stuck on the floorboard, the way he'd sobbed, unable to get up, and how his sister had reassured him. That day, she pulled him up and led him downstairs, holding the silkworm. And he found himself under a yulan magnolia. Far away stood Dragon Lustre Temple's pagoda, the golden finial like a wand. When he looked back, his sister was kneeling on the grass, making a heap of soil. She then joined her palms and told him the silkworm would fertilise the tree.

'She also told me,' Lin Feng said to Chen Di, his tone so gentle it made her heart squeeze, '"No one ever dies, because we're all connected."'

Chen Di pressed on the dressing table, her eyes watering. She must've stared too hard at the silkworms, eating tirelessly. She touched a caterpillar's head, and her fingertip traced along its back, smooth, and cold.

'Lin Feng, I'm not your sister,' she repeated as much to him as to herself.

'I know,' he said. 'I'm your apprentice.'

'You're not.' She couldn't allow herself to get more attached. *Stop! Stop now.* She had a feeling if she didn't, the kid before her would irrevocably change her life. She willed herself to add, 'I'm sorry but I don't need you.'

'No one does, I know.'

His words cut through her. She did all she could to not take back what she'd said.

Without looking at her, he spoke again. 'My existence has really hurt my sister.'

'How...do you mean?' Was he about to tell her the truth, finally?

Then came the sound of a key in the door.

'You're my new Chinese teacher,' Lin Feng said. 'My results are average.'

Only when he let go did she remember that, the whole time, he'd been holding her wrist.

Before Chen Di could fix her hair or take her seat on the living-room sofa, a man and a woman in their late forties came in. She hadn't expected the couple to be on good terms, let alone show up together after a night out. But Lin Feng pulled out a dining chair to sit and looked almost bored – he knew they'd come when she was here. Then it clicked. *Between eight-thirty and eight-forty-five would be perfect.* Chen Di checked her watch. 8:40.

Lin Feng's dad had a protruding stomach and an amiable look, his round glasses like a magnified version of his nostrils. He must've been fitter ten years ago, so fit he'd taken Tang's eye and beaten his uncle to death. Lin Feng's mum appeared even slimmer and taller in a grey trench coat, her bun out of fashion but perfectly pinned with a jade hairpin. She *was* elegant. Chen Di couldn't look away and wasn't sure how much it had to do with her whacking her son in public and how much with her working with Four Three.

'You must be Lin Feng's parents.' She extended her hand, again wishing she'd worn a newer sweater and proper trousers. At least the mum didn't look like she recognised her from that day on the street. 'I am Teacher Chen.'

Lin Feng's dad laughed with his paunch and shook her hand. 'So Teacher Jiang finally retired.'

'She didn't.' Lin Feng sat back in the chair. 'Teacher Jiang is still our class teacher, she still teaches Ideology and Politics.'

Chen Di took in the information, knowing it was for her reference. She let go of the meaty hand and put on a smile. 'I'm new, I teach Chinese.'

The dad laughed again. 'Home visit on Sunday, and you're not even their class teacher? Speaking of hard-working.'

The mum shook her hand too, frowning in suspicion.

'Please sit, Teacher Chen,' the dad said. 'You sound like you're from Sichuan.'

Chen Di took her seat on the much-too-soft sofa. 'I've lived here since university.'

'Oh, which one did you go to?'

'East China Normal University.'

'That's quite something.' The dad sat on the sofa too, leaving a seat between them. He raised a finger as if he was about to ask more, but then turned to the TV and let out an awkward laugh. Like his wife, he probably didn't believe her yet. Perhaps he was looking for a way to test her without making either of them lose face if she really were Lin Feng's East-China-Normal-University-educated teacher.

'I did my thesis on *Dream of the Red Chamber*,' she said, sounding more confident than she felt. Teacher Jia had left her only an abridged edition.

'Classic!' he said. 'I love that part where Lady Fèng jokes about a deaf man setting off firecrackers. Wait, which festival was it, it's not coming to mind…'

'Teacher Chen came to talk about *me*,' Lin Feng said.

'We'll get to that, Fengfeng.' The dad remained jolly.

Thankfully, the capable and cruel Lady Fèng was Chen Di's favourite character, and how could she ever forget… 'Lantern Festival,' she said. 'To me, though, such details don't matter. *Dream of the Red Chamber* exposes the feudal society in the Qing dynasty. At the same time, it's an elegy about life's impermanence. There is a lot to think about.'

Lin Feng's dad went silent, then mumbled, 'Impermanence, huh.' His tone was darker, his eyes fixed to a leg of the tea table. What a change in attitude. When he looked up again, he no longer seemed suspicious.

Lin Feng's mum set down four mugs of tea and a tray of snacks. The blue tin read *Danish Butter Cookies,* and the tea came in tea bags with tags that read *Earl Grey*. Chen Di took a sip. It tasted like soap. The mum disregarded the spare seats on the corner sofa and sat on a dining chair like Lin Feng had, but away from him.

'Lin Feng's mum,' Chen Di said, addressing her in the customary way. 'I hear you're a writer.'

'And I'm a behavioural biologist,' his dad said.

Chen Di concealed her annoyance at the interruption, then remembered Lin Feng saying his dad was more a businessman than a scientist. Perhaps that wasn't how the dad thought of himself. 'Lin Feng is lucky to have such a resourceful family. His results are average, but he has the potential to be more.'

Lin Feng's dad raised a hand. 'We know what you're getting at.'

Getting at?

The mum stood and headed to the master bedroom. She returned in no time, holding a box of wild ginseng. The dad took the box from her and passed it to Chen Di. 'Thank you for coming, Teacher Chen. Here's a little something.'

'Stop it!' Lin Feng's voice cut through.

'What's happening, Fengfeng?' his dad said.

'Must I spell it out? This is bribery.'

The dad looked flustered, while Chen Di set down the ginseng box and rose. 'It's good to meet you, Lin Feng's dad and mum. I have more home visits to do.'

'Please wait,' his mum said, the first time she'd spoken. She stood up too.

Chen Di remembered her voice from that day on the street,

but her crisp tone right now was nothing like that of the madwoman whacking her son. So she actually wanted to – cared to – talk about Lin Feng. Earl Grey's citrous-bitter scent lingered in the living room, and the wall clock ticked on. The mum looked away, seeming to change her mind.

Well, forget Lin Feng for a second, this was likely the only time she would ever meet his mum. Heart racing, she stepped closer. 'Lin Feng says you work with Four Three.'

The mum's lips parted.

'I just thought…' Chen Di tried to sound professional. 'I thought his writing could be good extracurricular reading material for the students.'

'It can't,' she said, her voice clipped.

'It's just… Four Three used to live in my home province, so…' Chen Di checked for the mum's reaction, hoping to confirm whether Four Three had actually lived in Sichuan, but her face showed nothing. Which probably meant he had. 'What was his family name again?'

'Do you know him?' Lin Feng's dad said, amused, then glanced at his wife as if to mock her. 'The big-deal author *is* exceptionally popular, isn't he?'

Lin Feng's mum opened the door. 'You do have more home visits to do.'

'R-Right, goodbye.'

The mum's reluctance made it all the more interesting.

Chen Di slipped on her shoes, shaking her head at the fact that they didn't care enough about their son to discuss him, which might've been why she'd managed to fool them.

Bribery saved the parents' energy to hear his problem, saved Lin Feng's need to behave, and kept the teachers happy. A win-win-win strategy.

Then it came to her: maybe Lin Feng stirred up trouble around town to get his parents' attention. Given his behaviour, home visits from teachers must've been a regular occurrence, but his parents still didn't seem to care. She refused their half-hearted offer to see her off downstairs, but before stepping out of the apartment, she stopped. At Yuanfen Eatery, Lin Feng must've stirred up trouble to get *her* attention too. He'd said he had already noticed her on the previous day.

'Teacher Chen!' Lin Feng came over. 'I have like six questions about the last class, can I go with you?'

'You stay,' his dad said. 'Teacher Chen is busy, ask her at school.'

'But, Teacher Chen!'

'Your dad is right.' Chen Di walked out, forcing herself to not look back.

She heard the door shut. But before the lifts, her hand stopped in mid-air, unable to press the down button. The dark eyes came to mind again – Lin Feng's eyes, Little Tiger's eyes – the eyes that said 'take me with you'. Lin Feng didn't want to be left with his parents...

But he was at least safe there. And this wasn't her business! She had come to study the layout of Lü's housing estate, and she was done. She'd go home, think it through, and carry out step three tonight. That was how Tang would proceed.

Mission first. Mission first. Mission first.

Chen Di stood transfixed in the eighth-floor hallway, her silhouette reflected in the sleek marble floor. She looked out the window. Everything below was tiny, two old men walking on a cobbled path, barefoot, to massage their feet. A part of her wanted Lin Feng to vanish along with her past that had spiralled out of control, but another part wanted to run back into the apartment and hug him close and see him grin like a happy child.

She heard his dad's loud voice. 'So, we're getting a divorce.'

28
Shanghai
Spring 2002

A divorce. Chen Di understood only then how unusual it was for Lin Feng's parents to show up together. She couldn't help but step back to the white metal door.

'We know this is hard for everyone,' she heard the dad say, as if reading from a script.

'No, it's *easy* for everyone,' Lin Feng responded, sounding like he meant it, the good actor he was. He must've expected the news and wanted Chen Di to take him away or be there when they told him. 'But why now?'

'It was my decision,' his mum said.

His dad laughed. 'All right! I'll take my leave then.'

Afraid he'd come right out, Chen Di stepped back. But then Lin Feng shouted, 'Don't go!' His words came out like a command. 'I don't give a damn if you divorce or not, but isn't it a miracle we're talking, the three of us? Has this ever happened? I have more to say.'

'Sure, sure, Fengfeng,' the dad said.

'The teas are cold,' the mum said. 'I'll make more.'

Chen Di put her ear to the door but heard nothing except the ticking of the family's wall clock, every note breaking the rhythm of her heartbeat.

'Dad, Mum, I had a sister, correct?'

Chen Di bit her lip, she couldn't believe it. It was true then: his parents had never mentioned their daughter to their son. Only Tang had. Thinking back, in the apartment, she hadn't seen a single memento of another child.

'I even remember her name,' Lin Feng continued. 'Lin Shun. Shunshun.' *Shun* and *Feng* put together meant *downwind*, good sailing condition.

Then came a woman's loud exhalation and a man's shout: 'We thought you were too young to remember!' He then lowered his voice. 'And with everything Doctor Wang told us, we totally thought... For how long have you known?'

Ever since Tang had told him the story?

'I know we used to live down in Dragon Lustre,' Lin Feng said. 'And that my sister had a heart problem, so you got to have another child – me. She died a few years later, we moved again and again, and you wiped her existence from my life. Is anything I said false?'

'It's all...true,' his dad said.

'How selfish you were!' Lin Feng's yell caught Chen Di – and perhaps his parents – off guard. 'Don't you realise *no other families* have two children? How could you have had me? How could you take advantage of her illness like that? It was like telling her to her face you expected her to die!'

Everything stilled, then Chen Di heard his mum sob. Having a second child under the one-child policy must've tormented the parents. Instead of focusing on their sick daughter, they'd made use of the exception in the policy to have another child. She stood still before the door, more sympathetic towards them now than just moments ago.

'Say that again?' his dad said.

'A dog ate your conscience,' Lin Feng said.

'You ungrateful... You ungrateful brat! We raised you with more effort than you can ever imagine. Now, instead of showing the least bit of gratitude, you— you—' He sounded like he was choking on his words. 'All those years when Shunshun was still alive, neighbours and colleagues thought we were exaggerating her sickness and kept saying how *lucky* we were to have two kids, jealous of our *special treatment*. And now you! You think *you* get to accuse us.'

'Enough...' The mum started weeping again.

'*Enough?*' the dad said. 'You can fool others, fool yourself, but not me. Deep down, aren't you sick of this situation, sick of yourself for being stuck?'

'It was my own fault,' she said.

'It *was*.' Something fell to the floor with a clang. Even across the door, Chen Di could hear the dad's heavy breathing. 'Time for you to learn some truth, Lin Feng.'

'I already know the truth,' Lin Feng said. 'My memories are coming back.'

'Including how Shunshun died?' his dad asked.

'Wasn't it her heart problem?'

'How, *exactly*?'

'Stop it!' His mum choked on her tears. 'It's bad for Fengfeng.'

'Bad for Fengfeng, or for you?' His dad raised his voice again. '*You* don't want to hear it, you think I don't know? Fengfeng remembers Shunshun now, he should learn about her death.'

The cold metal door fogged with Chen Di's breath. Whatever Lin Feng's dad was about to say could only hurt Lin Feng, and she desperately wanted to prevent that. Well, she could, if she knocked on the door. But it wasn't her place to step in. Besides, didn't she have things to do?

'Doctor Zhao let Shunshun spend the 1992 Spring Festival at home,' the dad continued. 'You were only five. Her reoperation had gone well, and though she needed rest, we all hoped she'd be fine...at least for a long time. That morning, your mum took you two downstairs to get some sun, and you sat on a bench under that yulan magnolia just inside the housing estate's entrance. Until this point, Fengfeng, everything was fine. But then you took off.'

'I took off?' Lin Feng asked.

'You ran towards the road! Look, I blame myself a hundred times more than I blame you. I should've gone downstairs with you instead of working on that, that, that damned paper. Who works on the Spring Festival? Fucking researchers! And I blame... I blame your mum for it!'

'For what, Dad? What are you—'

'Your mum was too slow, so it was Shunshun who chased

after you to save you from getting killed by a truck. But Shunshun couldn't—'

'Stop it,' the mum begged.

'Shunshun couldn't run.'

'Stop it...'

'And she had a heart attack. Right there.'

For a long moment no one spoke. The hallway remained so hushed it was as if the window, doors, and lifts were all holding their breaths. The digital numbers above the two lifts flashed, low to high to low. Every time Chen Di thought they'd stop at the eighth floor, they didn't.

'A neighbour banged on our door,' the dad said. 'Downstairs, Shunshun lay on the ground, face bloody. She'd hit her head on the edge of the pavement. You were also unconscious. The crowd said you passed out seeing all the blood.'

'But...' Lin Feng's voice quavered. 'But why did I run out in the first place?'

'You're asking *me* that?' His dad gulped the tea and gagged. 'Shunshun was studious and helpful. You were the opposite. You wouldn't sit still, always running around breaking things. The way I taught her just didn't work on you. Fine, we accepted you were a hard child, but that running wild... That's literally what killed my daughter!'

Run, run, run! Run to your death!

'If only... If only we did what everyone—' The dad cut himself off. 'I-I-I didn't mean to...to say these things, Fengfeng. Of course you ran, kids are supposed to run. You were only five years old. I just... I wish even now that *I* went downstairs with you, that *I* grabbed you before you could—' He let out a long, shaking sigh. 'That day, an ambulance took you both. You woke a changed person, and Shunshun died.'

Chen Di took a step backwards, and another, and slid against the wall to the cold marble floor. She wished Lin Feng wouldn't blame himself but knew he did. None of them should blame themselves. She had the urge to swing open the door and stride inside and talk sense into them all, and hug them all. If it wasn't for the one-child policy, Lin Feng's sister's suffering wouldn't have been the prerequisite for his birth.

Lin Feng's mum sniffled. 'It was my fault.'

'No,' Lin Feng said. 'Mine.'

His dad spoke again in a restrained voice. 'Doctor Wang said you lost memories, and it took forever for your speech to return to normal. We thought it best to start afresh. We moved all the way to Pudong, we didn't wait for time to clear all the gossip, and I quit academia for good. In a year we moved again, back to Puxi, and in a couple of years, yet again. Both your grandmas died. Both your aunts moved to Australia. We never brought up Shunshun again, and you didn't either.' He laughed painfully, then let out a wail. '*You* were supposed to be watching the kids. *You.* My last day as your husband, tell the truth, for once! When Fengfeng took off that day, what were you doing?'

Lin Feng's mum was quiet. Inside the apartment, there came a thud.

'Fengfeng?' the dad said. 'Fengfeng?'

'He'll wake soon,' the mum said.

Lin Feng must've fainted again.

Chen Di hugged her knees, tears brimming in her eyes. Were children of this nation manufactured goods? Home appliances? Limiting numbers and destroying extras, granting a replacement when one malfunctioned... She'd thought poor rural families were the only victims of family planning. Apparently, it also tore apart better-off urban families like Lin Feng's.

Chen Di put her forehead to her knees until bright light shone through the window down the hallway and lit up one family's *Welcome* doormat and another's three pairs of shoes. She didn't know how long she sat there until the white door before her creaked open.

Lin Feng stopped dead, a patch of dark pink showing on his chin, and the look in his eyes made her feel as if she'd opened a cabinet door to see all the glasses inside shatter. But then he smiled faintly, at her. He wanted her to know... everything.

Slowly she rose and watched him, and he did her. She noticed behind him his mum sitting on the same dining chair as before, hanging her head. Chen Di should press the button for the lift but couldn't. It arrived nonetheless. A slow-moving old couple got out and gave her an unsure nod and waved at Lin Feng. 'Fengfeng, how's school?'

He stood still in his doorway, his dark eyes begging Chen Di to take him away. She steeled herself to step into the lift alone.

The doors shut at an excruciatingly slow pace, and the lift budged. It slid to the ground floor without a stop in between. She got out, crossed the foyer, and walked down the marble stairs of Dragon Lake Court. The light was blinding. Numbly she pushed her bicycle down the street, around the corner, down the street again, around the corner again. She looked up after she didn't know how long.

And she halted, finding herself back on the street where Phoenix Sea Court was. She hadn't meant to return the same way. People walked past her on the pavement, old and young, Shanghainese and out-of-towners. Before she could turn around, one of them leaned over.

A heart-shaped face. On each side, a pointed ear with a long lobe.

Time stopped.

'Miss,' Lü Yuandou said, 'I know you from somewhere.'

29
Sichuan
Winter 1998

In Chen Di's dazzling dream, tiny black silkworms speckled mulberry leaves. They ate and moulted, over and over, and turned grey, then white, then translucent. They moved their heads left and right and spun silk cocoons. They metamorphosed inside and broke the cocoons and got out. Two moths made a pair. They laid eggs, tiny yellow ones that slowly turned black, awaiting the next cycle of life. But a fire swallowed all the mulberry trees. The eggs hatched, and the newborns starved. Piles of tiny dead bodies, dry like soot.

Then came noises: rushed footsteps, furniture being dragged around, people weeping. One voice said, 'Are we setting up incense sticks and fruits here? Or there?' Another said, 'You need bricks, cement, sand, and water.' A third said, 'I'll get the cook, your wives can help, and I'll bring some tables and stools over.'

More voices sounded, indoor, outdoor, indistinct.

Chen Di awoke, eyes dry, a sharp headache. She touched her head – it was bandaged. Beside her was their sewing machine and green mahjong table, and she felt she was twelve again, sleeping at home. But the mahjong table had never been moved to the back room before, and she was certainly sixteen. Her body recalled the vague sensation of being carried by someone trudging through the jungle. And she hadn't only been dreaming just now: the noises were real, inside and outside the house.

Someone barged in, her skinny second aunt living in a neighbouring village, her head covered with a white cloth. She didn't even look at Chen Di but grabbed a few candles from a cabinet and went out. Then Uncle Li entered, probably also to get something.

Chen Di sat up, head pounding.

'You're awake!' He turned around and called, 'She's awake!'

Just as Chen Di got off the bed, his wife – Chubby Aunty – came in, holding a white cloth. She lunged at Chen Di to hug her. 'My child!' She tied the cloth over the bandage on her head. 'Your mother... Your mother bled too much...'

Chen Di said nothing, not breathing.

'You hit your head and passed out in the jungle on the west,' Chubby Aunty continued. 'Your father bandaged you, but he's busy now, went to get Mr Yin-Yang. A lot to organise...'

Chen Di stopped listening, head hurting, mind buzzing. She slapped away the lid-attached enamel mug Uncle Li held out. Barefoot, she leaped to the front room crammed with relatives and other villagers, white cloths on heads, arms, everywhere. Disorienting. A young couple present at Mother's abduction now cried at the tops of their voices. The old woman who'd told Lü about her granddaughter's leadership skills kept wiping her eyes.

Despite the number of people, the air in the room was cold.

Then, in the gaps between the people, she saw it: a human body lying on a makeshift plank bed, someone leaning over and applying make-up. Mother. Mother's lifeless body, the belly still bulging.

Chen Di was hyperventilating. Not enough air.

No. This couldn't be real. She backed to a wall, legs shaking. Beside her, yet another new portrait of Mao watched the room, saluting, hand raised high. Chen Di's knees buckled, but she didn't fall. She shot out of the house, legs racing until her foot landed on a lantern, the one that had dropped to the ground before Lü's team had dragged Mother out of the house. A point of reality. Instead of letting the lantern trip her over, Chen Di's foot squashed it into a puddle of blood. The rest of the lanterns glared at her from above, giant bloodthirsty eyes.

'Take down the lanterns!' someone said.

Chen Di took one slow breath. She charged into the wintry field, barren but no longer empty. People burnt paper in a brazier, set up tents, moved tables and stools, and wept, and wept. One child kicked another. All blurry.

She took another slow breath and caught sight of Father, dressed in white. She touched her head, bandaged by him. She wanted to yank off the gauze but couldn't. Father looked oddly calm as he led the way for a Taoist priest with a yin-yang symbol on his robe. For an instant she felt that Father, like her, didn't fit in with the others.

She took yet another slow breath, her lips forming the word, 'Mother,' before the void in her chest swallowed her whole from the inside.

Chen Di howled like a beast, the sound piercing the golden afternoon, scaring away the birds, silencing everyone. When her voice died, her mind was blank apart from the image of a small man with pointy-topped ears and long lobes.

Lü Yuandou, the culprit.

A hand landed on her shoulder – Father's. She whipped around and smacked him so hard it burnt her palm. He opened his mouth only to shut it, his sunken eyes bloodshot. He turned away, revealing wrinkles at the back of his neck she'd never noticed before.

'Give me a minute,' he said to the priest.

Father pulled a leaf from his pocket as if he'd prepared it for this exact occasion. He folded it by the edge, lengthwise. He tucked it between his lips, holding one end with his thumb and index finger, the other with his middle and index finger. He played the leaf whistle. The quiver in his thumbless left hand created vibratos, like a songbird. A folk tune floated through the air, a love song with tidal waves of longing, sad beyond words.

Time flowed backwards. Chen Di had a flash of memory of Father playing the leaf whistle in her childhood, taking her into sleep. It used to soothe her, but now the melody drained her soul. She didn't know for how long she'd been clutching her head, eyes shut, her nails digging into her bandage, her skull. Everyone else seemed to have evaporated, leaving only Chen Di and Father in the world.

She swayed, and slumped to the earth.

Loudspeakers blasted from afar. A grating voice announced a funeral.

Almost simultaneously they both looked towards the west.

The sun was setting.

30
Shanghai
Spring 2002

Time stopped, but the words continued.

'Aren't you from Sichuan?' Lü Yuandou said in a tone anyone might use, seeing an old acquaintance. 'Daci Village, right?' He had on a grey knitted waistcoat and grey trousers and carried two plastic bags. Up close, she noticed light age spots on his cheeks, making his heart-shaped face look older than he really was. Lines extended from the corners of his small eyes, and his hair appeared grey at his temples.

The world morphed into high walls displaying TV static, human shapes flashing, ghostly. Chen Di knew her face gave away nothing, though she wasn't sure whether she was too shocked to react or she'd trained herself to not react.

'You're Old Chen's granddaughter,' Lü said, his voice strangely low.

Chen Di felt her insides being cut out, replaced with salty water. If she wanted to deny it, now was her last chance. In the end she nodded. She could not afford to make a mistake.

'Yes, that is me,' she said with respect. 'How are you, Chief Lü?'

'Call me Uncle Lü.'

'Excuse me?' *Uncle* Lü?

He switched from Mandarin to Sichuanese. 'You can call me Uncle Lü.'

Chen Di gave another nod and moved her lips to form friendly words. 'Hello, Uncle Lü.' Inside her waves surged and crashed, black and furious. She couldn't think. No, she didn't let herself think, afraid any imprudent thoughts would push the waves into a tsunami and burst from her and ruin step three. Ruin her mission. Ruin everything.

Lü watched her a long second and held up the plastic bags. 'I bought too much food. If you're not busy, come to my place. Let's chat over breakfast.' As any old acquaintances would, anywhere in China, bumping into each other.

Chen Di swallowed his words. Lü Yuandou might have an agenda too, but, regardless, Mother's killer was inviting her to breakfast! She didn't need to climb over Phoenix Sea Court's fences, she'd never get such a chance again. *Then what are we waiting for, little sis?* Tang's snigger rang in her head. She tied her ponytail high as she summoned her role model's strength, cruelty, shrewdness, experience, and resolution. She pushed her bicycle in the direction of Lü's outstretched arm, each step bringing her closer to slashing his throat.

Today was the day.

'So you're in Shanghai now.' Lü stared at a far spot. 'Do you live nearby?'

Chen Di snapped her head back, remembering the last few hours of her morning, a sudden ache inside her. Lin Feng's broad, brilliant grin was nowhere to be found.

'Are you all right?' Lü asked.

'Y-Yes.' She clutched her head. This was not like any other times – she'd never, ever forgive herself if she let any undesirable emotions interfere and screw up her face-to-face encounter with Mother's murderer. 'I work at Pizza & Apple Pie, the one at Xu Junction. I had to grab something, then decided to take a walk. What a...sunny day!'

'I'm glad you've done well for yourself.'

Pizza & Apple Pie *was* the best a girl of her background could've done for herself apart from getting a rich husband and a Shanghai household registration. And she couldn't thank Lü Yuandou enough for it. She wanted to laugh – a bitter laugh, a wry one, one that was more crying than laughing.

Chen Di nodded as Lü talked. He maintained a pitch that wasn't nearly as high as she remembered, so unlike the voice that had haunted her village through the loudspeakers. In fact, without looking at him, she wasn't sure if she'd be able to recognise it at all.

'What a coincidence,' he said, 'for us to bump into each other in Big Shanghai.'

Yeah, right. She'd only come to his street for them to 'bump' into each other.

By the stone that read *Phoenix Sea Court*, Chen Di locked her bicycle. She followed Lü up to the foyer and past the guards and the chandelier. It was like a copy of Dragon Lake Court, except she didn't smell any artificial fragrance. The two guards yawned one after the other. She took it all in as she added a bounce to her walk, not quite as relaxed as Tang's, but she was getting there. The next time she passed this area, Lü Yuandou would be dead.

One glass door had an *Out of Order* sign. Lü invited her through the other. In the lift, he pushed the unlucky number, 4. She could easily run down four flights of stairs.

The lift doors opened. The fourth-floor hallway was like in Lin Feng's building, with a window on one side. But six doors appeared instead of three, meaning the apartments were smaller. Lü stopped at a door covered with protective plastic. It read *406*, as expected. *Four* signified *death* and *six* signified *smooth*. She would give him a smooth death.

Indeed, apart from his gnawingly low voice, everything was within expectation.

'We moved here only two months ago,' he said.

We. Another crevice in her imagined reality. Chen Di's hand shook before she regained her concentration, and she tried to breathe evenly.

Lü pushed open the door. 'Meilin!'

'You're back,' said a woman.

'I brought someone.' He bent to pull off his shoes.

A wife made her task harder, but Chen Di would just have to kill them both. She'd already thought about it: whoever supported Lü Yuandou deserved to die too. She rested her hand on the doorjamb, stepped in, and changed into slippers. Calm. She shut the door to see a few quilted coats hanging at the back, red, green, and brown. All old fashioned. They reminded her of something.

The living room was furnished more like Grandma Chu's than Lin Feng's. On the carpeted floor sat a white linen sofa, a simple wooden tea table, and a stand with a bulky TV. By the door to the kitchen stood a low shelf and a square dining table. Judging by the number of doors, the apartment had just two bedrooms. The red character for *Double Happiness* was stuck on one wall – they were newlyweds. Another wall showed some framed awards, not surprising given Lü Yuandou's dedication to the Party.

Lü's wife came, wearing an apron and oversleeves, slightly overweight. She had short hair, her face ruddy and chubby, like a monkey's bottom, and her eyes were kind but set too close together. Tang would snigger.

'This is...' The wife looked from Chen Di to Lü. Her voice was also kind, her Mandarin accent announcing she was Shanghainese.

'I'm Chen Di.' She held out a hand. 'From Sichuan.'

'So you're an old acquaintance of Yuandou.' They shook hands. 'Call me Aunty Gu.'

'I'm ashamed, Young Chen,' Lü said. 'A decade there, I never learned your name.'

Lü Yuandou knew no shame. He had to be acting in front of this Gu Meilin. Chen Di didn't know in what unscrupulous way he'd lured a Shanghainese into marrying him. Well, he *was* a high official now. Gu could be as evil as Lü or else just hopelessly dumb.

'Thank you for having me, Aunty Gu. I'm sorry for...' *Killing you?* '...bothering you.'

'Welcome, Young Chen. Do you feel unwell?'

'Me?'

'I'm a nurse, I can tell.'

'But I'm completely fine, I'm just surprised. What a coincidence!' Chen Di tried to put on her smile. 'Seeing Uncle Lü in Big Shanghai! And that he got married, who would've thought? Wh-What I meant was I just didn't know, I didn't mean he couldn't... Sorry.' *Pull yourself together.*

They asked her to sit at the dining table and busied themselves in the kitchen, opening the plastic bags that contained breakfast, taking out bowls and mugs, boiling water. Chen Di sat in a chair by the window, her hands on the table, her back warmed by sunlight. Through the open kitchen door, Lü moved in and out of view. An oversized knife sat on the worktop, the blade gleaming. Made in America or not, it would do the job just fine.

Streams of water hit the sink as Lü whispered to Gu. Chen Di couldn't catch his words and didn't need to, it didn't matter what they talked about. She could head into the kitchen and take them down, now. Except... She inhaled, exhaled, her eyes fixed on a peach-coloured cake box on the low shelf beside her. Was it someone's birthday?

She pictured Tang's comical eyepatch to relax her mind, and her body. *Tread carefully. You have only one shot.*

'Are you...really all right?' Gu came out. 'You're sweating.'

'I'm fine.' Chen Di wiped her forehead. 'I really am.' And she noticed that Gu was sweating herself, a look of hesitance added to her kind face.

Gu carefully set bamboo baskets of flatbread, fried dough sticks, and tea eggs on the table. Lü came with a tray holding three mugs of oolong tea, his hands shaking slightly, his wrists looking weak. At last, the time had come for her to use her aikido wrist locks. They weren't as strong as Tang's but would also do the job. Just fine.

'Would you like some hot milk?' Lü asked.

'No, thanks,' she said.

Lü didn't push it the way most hosts would. The couple sat on either side of her, and Chen Di imagined herself in a courtroom, she the judge.

Lü sighed, then said quietly, more to himself, 'I didn't think I'd meet anyone from Daci again, but first him, then you.'

'First who?' she asked. Another Daci villager?

'Don't worry about it.' He sighed again. 'Heaven brought you here. Please eat, eat.'

Heaven had not brought her there. Hatred had. Years of hard work.

'How long have you been living in Shanghai?' Gu's smile felt like an apology. 'Life is so hard for out-of-towners. Do you have relatives here? Tell us if you need anything.'

Gu Meilin wasn't playing games – she was a genuinely kind person. Chen Di had the urge to expose the evil of the man she'd ended up with. She glanced at Lü, his long lobes that looked as unfitting on his ears now as they had then.

'Sorry,' Gu said, 'that was a lot of questions.'

'I've lived here for three years.' And today would be her last day. Chen Di couldn't wait to leave Shanghai. 'I'm getting by fine, thank you for asking.'

Lü wrapped a fried dough stick in a flatbread, the way any normal person might enjoy the food. 'Is your father well?'

Chen Di stared at him, jarred by the seemingly ordinary question, or perhaps his tone. It was as if Lü actually cared about her family. *My father's alive,* she wanted to say, *unlike my mother.* She pushed out the words: 'He's fine.' In truth, she didn't know whether he was. Her father could've died in the last three years. A leaf whistle sounded in her mind again, a folk love song conjuring up tidal waves of longing, draining her soul.

She grabbed a tea egg and broke its shell on the table. 'How did the two of you meet?' If they talked for a while, she'd have time to plan. Plus, the more someone blabbered, the more they dropped their guard.

Gu sipped some tea. 'Soon after Yuandou came here, his bicycle was hit by a truck.'

'That's awful.' Chen Di tried to sound like she meant it. She was six steps from the kitchen door. It'd take her three seconds to get there, another two to grab the knife on the worktop. She might not be as fast as Tang, but Lü and Gu wouldn't have even reacted in those five seconds. She would return with the knife in her right hand, seize Lü's left wrist with her left hand, slide behind him, stab his kidney from the back, and twist out the blade. *White knife in, red knife out,* she could almost hear Tang say.

'It was a bad accident, he almost died.' Gu gave Lü a benign look. Lü only munched his food. 'I happened to be Yuandou's nurse. Many years ago, my first husband had in fact passed away in a bus accident, and life hadn't been easy. Not financial-wise, but my son is autistic. Well, now, Yuandou and I take care of him together.'

But do you know this man murdered babies and mothers? Chen Di gulped the tea and barely chewed the egg before swallowing. How close was Gu to her relatives? How long would it take before anyone learned about the couple's death? Then she paused, having processed all of Gu's words. 'Where is your son?'

'At a tutoring session, but he's really there to help others. He's a little genius.' Gu looked proud, her ruddy cheeks reddening. 'Young Chen, I want to hear more about you.'

A kid with autism helping out at a cram school. Chen Di weighed the fact. Before she could conclude anything, Gu spoke again, her voice still so kind.

'Back when I was Yuandou's nurse, he already told me about your mother.'

31
Sichuan
1998–1999

The cold night wind whipped Chen Di's cheeks, stung her eyes. The moon was nowhere. She scanned the hilly burial site, lonely trees here and there, to check if anyone was around. No one, save for the dead. In Daci Village, women, menstruating and therefore filthy by definition, were not allowed to sweep the ancestral graves. They'd clash with the ancestors and break the peace of the dead, and in turn, cause them to stop protecting the family.

But Chen Di knew Mother would want her there.

'A ghost!' a voice shrieked in the distance. They must've seen Chen Di's shadowy form. 'Let's go, let's go, let's go!'

'The big pit's ghost woman?' said another.

'Go! She'll possess us.'

Chen Di stared at the two silhouetted figures as they scurried away and disappeared behind a hill. She laughed quietly. Fools.

The dozen ancestral graves before her appeared disorganised, each family having chosen their own style of headstones. But as tradition dictated, they were all positioned near the creek and against the hills to ensure later generations' prosperity. The eldest generation's headstones stood at the front of each grave, their sons' and daughters-in-law's in the second row, their sons' sons' and sons' daughters-in-law's in the third row, and so on. Unmarried daughters had no right to be buried in an ancestral grave as they were believed to cause deformities in the family's future newborns.

With no male child to continue the family name and her husband still alive, Mother had no right to be buried there. Except she *had* been, by Father.

Chen Di stopped at the right end of the third row of her family's grave and touched Mother's headstone, rectangular, cold and hard. She knelt before it and didn't cry. She put down bananas, tangerines, grapefruits, and a bowl of rice. She opened her plastic bag and poured out a pile of money for the dead: gold and silver paper folded into the shape of ingots used as currency in the Qing dynasty. She lit a match. The flames spread from one ingot to two to four to eight, swallowing the gold and the silver. They blackened and sagged and turned into ashes, disappearing to the other world like Mother had, for Mother to spend.

'Mother, I'll find justice for you.'

Chen Di kowtowed before the headstone, forehead to the earth. Once. Twice. Three times.

Just as she rose, a crescent moon poked out between the clouds. It lit the whole area, including, one row to the front, the back of Grandfather's headstone.

Right after Mother's death, Grandfather had collapsed at the village health centre. Brain haemorrhage, apparently, not the heart attack he'd been warned about. Thinking back, Chen Di simply hadn't registered his absence the afternoon Mother's body had been brought back, and it'd taken another week for him to stop breathing.

Now she stared at Grandfather's headstone, just like Mother's. *He was kind enough to let us keep our first child: you.* But regardless of how many lives he'd let Chen Di live, he had asked Mother for a grandson again. And that, was unforgivable.

'Be grateful, Grandfather, that I'm not spitting on you.'

It was too convenient for him to die like this. After all, Mother's death had extinguished his hope of having another grandson, and he'd had nothing else to live for.

Over the weeks, their story had spread fast because the abortion had led to the death of three generations in the same family. It'd also become Lü Yuandou's last intervention in family planning before he left the county. He was not returning to his original position in Chengdu but leaving Sichuan Province altogether. Awarded the honour of Advanced Worker, plus his connection with a big shot in the Ministry of Health, and given his deceased father had been Shanghainese to start with – sent to Sichuan decades ago to support interior China – Lü would be posted to the Family Planning Commission in Shanghai.

A gust of wind shook the scattered trees. Chen Di left the burial site and walked the paths back to the school, meandering and uphill.

Lü Yuandou is a monster. Between our fellow countrymen's outdated mindset and the Party's authoritarian policies, he's found an opportunity to prey on people. She stepped into the school office that night, realising she'd understood each one of Teacher Jia's words.

Outdated mindset, like valuing boys over girls.

Authoritarian policies, like family planning.

The school's electricity was no longer cut at night. She pulled off her green jacket and fished out a book from Teacher Jia's box. She read under the light from the dim bulb, immersing herself in the story, empathising with the characters, analysing the themes. In Chinese and foreign books, fiction and non-fiction alike, she was most inspired by the vigilantes: female assassins like Mistress Marcia, who poisoned Roman Emperor Commodus, and Nie Yinniang, who killed undetected with her martial arts skills.

With each reading, Chen Di understood Teacher Jia's words all over again.

Summer arrived. One humid night, Chen Di tied her ponytail high and headed to the burial site again, holding a bunch of incense sticks. A full moon brightened the path, the trees, the houses, the fields, and her. But she didn't think she'd be spotted. It was the middle of the night, and no one swept the ancestral graves at this hour.

Except this particular evening, a lanky figure crouched before Mother's headstone.

Father.

She stood far away and listened to the crickets. If it had been anyone else there, she would've turned back. But it was Father in the silvery light, reading from a booklet. As if all his sutras could truly help him make sense of life. His life. He tucked the booklet in his pocket and joined his hands before Mother's headstone, then rose. When he moved to wipe Grandfather's headstone, Chen Di marched over.

Father turned. His wrinkles had deepened like old bark, his eyes widening with a surprise that was both happy and sad. 'You came, Chen Di.'

'How faithful you are, to your owner.'

A tremor in his hands. 'Do you still hate your grandfather?'

'And his dog.'

'I...understand, but your grandfather—'

'Grandfather, what? He forced Mother to get pregnant again!' For the first time since Mother's death, Chen Di's eyes welled. Tears threatened to spill.

'No, your mother was willing.'

'She was *not*.'

'She wanted a son, too.'

'She did *not*.' Yet Chen Di remembered the night Father had gripped Mother's hand and kissed her. No, it wasn't just that night. Her parents had lived under the same roof since their teens. Father had always known Mother better than she had.

'Like your grandfather's wife – the grandmother you've never met – your mother felt it was her responsibility to give birth to a son.'

Chen Di stared at him, jarred by the mention of a 'grandmother'. Grandfather's wife had died so long ago that no one, not even Grandfather himself, had said much about her. Now she couldn't help but wonder how her life might've been different had her grandmother lived to this day. And suddenly they came into focus – two vague syllables she'd heard Grandfather utter. 'Was my grandmother named Xixi?'

'That was her nickname. She died during the Great Famine.'

Which Grandfather had outlived, eating bark and roots...

'Your grandfather made me kowtow to her grave once he'd brought me home. She was buried a few hills away then, but I've moved her here now to keep them together.' Father laid a hand on the headstone beside Grandfather's, and Chen Di leaned back. Had there really been a woman whom Grandfather loved, who loved him? 'Your grandmother felt she'd failed as a wife because she hadn't been able to bear a child. It was *her* dying wish for her husband to remarry and have a son to carry on the family name.'

Chen Di didn't want to look away, but did.

'And it wasn't just your grandfather who was stubborn...'

'What?'

'Your grandmother loved cotton and dreamed of growing

it. So fluffy and snug, she told him, unlike silk, lustrous, flashy, trying hard to stand out.'

Chen Di couldn't imagine Grandfather telling Father all this, but if he'd really made Father kowtow to his late wife's grave, wanting Father to treat her as his own mother... 'Enough of the excuses. If Grandfather truly cared about his late wife, he wouldn't have treated any women the way he did.'

Sweat trickled down the sides of her face, and his. Father remained silent and still, not arguing back. He removed his hand from the headstone.

'Back to your mother,' he said. 'She was fitted with a coil at the time, no real surgical procedure on her or on me. And after the...the loss of Little Tiger, she had the coil removed without official permission.'

'No!' Chen Di cried out, tears tracing down her cheeks.

'It is the truth.'

'It isn't!' She staggered back to Mother's headstone, incense sticks falling from her hand. 'Grandfather forced her to have it removed! He forced her and you did nothing!'

Mother had said Chen Di was enough.

Footfalls behind her. 'Your grandfather was not all bad.'

'He was only good to his dog!' Her cry cut through the crickets' chirps, words she no longer fully believed in. She turned to leave. 'I don't want to hear another thing you say.'

'Wait, please come home? It's just you and me left.'

She ignored his plea, walking away fast, trampling on the fallen twigs, headstones blurring past her in moonlight. The wind from her own momentum dried her tears.

'Don't forget me, Chen Di!' Father's voice chased her out of the burial site.

She *would* forget him.

Lying in bed that night, Chen Di heard a leaf whistle, a soothing melody rising, falling. She jumped up and looked out only to realise the tune was in her head. Father's voice echoed as she returned to bed. *Don't forget me, Chen Di! Don't forget me, Chen Di!* Like a curse.

When she finally drifted into sleep, eyes open, she saw the same nightmare she'd been seeing since the 1994 harvest. Again she stood alone on the precipice, eyes forced open, expecting to slip on the gravel but not slipping, legs paralysed.

Chen Di repeated to herself Lü Yuandou's role in causing Mother's death. It was his fault, all his. She murmured it while sweeping the school grounds, cooking, eating, hanging her laundry, stashing away her savings, and kowtowing before Mother's headstone. Every so often, she found herself amidst the bamboo without knowing how she'd got there.

She deserved to live, and live well.

Lü did not.

It was wrong for her to waste away in this village. Chen Di didn't care how Lü died, but he needed to. If no one and nothing else could do the job, then she'd be a public avenger. That'd be the most meaningful thing she could accomplish in this senseless world. On behalf of all families ruined by family planning policies, of all lives lost, she would execute the monster.

Spring Festival, 1999. While villagers working in cities

returned, happily flocking back into the village, seventeen-year-old Chen Di sold what she could and closed the covers of Teacher Jia's last remaining book. Getting her hands on a gun seemed unthinkable, and poison was unreliable if Lü had access to Shanghai hospitals, so a good knife would have to do. And regardless of the weapon, training would help. She just had to find the right martial art.

Two weeks later, under the full moon of the Lantern Festival, she disappeared alongside the villagers returning to work as she embarked on a journey to Shanghai.

Her mission in mind, she left behind her little village of big benevolence.

32
Shanghai
Spring 2002

Fury coursed through Chen Di.

Who are you, woman named Gu, to talk about Mother!

She had long stored in her head the series of events from the 1998 Lantern Festival. Now they returned all at once: Mother being tied up and hauled like a farm animal, her sweat- and tear-soaked face, her eight-month belly, the bright-red jeep.

As she mentally transported herself to Master Mu's dojo, Chen Di felt so over-prepared in her training she almost laughed. Sniggered. She didn't need to summon Tang's superior abilities. Lü Yuandou might've appeared fearsome back then, but the couple sitting before her in this apartment was defenceless. Chen Di killing them would be like slaughtering chickens with a knife meant for butchering cows. She scanned Lü's age spots that'd come too early, his wrists only strong enough to hold a flatbread. A kid could take him down.

Outside, the sun shone brighter, the day as beautiful as that late morning in Daci Village, except now the roles were reversed. Her eyes wandered from the woman with ruddy cheeks, who seemed nothing but kind, to the man focused on munching his food. This was not what she'd expected, but enough was enough. Tang would've killed and fled by now.

Just as she was about to rise, Lü raised a hand, alarming her. But he only rubbed his forehead, his eyes squeezed shut as if in pain.

Gu spoke. 'Yuandou regrets so much.'

'What?' Chen Di blurted, her palms pressed on the table.

Lü joined his hands and lowered his head, his forehead touching his fingertips. 'Young Chen, I'm so sorry.'

She sprang up, she did not want his excuses. He'd ruined her life, the lives of too many. This man was a monster! He deserved death! She glanced back through the open kitchen door at the knife.

'I'm no longer the person I was,' Lü said in that low voice. 'Today I invited you over so I could beg for your forgiveness.'

'Shut up,' she whispered, shaking.

Across the table, Gu snivelled. 'Circumstances made him do those horrible things.'

How dare she appeal to sympathy! Chen Di had none.

'That's unimportant, Meilin.' Lü looked up at Gu, then at Chen Di.

She hated listening to them. She would never forgive this man regardless of what he or his wife said. She was five steps from the kitchen door, seven from that knife. *Move!*

'But it's the truth.' Gu moved around the table to hug Lü's shoulders. 'If you met me, met Deke, all those years ago, you wouldn't have...'

'Deke?' Chen Di asked, and regretted. She did not want to comment, to ask anything.

'Deke is Meilin's son, our son,' Lü said. 'Meilin and Deke taught me love.'

Gu used her oversleeve to wipe her own eyes, then Lü's. Three years in Shanghai, Chen Di had planned for everything. Yet this reality before her: a remorseful man weeping, begging for forgiveness with his hands joined, his kind wife by his side, the child they shared...

'I regret,' Lü said to the table. 'I cringe at all the atrocities I committed back then. My last case in Sichuan, your mother's case—'

'Shut up,' Chen Di said, louder.

'Her case pushed me over the edge, she reminded me of... of my...'

His ex-wife. She'd figured that much from all his talks of a fox spirit. But so? She had no obligation to give a damn about his lousy life. 'Shut up!'

'All the death – babies, mothers – passed through me in one go. I had to leave, and I came to Shanghai feeling like a walking corpse. Maybe that was why my bicycle wandered into that truck...' Lü's hands joined so tightly they trembled together, his nails digging into his forehead. 'Whatever you need from me, say it.'

I need you to die.

Chen Di pictured Lü and Gu collapsed on the floor. She would go down, exit Phoenix Sea Court, stop a taxi, ask to be taken to her longtang, grab her backpack, get back into the car, head to Shanghai Railway Station, and buy the earliest ticket to Shenzhen. From there she'd get a pass to Hong Kong, Teacher Jia's real hometown. And some day, she'd escape China entirely and settle down in a warm place.

She had to do this! Do this, and she'd finally get there, finally be able to start a new life. She gave one last look to the teary couple, trying her best to disregard the loving way Gu hugged Lü's shoulders. Chen Di couldn't walk with a bounce, but no matter, she'd do it her way. She marched towards the kitchen for the knife.

Only her leg knocked that peach-coloured cake box off the low shelf. It flipped open, pouring things on the floor.

She gasped.

They were silkworms, dozens of them, in shades of grey. They squirmed on the floor, some struggling to orient themselves, others clinging onto mulberry leaves. One was moulting, half its body stuck in old skin. Another was deflated. Dead.

Chen Di could no longer head to the kitchen without stepping on the silkworms, and more, she felt a need to scoop them back into their home. Her legs gave out and she slumped back in the chair, panting.

The door creaked. 'I'm back.'

She snapped her head around to find a teenage boy, about Lin Feng's age, taking off his shoes. She looked back at the couple beside her. Child, mother, father. She had an impulse to kidnap the boy, to do to Lü what he had done to countless families.

'Wh-Wh-What's happening?' The boy put down a school bag.

Gu and Lü remained silent.

Chen Di shuddered. She hadn't considered the possibility of their son coming home. Had she slashed their throats two minutes earlier, he would've walked right into the scene.

And when the boy rose, she held onto the table, her lips parting. An image flashed across her mind, one from the night of this year's Lantern Festival, of a father-and-son pair strolling around. The son had had narrow shoulders and worn square glasses, like the boy before her eyes. And the father in the brown quilted coat had bent his head to talk to the son, his posture so humble that Chen Di had written him off as anyone but Lü…

Right now, that brown quilted coat was hanging behind the apartment door.

Chen Di clenched her teeth to pick herself up and went around the far side of the table to get to the door, not letting her steps falter, not looking back at the couple or the silkworms. She ignored the boy too, as well as all the quilted coats, but noticed the awards on the wall again: *Xinhui Cup Mathematical Competition*, *The Yifu Award*, *Youth Calligraphy Contest*. They were not Lü's but the boy's.

She put on her canvas shoes with difficulty, her feet seemed to have swollen.

Gu caught up to her, her ruddy face even redder than before. 'Please wait, Young Chen.' She held out a crisp note showing handwritten words and numbers. She folded it in half and passed it to Chen Di. 'Please come back for another visit.'

'Wh-Who is this, Mum?' the boy said. 'What's happening?'

'Come back for another visit,' Gu repeated. 'Please.'

Chen Di walked out, one heel not yet in her shoe.

———

She didn't know how she rode back to her longtang. All was blurry under the blinding sun: the traffic, the trees, the buildings – new or old, Chinese or European-style. In her unit, she poured hot water into cold rice for lunch, without adding a cube of fermented tofu or pickled mustard stems or even chilli bean paste. She lay in bed, the line of light under her door dimming.

Chen Di had to do the right thing for Mother. To spare the culprit was to deem Mother's life worthless – someone had to pay for her death! Well, who, if not Lü? She blamed the cultural obsession over sons, still rampant in rural areas, and she blamed the Party's policies. But you couldn't take revenge on such abstract things. Grandfather was dead, and Father was hardly a human with his own will. The only person she could pin her hatred on was Lü.

Or…

She wiped the cold sweat from her face and pulled her quilt over her head. The man behind it all *was* Lü Yuandou, who'd made Daci Village what it was. *Lü Yuandou is a monster. Between our fellow countrymen's outdated mindset and the*

Party's authoritarian policies, he's found an opportunity to prey on people.

But how could such a predator be a father? How had that man become this man? Apparently, Lü was capable of remorse.

'Teacher Jia,' she said to the ceiling, 'what should I do?'

Chen Di jumped up and swung open the door to her wooden wardrobe. She punched Lü's headshot, the door squeaking, and tore the paper into pieces and watched them flutter.

Then she glimpsed *The Art of Peace* on her chest of drawers. It'd been drenched and dried, the pages now wavy, but the large calligraphic circle on the cover remained solid and imposing. She thought she'd forgotten about the book, but a line from it sprang to mind. *We put ourselves in tune with the universe, maintain peace in our own realms, nurture life, and prevent death and destruction.*

She swept the book into a drawer.

She reached into her jeans pocket for Gu Meilin's note. It showed their home phone number, her mobile number, and Lü's mobile number. How thoughtful. Her mind lingered on Gu's kind face and their son. Lü Yuandou had risen from his guilt, while Chen Di herself...

The room had never felt so stuffy.

She flopped back down and closed her eyes and clutched her head. She imagined Teacher Jia's arms around her, so tight he was killing her.

33

Chen Di was woken by steady knocks on her iron door.
'Who?'

'It's me.' Master Mu's deep voice took her to the dojo.

She jumped to open the door and realised it was already night-time, the longtang dimly lit by overhead bulbs. She couldn't remember dozing off.

Master Mu's goatee made him look even sterner than usual, like a day of winter in the midst of spring. He walked right in, sat on the edge of the bed, and watched her with a probing gaze. His presence made her unit feel smaller than it already was.

'I don't have tea, not even hot water.' Chen Di's voice was tight. She poured a mug of cold water and put it down beside his feet, then took her seat on the small bamboo chair.

'Three things brought me here,' he said.

She waited.

'First, I know you're leaving Shanghai.'

'How...' Besides Tang, who obviously didn't side with

Master Mu, she'd only told Manager Chu and Grandma Chu that.

'So, my question is, have you let go of your thirst for vengeance?'

Chen Di looked down at her hands in her lap. 'I don't know what you're talking about.' Yesterday she would've said the line more spontaneously, Master Mu's voice entering her head from one ear and exiting from the other. But tonight, she attached meaning to his words.

'I'll be more direct then. Since you're leaving, does it mean you've changed your mind? About that revenge against an official?'

Her heart jumped. 'Y-You have no evidence!'

Master Mu sipped some water and kept the mug in his hand. He looked like he was debating something, then let out a long sigh, the concentration in his eyes she'd never seen before. 'Perhaps I should've told you this long ago.'

She sat stiffly on the chair, heart still throbbing. 'What?'

'Shortly after you left your village, your father did too. To look for you.'

'Sorry?' She must've misheard him.

'Your father spent seven months in Shanghai, sweeping the streets, thinking about his dead father, dead wife, dead son, dead infant daughters, and you, what you'd done, what they'd done to you. And in the autumn of 1999, when the roads reddened with banners celebrating our country's fiftieth anniversary, he found you.'

No, she mouthed.

'To search for one person in Big Shanghai is like to scoop up a needle in the ocean, it was nothing short of a miracle. But your father asked everywhere, mentioning your birthmark, and some people remembered seeing you outside the dojo. So for weeks, your father waited there, in the distance, watching you come and go. Until I approached him one day. He couldn't face you, he said, and he knew you didn't want to see him. He then knelt before me, imploring me not to say a word about him and look after you on his behalf.'

'No...' *Because of someone who knows you, though I promised to not reveal the identity.* Father had been the one asking Master Mu to meddle in her business?

'After which he went far away to shave his head, and became a monk.'

'A *monk?*' As outlandish as it all sounded, Master Mu was too charitable, too devout, to have refused such a request from a Buddhist monk.

Then she heard it again: a leaf whistle. Memories flashed across her mind, of Father taking away her baby sister, Father boiling medicine for Mother, Father watching Grandfather beat them, Father giving his seat to Teacher Jia, Father following Grandfather like a dog, Father calling her home, Father begging her to remember him. A part of Chen Di was so moved she wanted to cry. Another part wanted to yell, to hurl her chair across the room.

'So, Young Chen, don't bother denying anything, because your father told me everything.' Master Mu sipped some more water, giving her time. He lowered the mug and slowly deposited it on the floor, letting the silence deepen.

Chen Di's hands trembled in her lap. So Father had guessed, correctly, that she'd travelled to Shanghai for revenge against Lü Yuandou. Father knew her. He did more than she'd ever assumed. Father, the monk...

'And you are still vengeful, it's in your eyes,' Master Mu said before she was ready to hear more of his words. Well, no matter how much time he gave her, it wouldn't be enough to digest all this. 'I know it when I see someone vengeful because I, too, once sought revenge.'

She stared at him, still picturing Father with a shaved head, holding a booklet of sutra, chanting in a faraway temple. '*You*...sought revenge?'

'I went to Japan back then not only to build my company, but also to know my enemies and seek revenge.'

'Against the Japanese?'

'I spent my childhood during our Resistance Against Japanese Aggression, my hometown being Nanjing.' Nanjing, the only Chinese city whose name alone evoked images of a massacre. 'In my earliest memory, I hid in a cupboard, shaking as I watched four Japanese soldiers raping my mother and two sisters, slicing off their breasts after the fact.'

Chen Di couldn't even open her mouth, her jaw locked closed with shock. Outside the dojo, she'd caught passers-by giving Master Mu hostile looks. One man had called him 'Little Japs' running dog' and another had said to his face, 'Aren't you ashamed of yourself as a Chinese? Teaching Japanese martial arts on Chinese soil humiliates the people of China!' Never had she expected him to have such a personal history. If anything, she'd assumed him to be a Japan enthusiast, a mature version of some anime-obsessed kids at Pizza & Apple Pie. 'Then how… How did your life turn out as it did?'

'After the war, I was fortunate that a good Shanghainese family took me in. But as you can imagine, for decades I lived in utter hatred.'

Chen Di nodded. 'Then you went to Japan?'

'As soon as China opened up. And my experiences there were nothing like I expected. In Japan I met my wife, a devout Buddhist. I found aikido. As the years went by, I let go of my obsession with vengeance—'

'How could you!'

'I could.'

'But your mother and sisters… Are you not human?'

'I am, and that's why I could let go of it.'

'But you betrayed them!' Her hands shook. 'People literally call you "Little Japs' running dog". You know how some people think of you.'

He waited before saying, 'I do. My son is among them.'

Chen Di's mind zoomed to the small photo at his unit, of a smiling young couple posing in Tiananmen Square. 'But isn't your son half-Japanese himself?'

'That's not how he'd like to think.' Master Mu averted the eyes that no longer seemed so penetrating. For an instant he didn't look like some martial arts master, just a father in pain. It hit Chen Di that he could lose his cool too, that his life wasn't all set either. And perhaps... Perhaps he had connected with her father for more reasons than she'd assumed.

Master Mu looked back at her with a renewed intent on his face. 'I could let go of my desire for vengeance, Young Chen, and so could you.' Even as he picked up the mug and sipped more water, he didn't take his eyes off her again, the eyes that forced her to ask herself if she could forget her vengeance.

Could she? Her answer would've been a clear 'no', yesterday. But the Lü Yuandou in her mind today was a different person.

'This brings me to the second item I want to talk about.' He glanced at her wardrobe, covered with knife gouges. 'Have you thought about the Great Teacher's words?'

The Art of Peace. Chen Di moved around the bed and pulled it out from her top drawer. She held it out to Master Mu. 'Please have it back.'

He didn't take it. '*The Art of Peace is medicine for a sick world.*'

She recognised the line, and said nothing.

'*There is evil and disorder in the world because people have forgotten that all things emanate from one source. Return to that source and...?*'

'*Leave behind all self-centred thoughts, petty desires, and anger.*'

'*Those who are possessed by nothing?*'

'*Possess everything.*' It shocked Chen Di how much she remembered from the book. *The Art of Peace* had only been a disguise to help her stalk Lü, and yet it was as if she'd studied it the way she had Four Three's writing, as if she'd absorbed the messages.

'Keep the book.'

Silently she put it on her bed.

'I still trust you, Young Chen. I believe you can save yourself.'

She dropped back on her small bamboo chair, disturbed by the change she sensed inside herself. But Mother's life had meant something, and *someone* had to pay.

'Here.' Master Mu held out his palm, her Voyager folded on it. Chen Di's jaw dropped. She hadn't expected him to give it back – hadn't thought she deserved it back, not in his book. He placed it on *The Art of Peace,* at the centre of the calligraphic circle. 'Use a knife to protect people, not to kill. This brings me to the last item I want to talk about.'

She sat up again, breathing slowly.

'I want you to help me protect someone.'

'To *protect* someone?'

'He's your friend.'

'You must be joking, Master Mu. You know I don't have friends.'

'I'm talking about Lin Feng.'

Chen Di stiffened. She'd almost forgotten about everything that had happened before her breakfast at Lü's. Lin Feng's apartment, his pets, his 'take me with you', and her pretending to be his teacher, learning about his parents' divorce and his sister's death. What was Lin Feng up to now? Suddenly she wished Master Mu hadn't brought her Voyager but instead its thief.

'Young Tang bears a grudge against Lin Feng's family,' he said.

She knew that, but she'd already involved herself more than she should have. 'Neither Lin Feng nor Tang-senpai has anything to do with me.'

Master Mu placed the mug in his palm. 'How should I put it? I consider Lin Feng a linking thread in this circle of people. His fate will determine everyone else's fate.'

She couldn't buy that. 'Whose?'

'Yours, for one.'

'This is getting absurd. Lin Feng and I met by coincidence.'

'What is a coincidence? Yuanfen brought you together, brought us together. We, human beings, are all interconnected parts of a whole.'

Chen Di was reminded of not only Yuanfen Eatery but also Lin Feng's sister's words. *No one ever dies, because we're all connected.* 'There is no yuanfen between us,' she said, as much to Master Mu as to herself. 'We are not connected.'

'Well, I knew Lin Feng's family from a long time ago.'

She looked at him. 'Excuse me?'

'Back when I was helping Young Tang with legal trouble.'

Right. This had to be about Tang's lost eye and his uncle's death.

Master Mu drained the mug. 'One of my informants saw Young Tang with Lin Feng earlier today, having wonton soup down in Dragon Lustre.'

Chen Di shivered. *How I get my job done without getting*

my hands dirty? By guilting a kid who's already depressed – and, should I say, suicidal. Lin Feng had gone to Tang after learning about his sister's death, the worst thing he could've done to himself. She couldn't help but wonder how things would've been different for him, and her, had she taken him away from his apartment this morning and never gone to Lü's place.

'Linking threads are not to be broken,' Master Mu said.

Chen Di poured herself some water and gulped it down. She clutched the empty mug, wanting to tell him – and herself – that Lin Feng was none of her concern. She could no longer. 'As you know,' she said, 'I'm leaving Shanghai—'

'At the end of April.'

No, within days.

'Young Chen, even without your father's pleading, I would've done everything I could have. I'm responsible for you, and for Young Tang. You are my students.'

'*Former* students.'

He placed his palms on his knees. 'Since you're leaving Shanghai soon and it doesn't sound like you've let go of your thirst for vengeance, I can only assume the worst.'

She sprang up, but words failed her.

Master Mu rose too. 'I'm going to keep a closer eye on your every move.'

'You're *not*.'

'I will not let my students commit crimes.'

He opened the door and walked out fast. Chen Di's heart wouldn't stop pounding, even though it didn't sound like

Master Mu knew about her breakfast at Lü's. He was serious. He had the will and the means to ruin her mission.

She poked her head out of her unit and looked up the dark alley to see Master Mu and Grandma Chu nod at each other like acquaintances, half their faces lit by a dim bulb. She ducked back inside and closed her door. Grandma Chu had mentioned 'powerful people behind you' – she was referring to Master Mu. And that day, when Master Mu had come to Pizza & Apple Pie, Manager Chu had blinked non-stop, flustered like a shoplifter caught in the act…

Chen Di sat heavily on her bed. During her first year in Shanghai, she had lived in a more expensive longtang and worked in a disgusting eatery before Grandma Chu had materialised out of nowhere. She'd stopped Chen Di on the street, offering a cheap rental unit, saying her nephew was hiring at Pizza & Apple Pie. It'd all happened the winter after she had started aikido.

Had Master Mu followed the request of her father – *monk* father – and gone so far as to sort out her life for her?

She let her back fall on the bed and turned to her side, her face touching both her Voyager and *The Art of Peace*. From day one, she'd known Master Mu's good intentions for her. But, like Tang, she'd always laughed off his lectures. She'd never felt she was at risk of being convinced by Master Mu's philosophy, until now.

Except even if she let go of her hatred, she still had to do it.

No matter how Lü Yuandou had changed, she still had to do it. For Mother.

34

Legs paralysed, Chen Di stood alone on a precipice, looking down into the canyon. The surroundings darkened, the cliffs reddening as if smeared with fresh blood. Gusts of wet, chilly wind slapped her face, howled in her ears, and froze her from within. Then the bushes behind her rustled. She spun around before realising she *could* move, to find Lü Yuandou, still young.

'So you came to kill me?' he said in a high voice.

'You!' She lunged, seized his hand, twisted his wrist, and pinned him face down into the bushes. She knelt on his back and bent his arm in the most painful way she knew.

But Lü turned his head to look at her, a smile plastered across his heart-shaped face, his breathing steady. Then he chuckled.

'What's so funny?' Chen Di yelled, and heard her voice echoing around the canyon. *What's so funny? What's so funny?* A drip of her sweat fell on his cheek, and he kept chuckling, the pitch higher and higher.

'What's funny,' he said, 'is that you want me dead.'

'So Mother can rest in peace!'

'And she can't because?'

'*You* are asking *me* that?' She flipped him around and locked her hands around his neck, her thumbs digging into his flesh. 'Because she died a miserable death!'

A flash of lightning made Lü's face look ghostly, and thunder rumbled. His small eyes fixated on hers, and narrowed, his unspoken words clear to her: there would have been no death, no abortion, no pregnancy, had Little Tiger still been around.

Chen Di recoiled, almost letting go of him.

Lü spoke again, breezy despite her nails in his neck. 'How funny it is that you want *me* dead.'

When she'd been the one to lose Little Tiger.

Everything stilled, no wind, no sound. Even the dark clouds stopped moving, each blade of grass frozen in time. Then a large black bird swooped down. Chen Di ducked but its wing swept the back of her head, spreading a rotten odour. Two more black birds appeared. Four more. A flock. They let out a chorus of piercing calls as they circled overhead, attacking her at unexpected moments. Hard beaks pecked at her face, cold claws pulling out her hair. She frantically slapped away the birds and was forced to let go of Lü.

When she looked back, he lay comfortably in the bushes, brushing dust off his suit jacket. He interlocked his hands and placed them under his head like a pillow, leaving his body vulnerable to assault. But Chen Di could no longer strike.

Suddenly lines showed on Lü's forehead and the sides of his eyes, his short hair turning grey at the temples, age spots materialising. He said in a low voice, 'Young Chen, I've done something about my guilt, while you—'

'*You* turned me into a murderer! It was all you! You! You!'

Jarred awake by her own screams, Chen Di panted and felt like choking. She touched her neck, and swallowed. It had been a dream. She pressed a hand to her chest but quickly let go, reminded of Grandfather doing the same back then. She wiped her sweaty forehead and both sides of her face, feeling as if she was spiralling down, down, down.

After all these years, her familiar nightmare had changed.

And she knew what it all meant.

The bright line of light under her iron door signalled the sun being high in the sky. It must be late. She couldn't believe she'd slept for that long. She fumbled around for her tube of eye ointment and couldn't find it. She felt a creeping sense of something eating away at her, reaching into her soul for her darkest secrets. She flinched, and shut her painfully dry eyes.

Lü Yuandou had killed Mother, and Lü Yuandou had to pay for it. There was no other way for her to move on. Only by killing him could she put an end to it...

And stop blaming herself for Mother's death.

Chen Di perched on her bed, bowl in hand, and chopsticked rice topped with mapo tofu, too spicy even for her. She'd added chilli bean paste twice without realising. She was not Master Mu. Even if his philosophy made sense, he had betrayed his mother and sisters. An irrefutable fact. He was supposed to take revenge on the Japanese, not marry one! Even his own son didn't approve of him.

Chen Di would not let Mother down.

She gripped the chopsticks so tightly her hand hurt. She had to carry on. She must, she must, she must. She had found Lü after three years of blood and sweat, no way she could back out now. She would take up Gu Meilin's invitation for her to revisit, and she had to find a way to proceed under Master Mu's watch.

She gobbled her lunch, the spices numbing her tongue. Then an idea came. If Tang kept Master Mu occupied on her big day, then Master Mu wouldn't be able to ruin her plan. Except…were she and Tang still on the same side? He wanted to harm Lin Feng, after all. But that was all the more reason for her to see him. She wouldn't expect Tang to forget his own revenge, but she might just find a way to protect Lin Feng all the same.

Chen Di stabbed her chopsticks into her rice. People considered it bad luck, vertical chopsticks in rice looking like incense sticks burnt for the dead. She didn't care. She was still chewing when she picked up Gu Meilin's note and marched out.

At a corner shop, beside the Chupa Chups wheel on the counter sat a dirty white phone. The middle-aged plump owner said hello, her lipsticked mouth like a big cherry. Chen Di opened the piece of paper in her hand only to see it wasn't Gu's note but the one Lin Feng had left in her unit, a number scribbled on it in pencil. She stared at it, feeling like a schoolgirl summoning her courage to call the boy she liked. She almost turned back when she put a hand in her jeans pocket and realised she did also have Gu's note.

After a single ring, Gu Meilin picked up.

'It's Chen Di.'

'Young Chen!' Gu's voice shook as if she was moved by a great novel, and Chen Di imagined her ruddy cheeks redden. 'Are you coming again?'

'I am, Aunty Gu.'

'That's great! I can't tell you how glad I am. I'm sorry we were interrupted, there is so much we still want to say.'

Chen Di bit her lip. How kind Gu was.

'Yuandou's hours are quite standard.' As if Chen Di didn't know. 'But I have afternoon and evening shifts, Saturday to Wednesday. I'm about to return to the hospital now. When would you like to come?'

So Lü Yuandou was never home alone. When his wife was at work, their son would be there. Chen Di would never kill a schoolboy, but she could no longer imagine killing Gu Meilin either, a genuinely kind person, a mother.

'Hello?'

'Y-Yes.' She did all she could to harden her heart. She had to do it, it was only right for Mother. 'Friday morning, seven-thirty.'

'Morning, you said?'

'I'm only free in the mornings.' She tried to sound apologetic.

'Oh, it's just we were hoping to have a bit more time with you, so we could talk properly. Mornings are a bit... How about Thursday dinner at six?'

'I'm sorry but I work all evenings. Friday morning we'll have an hour. Besides, it's better if your son's out of our conversation, don't you agree?'

'All right then. Yuandou will be thrilled to see you again.'

Because he had repented and sought redemption... Chen Di clutched her head and shut her eyes to force the words: 'Give him my regards.'

'Let us know if you can make Thursday dinner instead, we can send away our son.'

'I will.' She put down the receiver.

The short call cost her not even one yuan, and she placed three coins on the shop's counter. All Chen Di needed now was Tang's cooperation.

A young man with acne on his forehead came to buy cigarettes. The plump owner scolded him for smoking while taking his money. She then fixed her lipstick and turned to collect Chen Di's coins. 'Girl, you're done?'

'Actually, one more call.' Chen Di pulled out Lin Feng's note. She should warn him about Tang, she owed it to him. Her finger rigidly moved about the numbers, hovering in the air before pressing the last button.

She wasn't yet ready when Lin Feng picked it up.

'Who?' He dragged the word as if he were a gang leader sprawled on a throne, flaunting the arrogance of the little emperor he was not. Chen Di tried to loosen her body as if getting ready to run a marathon. A gust of wind swept dust into her eye, and she rubbed it only to make it teary.

'Hi,' she finally said.

She heard his breathing, then he said, 'Boss Chen! What an honour.'

She laughed, a tear trickling down her cheek. She looked up at a plane tree, large leaves rustling in the dark as if forecasting a major change in the weather.

'You called at a good time,' Lin Feng said, the tone he used when he smirked. 'Can we meet? I need to talk to you about some important business. Very important.'

'Lin Feng.' Her voice almost broke.

'Yep?'

'Don't listen to Tang Bro.'

He was silent.

'I know you look up to him as some awesome dude, but he's not to be trusted.'

'Boss Chen, let's meet. It won't take long.'

'But—'

'You won't regret it.'

She gripped the receiver so tight her ear hurt. The shop's fluorescent light flickered, and the owner slapped it to stabilise the tube. 'Fine,' Chen Di said. She didn't want to admit the relief she felt, knowing she'd see him again. 'Tomorrow morning I'll drop by your housing estate, at seven.' After which she'd head to Dragon Lustre to see Tang.

'Excellent,' he said. She felt an ache picturing his childlike grin. 'By the way, Boss Chen, Four Three really means a lot to you, no?'

Her lips parted, and she pushed down the sudden heat in her chest.

'Did you know him from Sichuan?' Lin Feng asked.

She said nothing, holding her breath. What was he about to tell her?

He continued, 'The way you asked my mum about him, you're never so eager. You actually smiled, you did whenever Four Three came up. Are you smiling right now?'

Chen Di realised she was, and it alarmed her. She clutched her head to warn herself and said, 'Look, if this is the "important business" you need to discuss with me in detail, in person, then just forget about it.'

'This is separate. I just wanted to tell you I checked with my mum.'

'What?'

'You wanted Four Three's family name, right? It's Jia.'

35

Chen Di awoke the next morning, having slept badly. She vowed not to let whatever Lin Feng wanted to say bother her. This was not about Four Three, whether he was Teacher Jia or not. 'Jia' was a common family name! Today, she was out to seek Tang's cooperation to keep Master Mu out of her way. She was so close to ending it all, she couldn't afford to be distracted.

She did her workout as she recalled the day two years ago when Tang had taught her the routine. They'd both come a long way, he'd help her.

The Voyager back in her pocket, she jumped on her bicycle to meet Lin Feng on her way to Tang's recycling yard. The morning was balmy, and Chen Di zipped along the tree-lined streets. The plane leaves had spread like a pandemic, blocking the sky like giant parasols. Before turning into Dragon Lake Court's street, she braked abruptly. She'd just passed a tall woman walking in the opposite direction: Lin Feng's mum.

Thank Heaven, thank Earth she hadn't noticed Chen Di. Heart still throbbing, Chen Di got on the pavement and turned her bicycle around. She had on the same old seaweed-green sweater she'd worn when pretending to be Lin Feng's teacher. She really shouldn't risk being remembered in the area where she planned to commit a crime. Whatever 'important business' Lin Feng needed to talk to her about, they'd have to find another place.

Chen Di gazed at the back of his mum's grey trench coat, her pinned hair. The black satchel she'd used to whack Lin Feng hung from her shoulder, a jade bracelet appeared below her sleeve, and her black kitten heels reflected sunlight. Chen Di pushed her bicycle, unsure if it was wise to pass ahead of the woman and risk being seen.

Where was Lin Feng's mum headed anyhow? To some publisher? To meet her collaborator – Four Three?

Her heart raced.

Lin Feng's mum walked faster than others on the pavement and didn't get on a bus or into a taxi. Chen Di stayed metres behind. Was she heading to the Xu Junction metro station? People queued and pushed in front of an eatery. Lin Feng's mum didn't cut through them but went around, off the pavement.

The street widened, but the crowds grew denser, bicycles ringing bells, motorcycles honking. They arrived at the bustling Xu Junction. Lin Feng's mum put on a pair of sunglasses, an unusual practice in the city despite the bright day, and never once looked around.

Ahead was a giant intersection, and around them, soaring malls. Pizza & Apple Pie advertised on a large screen, and Chen Di had no desire to be seen by Manager Chu. Thankfully, Lin Feng's mum stopped before a different mall. She opened her satchel and extracted a pack of Chunghwa cigarettes, which took Chen Di aback. It was rare for mothers of her social class to smoke. But then again, Lin Feng's mum was anything but typical. She broke the seal with her long fingers and put a cigarette between her lips. She flicked a silver lighter, shielding the cigarette with her other hand, and took a drag.

Two white women strolled into the mall, laughing hard. People gawked at them, but Lin Feng's mum didn't even look up. She dropped the barely smoked cigarette and stomped on it like she was killing a cockroach. A street sweeper sneered at her. A swarm of shoppers blocked Chen Di's view, and after they passed, she saw Lin Feng's mum dabbing her eyes with her sleeve. Then she pulled out the whole cigarette pack and crushed it in her fist, her arm shaking, her face distorted. She tossed it into a rubbish bin.

Why? It didn't seem she was simply being wasteful.

Lin Feng's mum continued walking with more forceful steps. Chen Di maintained the distance between them, and they passed a series of clothing shops less fancy than the malls, heading further up north. Five minutes. Ten. Ahead was an old housing complex of six-storey buildings. Before an alleyway leading into the grounds, Lin Feng's mum stopped just as a middle-aged woman gripping a basket hurried out, followed by a man.

Chen Di tensed, but the man turned and waved Lin Feng's mum to come with him, his raised arm blocking his face. Chen Di followed, but they soon disappeared into a building at the other end of the short alley.

While wondering if she should get into the building, she glimpsed out of the corner of her eye an old woman in black flats, eyeing her. The thought of confronting the equivalent of Grandma Chu made Chen Di wince, jolting her back to reality. She had to go south. South! To Tang's recycling yard down in Dragon Lustre. She swung around her bicycle, focused again on her mission.

Past Dragon Lustre Martyrs Cemetery and Dragon Lustre Temple, Tang's palace and garden hadn't changed: the shed palace with upper floors knocked off and the garden of scrap metal. Chen Di jumped off her bicycle and let it fall. She shouldn't have wasted an hour, stalking Lin Feng's mum, but at least it was still early.

'Little Sis Chen!' It was Big Nose again, his buzz cut having grown out.

'Hello, big brother. Where is Tang Bro?'

'Yo, little sis,' Tang said from behind. 'Which wind brought you here again?'

Chen Di turned and almost didn't recognise him. She'd never seen Tang without his eyepatch before. On the right side of his face was a sunken socket, the eyelid dark, loose, and incomplete. No eyeball.

'Let me guess,' he said. 'I should congratulate you this time.'

'Not yet.' She felt embarrassed. 'I came to ask a favour.'

'Again? I'm honoured.' Tang told Big Nose to bring tea. He and Chen Di entered the shed, the same wall calendar dangling from the huge character for *Fortune,* and as before, they sat on opposite sides of the frosted glass desk. Tang pushed aside the computer and Chen Di's reflection appeared on its screen. She looked back at him and drew an uncanny parallel between the imperfect sides of their faces.

'Master Mu talked to me,' she said. 'He's keeping an eye on us.'

Tang rocked his chair. 'Well, he's doing a bad job.'

'How so?'

'Remember the kid whose thug dad took my eye? If the old fart's watching me, then how come two days ago, when I was with the kid—'

'He knew. He knew you and Lin Feng were having wonton soup—'

'Words travel fast! What else has he told you besides the kid's name?'

'I…know Lin Feng. We met recently.'

Tang looked at her with his one eye, his expression indecipherable. Big Nose brought a pot of Dragon Well tea. Tang poured for them and slurped the hot tea, then he put down the cup, hard, spilling the tea. 'Little bastard.'

'What's wrong?' Chen Di asked.

'The kid's smitten with you.' Tang rocked the chair harder. 'He's been pretty secretive about it, never mentioned your name. I thought it was some girl at his school.'

'Maybe it is,' she said, brushing away a sudden warmth.

'No, it's you, because apparently the girl wants to kill someone.' Tang laughed, belched, and laughed some more. 'Man, the kid's dedicated.'

Chen Di sat rooted to her swivel chair. She shouldn't feel flattered but was.

'Guess what, little sis, I know the kid is no one to you, so it's easy.'

But he's like my little brother, she almost said. 'What is easy?'

'You know I need his family to go down.'

Tang's laugh gave Chen Di the creeps. She drained the cup. 'Why don't you just blind his dad or something?'

He refilled her cup for her. 'Because an eye for an eye, a tooth for a tooth, a life for a life.'

Chen Di understood, perhaps better than anyone, Tang's desire to find justice. And she would've easily agreed with him, before. But this involved Lin Feng.

'Little sis, have you forgotten why you came?' Tang rocked forward and brought his cup to his lips. A small sip. 'You aren't the type to ask for favours.'

Chen Di considered her tea.

'You want revenge,' he said, 'and I want revenge. We should work together.'

She picked up the teacup. 'Yes.' This *was* her purpose for

coming here. Nothing else was supposed to be as important as making Lü pay for Mother's death. 'You might not be worried about Master Mu but I am. He has what it takes to ruin our plans – mine, at least.'

'And I have a proposal.'

'A proposal?'

Tang's good eye narrowed. 'A depressed rich Shanghainese kid is smitten with you. Why would you waste that opportunity?'

'What do you mean?'

'For people like us, if we get caught for murder, it's guaranteed death penalty.'

'I'll be able to escape,' Chen Di said into her tea. She wished she sounded more confident. 'I'll start a new life, down south.'

'But why go to the trouble of killing someone yourself?'

She looked up.

'When the kid told me about his *homicidal lady friend*, I already suggested him to be a man and do the killing for her.'

'Excuse me?' She almost stood.

'Now all you need to do is to go along with it.'

'No! No way.'

'Why not? The kid just needs a little training. Besides, the old fart's watching you and me, not him. Too bad there's no death penalty for minors, but Lin Feng *will* be jailed, which I'd *love* to see happen.' Tang sniggered. 'One arrow, two condors.'

'No! I don't want to involve—'

'The kid doesn't think he deserves to live anyway, so why not indulge him?'

'He deserves to live!' It came out louder than she meant… or did it? She did think Lin Feng deserved to live. She believed in it so strongly that no matter how loudly she said it, it wouldn't have been enough.

'He does not.'

'Well I—' *I want him to live.* 'You're wrong!'

The Dragon Well tea suddenly smelled pungent. A shadow. Chen Di turned to find Big Nose blocking the doorway, arms crossed, and she jumped up. Tang waved him off and stood too, leaning over the desk, his face close to hers, his sunken socket versus her birthmark.

'What, little sis? Itching for some sparring?'

'I am, in fact.' Chen Di knew she was getting carried away, but she wanted to win, badly. It was as if by winning in a fight against Tang she'd prove Lin Feng's right to live.

Tang held out his hand. 'Be my guest.'

They pulled off their sweaters and headed out, Chen Di in a black T-shirt and Tang showing off his abs. A thin layer of cloud hung in the sky. By the shed, three men chatted among themselves as if waiting for the start of a show whose ending they already knew. Big Nose propped two wooden swords against the wall.

Chen Di and Tang stood two metres apart. Right foot before left, she extended both hands in defence, one hand higher than the other, fingers splayed.

'Strong stance.' Tang's punch started from his centre line

and aimed at her face. This was not aikido. She moved to a side, panting, almost failing to block it. 'Now you know how useless aikido is,' he said. 'All defence, no attack.'

Except a defender in aikido was really a superior assailant who always managed to take down the original attacker – that was how she'd thought about it from her first day at the dojo. Chen Di moved in and tried to seize Tang's wrist, but he slipped past and hit the back of her neck. A dull pain. The side of his hand felt like a wooden sword. She faked an attack at his shoulder and kicked at his groin. But he grabbed her foot and pushed it – and her body – backwards, a new seriousness on his face. She did a back shoulder roll and rose.

'Little sis,' he said, 'balance is key.'

She lunged to his side and turned, her right arm trying to clamp his neck from behind, her left hand reaching for his left wrist. He grabbed her wrist first, his other hand on her elbow. She was going in circles, then her cheek pressed into the ground.

Tang's lips touched her ear. 'The kid's not worth your effort.'

Chen Di breathed hard and returned to her stance. She was stronger than most students at the dojo, but Tang was at a different level. Once she extended her hands again, he punched her midriff – a decoy – then a high kick on her left ear slammed her down. A sharp noise rang in her head, but again she managed to rise.

Another high kick was already on its way. This time, Chen Di saw it clearly. Tang sacrificed his balance for impact.

Master Mu had discussed the danger of performing high kicks, and Tang knew the basics. How lightly he took her. Just before the impact, she crouched and slipped under his approaching leg to the other side. Using his own rotational momentum, she added a push on his ankle, and he fell, saved by a shoulder roll.

Tang was stone-faced.

'Balance is key,' Chen Di said, 'isn't it?'

Before she knew it, her wrist was caught. She found herself in the air, head down, legs up. She tucked her head in the last instant, but her left shoulder crashed into the ground. A splitting pain. Dislocation.

Worried chatter came from the men watching them, but Chen Di stood yet again, drenched in sweat. She couldn't move her left arm, let alone hold a weapon, but she looked to the two wooden swords propped against the shed.

'You serious?' Tang said. 'Do you know how high the sky is, how thick the earth is? You want to fight me single-armed?'

'I'm not giving up.' She kept the pain out of her voice.

'Is the kid really worth it?'

'It's not about him.'

'Whatever you say.' Tang signalled Big Nose to throw over the wooden swords. Chen Di caught hers single-handed and pointed the blade at Tang's navel. Her dislocated left shoulder was killing her, but she stepped forward, raised the sword with her right arm, and cut it down, sharp and centred. Tang tossed away his own sword, slipped in, and took hold of hers, his other hand catching her neck. Forced to face up, she fell hard on her back. Her sword was now in his hand, its tip pointing at her throat. On her throat.

Chen Di rolled away. Metres from him, she rose yet again, ready for his next move.

'I give you face, but you don't want face,' Tang said. 'Fine!'

The sword high over his head, he shot towards her. She could crack her skull against the concrete, she could go deaf! She felt a rush of air. Like an instinct, her hand found her Voyager and flicked it open. She threw just as his sword sliced the air above her skull.

36

A fist-sized stone smashed into Tang's raised wooden sword, forcing him sideways. Chen Di's Voyager stabbed the ground. Across the yard, Master Mu stood tall like a pine tree, his brow furrowed in a way she'd never seen before. So he'd saved them. Chen Di sighed with relief only to stiffen, thinking he must've been watching all along.

'Yo.' Tang faced him, panting but sounding unsurprised. 'What an exceptional guest we have here, coming without a shadow, leaving without a footprint.'

'*To injure an opponent is to injure yourself.*' Master Mu approached, his deep voice reverberating through the yard. '*To control aggression without inflicting injury is the Art of Peace.*'

'Silence!' Tang said. 'You don't come to my territory to lecture me.'

Master Mu stopped before Chen Di and pulled her sleeve up above her dislocated shoulder, then he seized her forearm and her elbow. 'Don't move, and breathe evenly.' He lightly squeezed her upper arm, then wrapped both hands around her elbow and twisted it outwards.

'Ow!' she cried.

He touched the back of her hand. 'Can you feel me? Can you move your wrist?'

She nodded, not wanting to feel thankful.

Chen Di plucked her Voyager from the ground and returned to the shed. She downed some cold tea, staring at that *Fortune* on the wall, on so many households' doors and walls. She put on her sweater, careful about her shoulder, wondering if she'd done the right thing by fighting Tang. She was normally more prudent than that...

She came back out to see Tang holding the sword like a walking stick.

'I know how you feel,' Master Mu said, his deep-set eyes fixed on Tang. 'And I knew how you felt as a teenage boy back then. But there is another way—'

'You. Know. Nothing,' Tang said with menacing slowness. 'And your *help* did not help us.'

It occurred to Chen Di that he might've blamed Master Mu too – not just Lin Feng's family – for his lost eye and his uncle's death. Exactly how had it happened? Tang had told her the story of Lin Feng's family but seemed to have intentionally avoided talking about what had happened later, to him and his uncle.

'You don't have to hide your weakness, Young Tang.'

'I have no weakness!'

'Your uncle was the only person you had.'

Silence. Chen Di leaned on the shed and contemplated Tang's narrowed eye, filled with hate — and a glimpse of sorrow, the kind she'd seen in Father's eyes, and in her own. This was why she'd never kept a mirror in her unit. Tang was a more competent avenger than Chen Di, but still, something remained in his eye that wasn't hate.

'Your uncle meant a lot to you,' she heard herself say.

Tang turned to study her as if she had rice all over her face. 'Little sis, you were fighting me just minutes ago. Now you want to talk to me?'

'Well...' Chen Di glanced away from Tang, at Master Mu, who was watching her.

Tang laughed and hit the ground with his sword, three times. 'I'm always happy to chat with you, little sis, because I like you. You remind me of my younger self.' He'd told her this before, but then he added, 'My less capable self.'

She said nothing. She did not disagree.

'Back in my teens, when I collected cans, two things kept me going. Number one, my fantasies. I was that toad fancying swan meat for a meal.' Tang let out a series of dry laughs. 'How I fantasised! I imagined owning the biggest units in the fanciest housing estates, Shanghainese and out-of-towners alike bribing me to get stuff done, and most important, daughters of the rich families fighting over me.'

Something clicked inside Chen Di. 'Does that include Lin Feng's sister? But it wasn't fantasy.' She knew Tang had had a real connection with her.

The sun came out from behind the shed. It dazzled Chen Di and lit the imperfect side of Tang's face, dividing his body into two halves, light and dark.

'Number two,' he continued, dodging her question, 'my uncle. My uncle was the one who'd sold his blood and a kidney to get my whole family out of debt and get us started in Shanghai. He was the one who scraped by with me, laughed and cried with me, no matter how the Shanghainese abused us. He made me feel like I belonged, until! Until the 1992 Spring Festival, when the fucking kid walked out onto the street alone – my uncle was looking out for him! But his fucking parents beat us up.' Tang made a sweeping motion with the sword. 'I'll never forget the way the fucking daddy kicked my skinny uncle, making him cough blood: one of the last images I saw with two eyes.'

Chen Di's heart tightened. 'Did they assume your uncle would hurt—'

'You're sharp, little sis. All my uncle did was ask the kid if he was okay before his parents came, but he was accused of attempted kidnap. All xiangwunings are filthy kidnappers, aren't we? Later, the judge agreed the dad was acting in self-defence. So the fucking family walked away, while I lost my eyeball, and my uncle was left to die from organ damage.'

Master Mu spoke. 'It was clear at the court the parents were in grief. They lost their daughter, and they truly thought they would lose their son as well.'

'I. Don't. Care. And thank you, Great Master Mu, thank you so very much for helping us with legal trouble *and* paying our medical bills, all of which resulted in a grand total of nothing!' Tang pointed at him with the sword.

Chen Di found herself nodding. Perhaps more than blaming Master Mu for failing to save his uncle, Tang felt indebted to him because of the time and money Master Mu had spent trying to make things right for them... How helpless that teenage boy had been. Until now Chen Di had never considered Tang as someone to feel bad for.

He stepped up, sword still raised. 'That fucking family thought they could move again and again and vanish, but I'm about to defeat them.'

Master Mu came forward too and let his chest touch the tip of the sword. '*Defeat means to defeat the mind of the contention that we harbour within.*'

'Shut up!' Tang yelled.

Chen Di remembered the line from *The Art of Peace*. 'Master Mu, don't *you* want to educate people, change this society? Don't *you* want to fight injustice?'

'Only when you have achieved inner peace can you truly fight.'

'How? How do you expect us to achieve that when it's chaos all around?' She exchanged a knowing look with Tang. 'We want peace, yes, but we only know one way of getting it, and it's not your way.'

Tang's sword was still pointed at Master Mu's chest, but the next second, it was in Master Mu's hand and snapped into two halves. 'I won't let either of you commit crimes,' Master Mu said with finality. 'If you harm others, I will ensure you are punished by law.'

'Let's see if you can.' Chen Di crossed the yard.

'Little sis!' Tang shouted. 'You weren't fighting me for anyone's sake, it's in your blood, in any avenger's blood. Think about my proposal.'

Chen Di wished she could tell Tang he was right, that she felt no attachment towards Lin Feng and could use and discard him like Tang had suggested. But she could no longer lie to herself – she *had* fought Tang for Lin Feng's sake. Even if Lin Feng had what it took to kill and promised to never disclose her involvement, she'd never risk him being locked up. She didn't want prison for herself, so couldn't possibly want it for someone she considered her own brother.

She raised her bicycle. She could not let Master Mu ruin step three, but getting Lin Feng to kill Lü Yuandou on her behalf was not the solution. Her mission wouldn't be complete without step four – and the prospect of an easy escape once she'd achieved that was alluring – but using Lin Feng was not the solution.

'You're flinching.' Master Mu's voice sounded right behind her.

She spun around. 'I'm not.'

'Are you flinching at yourself? That means you still have a conscience. It's not too late.'

But it was. She couldn't go back in time to change what had happened at the 1994 harvest.

Master Mu's eyes pierced her, his voice calm. 'Ice your shoulder.'

'Thank you *as always* for your meticulous care.' Chen Di jumped on her bicycle and sped off. Her mission had already taken too much out of her, she'd come this far, there was no going back. Regardless of Lü's remorse, regardless of the sense in Master Mu's philosophy, Chen Di knew only one way to honour Mother. And it looked like she'd have to complete her last two steps all on her own.

Except she still owed Lin Feng a meeting.

She wasn't going back to his street. They'd find another place.

37

A misty morning drizzle veiled Dragon Lustre Temple's pagoda and red gates. Chen Di wore her single-use raincoat a second time, over her cardigan, even though it was ripped from the collar. A hawker in a red cap halved his umbrella price without her trying to bargain, and a white-haired couple warned her she'd get a cold in the rain.

Before she could look around for Lin Feng, a burst of shouts made everyone turn. A thin-faced woman came around the corner, her hair dishevelled, the blood on her forehead washed by the fine rain. She stepped forward, knelt, and pressed her palms and forehead to the wet ground. A man held an umbrella over her and caught her elbow to help her up. She rose and, despite her shaking legs, continued to kneel after each step. Chen Di moved out of her way, and the woman kowtowed through the gate into the temple.

'She lives near the botanical garden,' an old voice said beside Chen Di, 'praying from her doorstep, kowtowing step to step, all the way here. Imagine!'

'It's her daughter,' said another. 'Leukaemia.'

For a second, the woman's back looked like Lin Feng's mother's.

'Boss Chen!'

She turned to see Lin Feng waving two tickets, his hair wet. Warmth surged in her chest. She pulled off her raincoat and wadded it up. 'Why do I need this if you don't?'

'Because it's raining,' he said.

They both laughed. A flock of sparrows sailed overhead.

Lin Feng had been the one to suggest the temple as a meeting place. Now he led Chen Di through the open red gate, water trickling from the flying eaves. The cement courtyard centred a bronze censer, and beyond was a temple hall with yellow walls and crimson gates, guarded by stone lions. The woman from earlier kowtowed indoors.

'I'm not a believer,' Chen Di said.

'Me neither,' Lin Feng said. 'But there's a good spot to talk.'

He pointed to a pathway on the left that went around the temple hall. But she stood still and stared into the hall, then entered, drawn by familiarity.

The smell of old wood and incense wafted in the air. The earlier woman and a few others joined their palms, some bowing, others kneeling on a row of yellow cushions. When the woman turned around, despite the strands of hair blocking her face, her eyes caught Chen Di's, and Lin Feng's. She gave them a stiff smile, like a mannequin's.

'She reminds me...' Lin Feng said.

'Of your mum?' Chen Di asked.

He nodded.

At the front of the hall were three enormous golden statues, Buddha and his disciples, long earlobes reaching their shoulders. Chen Di gazed at them without praying as she thought of Lü Yuandou, his earlobes as long as the Buddha's, symbolising goodness.

Lü had acknowledged his guilt, learned to love, and was loved. He was no longer a monster, a murderer...

I am. I am the murderer here.

She felt tears building. She turned away to prevent Lin Feng from seeing her expression and held onto the merit box. She could not stop what she'd set in motion by losing her brother. Until someone paid for Mother's death, she would not be able to move on.

A young monk knocked on a wooden fish as he chanted, a book of sutra opened beside him. An image flashed across her mind, of her nine-fingered father doing the same in a faraway temple, head shaved, wrapped in an orange robe.

Chen Di backed out of the hall and followed Lin Feng to the next courtyard, and the one after that. A small wooden door – an opening in the tall wall – stood on the left, yellow paint peeling. The door was ajar. Lin Feng peeked inside, and his expression crumpled.

'What is this place?' she asked.

He shut the door but it squeaked and bounced back. 'Don't come.'

'Let me see it.' She pushed past him, but he put his hand over her eyes, his palm as wet as her face, but warm. She sensed his breathing, her head against his chest, and felt as if she was being comforted by not a younger brother but an older one who knew about life more than she did.

He kept his palm over her eyes. 'I'll tell you about this place.'

'What game are you playing?'

'Give me five minutes. Close your eyes.'

She moved her eyelids under his hand, and he let go. 'Just five,' she said, eyes shut. 'Then move onto whatever "important business" you need to discuss with me.'

'You're entering a secret forest.' A firm grip on her hand led her inside, one measured step after another. 'Can you feel the soft earth under your feet?' He paused, and she felt it. 'Can you hear sparrows sing through the rain?' He paused, and she heard it. 'So many trees are around you, ancient trees here from the beginning, not planted by humans. They know about life much more than we do.' Lin Feng didn't sound like himself, or rather, he sounded the same as when he'd divulged his memories with his sister. 'Now take a deep breath.'

Chen Di did without opening her eyes, her chest rising and falling, raindrops flecking her face. The soles of her feet connected with the soil, the tree roots.

'The trees have yellow-brown bark and deep green leaves,' he said. 'You touch a leaf's smooth surface. Your fingertip traces around its jagged edge, its heart shape.'

'Mulberry trees?' Her voice quavered.

'Mulberry trees,' he said.

They trod gingerly on the soil, the air permeated with the smell of something primal. Chen Di felt the canopy formed by the trees above her. Light filtered down, and when the leaves rustled, some beams vanished while new ones emerged. One tree leaned over her like a caring mother, another pointed towards the sky like a guiding father, and a third one brushed her with its leaves like a loving sister or brother.

A force swept through her, touching every cell in her body. Lin Feng picked up both of her hands and squeezed them, and when he let go, she wished he hadn't, her hands stopped in mid-air.

'Have you kept silkworms before?' he asked.

'My mother.' Her voice was small, but then her eyes sprang open. 'I haven't come for this, I can't afford to—' Chen Di took a huge step back, finding herself in a construction site. Lifeless. It was the size of a basketball court, a small crane parked on the left. High walls surrounded it, the concrete mortar gone from the bottom half, revealing blackened bricks. On one side was the small door they'd entered from. Opposite it was a large pair of solid wooden gates.

She stood, transfixed. Where was the secret forest? All the mulberry trees? She couldn't believe Lin Feng had made it all up.

'Your mother kept silkworms?' he said.

'And she was murdered by that man.' Alarmed by her own words, Chen Di snapped her head back at Lin Feng. She'd never told anyone the exact reason for her mission.

'So it was your mother. I thought you were avenging your siblings.'

'Wh-Where do you get that idea from? It has nothing to do with my br— I want to avenge my mother. Just my mother.'

He nodded. 'Did you believe me?'

'What?'

'What I said about the secret forest.' He seemed to be holding his breath.

She willed herself to harden and managed the softest 'no'.

Lin Feng sighed.

'Yes!' she blurted. 'Yes, I did. I did believe your forest.'

'Really?'

'Really.'

He grinned, his white teeth showing, his features soft. That childlike grin, again, making her heart clench. 'A couple days ago, Boss Chen, there really were mulberry trees here, and I thought you'd want to see them.'

'Well, I did see them.'

He grinned again. 'This is also a great place to talk business, of course.' The grin turned into a smirk, and his tone changed. 'So, you need that man dead.'

She nodded, hating the doubts she felt.

'Then I'll kill him for you.' His crisp voice sliced through the rain.

Chen Di opened her mouth, then wiped her drenched face. 'I know Tang Bro told you to do this, to kill for the girl you're…' She couldn't bring herself to say 'smitten with'.

'I want to anyway. This is the important business I need to talk to you about.'

'Listen, Tang Bro doesn't have your best interests at heart.'

Lin Feng huffed. 'He wants revenge for his uncle, I get that by now. But I think he's also doing this because the rest of my family, myself included, did a horrible thing to my sister. He *was* in love with her.'

'And he's desperate to guilt you.'

He huffed again. 'Why not? I should be guilted. I was born only thanks to my sister's suffering, my existence made her suffer more, *and* I ended up killing her.'

'You didn't.'

'You heard my parents. I caused her heart attack, I literally did.'

'Not on purpose. You didn't intentionally kill anyone, which makes you better than...' *Me.* Chen Di cringed. The thickening rain made the earth muddier and muddier.

'Whatever, Boss Chen. Just trust me to kill the man for you.'

'No way, I won't let you go to prison.'

'I wouldn't.'

'You wouldn't?'

'Well, look.' He cleared his throat. 'I'm underage, and my dad knows *a lot* of people, the higher-ups of the higher-ups. They won't make it hard for me.'

'I'm not so sure.'

He crossed his arms. 'I am.'

'How?'

'How about this? I swear on my sister's name I wouldn't go to prison.'

Chen Di stared at him, overpowered by his calm, the certainty in his voice. Lin Feng's family *had* got away with the death of Tang's uncle. Hadn't life taught her enough? With money and power, you could get away with anything. Except Lü Yuandou was not Tang's uncle – he was not a can collector but a government official. 'You're naïve to think that, Lin Feng.'

'I don't *think* that, I *know* that.'

'How can you be so sure?'

'I don't joke about swearing on my sister's name.'

Chen Di's voice died. She'd heard few things in life as convincing as this.

'Boss Chen, go and make a clean break from that man, from your past. Okay? I want you to live your new life without a criminal record.'

A lump rose in her throat. Lin Feng hadn't used the word, but it sounded like his sacrifice was for her. Even if he was right about not going to prison… 'I still can't—'

'It's not like I'm sacrificing myself,' he said, as if reading her mind.

'But you *are*.'

'Come on, don't get so mushy. I've always wanted to do something crazy, I should thank you for the opportunity. And *no one* is going to lock me up, as I said, it's good for us both. One arrow, two condors.'

The sky hung heavily over them, and Chen Di couldn't bear to look at him. She paced about, but no matter where she looked, she saw no living things. She stopped by the heavy wooden gates and touched their rough surface. She raised a hand, rainwater pooling in her palm. The warmth inside her wasn't enough to dry the rain-soaked world.

Lin Feng joined her, arms still crossed.

'Lin Feng, is it that you want to do something for your sister? That you think you owe her?' She turned to him despite the ache it caused her. 'It's not your fault.'

'Boss Chen, just let me kill the man for you. Please.'

'But have you heard me?'

'Let's talk business. Give me the details.'

Chen Di shrank. She closed her eyes and the secret forest reappeared, catching her off guard. She saw the dense thicket of mulberry trees, an oasis in the middle of the chaotic city, a paradise for silkworms. She reached out, but her hand fell through emptiness.

38

What had brought her to Shanghai? What had she worked for for the last three years, going up mountains of knives, down seas of fires? A blood debt had to be paid by blood! With Lü Yuandou dead, at last, she could break free.

Chen Di chewed on her lip so hard she tasted blood, and she clutched her head, eyes shut, her nails digging into her skull. There must've been a whole world of how rich and powerful Shanghainese got around things she wasn't privy to. Unlike her – a lowly out-of-towner, a xiangwuning – Lin Feng would be fine. He'd sworn on his sister's name he would not go to prison.

This was her real chance to live on, and live well.

Her eyes cut to him. 'First I need you to prove yourself.'

'Try me,' he said.

Chen Di pulled out her Voyager and put it in Lin Feng's palm the way she'd given him the stack of mulberry leaves. 'It's a good knife. Made in America.'

He stared at the inscription. 'Was it on the '98 Lantern Fest—'

'That my mother was murdered, yes. Now show me what you're capable of.'

He smirked and flicked out the blade. 'Aren't you afraid to get hurt?'

'You think you can hurt me?'

'Here I go.'

'No attacker would announce that.' She trapped his hand. 'Again.'

Lin Feng said nothing this time. He threw a punch at her face with his left hand and his right aimed the knife at one side of her waist.

Chen Di blocked his fist and slipped out. 'A few things,' she said, not dissatisfied. 'You did well by holding my eyes, and you successfully distracted me with a punch, but both your punch and your knife attack were inefficient. Let me show you.'

She took his hands and guided them through space. For a few seconds she felt they were in the middle of a family outing, playing eagle-catching-chicks. Lin Feng was the hen, dodging left and right, protecting the chicks behind him. Chen Di was the eagle, reaching for the chicks but failing, blocked by the hen. They laughed in the sun like they were real family.

But it was rainy, the area was deserted, and he held her deadly knife.

'When you came for me,' she said, 'your arms were drawing half-circles in the air, meaning your hands travelled more distance than needed. Understand?'

'Yep.'

'Find the *shortest* path between us and come *straight* at me.'

Lin Feng lunged and grabbed her shoulder – her injured left shoulder. Her motions slowed. He aimed the knife at her heart, and she thought he'd manage to cut her, but he stopped just as the blade tip touched her cardigan.

Chen Di reached for her shoulder. She'd ignored Master Mu's direction to ice it.

'Sorry,' Lin Feng said. 'Is your shoulder—'

'It wasn't you, a previous dislocation.'

'Are you okay?'

'Did I tell you to stop? You should've stabbed me.'

He folded back the knife. 'I would have if you had those funny ears.'

She gave a cold smile. 'You're a quick learner, Lin Feng, and naturally agile.' Indeed, ever since Yuanfen Eatery, she'd thought the boy had good potential.

'Is there a but?'

'But penetrating the ribcage can be difficult. Let's see if you can do this my way.' She took his hand and offered her other arm. 'Hold the knife in your right hand. Now grab my *left* wrist with your *left* hand. Then slide behind me.' She gestured. 'And push the blade into my kidney.' Chen Di reached over as if she was about to embrace him, and she almost did, but her hands only touched his back, below his ribcage. The position of kidneys.

'Sorry I hurt you,' Lin Feng said.

Neither of them moved, her hands still indicating his kidneys, her body tenser than his. The rain thickened again.

She dropped her hands. 'You didn't hurt me.'

'I did,' he said.

'A good stab to the kidney disables me, allowing a subsequent strike to my chest, solar plexus, or throat.' She almost stopped talking, remembering having learned the fact from Tang. 'I suggest you twist the knife before pulling it out, then cut my throat.'

'Got it.'

'Now take me on.'

He'd already seized her wrist. Without flicking out the blade, he slid behind her and aimed at her right kidney, an imaginary blade coming in low but at an upward angle. She escaped his grip, but the handle landed on her throat.

'You already know to use your hips for power.' She was impressed. 'Remember, in this kind of attack your target often reacts reflexively, not deliberately. Though I don't think it'll happen, if he catches your arm, then do this.'

'*He*, you said? So you've given me the job.'

She demonstrated the moves, and he got them in one go, escaping her wrist holds. 'Good job, Lin Feng. I'd recommend you train formally—'

'In the next life.'

'In *this* life!' She enclosed his hand in both of hers.

The rain suddenly thinned. Lin Feng looked vulnerable, somehow. She forced herself to let go of his hand, backed off, and studied the muddy ground. Her shoes were stuck in the soil. *Mission first. Mission first. Mission first.* She squeezed her injured shoulder to stay alert and pictured Mother's limp body, lying on a makeshift bed, with make-up on.

Her eyes cut to him again. 'I'll arrange for dinner with him tomorrow at six, you go instead. It'll be Lü Yuandou, that's his full name, and his wife.'

'His wife?'

'Spare her, but don't let her call an ambulance too soon.'

'Got it.' Lin Feng gently took her wrist. 'I'll grab Lü Yuandou's wrist, slide behind him, stab his kidney, twist out the blade, and slit his throat.'

'If you press the intercom button at Phoenix Sea Court, at six, I'm sure they'll let you in without you needing to talk. So you don't have to worry about the guards.'

'I have classmates there. The guards know me.'

'Do they?'

'Remember. I've been there before.'

She nodded. 'This is the one and only chance I'm giving you, failing isn't an option. I'm leaving Shanghai after that.' Then she leaned – fell – back on the gate, feeling like she'd used all her strength. It continued to drizzle.

'Boss Chen, I have a task for you too.'

'Tell me.' She looked at him. 'You know I believe in returning favours.'

'I want you to go to a place for me.' He reached into his pocket and pulled out a note, crisp and dry. He stared at it a moment then held it out.

She brought it before her eyes to find an address. 'What's this place?'

'You'll know when you get there. Go tomorrow.'

'Am I supposed to retrieve something? Or do you need me to bring a message? Am I meeting someone important?'

'You're important, to me.'

Her heart clenched so badly she felt she'd implode. *You're important to me too, Lin Feng.* She tore her eyes away from his and stared at the opposite wall. 'It's not too late to change your mind. After all, I'm just a—' Her voice broke.

'You aren't, you won't be one.'

'I already am. I've been one…for years.'

'No, you're—' He crossed his arms and turned to hide his flush. 'I first noticed you because of my sister, but you're just someone I like.'

Chen Di searched his dark eyes, and found truth.

'And I was right.' He grinned.

'About…'

'I knew you'd teach me knife tricks.'

'Listen, Lin Feng, listen,' she said, breathless. 'Deep down, I'm not sure if I'm doing the right thing. In fact, my aikido master made it clear that I'm not. I'm glad you're here with me, but… But the truth is, I'm scared.'

He embraced her in a hug, startling her, both of them soaking wet. 'Don't be scared, Boss Chen.' He rubbed her back. 'Just put your arms around me now. Keep it simple, I already know where my kidneys are.'

She couldn't believe he made her laugh, and wrapped her arms around him. Slowly, her shoulders relaxed. A hint of warmth came from his body, and warmed her. He continued to rub her back as they listened to the fine rain.

'Your brother would've done the same for you,' he said.

Chen Di's whole body spasmed. 'But I lost him!' she cried. 'I was the one, Lin Feng, who lost my brother…'

'You miss him, I can tell.'

Still holding each other, she took the deepest breath of her life and held it all in, and let it all out, not surprised by Lin Feng's words, or hers, his actions, or hers. The trust between them.

'What's your brother's name?' he asked.

'We called him…Little Tiger.'

'Really? I was born in the year of the Tiger.'

She nodded into his chest. She'd already suspected it, having calculated it from his age – a fact she hadn't wanted to think about.

'As I said, Boss Chen, it's entirely possible Little Tiger is still alive. So wherever you go, I hope you'll find him. That'd be a perfect ending to your mission.'

She nodded again.

'You're not as cold a person as you think,' he said.

Finally, the drizzle came to a stop. She felt the way their bodies fit together. It was as if they were no longer two separate people, as if they'd come from the same source and any separation was only temporary.

'Leave it to me now, Boss Chen.'

Her arms tightened around him. 'Don't...go.'

'I have to, but remember I'm always with you.'

'You are?'

'Always. Now close your eyes again.'

She did, and they let go of each other. She felt his gaze on her, a gaze that woke every part of her skin to life. He brushed aside strands of her wet hair, and she knew he was looking at her birthmark again. Then she felt his fingertips caressing it, his gentle touch like what she remembered from weeks ago, but warm. Ever so warm.

'I remembered this only recently,' Lin Feng said. 'But when I was little, I always wished I had my sister's birthmark. No matter how I rubbed my chin though, it never got dark enough to look like one.' He laughed quietly. 'But the habit stayed, silly of me.'

She couldn't speak, her eyes still shut. She knew if she made one more sound, she'd end up sobbing.

'The sun is coming out,' he said. 'Can you feel a gust of wind whooshing through the secret forest? It rustles the mulberry trees, every leaf like a small bell.'

She heard him take a quiet step backwards.

'Goodbye, Boss Chen. Live well.'

Yet again Chen Di stood in a forest of mulberry trees, an ancient forest after the rain, where the earth exhaled from underneath, and refreshing air filled her lungs. She inhaled, and exhaled, the surroundings so quiet she felt she could hear clouds move. She opened her eyes to the sky, which suddenly looked more blue than grey, the sun having peeked out of the clouds. For a second she saw Lin Feng's broad, brilliant grin.

But he was gone, the barren area still barren.

A wave of loss washed over her. She swayed. She tried to step to the door but slumped on the damp earth. The rain had turned the black soil into slimy brown mud, murky puddles everywhere, dirt on her shoes and jeans, on her shaking hands, the earthy smell unbearable. She wanted to howl, it felt as if someone had died. She could only weep like a child.

The sound of chains, a lock clicking, a screech.

The pair of gates opened. Two workers came in, wearing white safety helmets and heavy work boots, one of them whistling. Still on the ground, Chen Di squinted at the space behind them: Dragon Lustre Martyrs Cemetery. Outside these gates was where she'd found those twigs laden with mulberry leaves! So the gates didn't directly connect the cemetery and the temple but opened to this in-between area. There had really been mulberry trees here, a secret forest Lin Feng had seen...and recreated for her.

'Oi!' Both workers' eyes raked over her. 'What you doing here?'

Chen Di couldn't rise. She fumbled and pushed on the ground, forgetting her injured shoulder. She struggled up and rushed out the gates to the cemetery, not knowing why she'd decided against returning to the temple.

The cemetery after the rain looked like a dead reservoir. Her steps faltered, her shoes making muddy prints on the path, and inadvertently she went between an old couple and squashed a snail. Then, intentionally, she slammed her aching shoulder into a plane tree's infected trunk. It numbed her emotions, a little. She bent over in pain but bumped against the trunk again, and again, breaking her flesh.

She bolted out of the cemetery's stone entrance. A phone box stood steps away as if waiting for her. She'd never used a phone box before, only phones at small shops. With one usable arm, she put in a few coins, and one fell, bounced, and rolled away. She drew out Gu Meilin's note and punched in her number fast, almost flipping two digits.

Getting Lin Feng to kill Lü meant that Gu Meilin, a mother, didn't need to die. This small benevolence made her feel better.

After one ring, Gu Meilin picked up.

Chen Di skipped the greetings. 'Tomorrow dinner at six works. Send away your son.'

39

Before dawn, Chen Di woke with a jerk. Today was the day when everything would end. She'd spend the night at the train station's waiting room, where she'd see confirmation of Lü Yuandou's death in the early morning news. If it wasn't reported, she'd call Phoenix Sea Court from a public phone to verify it. She'd then leave Shanghai.

Her clothes were scattered on the floor as she'd left them last night, all green and entangled like seaweed. She picked up just a few items she'd bring along, and her eyes landed on her jacket from Teacher Jia. For practical purposes she'd keep it, but she would leave behind all her literary magazines.

Chen Di split them into four stacks and hefted one to her door, her injured shoulder throbbing. Yesterday she'd slammed it into that plane tree. No wonder the pain had worsened. She slipped into the empty alley, dimly lit by a bulb hanging from an overhead wire. She cradled the magazines to the recycle bin to see banana skins inside.

With the family name confirmed, thanks to Lin Feng, Chen Di was ninety-five percent sure Four Three was Teacher Jia. A part of her longed to see him again before leaving Shanghai, but another part knew she had to forget everyone in her past to start a new life. The magazines landed in the bin with a loud *thump* and she glanced around, alert. Master Mu could be watching. Vexed, she quickly fetched the rest and threw them all out too.

Chen Di slipped back into her unit. As she packed, she caught sight of Lin Feng's running award certificate. She picked it up, willing herself to tear it in two, but couldn't. In the end, she threw it in the rubbish with the note he'd left of his phone number.

Chen Di drew out her cardboard box from under the bed only to see her stack of rental receipts, now arranged from the oldest to the newest. She paused: 2000-2-29. Hadn't Grandma Chu welcomed her to the longtang, inviting her to the reunion dinner held for out-of-towners who hadn't been able to head home for the Spring Festival? The 2000 Spring Festival was at the start of February, yet her oldest receipt came from the end of February... Had she really stayed before paying? She shook her head, went out again, and threw away the whole box.

Backpack zipped, unit cleared of her possessions, Chen Di considered the next step. Though she didn't have to go all the way to Shanghai Railway Station to buy a train ticket, that was where she would go next. She wanted to check out the waiting room ahead of time.

She hopped on her bicycle, shoulder still throbbing.

Three huge characters, *shang hai zhan,* stood atop a squat building that eerily resembled Lü's workplace, and the gigantic square in front of the station was crowded with people. A thin man with a big moustache carried six wooden chairs. A young couple shouldered bags big enough to fit themselves inside, and a girl trailed them, a baby tied to her back the way Chen Di had once carried Little Tiger.

She brushed away the image and entered the building. The noisy waiting area had a small TV. Under the high ceiling, people queued and pushed behind the ticket counters, and she joined them, not allowing her thoughts to stray, not allowing a brittle old man to cut in line before her. The family in front of her changed their mind, so she stepped forward.

'Where to?' The young woman behind the glass used too much skin-whitening cream.

'Shen—' Chen Di stopped. What had she been thinking all along, planning to head to Shenzhen, to Hong Kong? She had to forget Teacher Jia if she truly wanted to start a new life. She should travel north, not south! From a northern city, she might just sneak out of China into a cold country.

'People are waiting.'

'Ürümqi,' Chen Di said, and she'd figure out a way to get from there to Mongolia or Kazakhstan. 'Or Harbin.' In which case, on to Russia.

'Ürümqi *or* Harbin? Do you even know where you're going?'

'I do, and either is fine.'

'*Either is fine?*'

'Are there many trains?'

'A few.' The woman frowned. 'To Ürümqi via Xi'an, to Harbin via Tianjin.'

Chen Di wished she could take the next one but needed to confirm Lü Yuandou's death first. Besides, she had an obligation to Lin Feng to go to the address he'd given her.

Then she heard someone call, 'Boss Chen!'

Her heart leaped and she glanced around, warmth rising inside. But she had only imagined it. Lin Feng couldn't have come, he had things to prepare for today, and she'd never...

She'd never see him again.

'People are waiting,' the woman said again.

Chen Di pressed on the glass. 'Any trains leaving tomorrow morning?'

'To Three Trees, yes.'

'Three Trees?'

The woman's brow went up. 'Station in Harbin. Do you really know where—'

'Yes, yes. To Three Trees.'

'Soft sleeper? Hard sleeper? Seat?'

So Harbin would be her new home. How hard would it be to sneak into Russia from there? To learn the language? Suddenly Chen Di was unsure whether Lü's death in Shanghai would make a difference in her new life. She pictured herself in a snowy land, alone, and felt an unprecedented hollowness. Loneliness. What she'd always wanted was to live well, but that didn't seem to be in tune with the life she was picturing right now.

'People are waiting!'

'Seat.'

A piece of paper the size of her palm, in a happy baby pink, with a barcode at the bottom. The ticket to step four – her final step. To her new life.

Chen Di took a long shower at the communal bathhouse. It was supposed to relax her but left her scalded, a trio of old women scrutinising her body and telling her to eat more in order to give birth to a fat baby some day.

She headed to a nearby eatery and ordered a century egg and yellow-croaker-and-pickled-vegetable noodles. It felt like the appropriate choice, 'yellow croaker cycles' being a common name in Shanghai for cart-attached tricycles. One explanation held that the vehicles transported the fish, and another said they moved about like schools of yellow croaker. She preferred the latter, an army of out-of-towners roaming about Big Shanghai.

Farewell, Shanghai.

The sun faded just as she took her seat at a table outside. A gust of wind rustled the leaves of a plane tree, causing one to land on her table. It looked green and healthy, how strange.

The century egg didn't go with the noodles, the strong flavours clashing, and she confused the waiter by asking for chilli bean paste. She didn't care, she wolfed them all down.

Chen Di marched back towards her longtang.

'Girl!' the plump corner shop owner called out with her lipsticked mouth.

'Yes, aunty?'

'Your nephew left you a message.' The woman tapped the white phone on her counter.

'My wh—' Chen Di cut herself off and approached. She held onto the counter, almost knocking over the Chupa Chups wheel.

'Are you all right?' The woman took a bite of a hot dog.

'Yes,' she said, unsteady. A small dog with V-shaped ears trotted past, its back leg missing, the wound still fresh. A bad sign. Lin Feng would've done something to help it.

'Are you really all right?'

'Yes, yes. I am.'

'It was a short message. He says not to worry, he'll get it done.' The woman stopped chewing and looked at her for an explanation, which she didn't give. 'He also wishes you happiness in life. Are you getting married or what?'

Chen Di's jaw tightened, she couldn't stop the surge of fear inside her. She turned to leave, a needle lodged in her skull.

'Wait, girl, you're not calling him back?'

She quickened her pace, barely avoiding someone's spittle as she passed.

'Oi! How about a "thank-you, aunty"?'

She ran.

Back in her unit, Chen Di lay still with the feeling she'd fall through her bed. She imagined Lin Feng's shrimp raising its pincers and tearing apart his guppies and angelfish. She imagined his turtles devouring the shrimp. She imagined his mother cooking his hard-shell pet turtles with oyster sauce, like how you might make soft-shell turtles. And she imagined him sliding open a window and pouring out his silkworms.

They'd fly, helpless, carried into oblivion on the wind.

Chen Di clutched her head and shut her eyes to settle the jumbled information inside. Then she did her final checks of the room, feeling an impulse to break her hanging bulb. Her green jacket didn't fit inside the backpack, so she threw it on, and it made her hot. She exited and locked the iron door behind her. A loud squeak.

The longtang was unusually quiet, as if conspiring to help her with her final step. She jumped on her bicycle and left her city home forever.

Though weighed down by the goods on their backs, a group of hawkers ran from two city inspectors at incredible speed. Chen Di missed nothing in this city. She rode fast, every pump on the pedals heightening her senses. The world appeared bright and sharp, the slightest differences in the colours of people's clothes leaping out at her. Even bicycle bells sounded rich and amplified. Was this how everyone felt at the cusp of a turning point in life?

She passed Lü's workplace. The national flag flapped like

a bloody hand, bidding her farewell. Across the road stood the same old Yuanfen Eatery. *Yuanfen brought you together, brought us together. We, human beings, are all interconnected parts of a whole.*

Except she was leaving everyone behind.

She arrived at the address on Lin Feng's note and double-checked the street name and numbers. The group of six-storey buildings looked familiar – it was the housing complex she'd seen Lin Feng's mum visit the other day. Lin Feng's mum had met a man here, and…

Heart racing, Chen Di pushed her bicycle into the short alley and emerged in a concrete courtyard, where she locked her bicycle. All the ground-level windows were barred, and above, AC units protruded precariously. The building on the right was marked 64 – the number on the note.

She entered through a rusty front door to smell the musty air. It was dark inside, more run-down than Lin Feng's and Lü's housing estates but newer than Chen Di's longtang. The dozen doors along the hallway were equally spaced, boxes for milk delivery here and there. One door had half a *Civilised Household* sticker. A sign by the stairs read *Maintain indoor and outdoor hygiene; keep the environment clean.*

She was about to head upstairs when she yelped: Master Mu had materialised beside her.

'Young Chen,' he said, his eyes penetrating.

Cold sweat ran down her spine. Thank Heaven, thank Earth she wasn't trying to kill Lü herself, that Master Mu hadn't followed her to Lü Yuandou's apartment.

Two doors opened and residents poked out their heads at the sound of her cry.

'What are you doing here?' Master Mu disregarded the others.

'Just paying a visit.' Her voice rose.

'Who are you visiting? What have you come to do?'

Another door opened and residents approached. So people here were as nosy as those in her village and her longtang, as nosy as Master Mu. They speculated among themselves. 'I haven't seen them before, have you?' 'I don't think so.' 'The man has a style.' 'Didn't Crooked Nose say his brother and niece were coming?' The voices brought even more people.

'What is this about?' a young mum asked them, baby in arm. 'Do you live here?'

'No,' Chen Di said, in exasperation.

A very old man hobbled over, his long brows reminiscent of the Great Teacher. 'Who are you looking for?' he said with a lisp. 'I will help you.'

'I'm asking you, Young Chen.' Master Mu's voice resonated through the hallway, drowning out others. 'What are you here for? Who are you here to see? I know you went to the train station this morning. Are you leaving?'

Sorry, Lin Feng, I tried.

Chen Di spun around and walked towards the exit. Only to be stopped by a voice.

'She's here to see me. She is my student.'

The voice had an accent she now knew was Cantonese.

Was she in a dream? Her body came to a boil. Slowly, carefully, she turned around.

He stood in the middle of the stairs, in jeans and a flannel shirt. Longer-than-usual hair, a high-bridged nose, two faint wrinkles added to his forehead. She was nine again, tiptoeing outside a school building surrounded by bamboo. She held onto a big, smooth hand. She felt an upward momentum and was pulled through the window into a classroom.

'Teacher Jia.'

'Hi, Chen Di.'

40

She ran, cutting past the residents, rushing up the stairs two at a time, and stopped before him, her face almost touching his flannel shirt, her breathing ragged. She took in his scent, clean, calming, and everything flooded back. Her first day at school, his home visits, the office-home he'd organised for her, the Lantern Festivals they'd spent together, and his departure, which had broken her heart. How she'd hungered for him, year after year...

People chattered, but Chen Di heard nothing. She didn't even look up, afraid she'd discover someone else's face. She felt him reaching over and placing his hand on her shoulder, over the jacket he'd given her. She knew this hand.

Eventually the others left, and quiet descended. Teacher Jia smiled, his eyes teary though filled with a new confidence. Only when he beckoned her to follow did she remember Master Mu, but he was gone. It must have become obvious she hadn't come to harm anyone. Perhaps Master Mu had decided he was wrong about her reason for being in Shanghai.

Had Teacher Jia really been a reason, one of the reasons, for her to come to this city?

Chen Di followed him up the stairs, watching the one diagonal wrinkle on his shirt, appearing, disappearing. He hadn't changed. Only his sleeves weren't rolled.

He stopped at the door to Unit 204 – the address on Lin Feng's note. So Lin Feng had found out from his mum her collaborator's address, and he'd sent her here because he'd sensed Four Three's importance in her life. Lin Feng was not only helping her start a new life without a criminal record but also sending her to the person she loved.

Something jolted inside her. She glanced at the unit number again. In Mandarin, *two* sounded like *child*, *zero* sounded like *approaching*, and *four* sounded like *death*. 204, ominous. She checked her watch: 4:44, again ominous.

A burst of light. The door opened, revealing a carpeted living room, low-key. Despite Teacher Jia's minimal furniture, the space looked cramped. It was so him. The tea table was made of light-coloured wood, as were the armrests and the legs of the matching red sofa and armchair. The wooden bookshelf was also light-coloured, with books and magazines and piled documents. She glimpsed a paperweight – a little national flag poking out of a block.

Teacher Jia shut the door and met her eyes. They were hardly one metre apart, she could hear his breathing. She didn't care if he was married, she wanted him so badly her body was melting. If he made one step towards her, she would give him her all.

He blinked away his tears. 'You kept the jacket.'

'Always.' Her voice quavered. She left her backpack on the carpet and took off the jacket, one arm, and the other, and hung it behind the door.

'The first day you came to school, I called you *girl with a sweet smile.*'

'I remember.'

'Your smile is still so sweet.'

They stared at each other and Chen Di wanted the moment to last forever, but Teacher Jia told her to sit and went to bring tea. She dropped onto the sofa and buried her face in her hands. She'd never felt so hot before, as if she'd been wrapped in plastic in the sun.

Teacher Jia returned with two lid-attached enamel mugs, which brought her back to Daci Village. She thought she caught a whiff of chrysanthemum tea, but he opened a lid to reveal jasmine tea. Green leaves lay at the bottom, white flowers floating on top.

He sat around the tea table in the armchair, the tips of their armrests in contact. His two socks were the same – both maroon – and he didn't rest one ankle on top of the opposite thigh. If Chen Di reached out, she could touch his knee.

'So Author Peng gave you my address,' he said.

She looked up from his knee. 'Who?'

'Author Peng, Dried Bamboo Shoot. Or you might simply know her as your student's mother. We're working on a piece of writing together.'

Right. Lin Feng's mum must've told Teacher Jia about her, including her looks, and he'd realised it was Chen Di. 'If you knew about me, then why didn't you…'

'Oh, Chen Di, don't get me wrong. I wanted to see you. Which teacher wouldn't?'

Teacher. Was she still just his student?

He picked up his mug. 'It's hard to face you. The way I left…'

'It's okay.'

'I've hurt you. I knew how you…felt about me.'

She wrapped her hands around her mug, then removed its lid. She picked it up, and put it down. 'Where is your wife?'

He blew at his tea to cool it. 'Do I have to answer?'

'No, if you don't want to.'

He put down the tea. 'She's back in America. She's with an American.'

The concept of running off with a foreigner sounded alien. Regardless, Chen Di should feel happy. He was single now, right? How convenient for her. But observing him – his sad eyes – only hurt her. 'I'm sorry.'

'Outside China, it's easier for her to find her freedom.'

Chen Di recalled the photo in his pocket watch, the beautiful woman in a red-and-blue striped headband, her face without blemish. Large eyes, full of light. Not that Chen Di cared to think about her, but America might actually serve the woman better. She sipped the hot tea. 'It's good to see you, Teacher Jia, after so long.' Four years and five months.

His eyes crinkled, his lips curling up with confidence. 'Author Peng said you went to East China Normal University and now teach at Wende Private. I can hardly believe it. I almost thought she was talking about someone else after all. I'm so proud of you.'

Perhaps, with him, she could spit out the truth?

'How did you do it, Chen Di? You just turned twenty.'

Even the birthday on her resident ID was an estimate, but Teacher Jia kept track of her age. A match flared inside her, a bonfire. 'Well, how's life been for *you*, after your wife...'

'I am fine.' The words seemed to cause him pain. He gripped the armrests.

Chen Di rested her hand on his.

Their eyes locked. His hand turned over under hers, and their fingers entwined, his hand bigger than hers, smoother than hers. For too long she'd yearned for this touch.

'Look at me,' she said. He already was. 'I still feel the same, Teacher Jia.'

He didn't look away.

She leaned closer. He reached towards her face and tucked her loose hair behind her ears, and she let down her ponytail, hair falling to her shoulders. She closed her eyes as his fingertips travelled from her forehead to her eyelids, her cheeks, her birthmark. His thumbs touched her upper lip, lower lip, every contact lighting a small fire underneath her skin.

Her breathing shook with his, her breasts swelling as if trying to break out of her chest, and their foreheads met.

Chen Di knew then he wanted her as much as she wanted him.

But his touch vanished.

Her eyes snapped open and she found him leaned back on the armchair, touching his clean-shaven chin, frowning at her as if she were a faulty specimen.

A chill settled inside her.

'What's wrong?' she murmured.

'It doesn't feel right.' Teacher Jia picked up his enamel mug and stared into it as an awkward silence passed between them. 'No, it's not that. I left you alone there, in that state, with all those ideas…'

'It's okay, as I said.'

He still faced his tea.

'For all you've done for me, Teacher Jia, I can never repay you. You fought for me, you gave me a home, and you taught me how to think.'

'That's the problem.' He looked up but his frown only deepened, pain seeping through his solemn eyes. 'I've done wrong to you, so wrong I can never redeem myself.'

She looked at him, not comprehending, her throat dry.

'I taught you wrong, I misled you.'

'Sorry?'

'It's been bothering me for a long time now. How do I even start…' He took a sip of his tea and didn't put down the mug. 'What makes us human? Does being free individuals really make us human? Shouldn't one person be sacrificed so ten thousand others could live better?'

She'd heard him, and yet she hadn't. 'What are you talking about?'

'Above all, it's hard to see you because I regret having taught you in such an un-Chinese way.' He put down the mug on the tea table but didn't let go. 'It's much too late now, but since we meet again, I have to correct some things I said.'

She struggled to wrap her head around his words. 'Are you joking?'

'I'm serious.'

Her eyes darted to that national flag paperweight on his bookshelf, to his buttoned sleeves, not rolled, and to his two maroon socks. She recalled Four Three's story set in Sichuan, about a village girl who grew up to realise everything she'd been taught was wrong. She waited before she trusted herself to speak. 'You taught me well, Teacher Jia.'

'I did not. The Party made a mess of things, but not everything, and it almost always had good intentions for us, the Chinese people.'

She couldn't believe these words were coming out of Teacher Jia's mouth. The room felt more constricting by the second, the light glaring, the furniture towering as if about to fall on her. She gulped the jasmine tea, swallowing a deathlike white flower. The tea had become lukewarm.

He sat forward. 'Have you noticed all the European-style buildings here?'

She nodded. What was he trying to say?

'And the plane trees?' he said.

'Plane trees almost define Shanghai.'

'And they have an interesting history: the French first grew them in the Shanghai French Concession. But really, they're London planes, discovered by a Brit. And the trees are actually a hybrid between the oriental plane and American sycamore.'

'But so what?'

'Before the Japanese invaded us, and long before the Party came along, Shanghai was cut up like a cake and eaten by the French, British, and Americans. Funny coincidence.' He turned his mug ninety degrees. 'My parents would've accepted the Party had Britain never colonised Hong Kong, and then so would I. And I can't help but think *you* would've been a happier person if I weren't your teacher, if you hadn't been swayed by my anti-Party sentiments.' He finally let go of the mug. 'Back then, Teacher Jia was just an ignorant outsider wanting to fix China.'

'And you aren't anymore.' Her voice shook. 'Was that why your America-loving wife ran off? Or did she run off first? Her leaving for an American man must've—'

'Keep our personal lives out of this.'

Chen Di sat up. She straightened her sweater. She tied her ponytail high. Despite being shocked by where their reunion was going, her mind sharpened as she prepared herself for an intellectual discussion, an ability given by him that she would now, ironically, use against him. 'Can you honestly say your wife's betrayal didn't change your thinking? You said you wouldn't be you without her.'

'My divorce acted as a catalyst, I admit that, but to think

it was the only thing that changed me is one-sided. In Big Shanghai, I see change year by year, month by month, day by day. Only now do I feel I can truly step out of my personal life and see the full picture.'

'Except in the end, our personal lives matter the most. You can't expect me to forget my pregnant mother's murder and love family planning, can you?'

Teacher Jia finished his tea and wiped off the tea leaf on his lip. Mother's death didn't seem to surprise him even though he'd left Daci Village before the incident. He must've heard about it from someone. Then words sprang to mind. *I didn't think I'd meet anyone from Daci Village again, but first him, then you.* Lü Yuandou's words. Chen Di couldn't believe it.

'Truth be told,' she said, 'I'm in Shanghai to kill Lü Yuandou.' Yet she heard hesitance in her voice, her words without the punch she'd intended. She tried to summon her hate, but it wouldn't come. She wanted to think like Tang but didn't. 'I'm in Shanghai to kill Lü Yuandou,' she repeated, and felt she'd further weakened her statement.

'That's what I mean by saying you would've been a happier person if I weren't your teacher.'

She opened her mouth. Teacher Jia ascribed her desire for revenge to her 'un-Chinese' education – he really blamed himself for having turned her into the person she was.

'Lü Yuandou only did his job,' he said.

'But he is a monster, no? Between our fellow countrymen's outdated mindset and the Party's authoritarian policies, he's found an opportunity to prey on people, no?'

Teacher Jia's posture didn't change. 'He only did his job.'

'And he did it like a monster.' Chen Di's voice was feeble. She shifted on the sofa, knowing that deep down she now considered Lü a changed man, and she needed him to die just to break free from her own guilt. But the hollowness she'd felt at the train station hit her again. Would his death really make her free?

Teacher Jia held her gaze, the calm in his eyes reminiscent of Master Mu. 'Following the Party was Lü Yuandou's solution to a better life, for himself and for everyone.'

She forced a wry laugh. 'Smart solution.'

'Chen Di, I'm sympathetic to your family, but—'

'You're *sympathetic to my family?*'

'But other families became richer, simple. Ask around. Most young people here trust the state, because life *is* better, the Party *has* created more opportunities. Human rights are secondary to getting citizens out of poverty – only people oblivious to their lifelong privilege would disagree. Policies like family planning help, they help people think.'

She downed her tea. 'I think for myself!'

'Most can't. Remember the villagers set on having babies until they got a few sons? Imagine if such ignorant people were *elected* to a government. Their children, grandchildren, would've all been stuck in poverty.'

'But they— We— I mean, I…'

'But the Party lifted them out of poverty, through various officials' hard work, encouraging them to make smart choices.'

Chen Di stiffened, recalling the new houses and roads, villagers bragging about being able to afford university for their kids... 'But can you credit all that to the one-child policy?'

'At least partially, and at least for these few decades – with fewer kids to raise. As to the future, we're facing an ageing population, but the higher quality of our new labour force compensates for its smaller size. The point of the one-child policy is for parents to concentrate their resources on their only child so they grow up better educated. Can you even compare one engineer with two, or four, or ten factory workers? So far, China has been getting richer because of our cheap labour powered by our massive population, but our future economic growth won't need to rely on that.'

Chen Di felt she needed more time to consider all this, but... 'Regardless! Life is about more than just getting rich.'

'It's the first step. It's what developing countries need the most.' Teacher Jia sat forward again. 'Not to mention other good things that came about these years. For one, after introducing the one-child policy, the Party worked even harder than before to combat people's mentality that boys were better than girls.'

One is good; a son or a daughter, equally good. The message the Party had tried to drill into people was clear. It hadn't worked on Grandfather but had on many others. Families without sons *had* put their resources into raising daughters... 'But the state knew villagers valued boys more than girls – they knew such family planning policies were recipes for tragedies! You call it *combating*, I call it *cleaning up their own mess*.'

'And they tried very hard.'

'But still so many individuals were sacrificed!'

'That's unavoidable in order to help the Chinese people as a whole.'

Chen Di shut her eyes to think, knowing if she looked deep inside herself, she would find something human, something indisputable. 'When a government sets rules like this, against human nature, the whole society becomes hypocritical. It destroys our hearts – our minds.'

'I don't disagree. Our level of consciousness is lagging behind all the external changes imposed on us, good or bad. Sometimes I fear the Party's methods are like pulling budding plants by hand to "help" them grow... But would they necessarily die?' Jia Guo's gaze remained steady before he sighed. 'The one-child policy won't last forever.'

'Then what?' Chen Di clapped her knees. 'Will my mother— Will all be forgotten?'

'They won't. We're always told to look forward in this nation, but I do believe in learning from past mistakes too. That's why we, writers, record things.'

'But how can you record anything truthful if you're not allowed to critique society?'

'We, Chinese writers, self-censor to avoid censorship.'

'What then *can* you record? If you write a novel about family planning, who can you have as the protagonist? A repentant abortion enforcer?'

'That's about the extent—'

'I have read every piece of your published writing, Four Three, and I really thought...' *You were on my side.* Chen Di felt like crying. She had never felt she'd truly lost him, until now. When he'd written lines like, *It is the man who has gone insane, not the society in which he lives,* had he meant it literally? Fine, if Teacher Jia had never loved her. Fine, if he'd left her behind. Never had she imagined him losing his way when it came to his politics.

Chen Di shivered, feeling she was losing her own way too. Gone was the clarity she'd experienced since Mother's death. Might good intentions have truly accompanied family planning officials' barbarous acts? Lü Yuandou was now a remorseful man, but the question wasn't how that man had become this man. Rather, had he ever been a monster?

'I do hope to do better, Chen Di, to bring out personal stories.' Teacher Jia told her to wait and he rose and headed to another room. Before she was ready, he returned with a laptop and flipped it open on the tea table. 'We're working on a piece of narrative non-fiction. The core was in fact written by Author Peng's daughter, Lin Shun.'

Chen Di tensed. What might have Lin Feng's sister written before her death? She checked her watch again. 5:24:34, 35, 36... 'I know she passed away.'

'And Author Peng blamed herself for it.'

'Right...' Everyone in Lin Feng's family blamed themselves.

'While watching the kids that day, she went for a smoke.' Teacher Jia paused as an image flashed across Chen Di's mind, of Lin Feng's mum stomping on her cigarette and throwing out the whole pack. 'When she got back, her daughter was chasing after her son and had a heart attack. After the daughter's death, they removed all traces of her life to start anew, thinking it'd not only help their son but also help themselves cope.' Teacher Jia double-clicked a document. 'But in truth, guilt had been biting at them ever since their son's birth.'

'Because having a second child…was like giving up on their first.'

He nodded at the screen. 'In other countries, a child's illness can only be the family's pain. Yet here, it becomes the family's pass to a second child, an opportunity to be taken advantage of. If the first child gets cured, the illness is almost a blessing.'

'And that's screwed up.'

Teacher Jia looked up from the screen. 'Our piece is based on the letters Lin Shun wrote to her little brother – your student – on his birthdays.'

'Lin Feng is not my student, don't make me explain.' Chen Di clenched her fists, seized by an inexplicable fear. 'So what did Lin Feng's sister write? If you're publishing it anyway, then can you show me?'

'That's why I brought it.'

She pulled over the laptop. Every letter began with *Dear Little Fengfeng, Happy Birthday!* As a young girl, Lin Shun wrote about the ugly shape of her own heart, about what a soft-hearted child her little brother was, about all the pets their biologist dad had got them, about their mum kowtowing to Dragon Lustre Temple to pray for her surgeries.

Chen Di read twice the words, *a boy collecting cans with his dad downstairs.* Lin Feng's sister was referring to Tang and his uncle. *I still feel bad about how Second Aunty treated him, but I know he'll be fine. He strides around so confidently he's like flying, like he can conquer the world. I watch him from my window and dream of us becoming friends.*

The last letter didn't begin with *Happy Birthday!*

Dear Little Fengfeng,

It's my birthday, not yours, but I have a bad feeling and I know Dad and Mum are hiding things Doctor Zhao said, so I'll write now.

This morning Dad brought me a birthday cake and we all ate it together in the hospital. Dad and Mum both ended up crying though, saying you could never replace me. I get that, but I'm still upset they didn't celebrate your last birthday. Why are you being punished?

To be honest, at first I didn't want them to have you. I hated Grandma for telling them: 'You don't want to end up childless! Think about your old age!' Later, your birth embarrassed me – my friends are all only children, and I felt our family did something wrong. Classmates laughed about how Dad and Mum had you because they didn't love me, and two boys even asked when I was going to die.

But Little Fengfeng, deep down, I've always known you did nothing wrong. The truth is, I've loved you from the day you came into the world, looking like a cute little potato in Mum's arms. Yes, I'm scared to die. But precisely because of that, I want you to live a good life. I really, really, really mean it. Please take care of Dad and Mum on my behalf, and please, live well.

Love you always,
Your sister

Chen Di mechanically pushed the down arrow key, her teeth chattering. Lin Feng had said no one wanted him to be alive, but it wasn't true. Herself aside, at least one more person wanted him to live: his sister. She had passed away, not resenting him, but wishing him a good life.

Teacher Jia spoke again. 'Author Peng didn't let herself love her son because she felt she betrayed her daughter if she did. But really, she is deeply worried about him.'

'Is she?' Chen Di saw little evidence of it, but then again, the family dynamics were complicated.

He nodded, sighing. 'The boy hurts himself, he has suicidal tendencies.'

She knew this but still shuddered.

'A couple of days ago,' Teacher Jia said to the screen, 'Author Peng actually confronted her son about it.'

'Really? So what did he say? What did Lin Feng say?'

'That he wasn't going to die yet, he first had "a mission to accomplish".'

Chen Di found herself shaking.

'It sounded like a joke,' Teacher Jia continued, 'though Author Peng did feel a little easier, knowing her son had something to look forward to. She said he must've been talking about Xuhui District's high-school running competition next month. So after our discussion today, she actually went to shoe stores to get him a new pair of—'

'No,' Chen Di said, her voice hollow. 'Lin Feng likes his old sneakers. He said he'd always be able to run as long as he wore them.'

'But they're breaking, I suppose, so Author Peng—'

'You don't get it.' Her eyes hurt but she stared back at the screen. In her mind, Lin Feng's fair skin turned pale, then translucent, as a silkworm would before spinning a cocoon. Once he accomplished 'the mission', then what? *I swear on my sister's name I wouldn't go to prison.* How *could* he have been so sure about not going to prison?

Then she froze.

Lin Feng wouldn't go to prison because he planned to kill himself.

'Call Lin Feng's mum!' Chen Di shouted, her voice scratchy. 'Call Author Peng!' The more she thought about it, the more certain she became. As soon as Lin Feng killed Lü for her, he'd have no more reasons to live.

'Why?' Teacher Jia asked. 'Are you okay?'

'Just call her! Now! Please!'

Though he looked unsure, he picked up his phone and thumbed a few buttons. She grabbed it from him and pressed it to her ear, but the ringing continued, one beep per second. Long beep. Long second. She tossed the phone on the tea table and jumped up and hurried to the door, light-headed.

She picked up her backpack but bumped sideways into the wall, and her bad shoulder screamed in pain.

'Are you leaving?' Teacher Jia asked.

She glanced at her green jacket and left it hanging. She turned the doorknob.

'Fundamentally, Chen Di, I haven't changed. If you know what I mean.'

She no longer knew what anything meant. But whether Teacher Jia was right then or now, whether family planning had any merit, it didn't matter. Only she had to stop Lin Feng – to save him. She pulled open the door. 5:48.

'Chen Di.'

She stood still but didn't look back.

'How beautiful you've become, how strong you've always been. You are one of the most amazing women – amazing people – I've ever met. How can I not have feelings for you?' Teacher Jia's voice was tender and, for two seconds, the longing flooded her body again. 'Just remember, nothing is black and white.'

She stepped out and ran down the stairs.

41

She jumped on her bicycle and sped off. She didn't reflect, didn't think. If you focused, the traffic of Xu Junction could be dealt with. The sun dipped, and between two buildings under construction rose a full moon – it'd been one month since the Lantern Festival. She concentrated on the roads, getting on the pavements when needed, avoiding humans and vehicles, cautiously ignoring the traffic lights.

Unlike two hours earlier, she felt that if she were to leave as planned, she'd miss everything in this city. The rhythm, the chaos, the ubiquitous plane trees. The snobbish malls and mindless shoppers, victims of a global scheme, who only wanted a good life, not knowing what a good life meant.

Well, did anyone?

Master Mu probably did. If only Master Mu had followed Lin Feng instead of her today! *We put ourselves in tune with the universe, maintain peace in our own realms, nurture life, and prevent death and destruction.* There must be a way out within life. For her, for Lin Feng, for the world. A middle ground built with peace.

Chen Di felt a corner of the darkness inside her recede.

She was out of Xu Junction but vehicles still crowded the streets. Housing estates appeared, and she reached Phoenix Sea Court at 6:04. Lin Feng might already be in the building, in Lü Yuandou's apartment. Once he stabbed Lü, he'd move onto...

No, she couldn't let Lin Feng die! She had to stop him at all costs, and she would, even if it meant exposing herself, ruining her mission once and for all. And as she thought that, a wave of relief washed over her. It felt as if she'd been trapped under rubble for years and had finally crawled out. She could breathe again. She saw light, light swallowing more corners of the gnawing darkness inside her.

Chen Di jumped off her bicycle. For too long she'd lived for the sake of revenge, which had never felt so trivial. She couldn't care less about the man named Lü Yuandou.

She let her bicycle fall and started to cross the street, but a motorcycle nearly hit her, forcing her back to the pavement. Street lights flickered on, dazzling her. The stone engraved with *Phoenix Sea Court* stood right on the opposite side. She only had to head up the marble stairs, tell the guards she was visiting friends, and press *406* on the intercom.

A young man in tattered clothes hopped on her bicycle and rode off. She didn't care. She lurched across the street, but before the stairs, a hand clapped her injured shoulder. She cried out and turned to find an old woman, her bob wig like Grandma Chu's, her face wrinkled with concern. 'Girl, you look ill. Tell grandma, what happened?'

Another woman cut between them. 'Move! You're blocking the way.'

'P-Please leave me alone.' Hit by a wave of dizziness, she almost fell but was pulled up by the old woman and another nosy – no, good-hearted – passer-by, hurting her shoulder further. Her body felt weak, her mind numb, and for the first time in Shanghai she joined her hands in prayer.

Perhaps Lin Feng hadn't come. *Please, let that be the case!*

Then she stopped: Lü Yuandou hurried over from down the street. A phantom? He carried a plastic bag, panting, his face as pink as his wife's.

'Young Chen! Sorry I'm late, we said six. Have you been waiting down here? Aunty Gu should've let you in, we're such terrible hosts.' He held up the plastic bag, mulberry leaves inside. 'I had to get these before the animal markets closed. Please, come on up.'

She examined him, his heart-shaped face, his pointed ears and long lobes.

No, she didn't need this man dead.

She didn't need anyone dead.

Lin Feng had sent her to Teacher Jia because he knew what she actually needed: love. A person who cared about her, whom she cared about.

Except that person was Lin Feng.

All she wanted now was to find him and hold his hand and never let him go. She pictured his childlike grin. She wanted to see it again, to see it every day.

She felt a sudden calm, a hopefulness that was so unlike her, which she'd never experienced before. A ball of light radiated from the centre of her body, bright beams pushing away the rest of the darkness.

'Lin Feng,' she murmured. 'Together let's live on, and live well.'

She looked back at Lü. If Lü Yuandou wasn't in his apartment, then Lin Feng should go home. Why hadn't he come out? He must've not come, he must have not...

But she knew he had.

'Are you all right?' Lü said.

She clutched her head but it didn't help, and she made a step up the stairs only to trip over. Hands on a step, weighed down by her heavy head, she pictured Gu Meilin's ruddy cheeks. Lin Feng could be chatting with the kind woman, drawing out information on her husband's whereabouts. Right? He was good at playing games, making up stories. But she felt no relief. *This is the one and only chance I'm giving you*, she'd told him. *Failing isn't an option. I'm leaving Shanghai after that.* Lin Feng must have realised he couldn't accomplish the mission, that he had failed. And upon realising that, what would he do next?

She convulsed, her face almost touching the steps. Worried bystanders circled around her at the bottom of the marble stairs, young and old, Shanghainese and out-of-towners. Lü Yuandou crouched, offering his hand.

'Help me,' she said, faint.

'Of course,' Lü said. 'Shall I get Aunty Gu? She's a nurse—'

'Help me up. Help me walk.'

He pulled her arm around his shoulders and lifted her body.

'Let's go up to your place, Uncle Lü. Please, quick.'

'Of course.' He helped her labour up the stairs, one step at a time.

She slipped. He caught her. But she could no longer raise her foot, her legs paralysed like in her nightmare. Lü said something to the guards that she couldn't make out, and all surrounding voices turned into static.

A beggar child sat by the wrought-iron fence, curled into a foetal position. A bony woman tripped over him as she passed, her face white apart from smudged eyeshadow, ghostlike. With her weight supported by Lü, she threw back her head and found herself in an apocalyptic world. The grey of the sky darkened, engulfing her, engulfing everyone in the nation. Was this what a cocoon looked like from the inside?

She gazed back at the tall building, which had a red glow that she wasn't sure was real. She counted to the fourth floor, but which window?

Then, on the very left, she saw a shadow – a person – in the window.

The window slid open.

The person stepped up to the ledge.

At first her heart leaped to see him. *Lin Feng!* she cried, but no voice came out. Except another woman's cry brought a moment of clarity – it was Gu Meilin's voice from the window, screaming, 'Stop!' Yet memories clouded reality, yanking her back in time to the 1994 harvest, to Daci Pit. To the edge of a precipice.

Where she had brought her little brother, hand in hand.

With the intention to throw him down.

Into the canyon.

She collapsed to the ground, but the street now looked like a riverbed. She stared up at the building, which now looked like a cliff. She heard a howl, the hoarse voice not a ghost's but her own. Eyes forced open, she saw her two-year-old brother flying, plummeting.

Before her, Lin Feng's arms opened like wings.

42
Two Weeks Later

She turned to her side, her arm dangling out of the bed, and stared through the doorway, listless. She could see a dark corridor with white walls, a green sign looming above. Her mind couldn't process the characters on it but she knew it was an emergency exit. Underneath the sign stood a man in a long white coat and a woman in a white shirt and hat. Her head felt fuzzy and it took a moment before she understood they were a doctor and a nurse.

'She is stable enough today.' The doctor glanced back into the ward. 'We can let her visitors come up.'

'She won't recognise them though,' the nurse said. 'She won't get a thing they say.'

'Still it will be good for her recovery.'

'But the boy... The boy might be too much for her to handle.'

'You are right. Not the boy.'

Their words were a buzz. Saliva pooled in her mouth.

She looked back at the ceiling, panel lights here and

there, and scanned the ward. The other beds were empty, and hers was closest to the barred window. It was sunny outside. The shadow of the steel bars formed a pattern on her blue-striped hospital gown. She glimpsed hair – her own shoulder-length hair – spread on the pillow. Her arm jerked on its own and almost knocked everything off the bedside table. There lay a folded green jacket. On top of it sat a small book, its white cover showing a large calligraphic circle.

Her leg twitched, then her whole body.

Footfalls echoed through the corridor. A woman with ruddy cheeks came into view at the doorway, followed by a man with a heart-shaped face and strange-looking ears that seemed to mean something. She felt she'd seen them before. Then an old man emerged from behind them, lanky like a withered tree. His head was shaved, his body wrapped in an orange robe. A monk.

'Here she is,' the woman and the man said to him.

The monk joined his palms at them, then his eyes met hers. He held onto the door frame, and she noticed his missing thumb. He entered the ward.

'Chen Di.' His voice quavered, water leaking from his light-brown eyes that felt familiar. 'I am sorry, so sorry.' He sat on the chair beside her, under a panel light, his skull almost visible under his skin. 'Perhaps I should have come to you years ago, or perhaps I should have never appeared in your life again… But I came now. I came to tell you I know everything, and I understand. Please, forgive yourself.'

Saliva trickled from a corner of her mouth and she looked behind the monk. In the corridor, the woman with ruddy cheeks sat in a waiting chair, and the man with strange-looking ears paced about. She turned away from them all and stared out the window. Above the high wall outside was blue sky.

'That night in the 1994 harvest…' The monk took a shaky breath. 'That night, I was the first to reach Daci Pit. Heaven offered the full moon to help us in our search, lighting up the grounds save for the places concealed in shadows. I looked down those cliffs into blackness. The ghosts of my three babies, your three little sisters, whom I had thrown into oblivion… Would they return to haunt me? Then I saw something sparkling in the grass at my feet. I picked it up. It was the leaf hair clip I had bought in the county town. My gift for you, Chen Di.'

A strange feeling overcame her at the monk's words, and slowly she turned back to him. With a tremor in his hand, he reached inside his robe and drew out a clip, rusted, its shape indistinct. Her lips parted. Her eyes followed the clip as he placed it on her bedsheet.

'But I believed you,' he said, 'and still do. I have asked myself over and over, hundreds of times, if you could have gone to the big pit and…and done it the way I had, with your three little sisters. And no, I could not picture you doing it. Twelve-year-old you would not have carried it through even if you had had the idea. When you reached the canyon, saw how deep it was, you must have been shocked. I could almost see you raising your hands to clutch your head, the way you always did when you were scared or did not want something to be true, and shutting your eyes, hoping to expel such a harrowing thought. Only you would have let go of a small hand in the process. The gravel there…was slippery…'

She was still. She could feel herself attaching meaning to his words.

'As you said, Chen Di, when you opened your eyes, he was gone.'

She heard a sound – her own breathing.

The monk spoke again. 'But whether it was a mishap at that last moment made no difference to you, because you did bring your brother to Daci Pit.'

A dawning realisation. She convulsed.

'And now, years later, to see that teenage boy fall off the building – what must it have done to you?' His hands clasped his knees. 'You have suffered enough. Forgive yourself.'

She stared at him.

'Forgive yourself, Chen Di. How many times have you considered the love we showered your brother with? How many times have you pondered the way your existence was denied? How many times have you contemplated the truth of your sisters' fate? A brother is to be revered; sisters we toss down the canyon…' He shifted his body slightly, light filling his eyes. And when he shifted again, those eyes reflected her image back at her. 'How is it right for you to be the one to endure guilt?'

Her breathing grew ragged. She tugged the bedsheet. She pounded the bed. She opened her mouth with the urge to speak, but nothing came out. She tried again and let out a croak that almost sounded human. She picked up the hair clip and flung it at the window.

They both looked to the glass.

Though it was shut, she heard the wind rise outside, like a calling from far away. Slowly she pushed herself up from the bed and onto her feet. She stepped towards the window, and placed her palms on the glass. In the courtyard, among red roses and green grass, sat a teenage boy in a wheelchair. His head was bandaged, but he rolled the wheelchair forward, strong, his feet resting in an old pair of black sneakers, both soles coming off from the front.

Suddenly he stopped, as if sensing her gaze, and looked in her direction with his large eyes, dark but radiant.

'Boss Chen!' he shouted. 'You look good with your hair down!'

Water spilt from her eyes, traced down her cheeks.

'Lin Feng,' she murmured.

She touched the left side of her chin. He did too. And he grinned.

Author's note

The one-child policy[1&2] ended in 2015, having prevented at least 400 million births according to the Chinese government.[3] In addition, the Chinese population skews male[4] due to countless incidents of selective female abortion and female infanticide. The exact numbers are unknown.

The avengers who succeeded in murder were sentenced to death under Chinese law, but to this day are often lauded as 'heroes' by the Chinese people, in daily life and on online forums.

In 2016, a two-child policy was formally implemented.[5] In 2021, it was relaxed to a three-child policy.[6] In 2023, the country recorded its first population decline since the Great Chinese Famine six decades ago.[7]

The National Family Planning Commission was renamed in 2003 to the National Population and Family Planning Commission, renamed again in 2013 to the National Health and Family Planning Commission, and dissolved in 2018, its functions integrated into the current National Health Commission. From population control to promoting population growth, family planning remains a government intervention in China.

End Notes

1 *On the Problem of Controlling Population Growth in Our Country: An Open Letter to the General Membership of the Communist Party and the Membership of the Chinese Communist Youth League*, Central Committee of the Communist Party of China, 25 September 1980.

2 '...in most rural areas, a second child should be allowed if the first is female. This is to be implemented during the actual work, not publicised...' Notice of Meeting Decisions of the Central Committee of the Communist Party of China, 5 April 1984.

3 '...over the past forty years, our country's family planning has prevented more than 400 million births, greatly reducing the pressure on resources and the environment caused by excessive population growth.' Mao Qun'an, spokesperson of the National Health and Family Planning Commission, 11 November 2013.

4 The Seventh National Population Census of the People's Republic of China, National Bureau of Statistics of China, 11 May 2021.

5 Population and Family Planning Law of the People's Republic of China, Article 18, 01 January 2016.

6 *On the Optimisation of Family Planning Policies to Promote Long-term Balanced Population Growth*, Meeting of the Politburo of the Communist Party of China, 31 May 2021.

7 National Bureau of Statistics of China, 17 January 2023.

Acknowledgements

This book wouldn't exist without my family: my parents are the most diligent people I know (and had to settle with me as their only child!); Dingzi is more than a real sister to me; DG and Eski make every moment of my life worth living; and everyone in my extended family in China, Australia, and Pakistan contributes to my inspiration. Thank you, and I love you.

The Art of Peace collects the teachings of the Great Teacher of aikido, Morihei Ueshiba. The English edition from which I quoted was translated by John Stevens.

I am indebted to two incredible agents: Hayley Steed of Madeleine Milburn Literary Agency, whose insights and belief in this project helped me shape the story since its early days, and Deborah Schneider of Gelfman Schneider Literary Agents, who has been supporting my various works since before she was my agent. Nothing would have been possible without them.

I am equally indebted to everyone at Atlantic Books/ Allen & Unwin. My brilliant editor, Kate Ballard, not only gave this story a perfect home but also helped me hone it into what it is today. She is also the kindest person I know!

My work was brought to a new stage thanks to Ella Carey and the generous support of the Australian Society of Authors and Copyright Agency. I am also thankful to Jennifer Kerslake, Nikita Lalwani, and Karolina Sutton at Curtis Brown Creative for sage advice, and to the Association of Writers and Writing Programs for connecting me with the amazing Bill Beverly, who volunteered so much of his time and energy to guide me.

My deepest appreciation goes to GrubStreet: Michelle Hoover saw my potential before I knew how anything worked; Rachel Barenbaum, Steven Beeber, Lise Brody, Henriette Lazaridis, Rebecca Rolland, and Nicole Vecchiotti shared insights; and my wonderful cohort, especially Nancy Crochiere, Shalene Gupta, Madeleine Hall, Eson Kim, Meghana Ranganathan, Reid Sherline, and Rich Sullivan provided feedback on this story before it was in shape and made my journey doubly enjoyable.

Writing was not my childhood dream. I stumbled upon it in my late twenties thanks to two writing groups in Porter Square and their talented members: Shannon Browne, Kenneth P. J. Dyer, Greg Stanley, Ken Moraff, Randall Childs, Miguel Balboa, Sara and Kate, and especially Jenna Moquin and Lucy Weltner.

My most sincere thanks to friends from all walks of life who shared thoughts on this book: Michael Amrozowicz, Ada Fredelius, Vanessa Hua, Jane Hung, Tina Jobs, Michal

Korzeniowski, Kristen-Paige Madonia, Vaibhav Mohanty, Stirling Newberry, Mark Pantano, Rachel Reyes, Mae Hwee Teo, Cheryl Lu Xu, and especially Dana Berube and Eve LaPlante.

Finally, I will forever be grateful to Harvard Physics: Bruno Balthazar, Temple Mu He, Marina Werbeloff, and Mobolaji Williams are among this book's early readers, and Andy Strominger, the nicest advisor one could ever ask for, tolerated my change of plan about what to do with a Ph.D. in black-hole physics: fiction writing, obviously!

Further Reading

For further reading on the one-child policy and female infanticides in China, I recommend the masterful novel, *Frog*, by Chinese Nobel Prize winner in Literature, Mo Yan; the heartfelt documentary, *One Child Nation*, directed by Nanfu Wang; non-fiction books, the informative *One Child*, by Mei Fong, and the poignant *Message from an Unknown Chinese Mother*, by Xinran.